Kung Food

Created by: Thomas Astruc
Comics adaptation by: Nicole D'Andria
Written by: Matthieu Choquet & Fred Lenoir
Art arranged by: Cheryl Black
Lettered by: Justin Birch

Bryan Seaton: Publisher/ CEO
Shawn Gabborin: Editor In Chief
Jason Martin: Publisher-Danger Zone
Nicole D'Andria: Marketing Director/Editor
Danielle Davison: Executive Administrator
Chad Cicconi: Akumatized
Shawn Pryor: President of Creator Relations

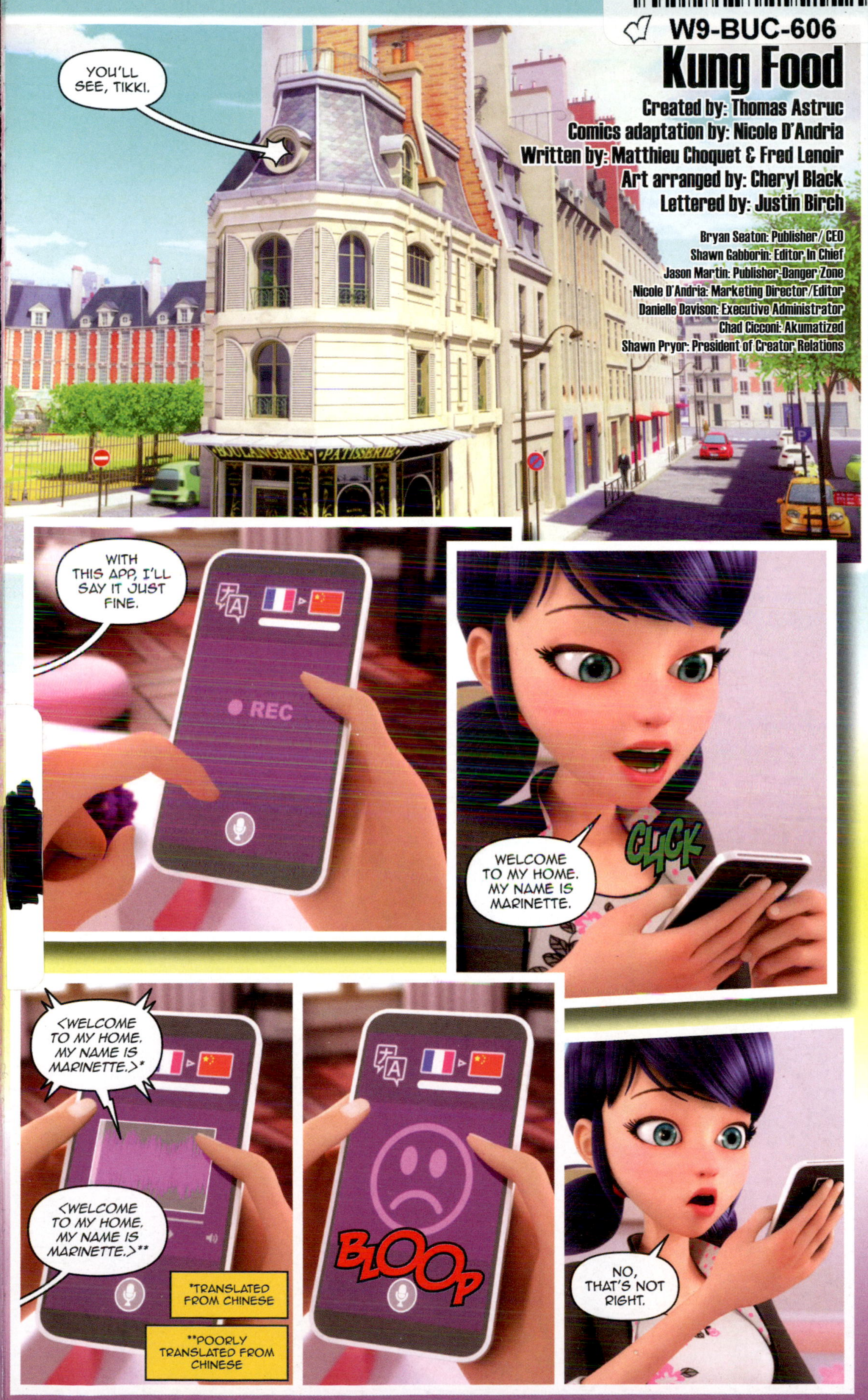
YOU'LL SEE, TIKKI.
BOULANGERIE PATISSERIE
WITH THIS APP, I'LL SAY IT JUST FINE.
REC
WELCOME TO MY HOME. MY NAME IS MARINETTE.
CLICK
<WELCOME TO MY HOME. MY NAME IS MARINETTE.>*
<WELCOME TO MY HOME. MY NAME IS MARINETTE.>**
*TRANSLATED FROM CHINESE
**POORLY TRANSLATED FROM CHINESE
BLOOP
NO, THAT'S NOT RIGHT.

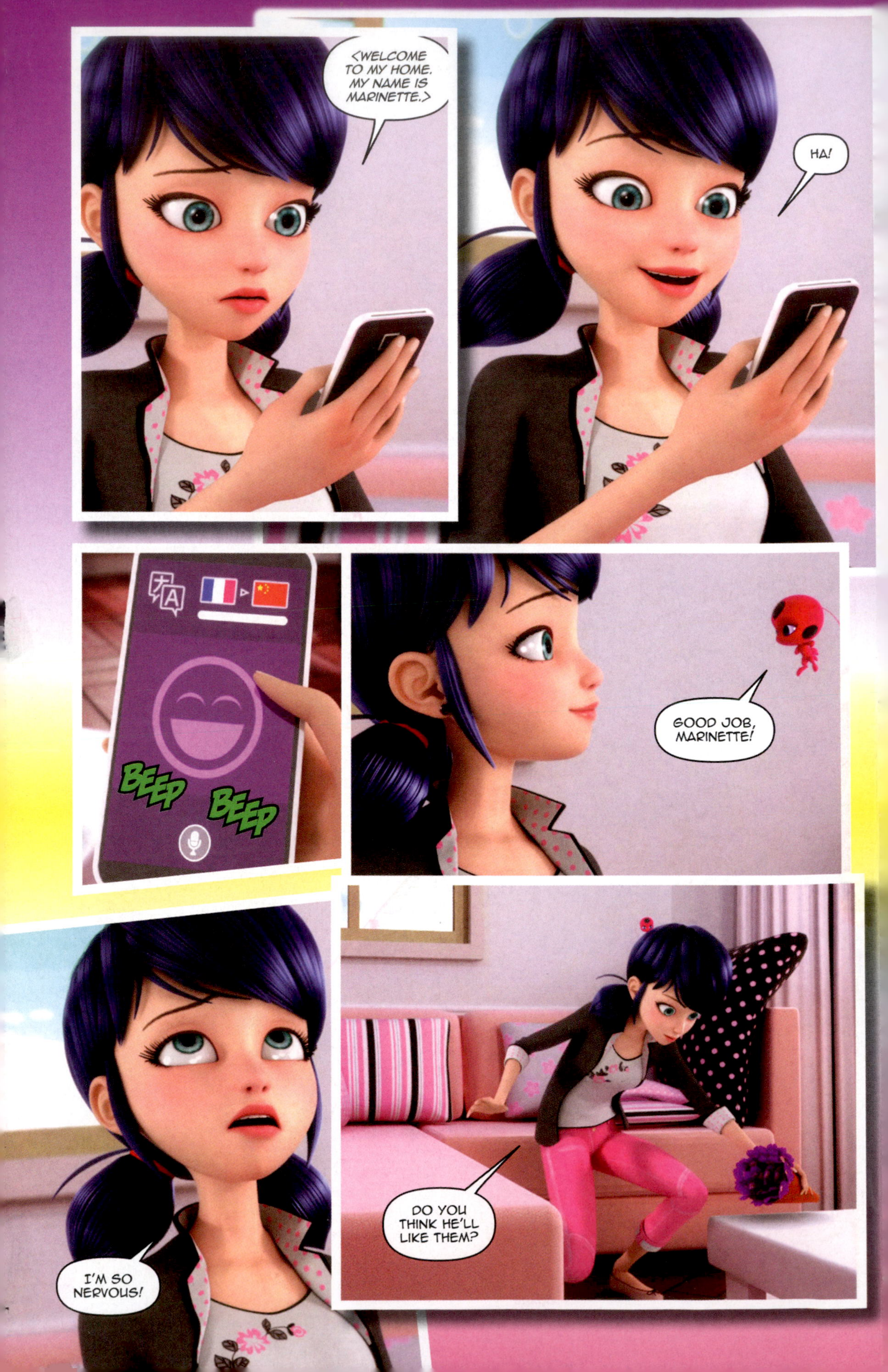
<WELCOME TO MY HOME. MY NAME IS MARINETTE.>
HA!
BEEP BEEP
GOOD JOB, MARINETTE!
I'M SO NERVOUS!
DO YOU THINK HE'LL LIKE THEM?

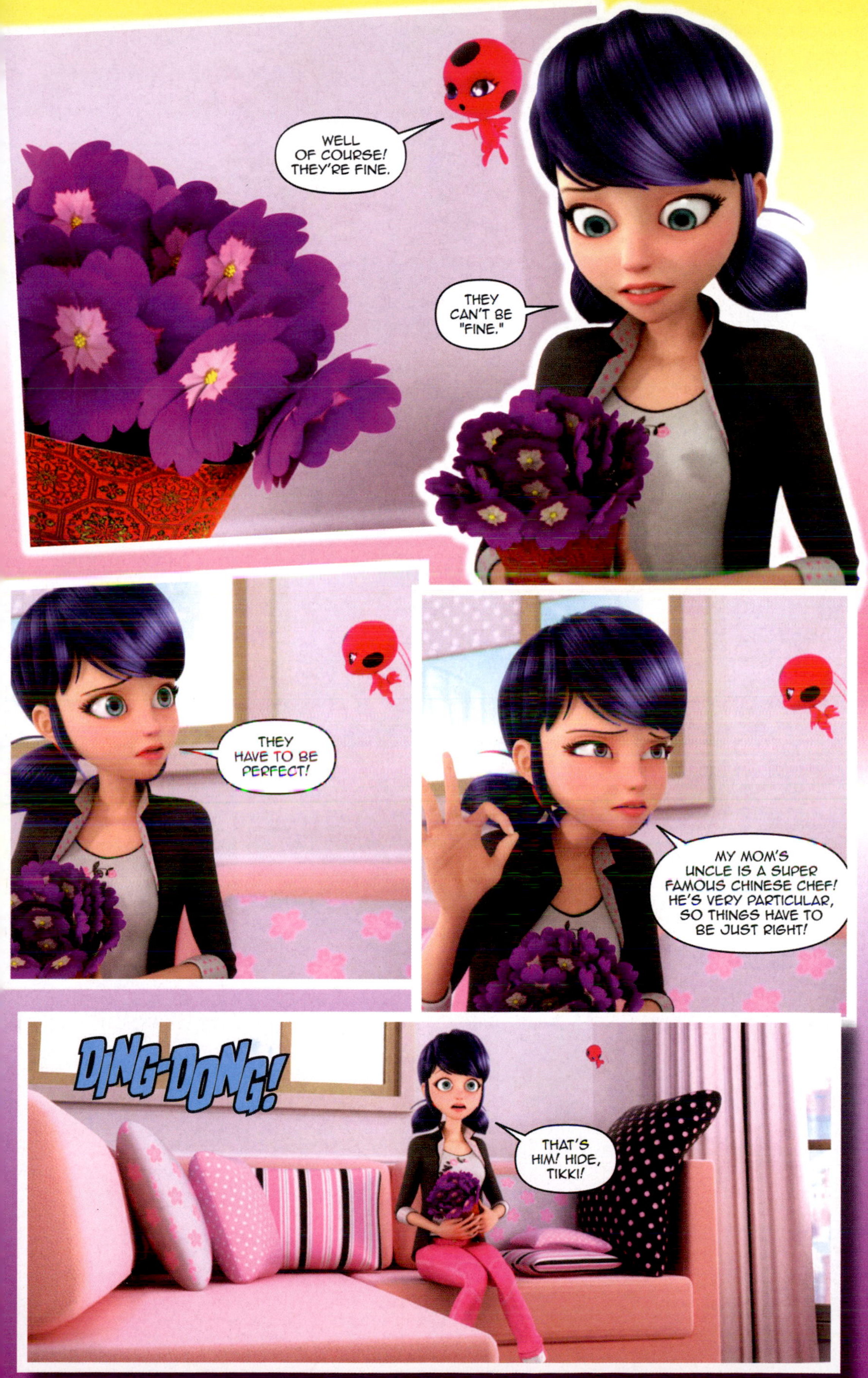
WELL OF COURSE! THEY'RE FINE.
THEY CAN'T BE "FINE."
THEY HAVE TO BE PERFECT!
MY MOM'S UNCLE IS A SUPER FAMOUS CHINESE CHEF! HE'S VERY PARTICULAR, SO THINGS HAVE TO BE JUST RIGHT!
DING-DONG!
THAT'S HIM! HIDE, TIKKI!

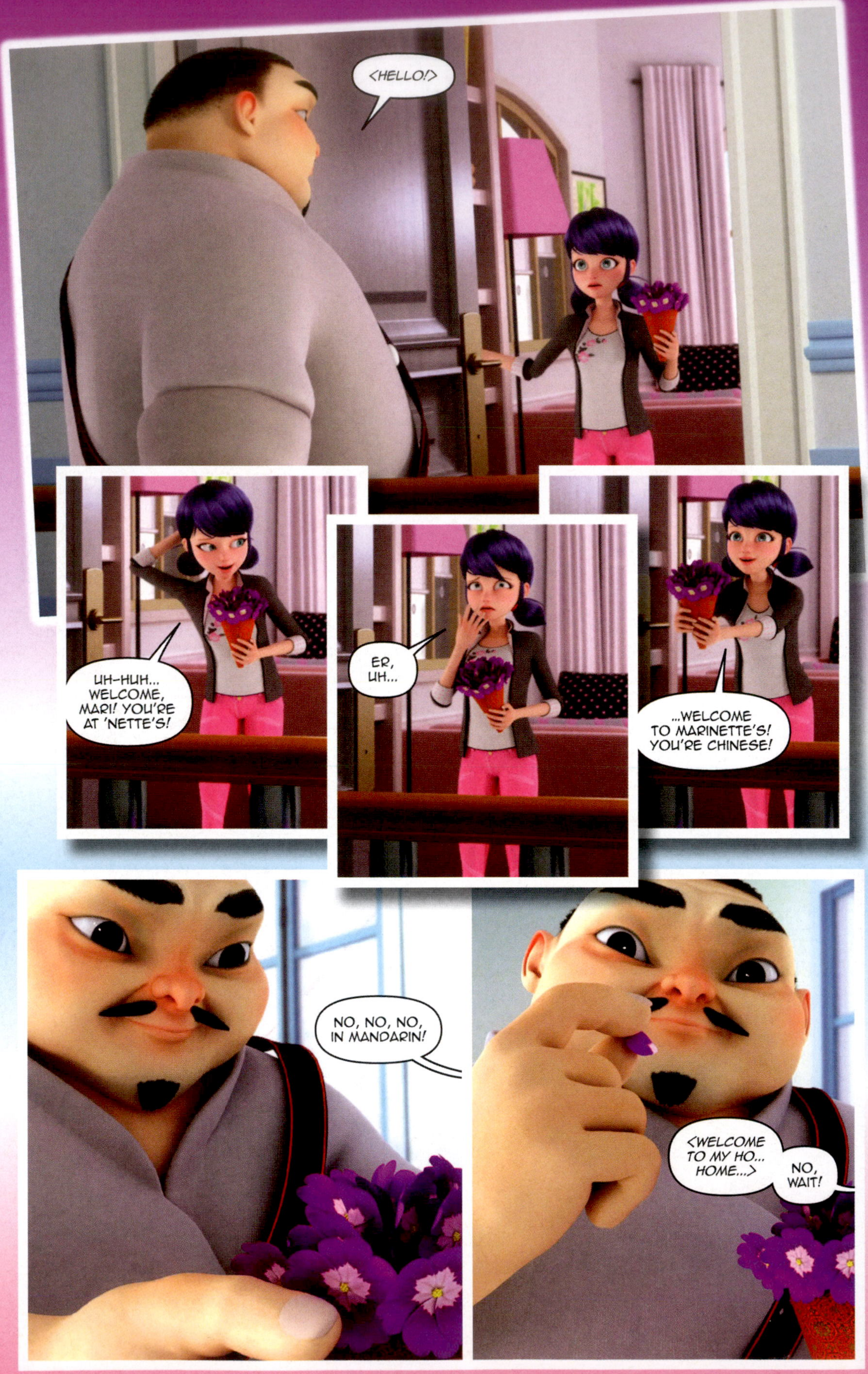
<HELLO!>
UH-HUH... WELCOME, MARI! YOU'RE AT 'NETTE'S!
ER, UH...
...WELCOME TO MARINETTE'S! YOU'RE CHINESE!
NO, NO, NO, IN MANDARIN!
<WELCOME TO MY HO... HOME...>
NO, WAIT!

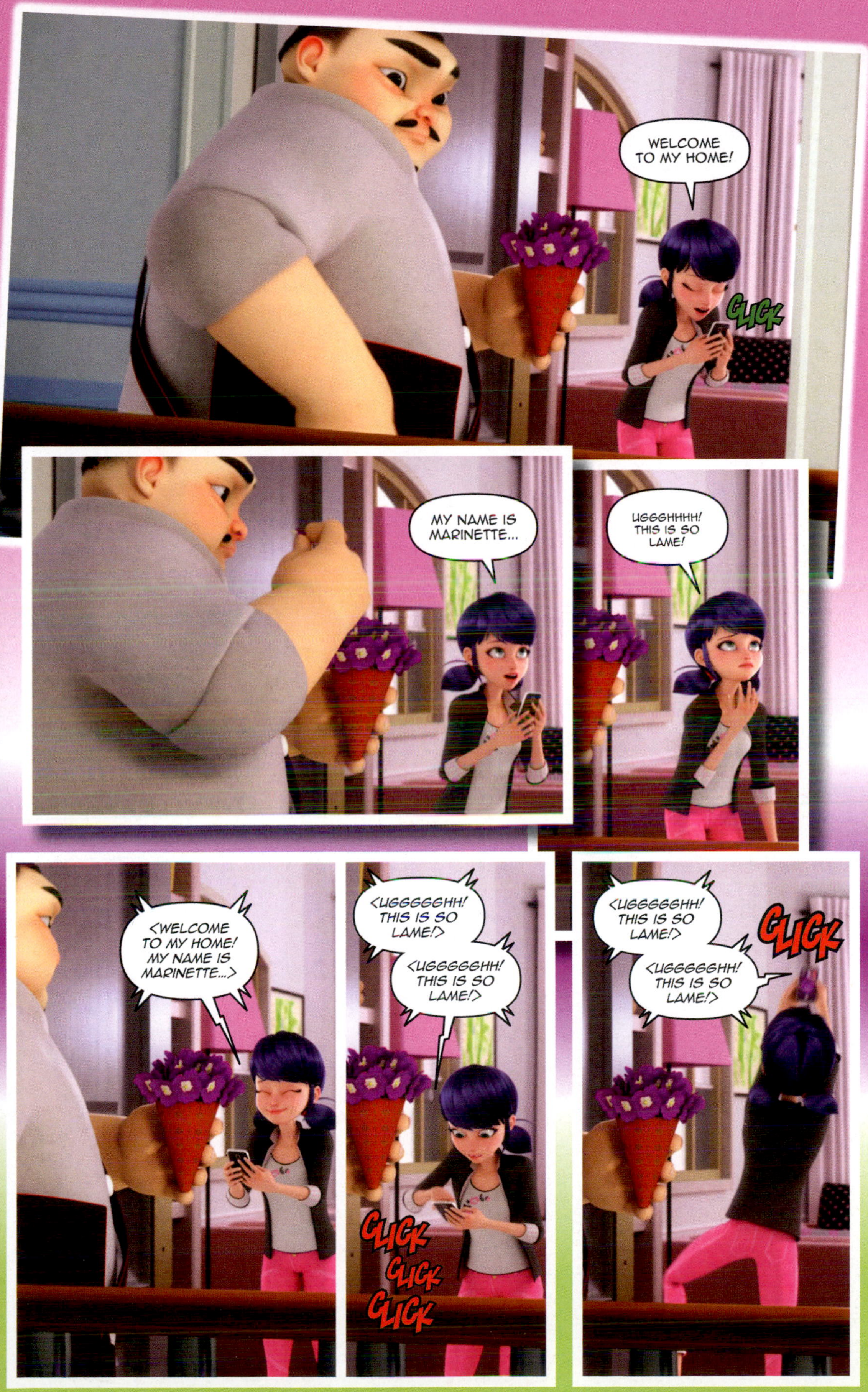
WELCOME TO MY HOME!
CLICK
MY NAME IS MARINETTE...
UGGGHHHH! THIS IS SO LAME!
<WELCOME TO MY HOME! MY NAME IS MARINETTE...>
<UGGGGGHH! THIS IS SO LAME!>
<UGGGGGHH! THIS IS SO LAME!>
CLICK
CLICK
CLICK
<UGGGGGHH! THIS IS SO LAME!>
CLICK
<UGGGGGHH! THIS IS SO LAME!>

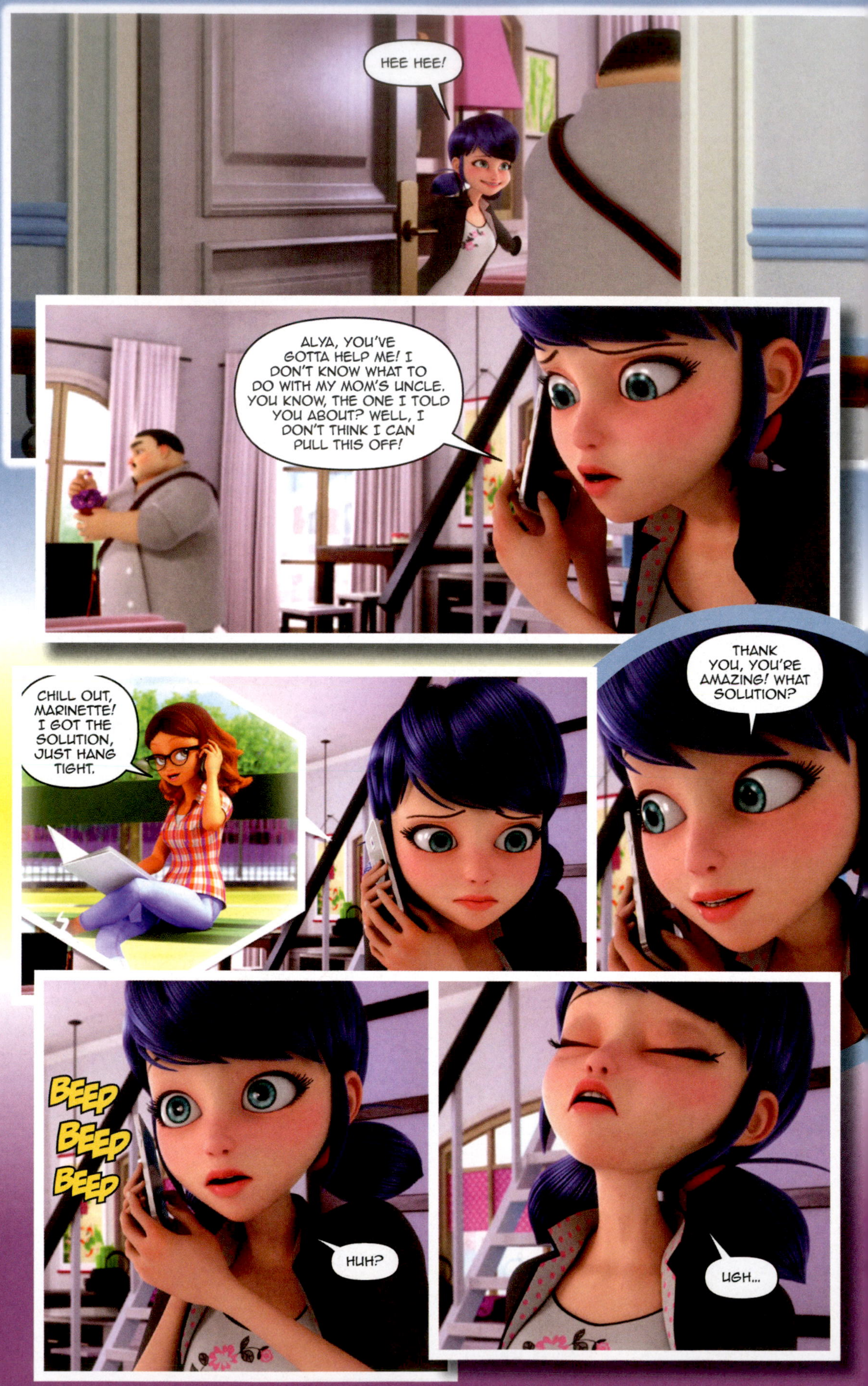
HEE HEE!
ALYA, YOU'VE GOTTA HELP ME! I DON'T KNOW WHAT TO DO WITH MY MOM'S UNCLE. YOU KNOW, THE ONE I TOLD YOU ABOUT? WELL, I DON'T THINK I CAN PULL THIS OFF!
CHILL OUT, MARINETTE! I GOT THE SOLUTION, JUST HANG TIGHT.
THANK YOU, YOU'RE AMAZING! WHAT SOLUTION?
BEEP
BEEP
BEEP
HUH?
UGH...

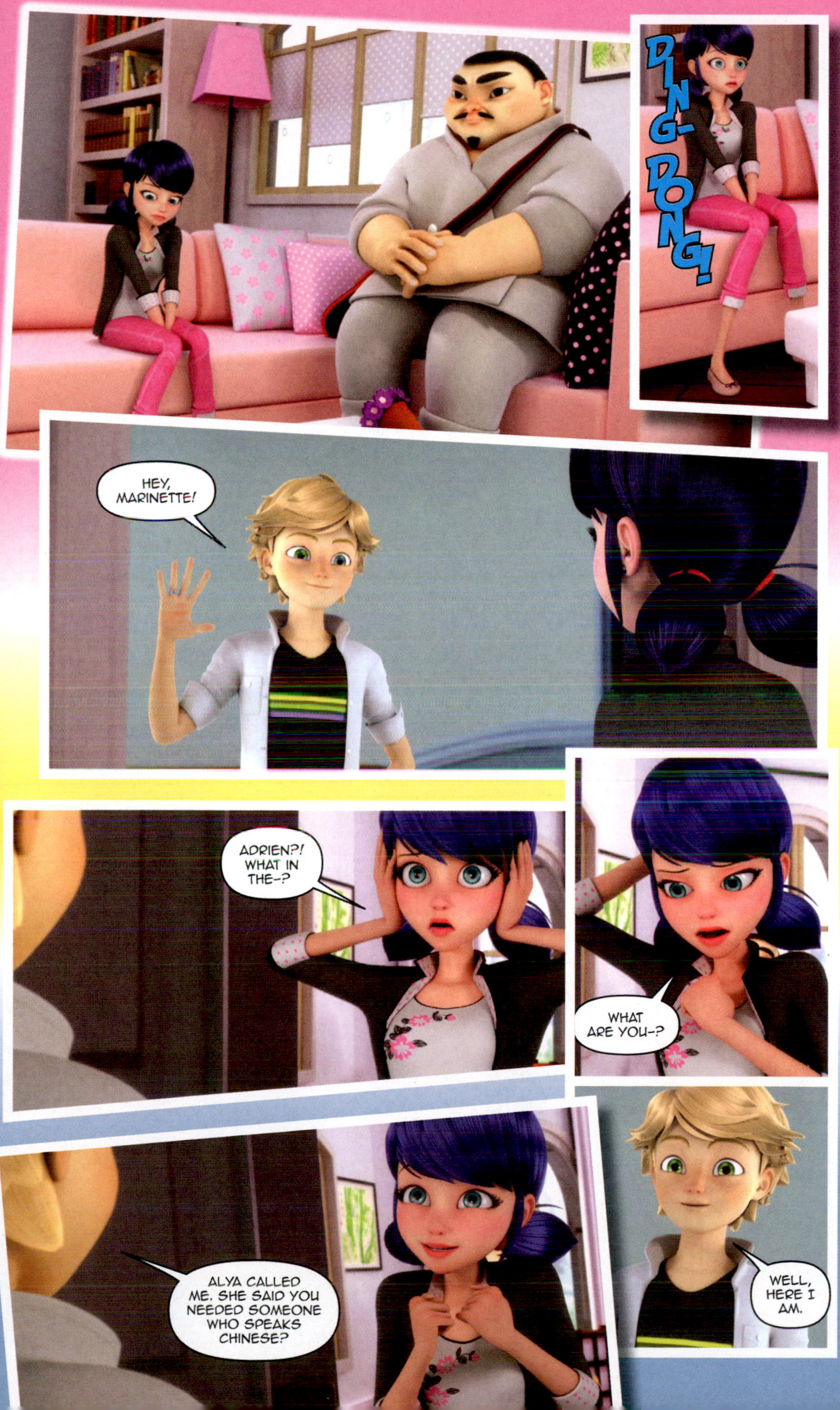

DING-DONG!
HEY, MARINETTE!
ADRIEN?! WHAT IN THE-?
WHAT ARE YOU-?
ALYA CALLED ME. SHE SAID YOU NEEDED SOMEONE WHO SPEAKS CHINESE?
WELL, HERE I AM.

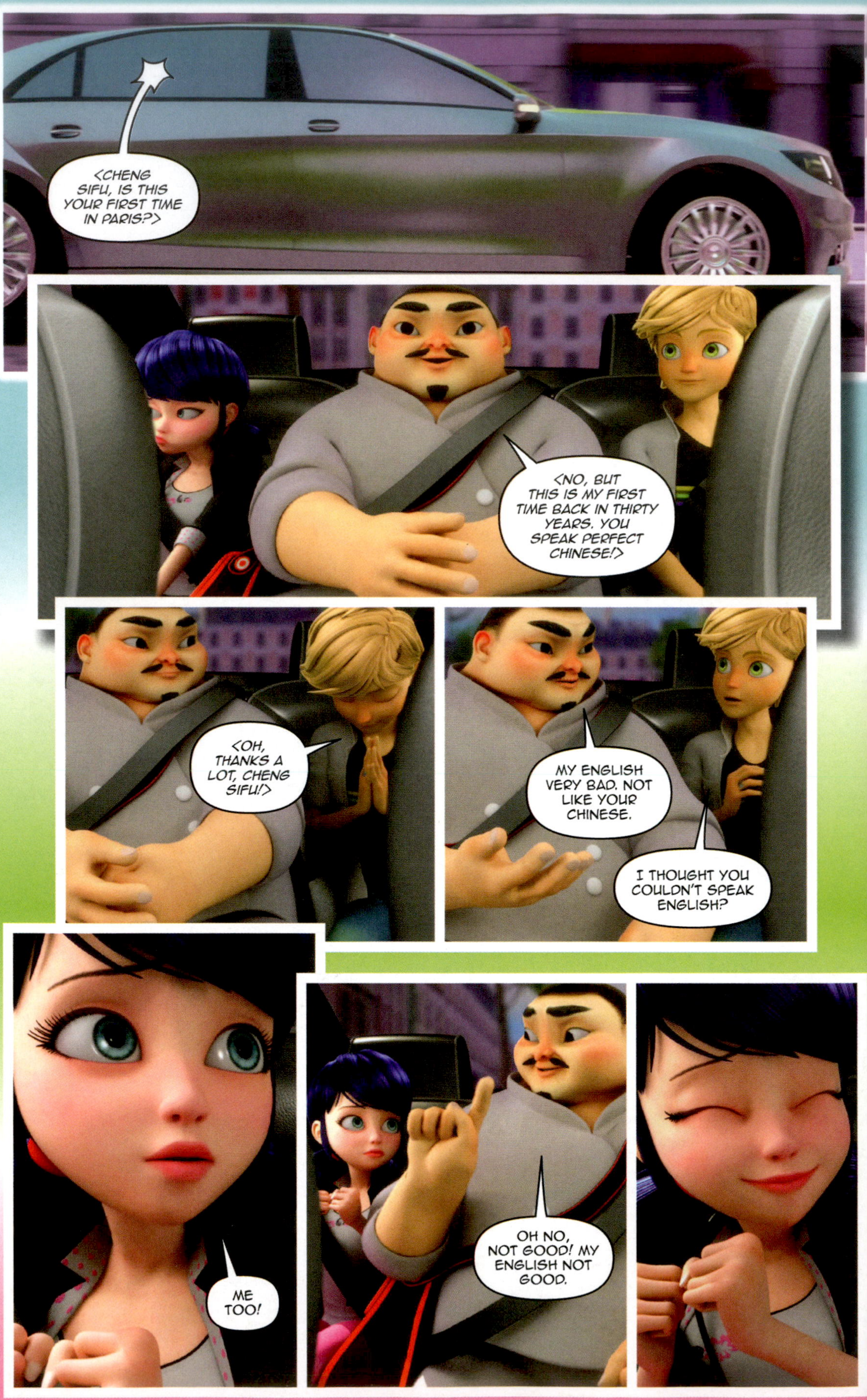
<CHENG SIFU, IS THIS YOUR FIRST TIME IN PARIS?>
<NO, BUT THIS IS MY FIRST TIME BACK IN THIRTY YEARS. YOU SPEAK PERFECT CHINESE!>
<OH, THANKS A LOT, CHENG SIFU!>
MY ENGLISH VERY BAD. NOT LIKE YOUR CHINESE.
I THOUGHT YOU COULDN'T SPEAK ENGLISH?
ME TOO!
OH NO, NOT GOOD! MY ENGLISH NOT GOOD.

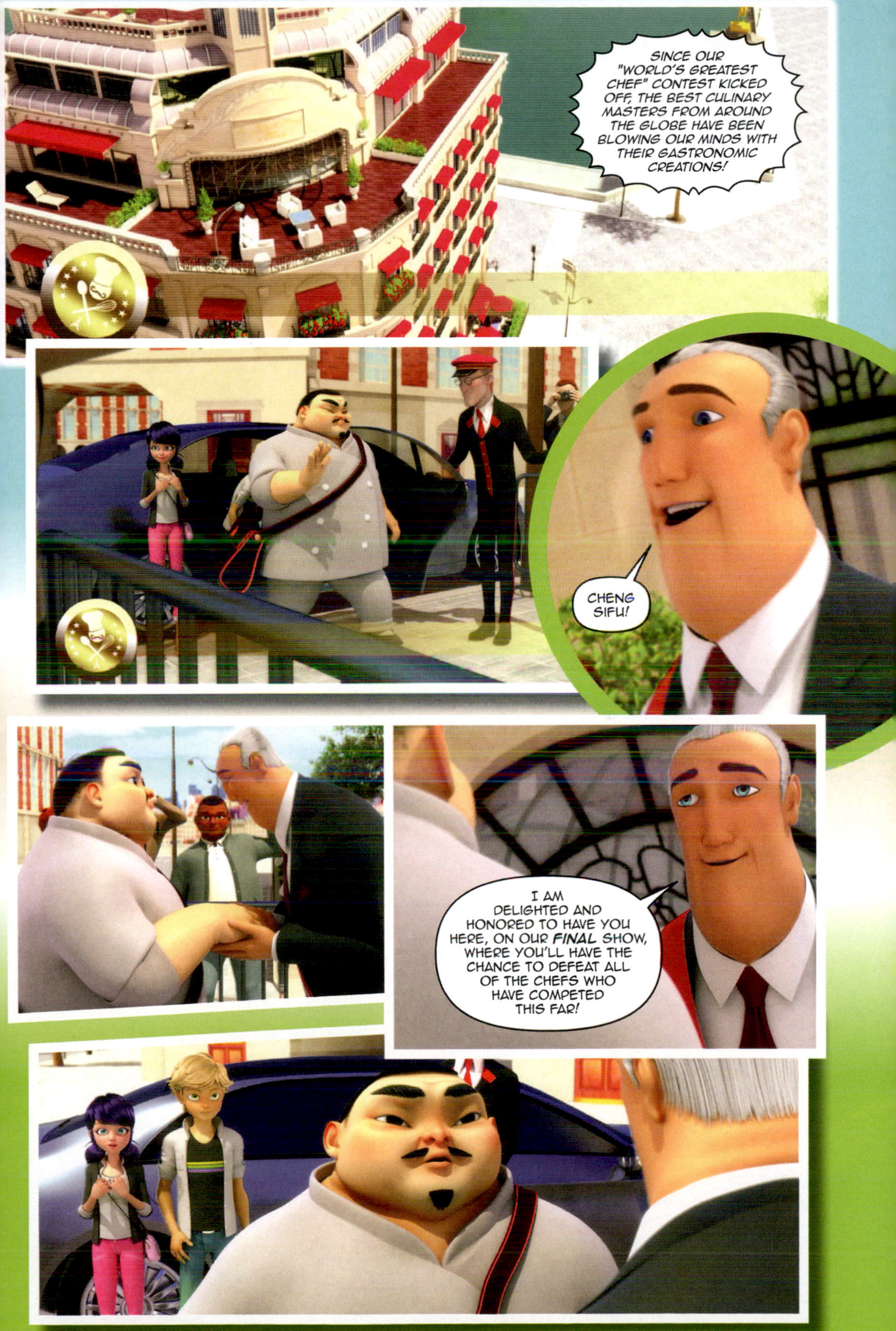

SINCE OUR "WORLD'S GREATEST CHEF" CONTEST KICKED OFF, THE BEST CULINARY MASTERS FROM AROUND THE GLOBE HAVE BEEN BLOWING OUR MINDS WITH THEIR GASTRONOMIC CREATIONS!
CHENG SIFU!
I AM DELIGHTED AND HONORED TO HAVE YOU HERE, ON OUR *FINAL* SHOW, WHERE YOU'LL HAVE THE CHANCE TO DEFEAT ALL OF THE CHEFS WHO HAVE COMPETED THIS FAR!

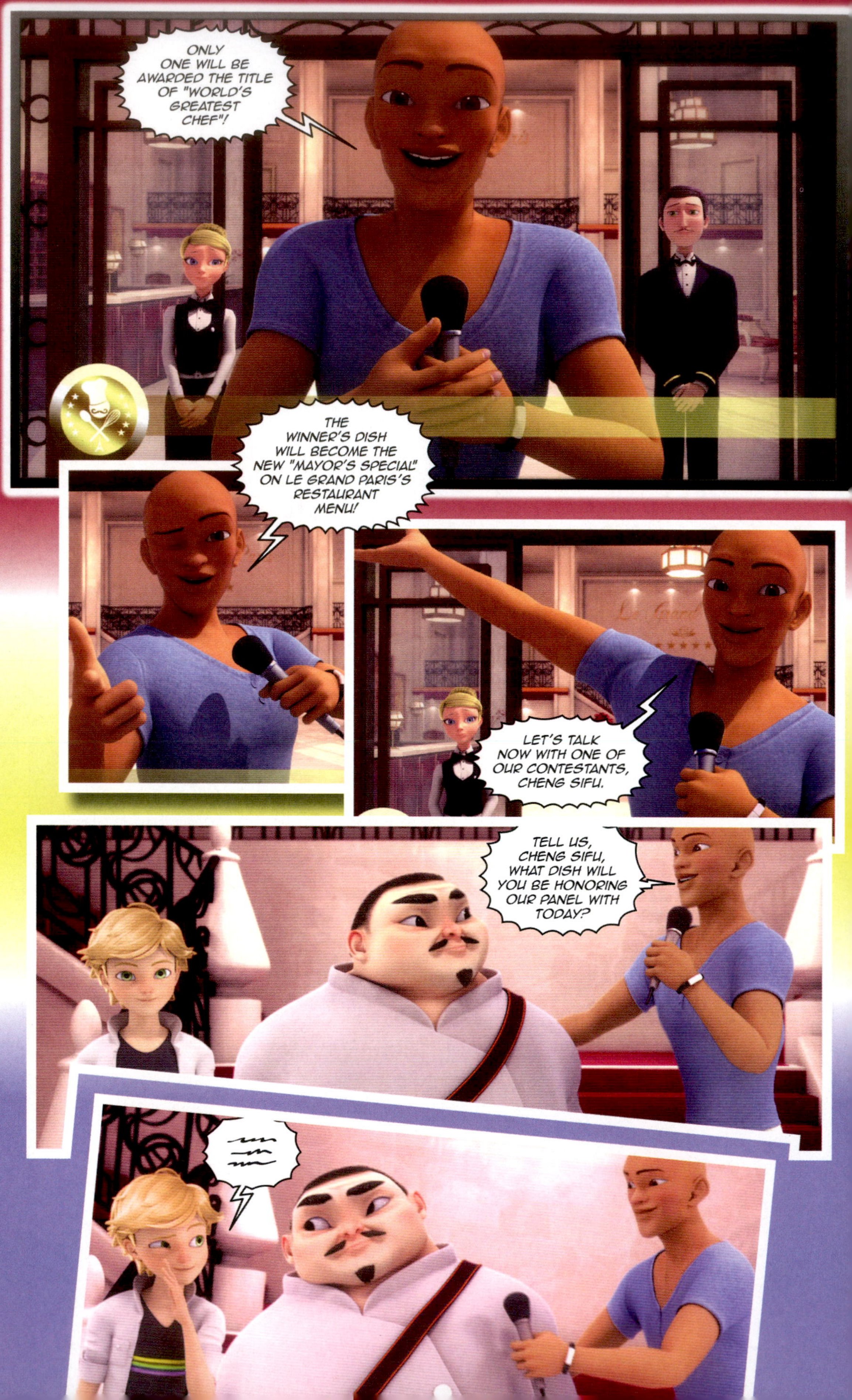
ONLY ONE WILL BE AWARDED THE TITLE OF "WORLD'S GREATEST CHEF"!
THE WINNER'S DISH WILL BECOME THE NEW "MAYOR'S SPECIAL" ON LE GRAND PARIS'S RESTAURANT MENU!
LET'S TALK NOW WITH ONE OF OUR CONTESTANTS, CHENG SIFU.
TELL US, CHENG SIFU, WHAT DISH WILL YOU BE HONORING OUR PANEL WITH TODAY?

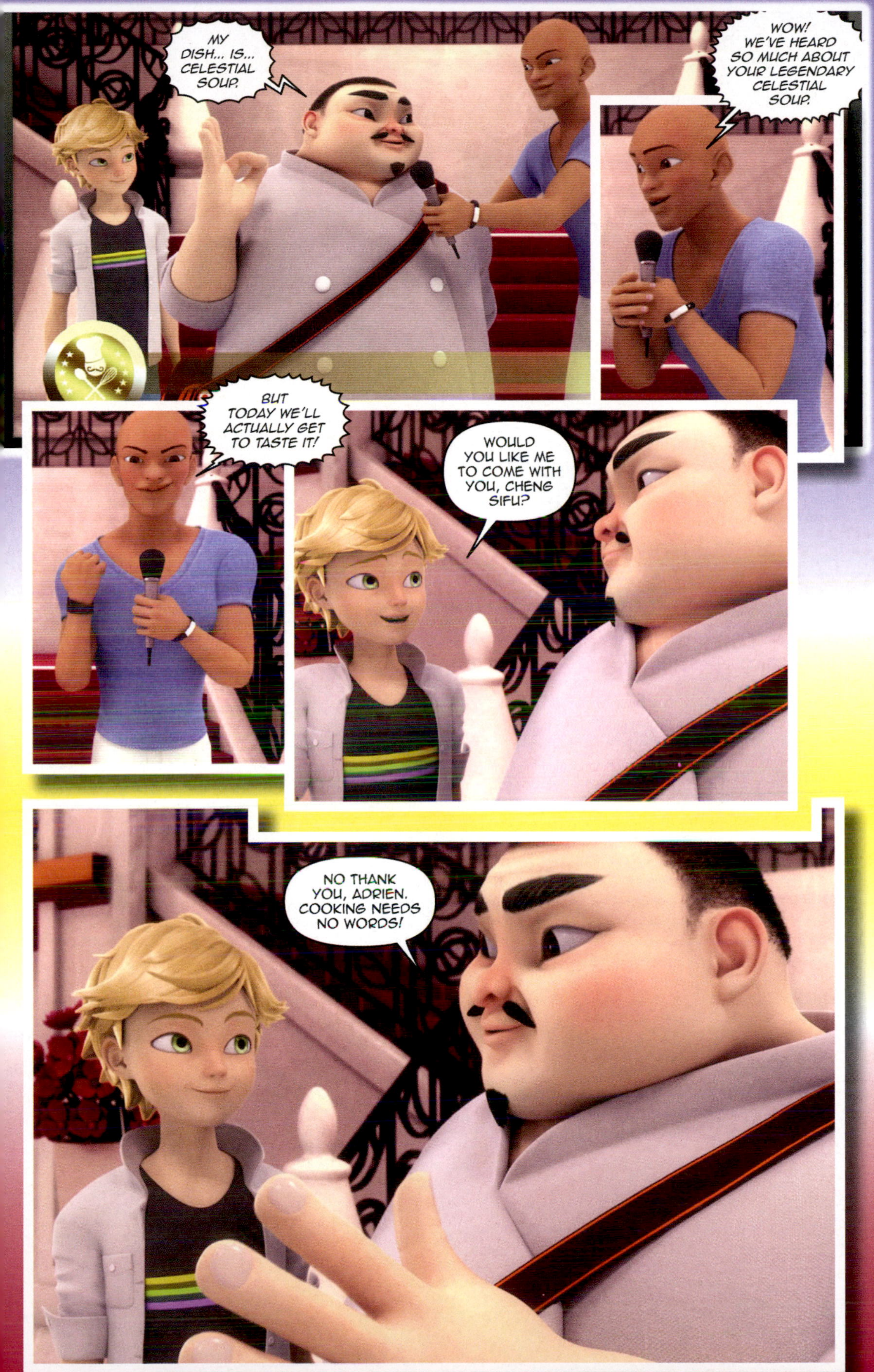
MY DISH... IS... CELESTIAL SOUP.
WOW! WE'VE HEARD SO MUCH ABOUT YOUR LEGENDARY CELESTIAL SOUP.
BUT TODAY WE'LL ACTUALLY GET TO TASTE IT!
WOULD YOU LIKE ME TO COME WITH YOU, CHENG SIFU?
NO THANK YOU, ADRIEN. COOKING NEEDS NO WORDS!

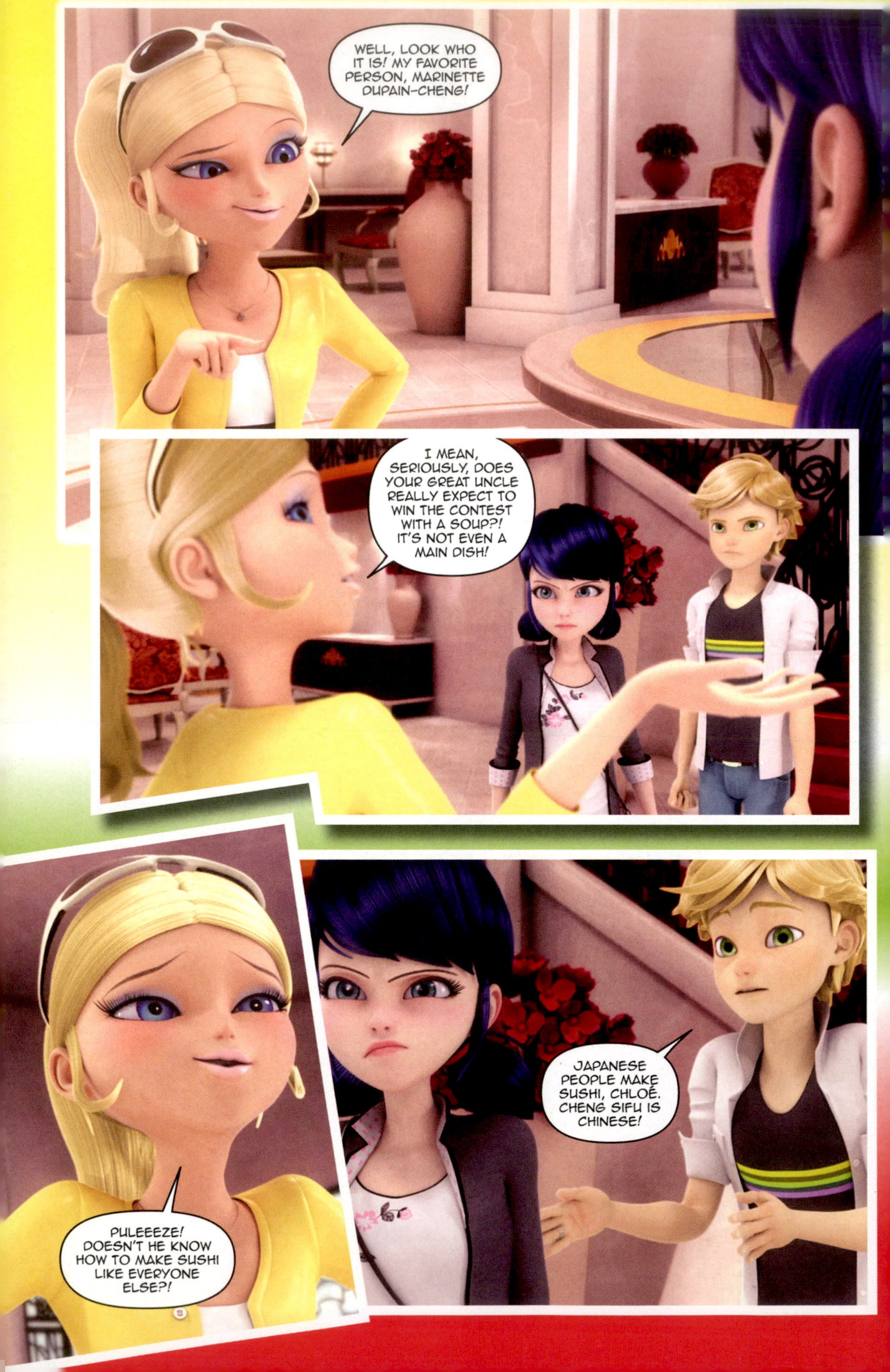
WELL, LOOK WHO IT IS! MY FAVORITE PERSON, MARINETTE DUPAIN-CHENG!
I MEAN, SERIOUSLY, DOES YOUR GREAT UNCLE REALLY EXPECT TO WIN THE CONTEST WITH A SOUP?! IT'S NOT EVEN A MAIN DISH!
PULEEEZE! DOESN'T HE KNOW HOW TO MAKE SUSHI LIKE EVERYONE ELSE?!
JAPANESE PEOPLE MAKE SUSHI, CHLOÉ. CHENG SIFU IS CHINESE!

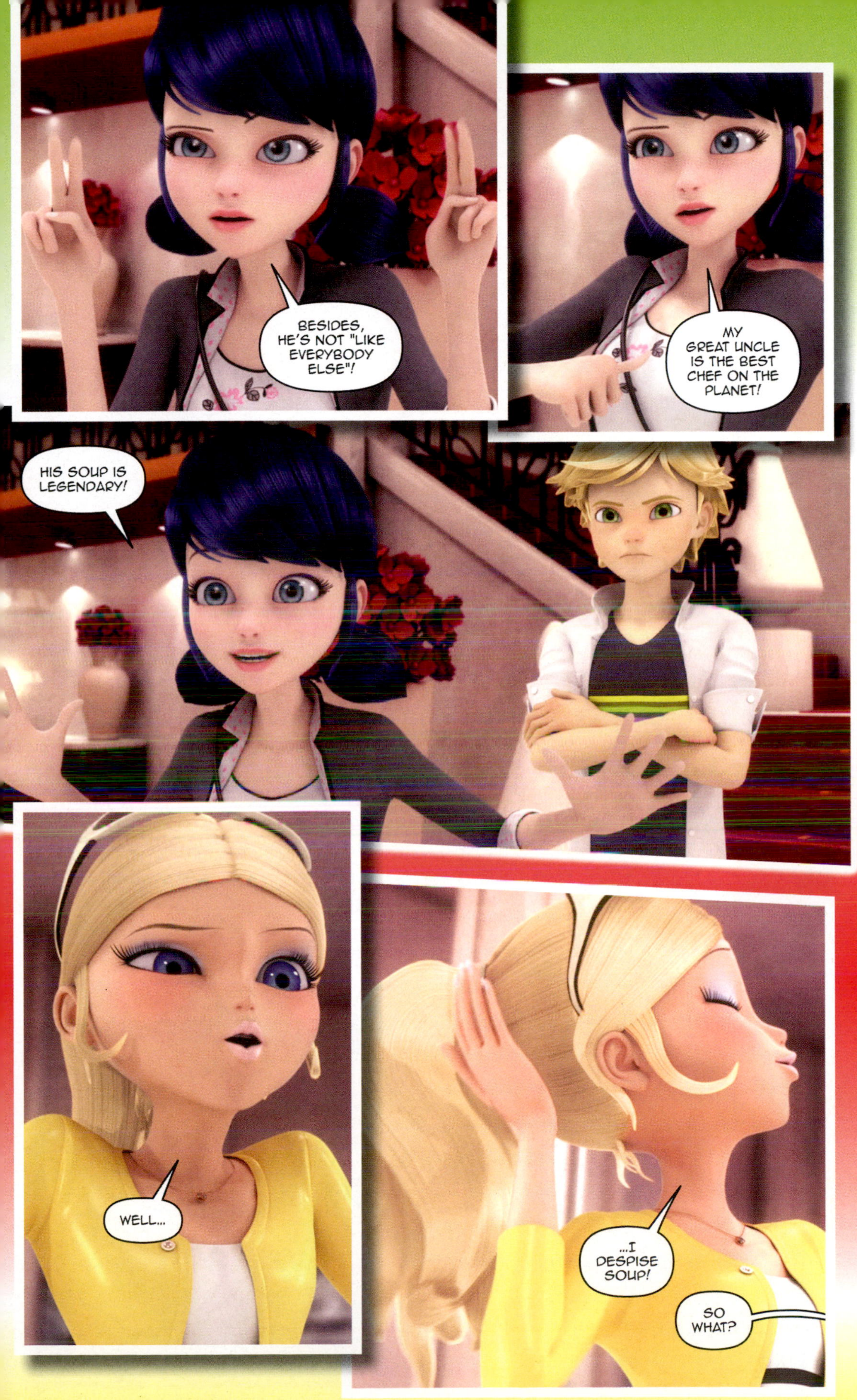
BESIDES, HE'S NOT "LIKE EVERYBODY ELSE"!
MY GREAT UNCLE IS THE BEST CHEF ON THE PLANET!
HIS SOUP IS LEGENDARY!
WELL...
...I DESPISE SOUP!
SO WHAT?

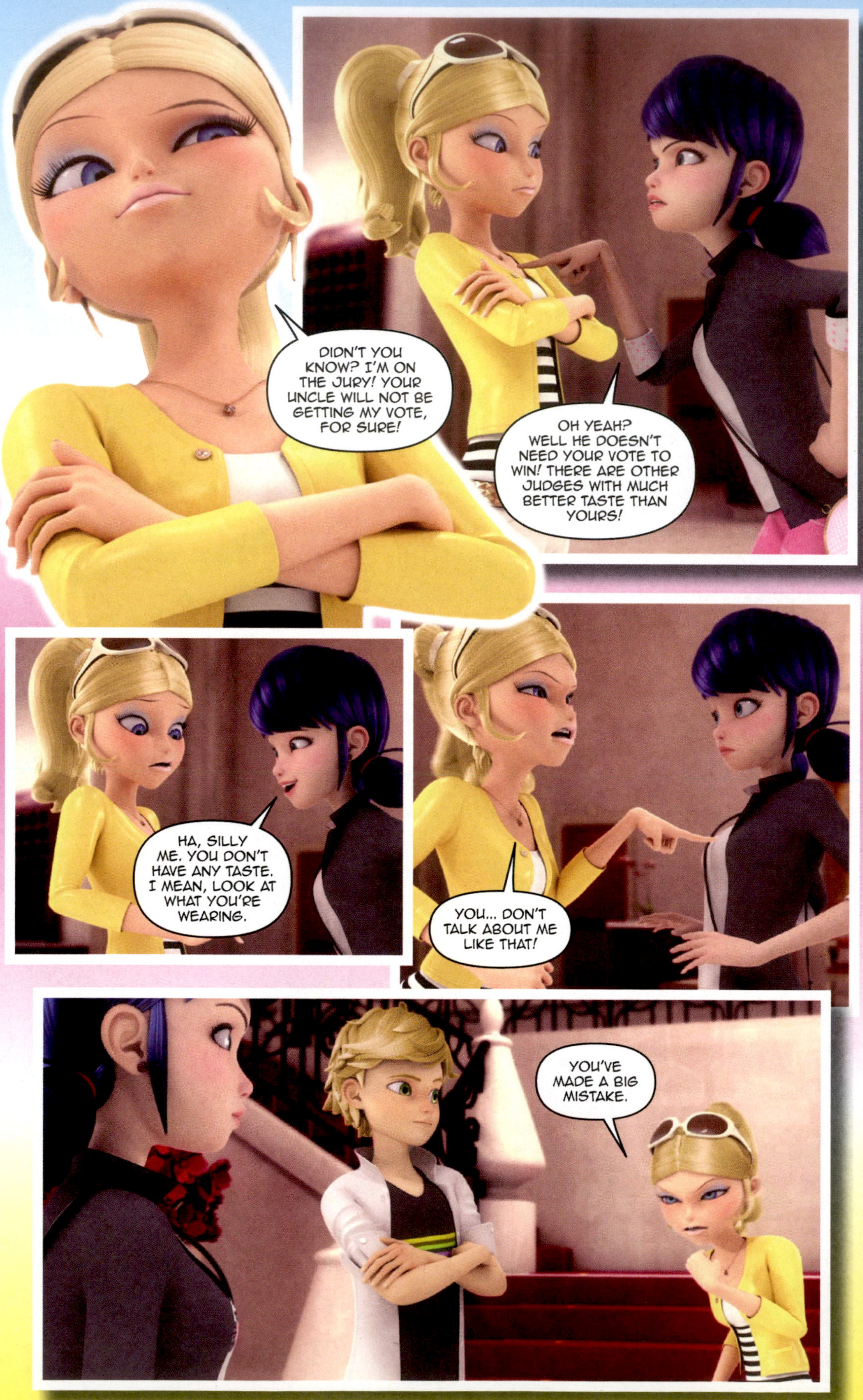
DIDN'T YOU KNOW? I'M ON THE JURY! YOUR UNCLE WILL NOT BE GETTING MY VOTE, FOR SURE!
OH YEAH? WELL HE DOESN'T NEED YOUR VOTE TO WIN! THERE ARE OTHER JUDGES WITH MUCH BETTER TASTE THAN YOURS!
HA, SILLY ME. YOU DON'T HAVE ANY TASTE. I MEAN, LOOK AT WHAT YOU'RE WEARING.
YOU... DON'T TALK ABOUT ME LIKE THAT!
YOU'VE MADE A BIG MISTAKE.

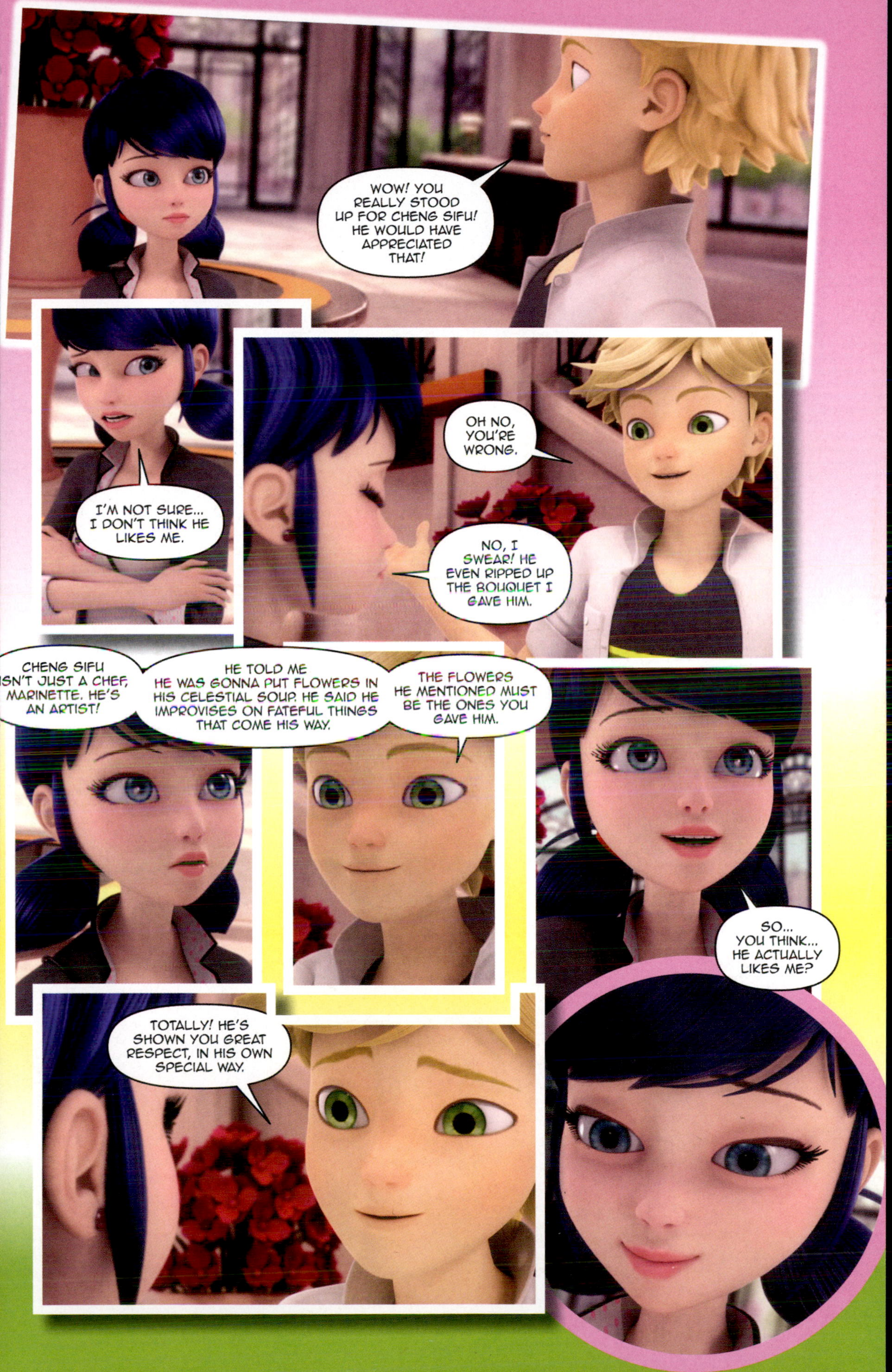
WOW! YOU REALLY STOOD UP FOR CHENG SIFU! HE WOULD HAVE APPRECIATED THAT!
I'M NOT SURE... I DON'T THINK HE LIKES ME.
OH NO, YOU'RE WRONG.
NO, I SWEAR! HE EVEN RIPPED UP THE BOUQUET I GAVE HIM.
CHENG SIFU ISN'T JUST A CHEF, MARINETTE. HE'S AN ARTIST!
HE TOLD ME HE WAS GONNA PUT FLOWERS IN HIS CELESTIAL SOUP. HE SAID HE IMPROVISES ON FATEFUL THINGS THAT COME HIS WAY.
THE FLOWERS HE MENTIONED MUST BE THE ONES YOU GAVE HIM.
SO... YOU THINK... HE ACTUALLY LIKES ME?
TOTALLY! HE'S SHOWN YOU GREAT RESPECT, IN HIS OWN SPECIAL WAY.

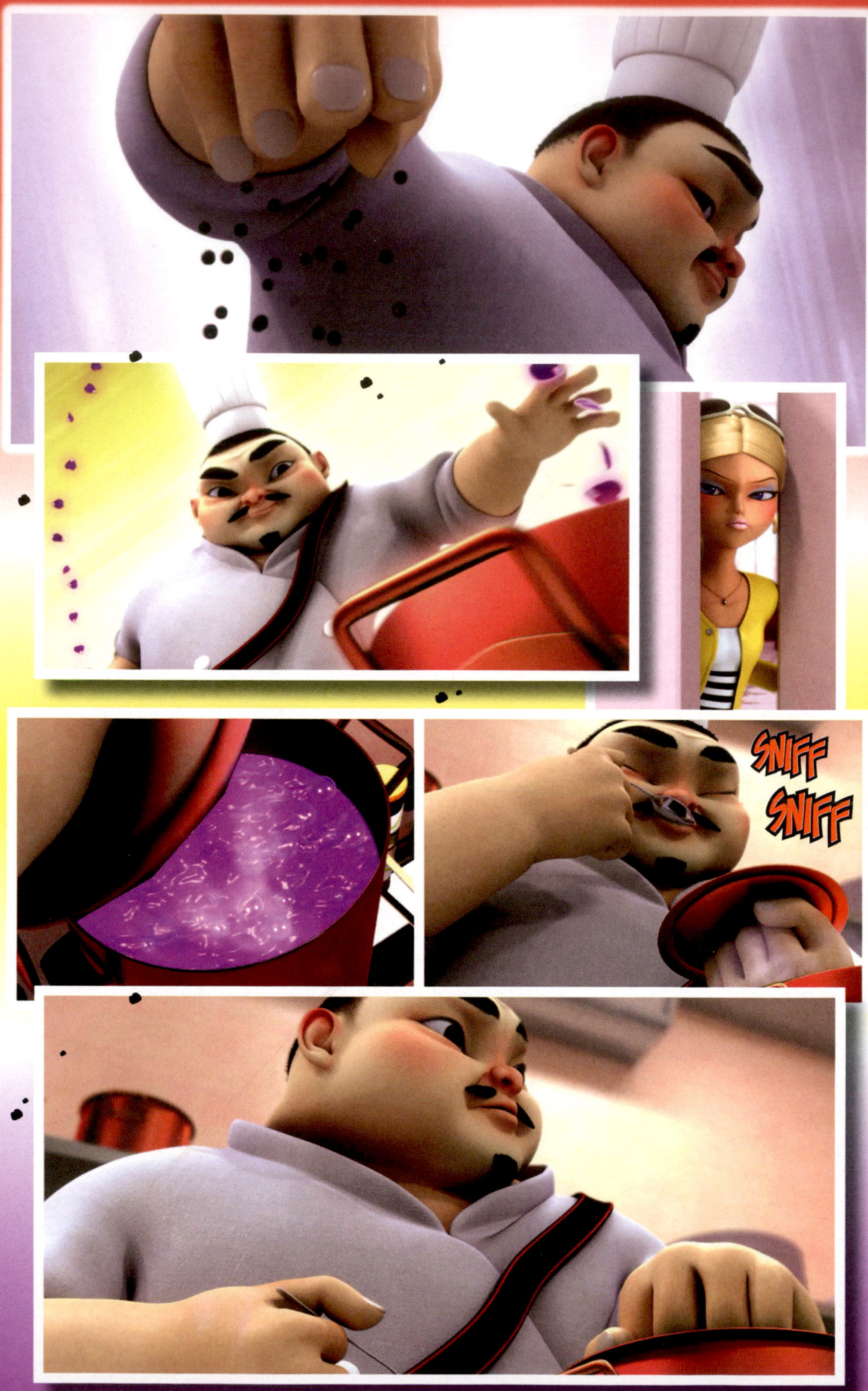
SNIFF
SNIFF

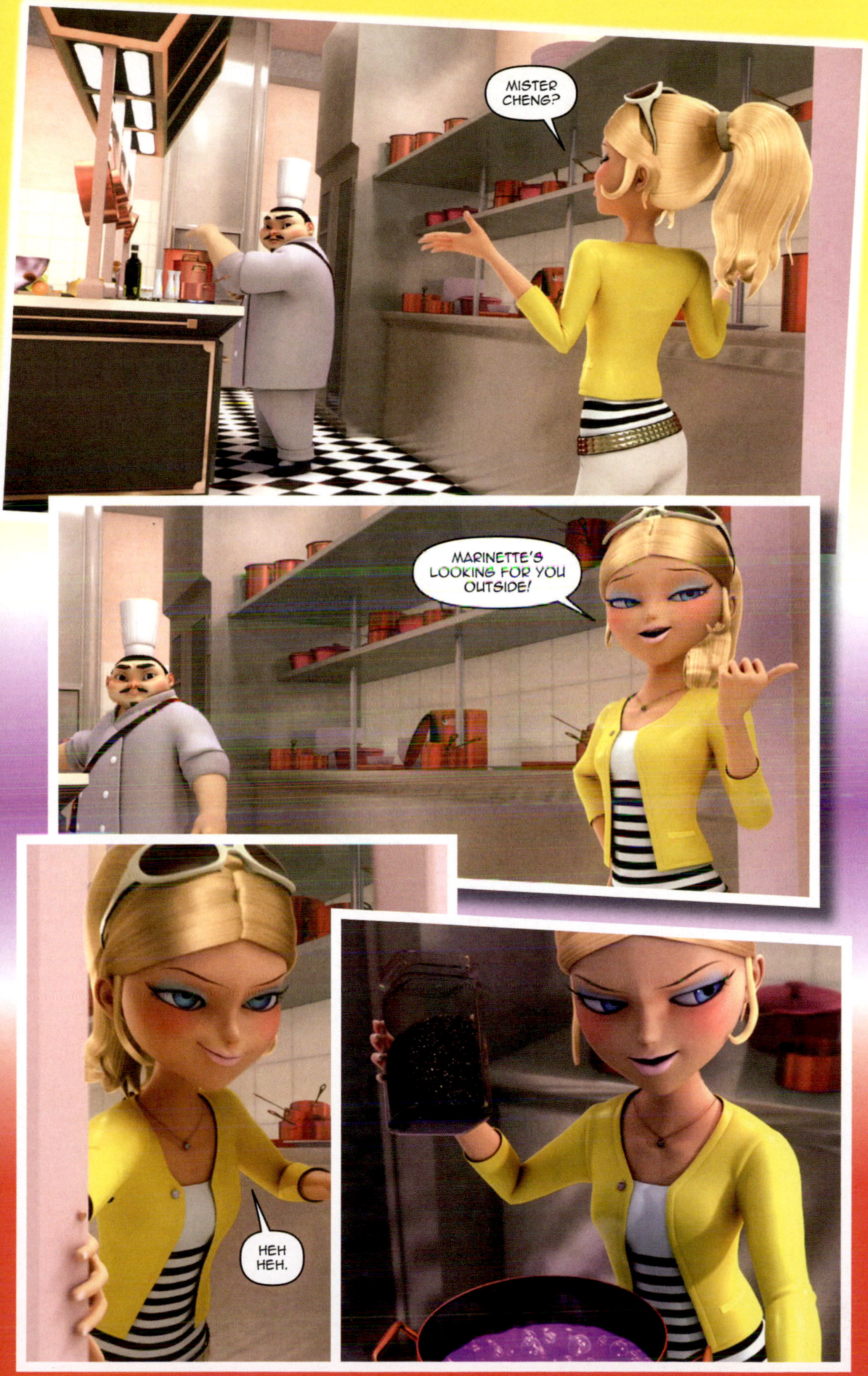
MISTER CHENG?
MARINETTE'S LOOKING FOR YOU OUTSIDE!
HEH HEH.

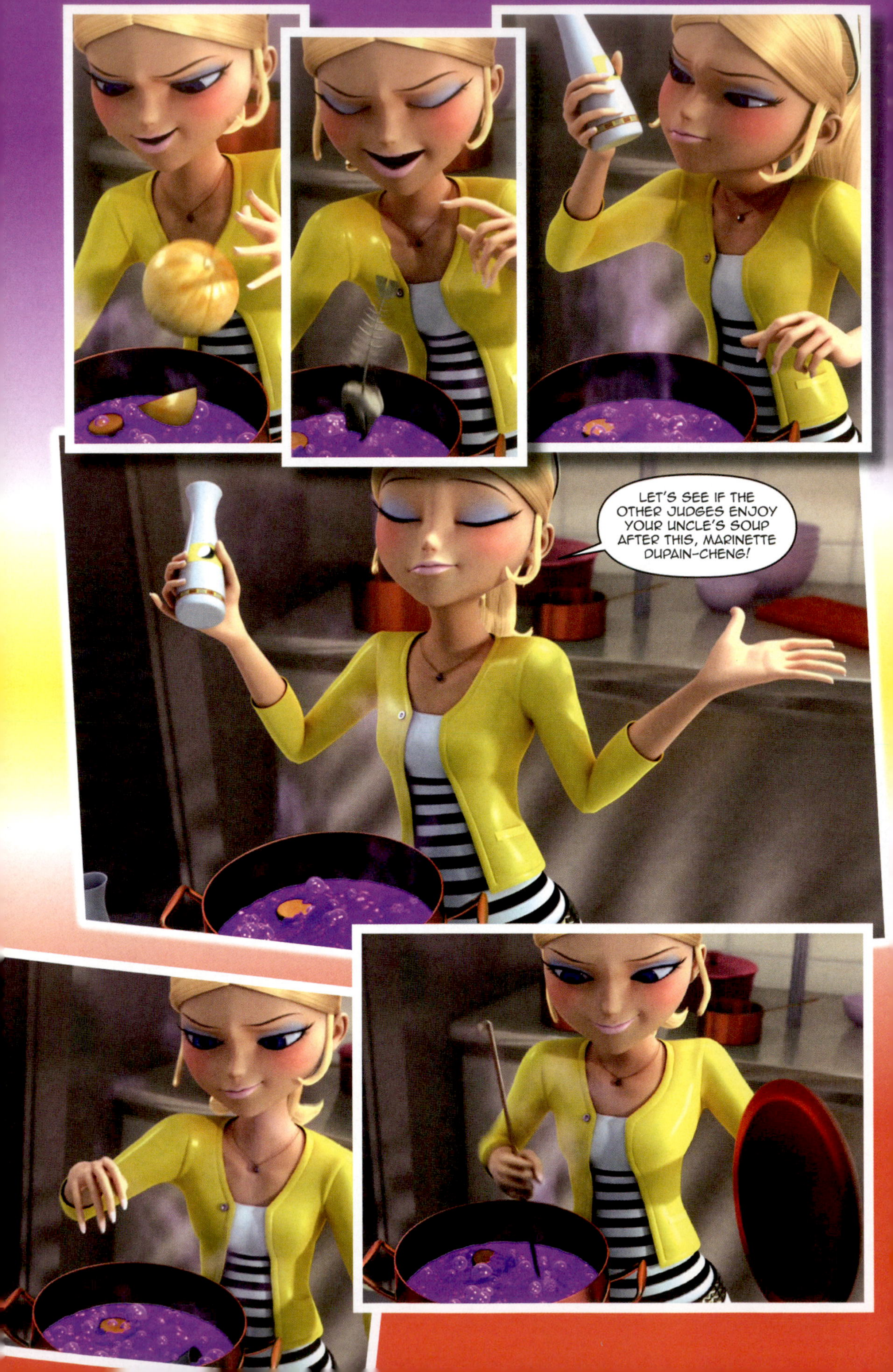
LET'S SEE IF THE OTHER JUDGES ENJOY YOUR UNCLE'S SOUP AFTER THIS, MARINETTE DUPAIN-CHENG!

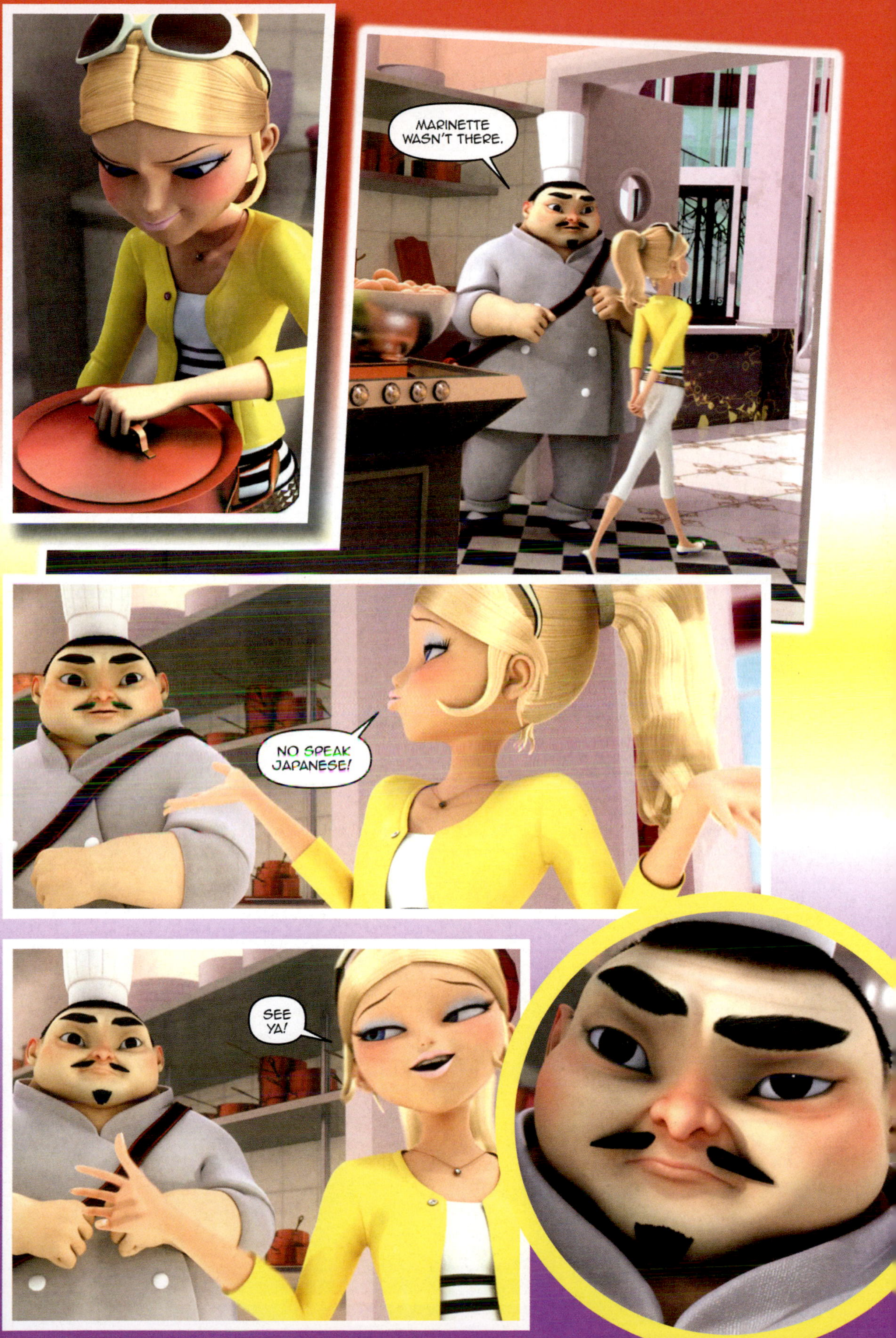
MARINETTE WASN'T THERE.
NO SPEAK JAPANESE!
SEE YA!

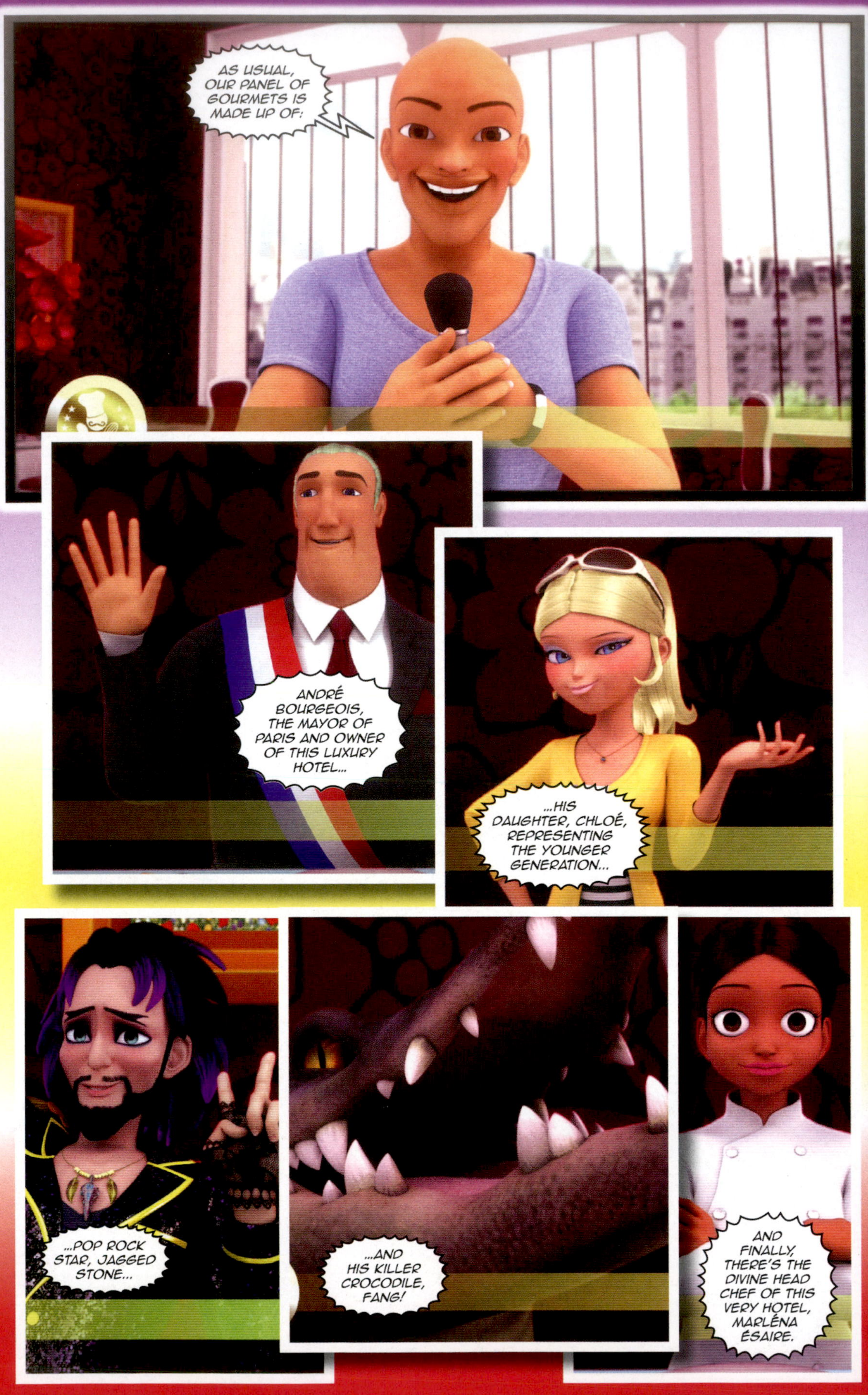
AS USUAL, OUR PANEL OF GOURMETS IS MADE UP OF:
ANDRÉ BOURGEOIS, THE MAYOR OF PARIS AND OWNER OF THIS LUXURY HOTEL...
...HIS DAUGHTER, CHLOÉ, REPRESENTING THE YOUNGER GENERATION...
...POP ROCK STAR, JAGGED STONE...
...AND HIS KILLER CROCODILE, FANG!
AND FINALLY, THERE'S THE DIVINE HEAD CHEF OF THIS VERY HOTEL, MARLÉNA ÉSAIRE.

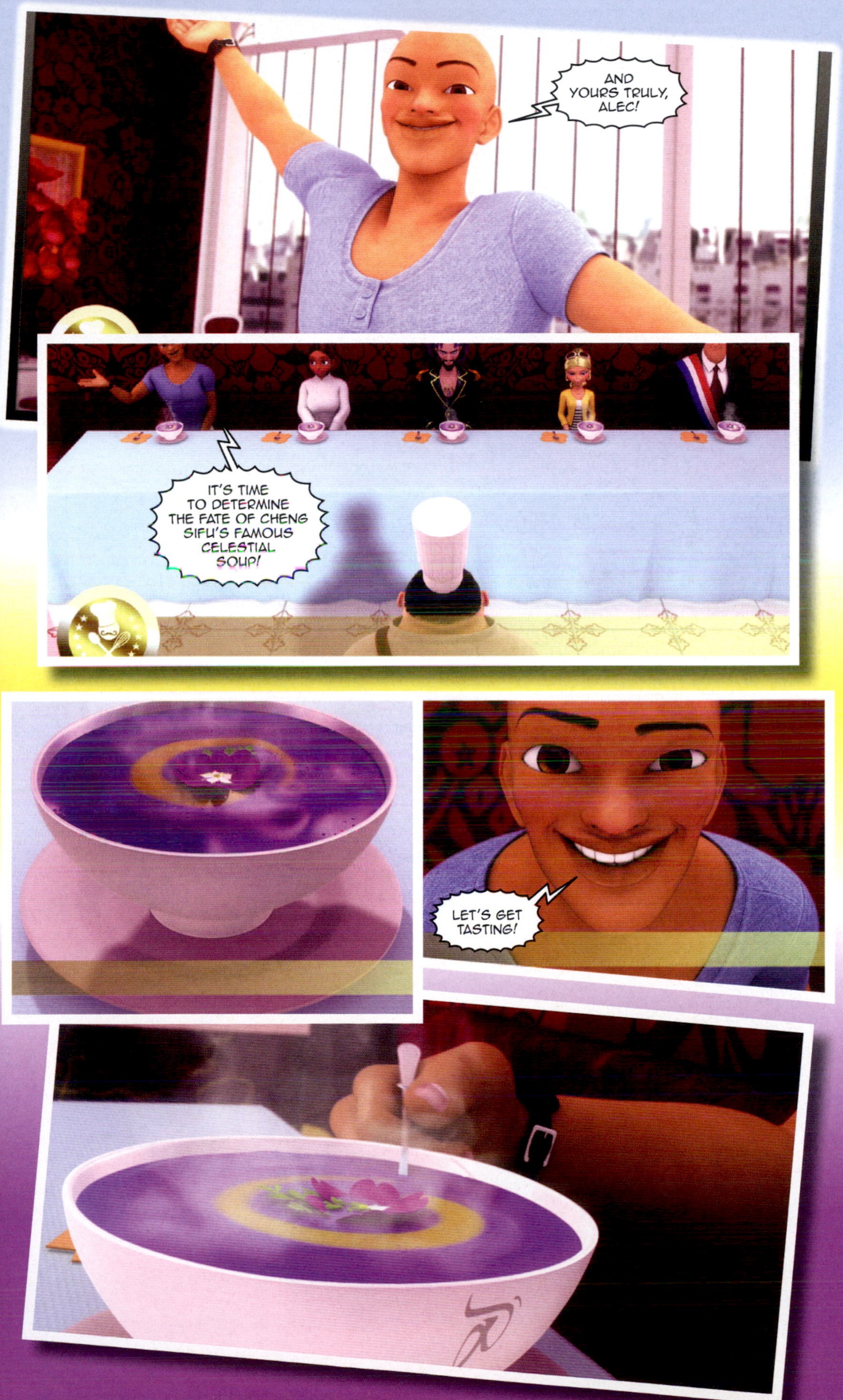
AND YOURS TRULY, ALEC!
IT'S TIME TO DETERMINE THE FATE OF CHENG SIFU'S FAMOUS CELESTIAL SOUP!
LET'S GET TASTING!

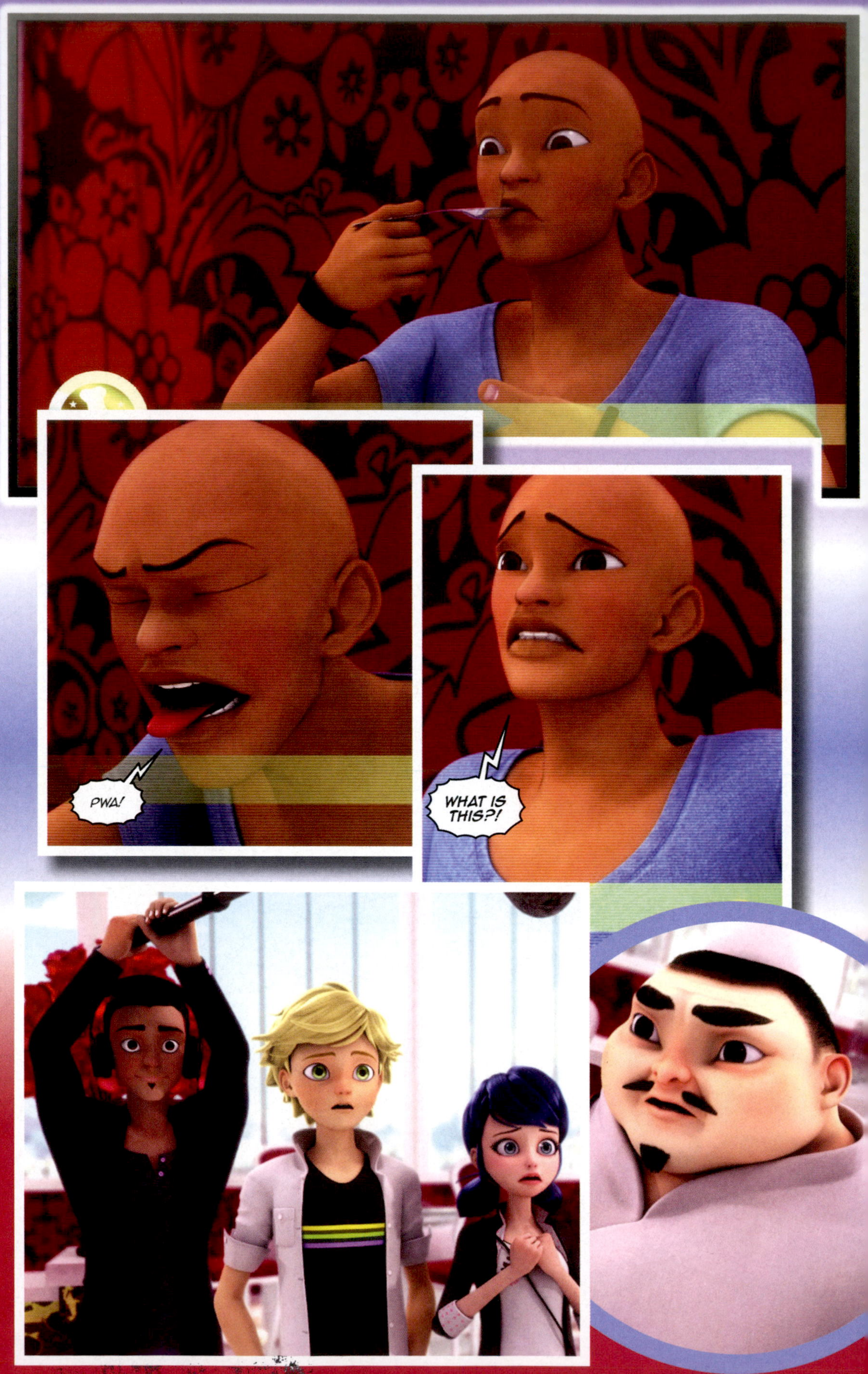
PWA!
WHAT IS THIS?!

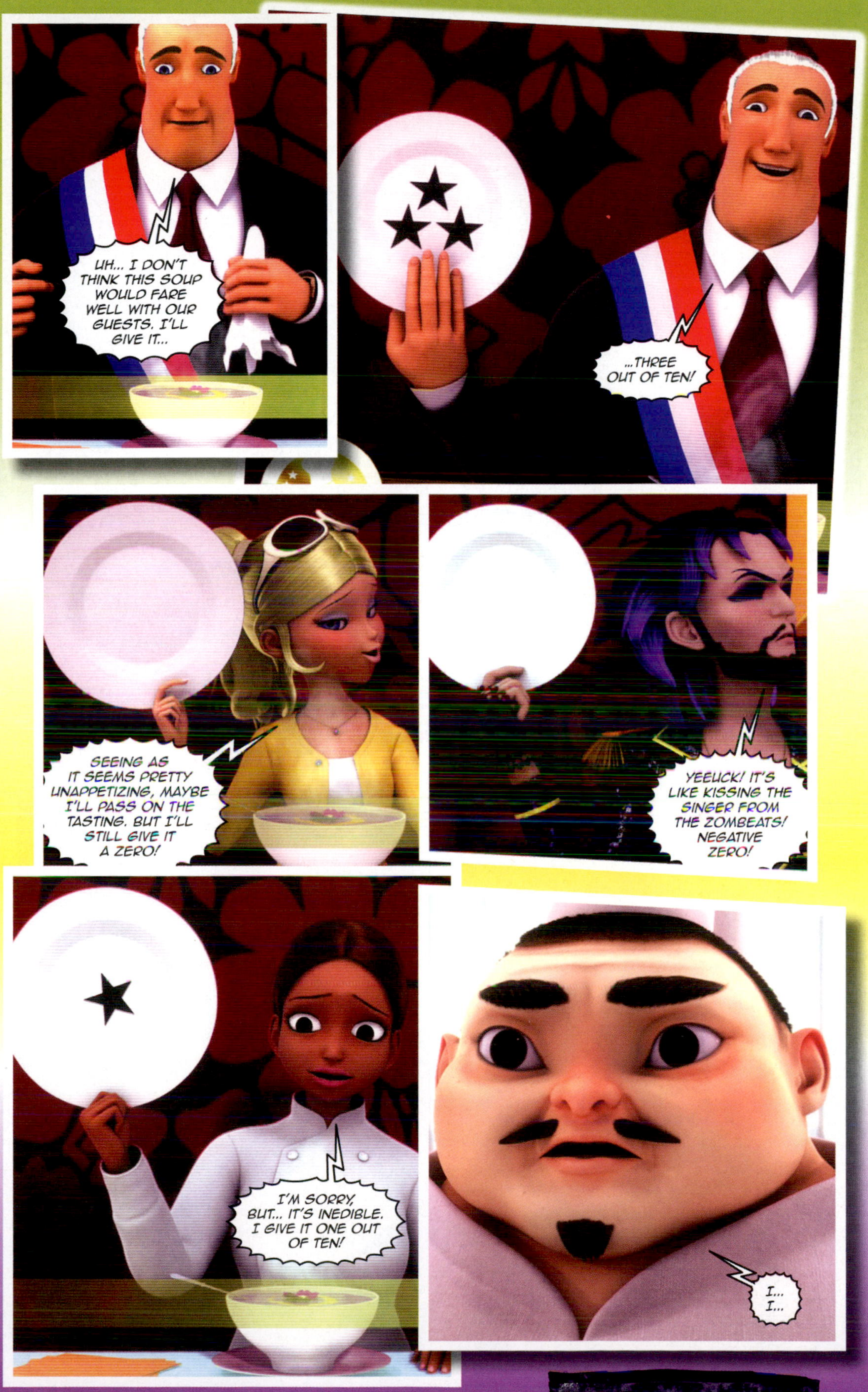
UH... I DON'T THINK THIS SOUP WOULD FARE WELL WITH OUR GUESTS. I'LL GIVE IT...
...THREE OUT OF TEN!
SEEING AS IT SEEMS PRETTY UNAPPETIZING, MAYBE I'LL PASS ON THE TASTING. BUT I'LL STILL GIVE IT A ZERO!
YEEUCK! IT'S LIKE KISSING THE SINGER FROM THE ZOMBEATS! NEGATIVE ZERO!
I'M SORRY, BUT... IT'S INEDIBLE. I GIVE IT ONE OUT OF TEN!
I... I...

[redacted]

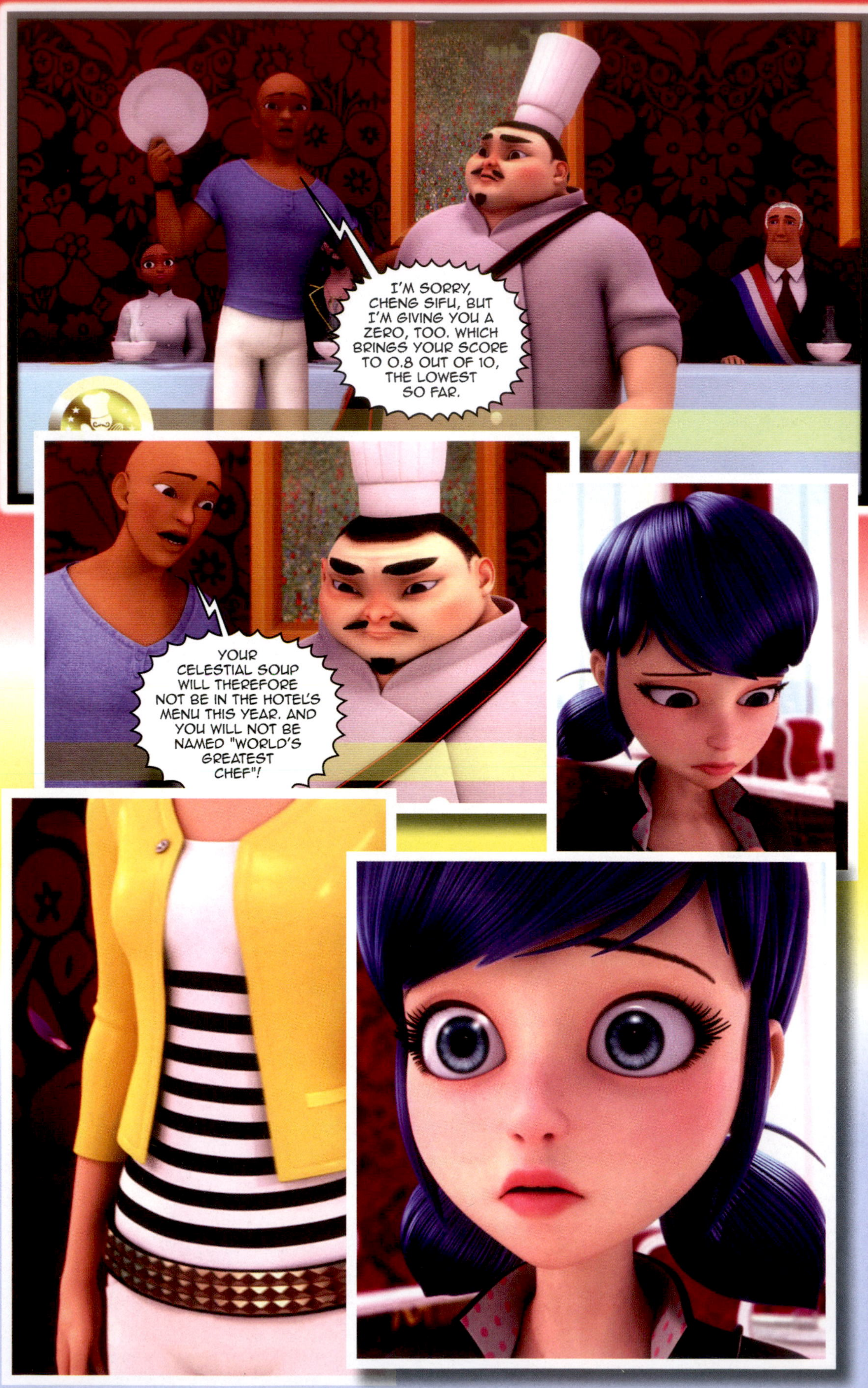
I'M SORRY, CHENG SIFU, BUT I'M GIVING YOU A ZERO, TOO. WHICH BRINGS YOUR SCORE TO 0.8 OUT OF 10, THE LOWEST SO FAR.
YOUR CELESTIAL SOUP WILL THEREFORE NOT BE IN THE HOTEL'S MENU THIS YEAR. AND YOU WILL NOT BE NAMED "WORLD'S GREATEST CHEF"!

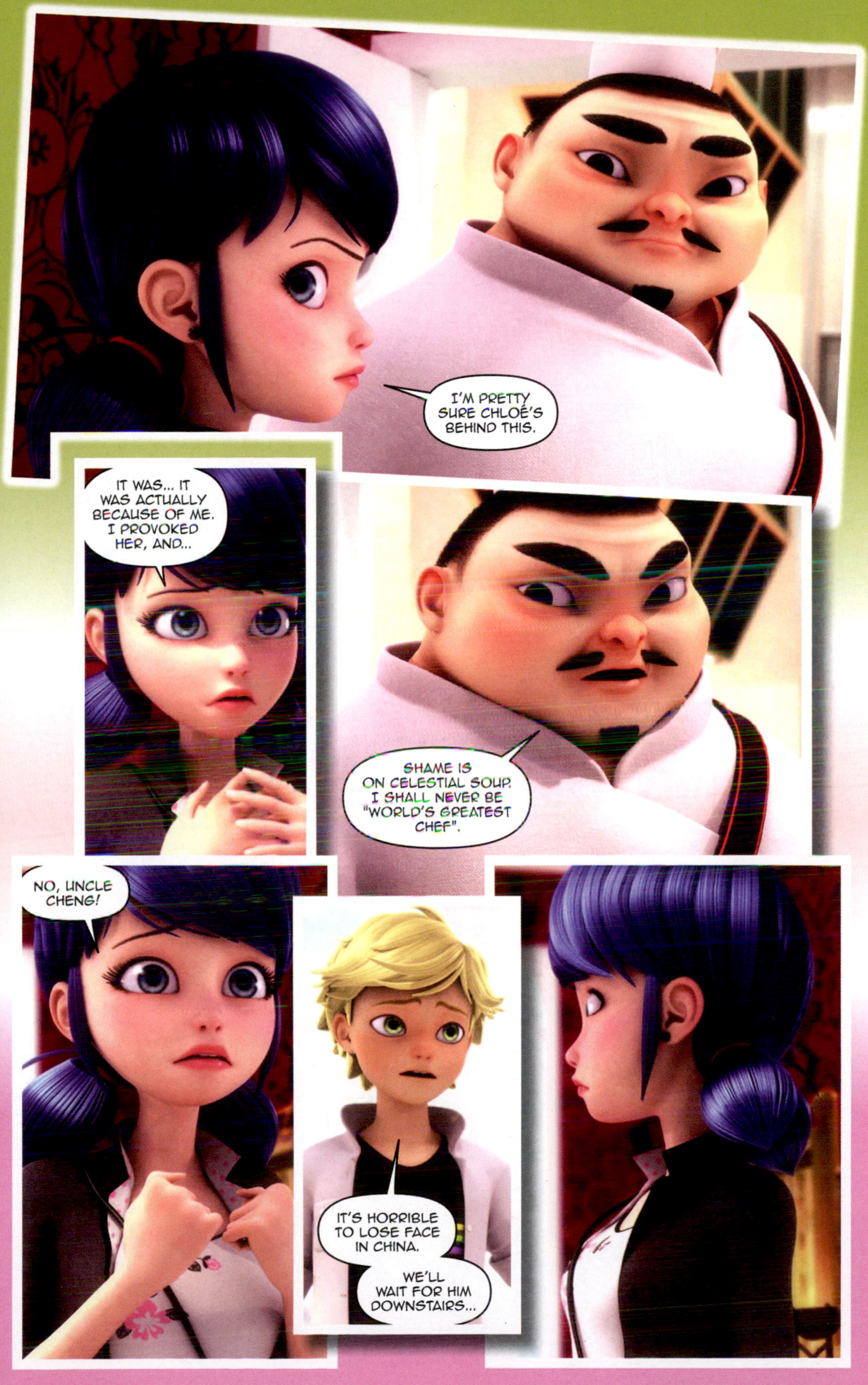
I'M PRETTY SURE CHLOÉ'S BEHIND THIS.
IT WAS... IT WAS ACTUALLY BECAUSE OF ME. I PROVOKED HER, AND...
SHAME IS ON CELESTIAL SOUP. I SHALL NEVER BE "WORLD'S GREATEST CHEF".
NO, UNCLE CHENG!
IT'S HORRIBLE TO LOSE FACE IN CHINA.
WE'LL WAIT FOR HIM DOWNSTAIRS...

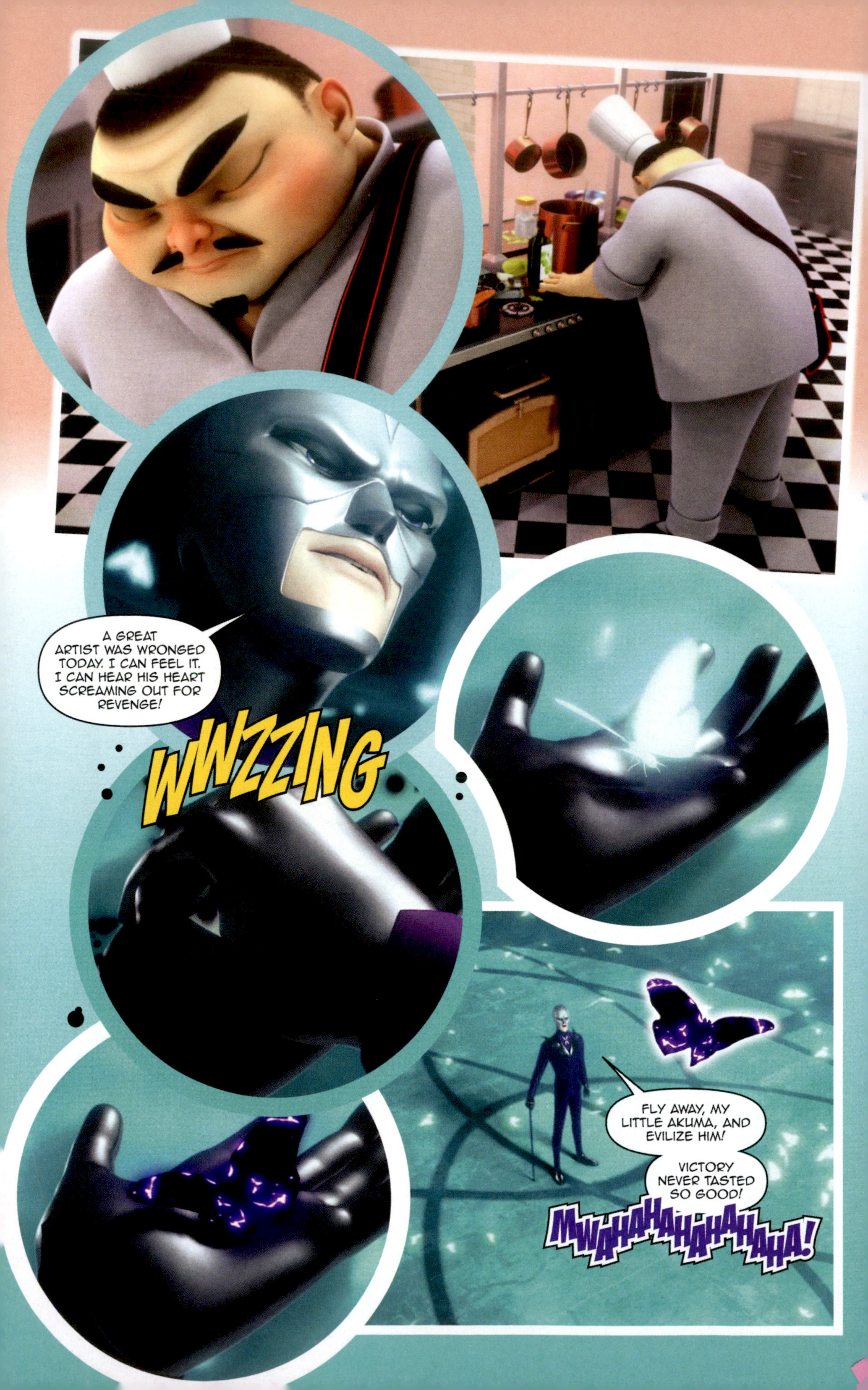
A GREAT ARTIST WAS WRONGED TODAY. I CAN FEEL IT. I CAN HEAR HIS HEART SCREAMING OUT FOR REVENGE!
WWZZING
FLY AWAY, MY LITTLE AKUMA, AND EVILIZE HIM!
VICTORY NEVER TASTED SO GOOD!
MWAHAHAHAHAHAHAHA!

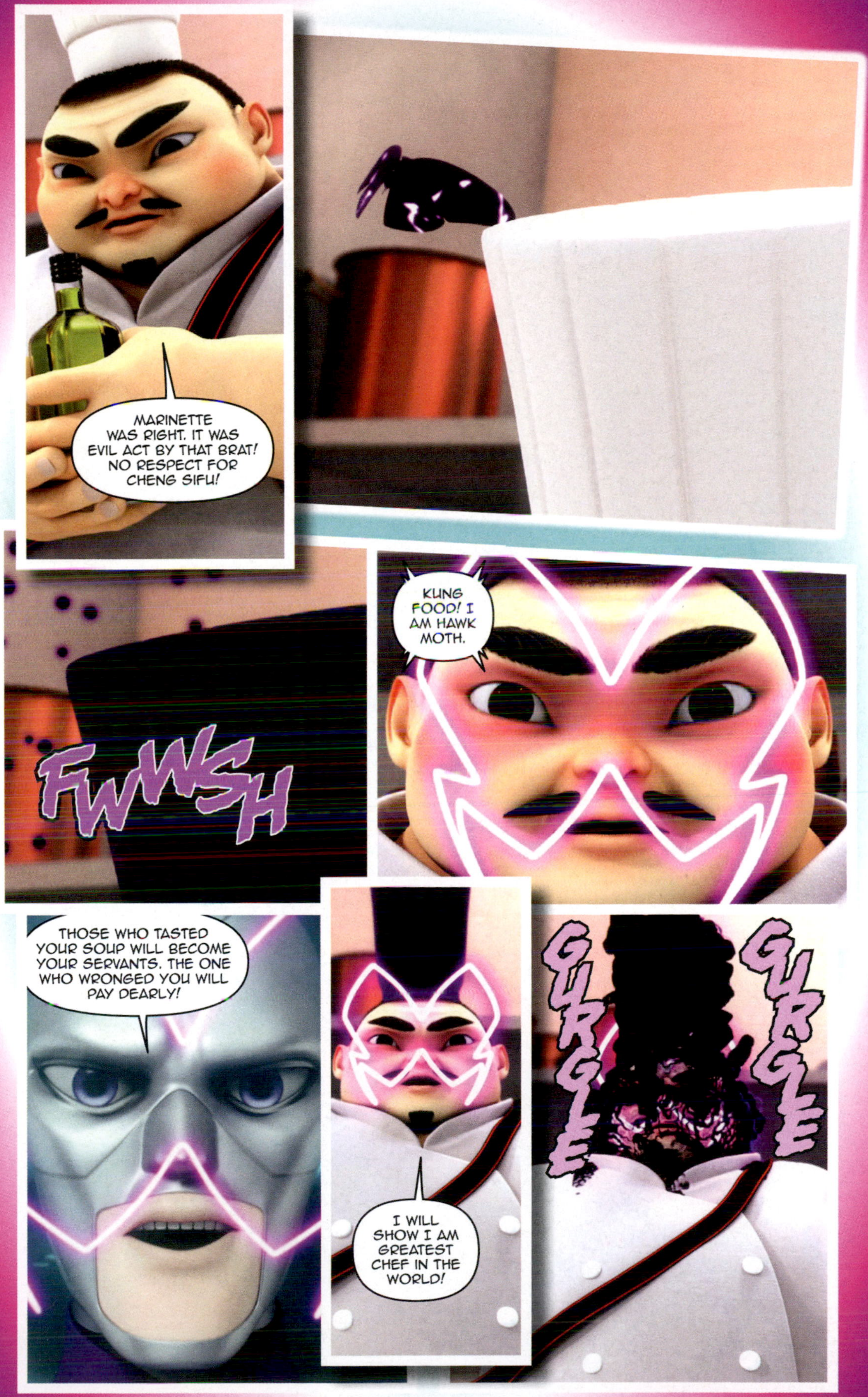
MARINETTE WAS RIGHT. IT WAS EVIL ACT BY THAT BRAT! NO RESPECT FOR CHENG SIFU!
FWWSH
KUNG FOOD! I AM HAWK MOTH.
THOSE WHO TASTED YOUR SOUP WILL BECOME YOUR SERVANTS. THE ONE WHO WRONGED YOU WILL PAY DEARLY!
I WILL SHOW I AM GREATEST CHEF IN THE WORLD!
GURGLE
GURGLE

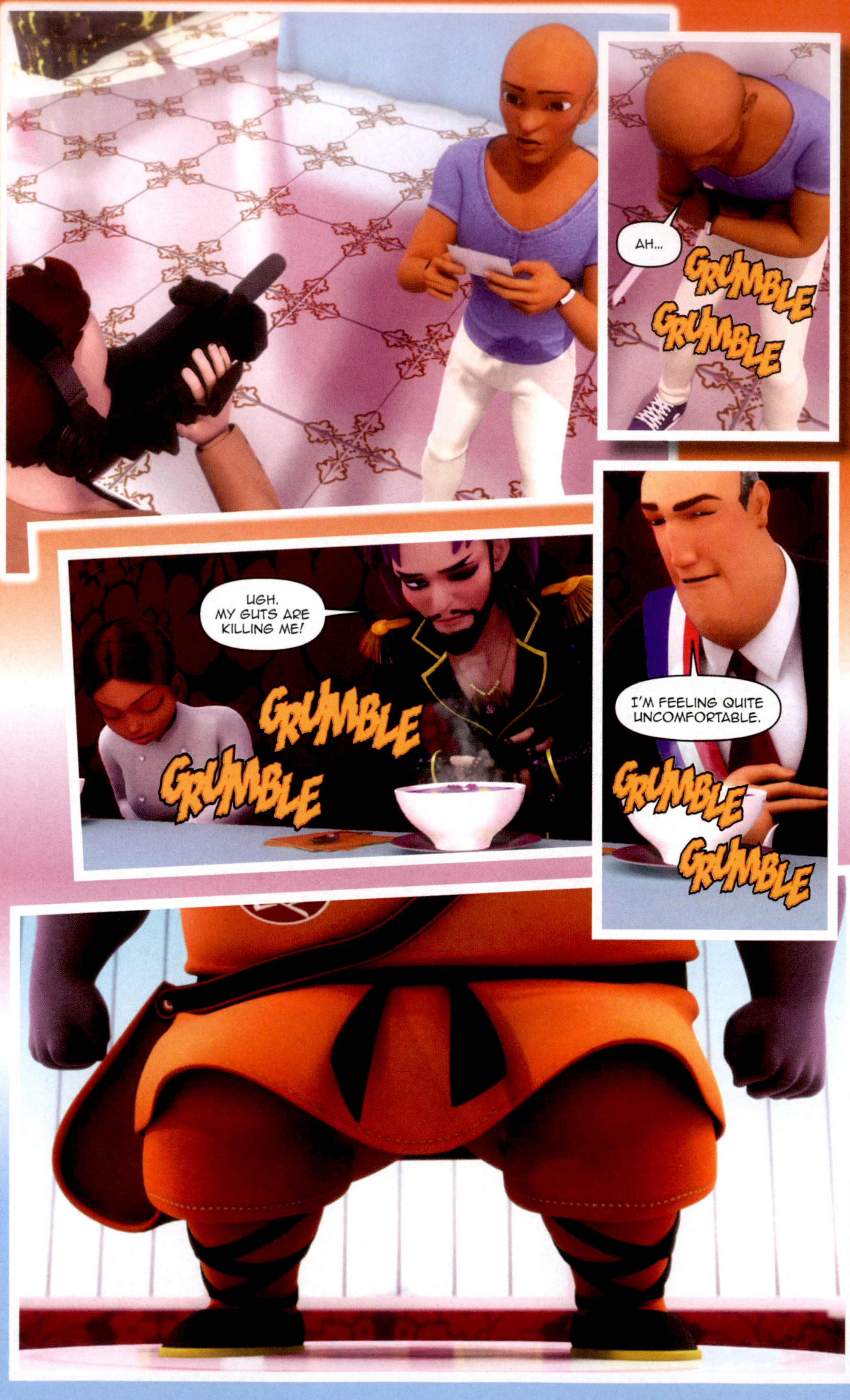
AH...
GRUMBLE
GRUMBLE
UGH. MY GUTS ARE KILLING ME!
GRUMBLE
GRUMBLE
I'M FEELING QUITE UNCOMFORTABLE.
GRUMBLE
GRUMBLE

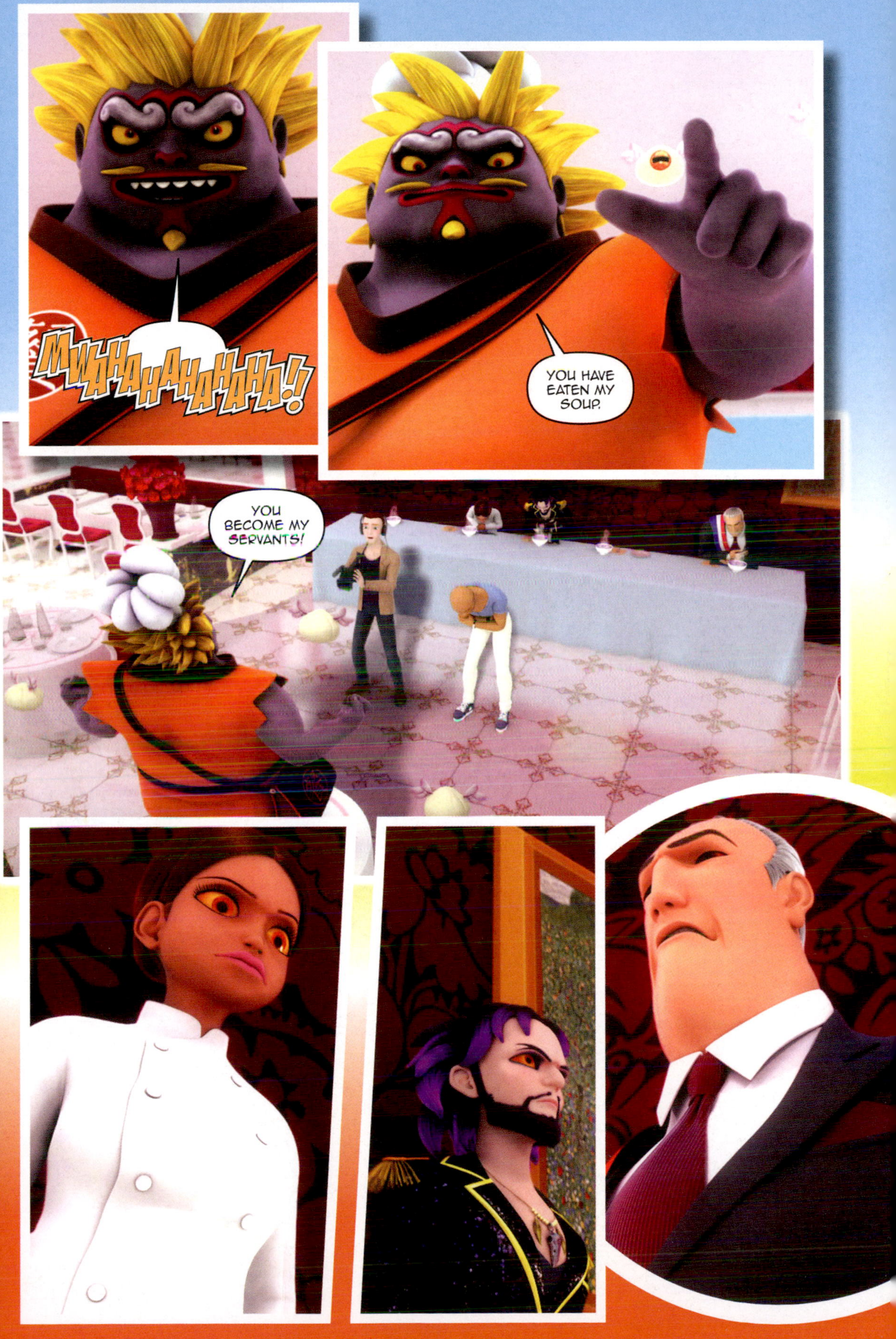
MWAHAHAHAHAHAHA!!
YOU HAVE EATEN MY SOUP.
YOU BECOME MY SERVANTS!

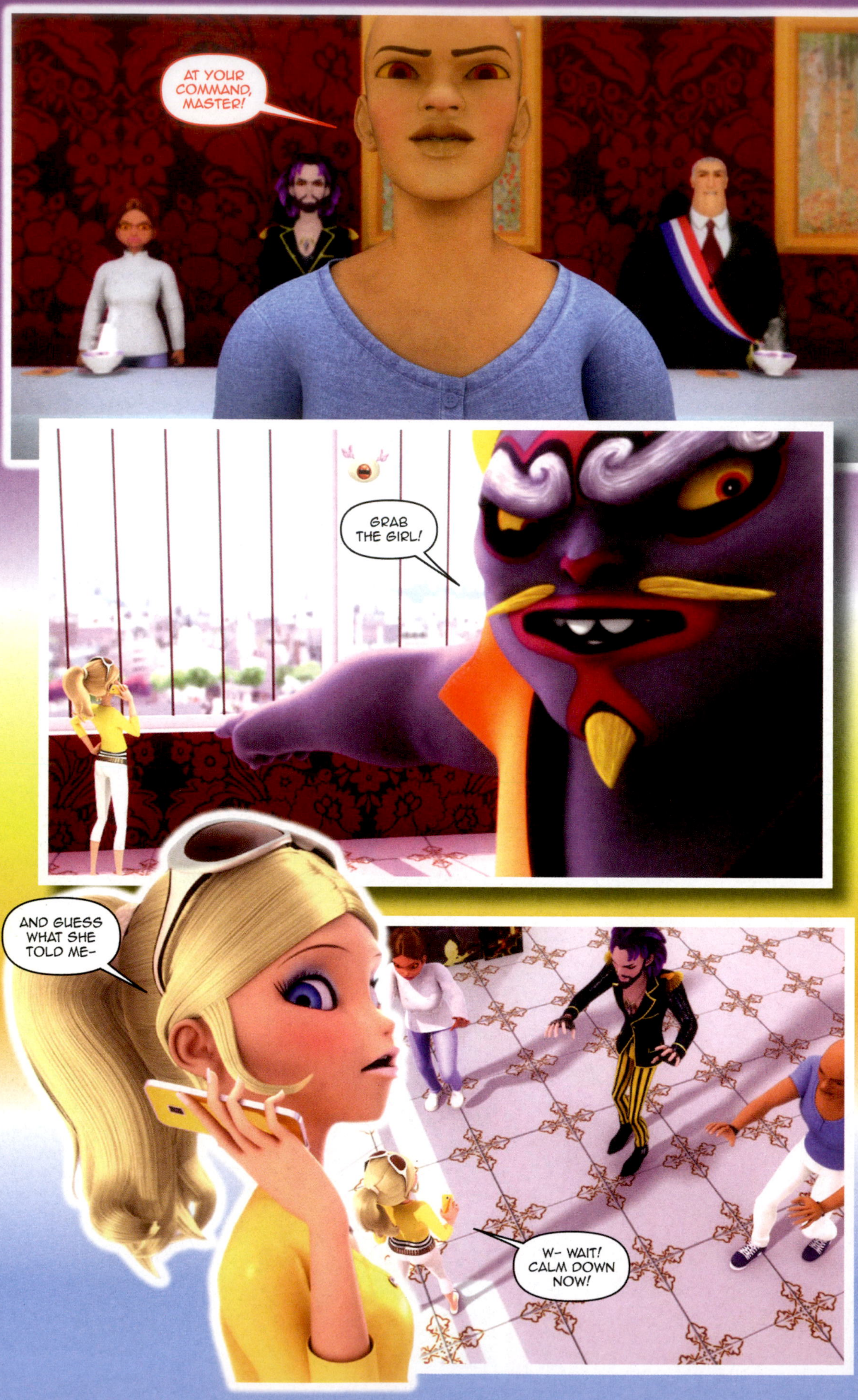
AT YOUR COMMAND, MASTER!
GRAB THE GIRL!
AND GUESS WHAT SHE TOLD ME-
W- WAIT! CALM DOWN NOW!

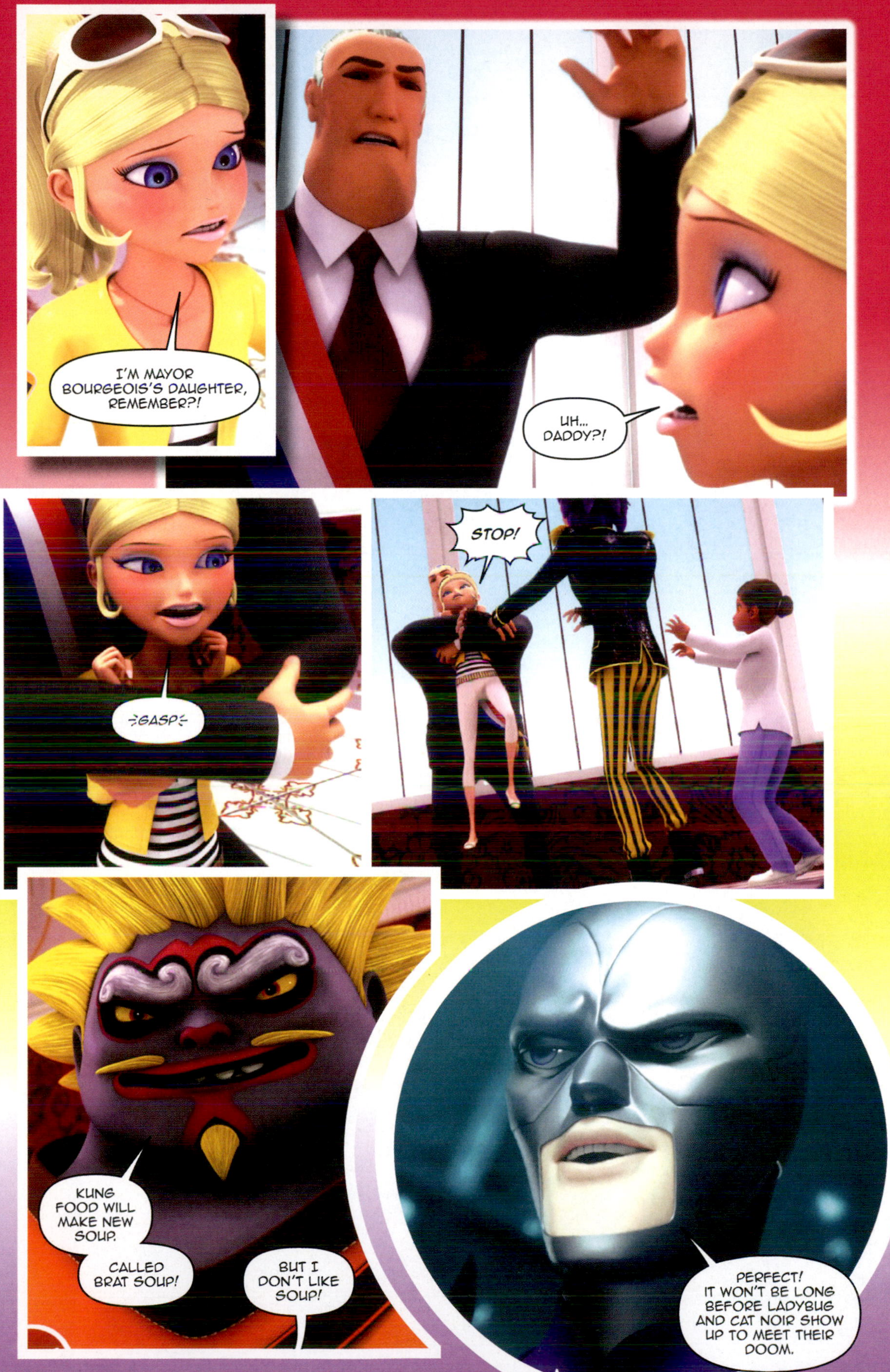
I'M MAYOR BOURGEOIS'S DAUGHTER, REMEMBER?!
UH... DADDY?!
GASP
STOP!
KUNG FOOD WILL MAKE NEW SOUP.
CALLED BRAT SOUP!
BUT I DON'T LIKE SOUP!
PERFECT! IT WON'T BE LONG BEFORE LADYBUG AND CAT NOIR SHOW UP TO MEET THEIR DOOM.

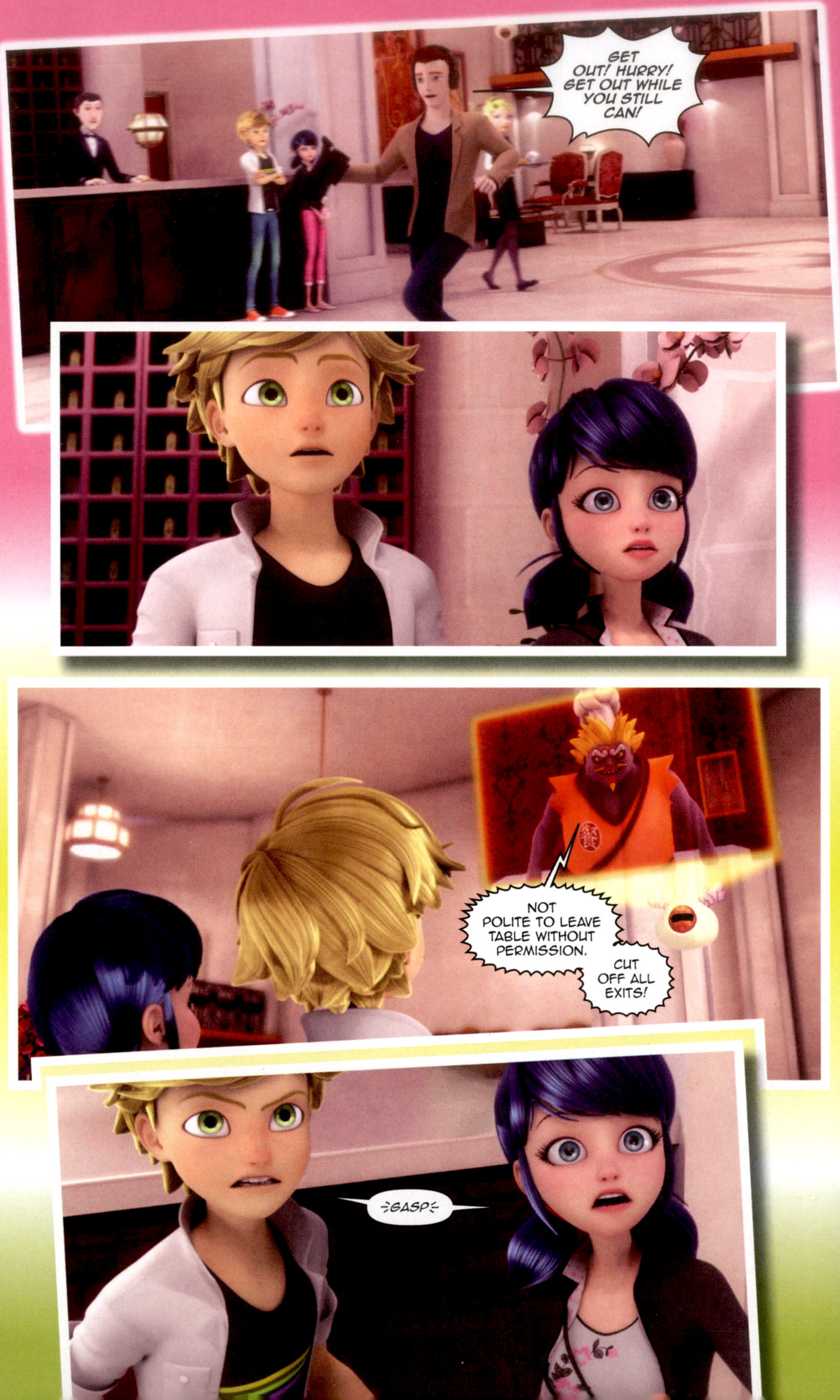
GET OUT! HURRY! GET OUT WHILE YOU STILL CAN!
NOT POLITE TO LEAVE TABLE WITHOUT PERMISSION.
CUT OFF ALL EXITS!
GASP

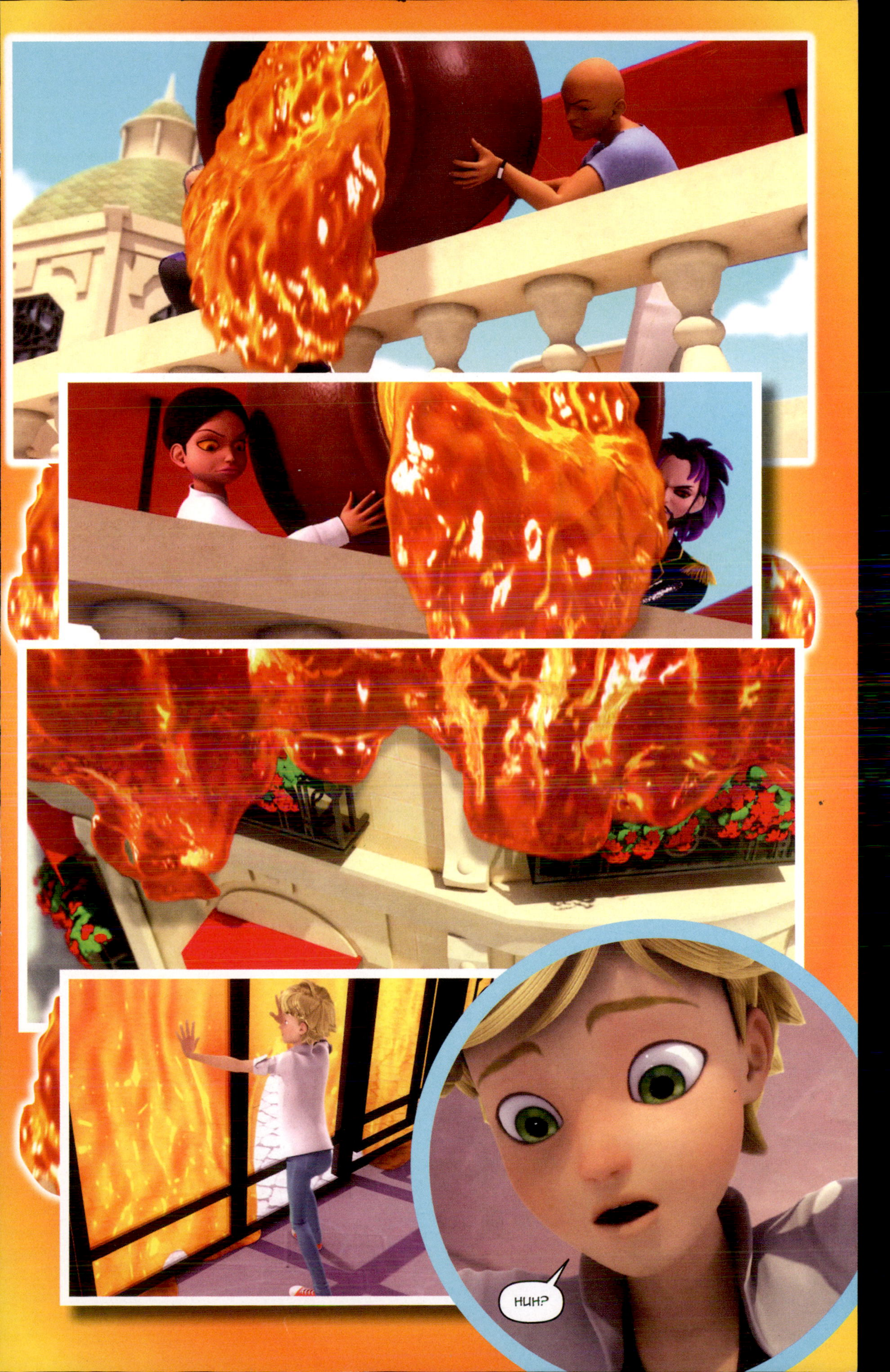
HUH?

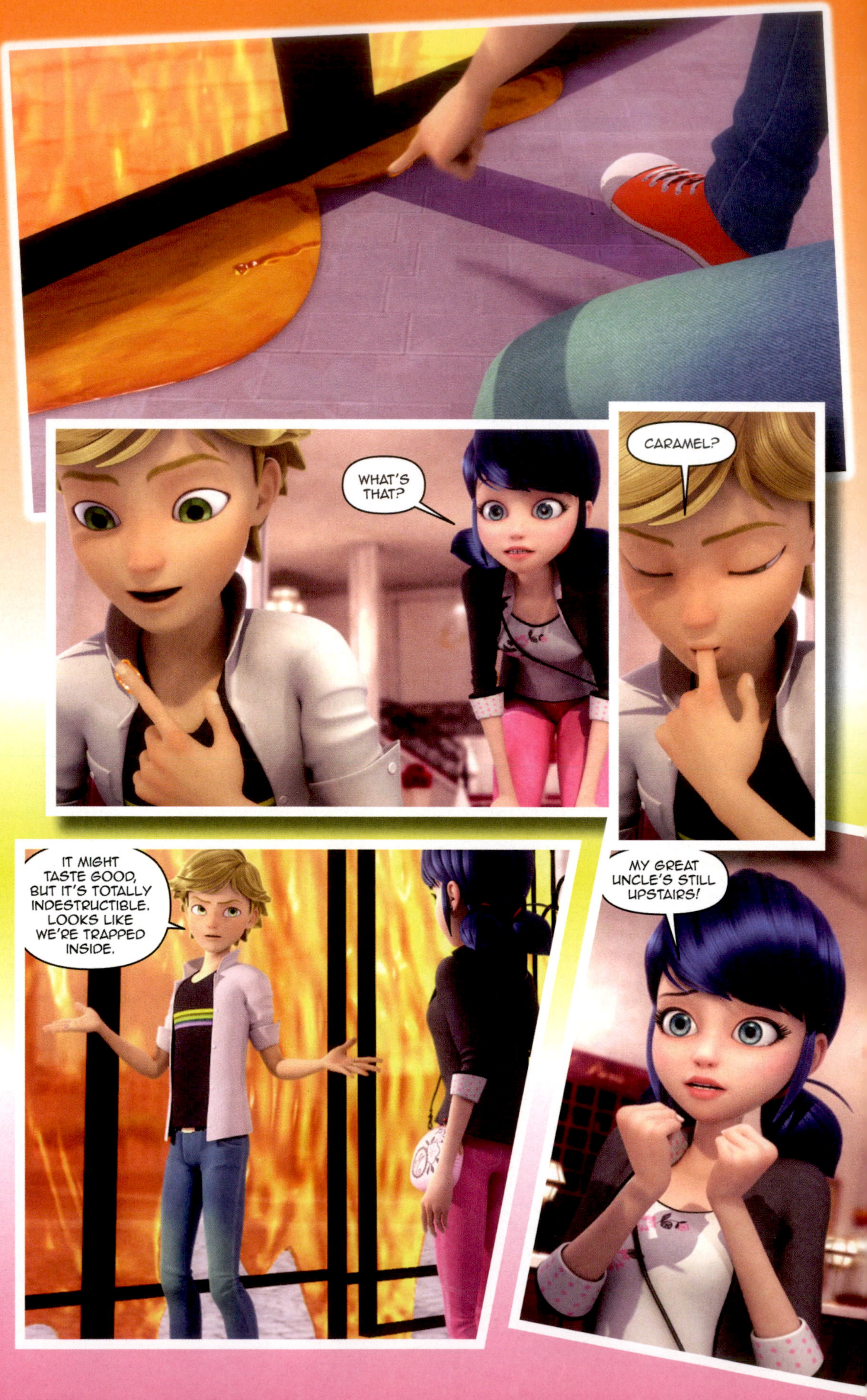
WHAT'S THAT?
CARAMEL?
IT MIGHT TASTE GOOD, BUT IT'S TOTALLY INDESTRUCTIBLE. LOOKS LIKE WE'RE TRAPPED INSIDE.
MY GREAT UNCLE'S STILL UPSTAIRS!

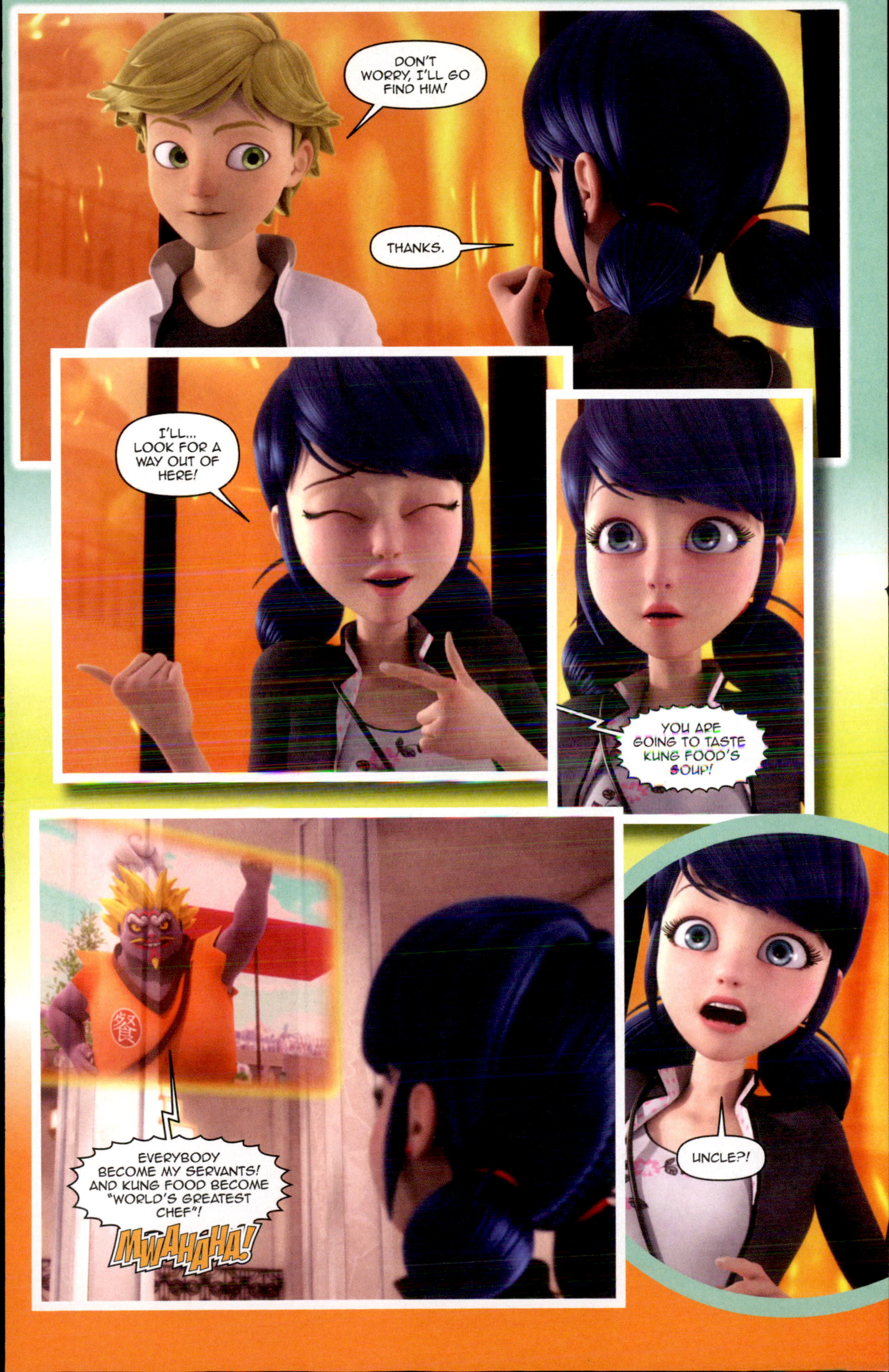
DON'T WORRY, I'LL GO FIND HIM!
THANKS.
I'LL... LOOK FOR A WAY OUT OF HERE!
YOU ARE GOING TO TASTE KUNG FOOD'S SOUP!
EVERYBODY BECOME MY SERVANTS! AND KUNG FOOD BECOME "WORLD'S GREATEST CHEF"!
MWAHAHA!
UNCLE?!

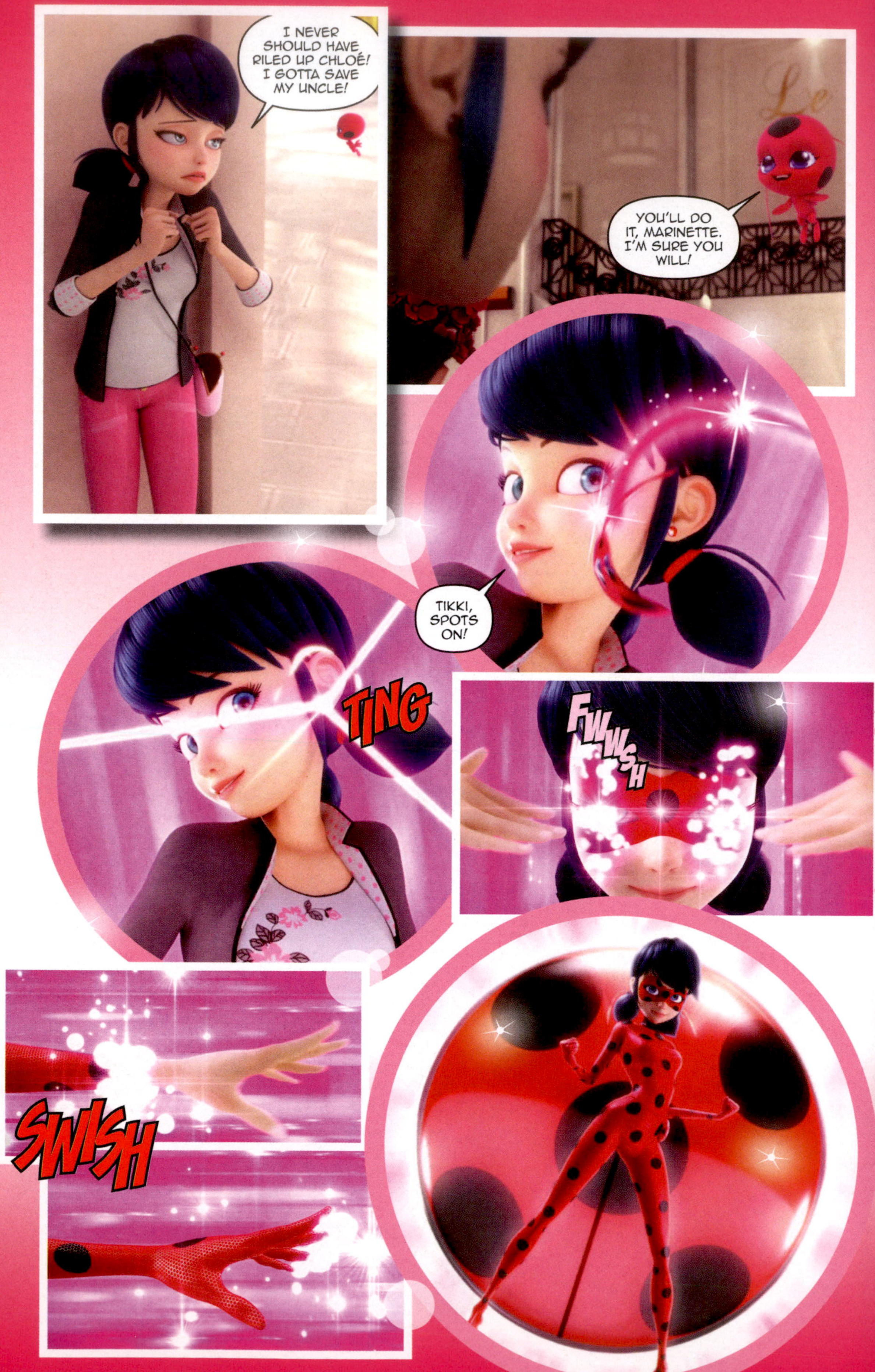
I NEVER SHOULD HAVE RILED UP CHLOÉ! I GOTTA SAVE MY UNCLE!
YOU'LL DO IT, MARINETTE. I'M SURE YOU WILL!
TIKKI, SPOTS ON!
TING
FWWSH
SWISH

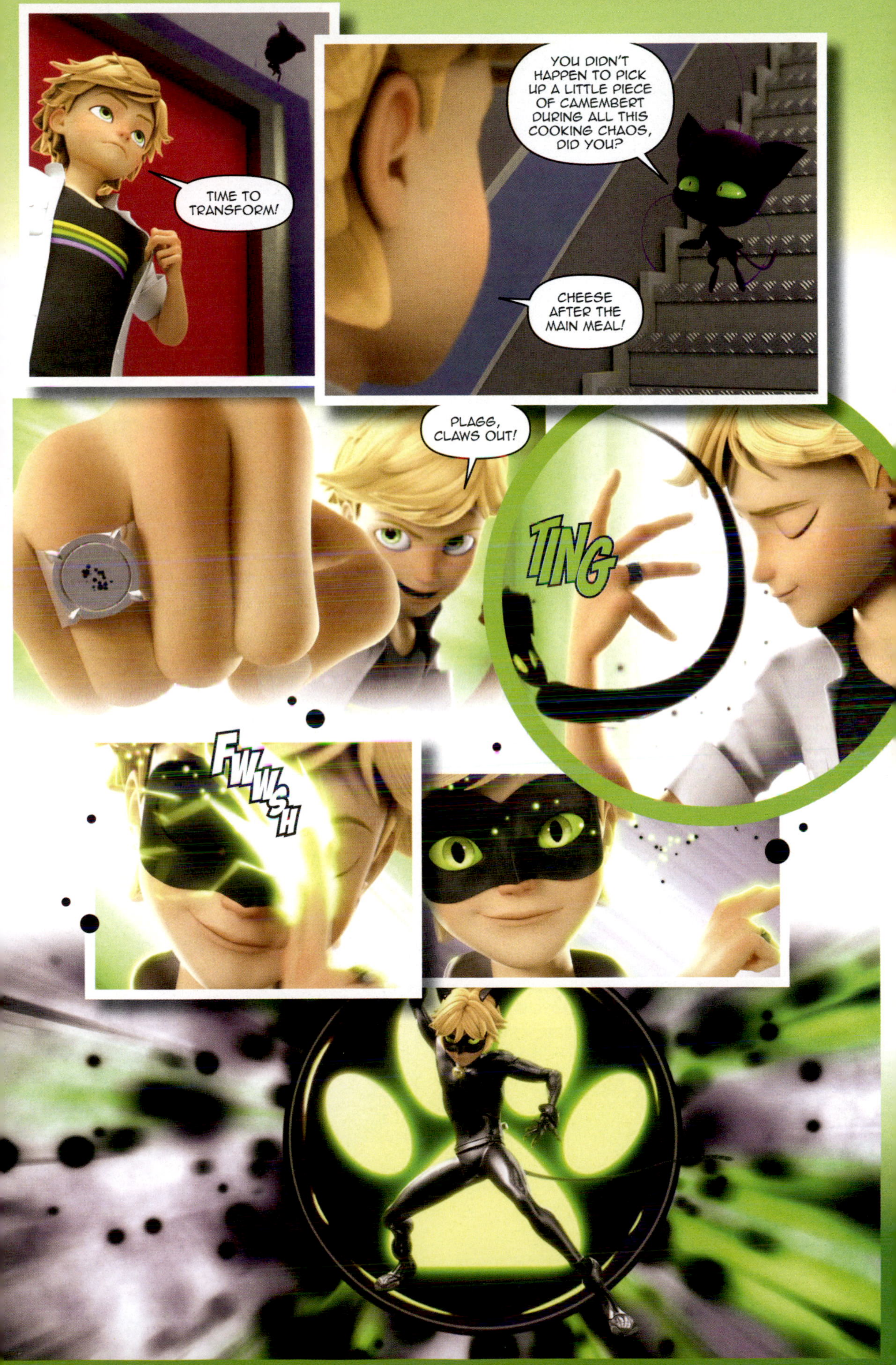
TIME TO TRANSFORM!
YOU DIDN'T HAPPEN TO PICK UP A LITTLE PIECE OF CAMEMBERT DURING ALL THIS COOKING CHAOS, DID YOU?
CHEESE AFTER THE MAIN MEAL!
PLAGG, CLAWS OUT!
TING
FWWSH

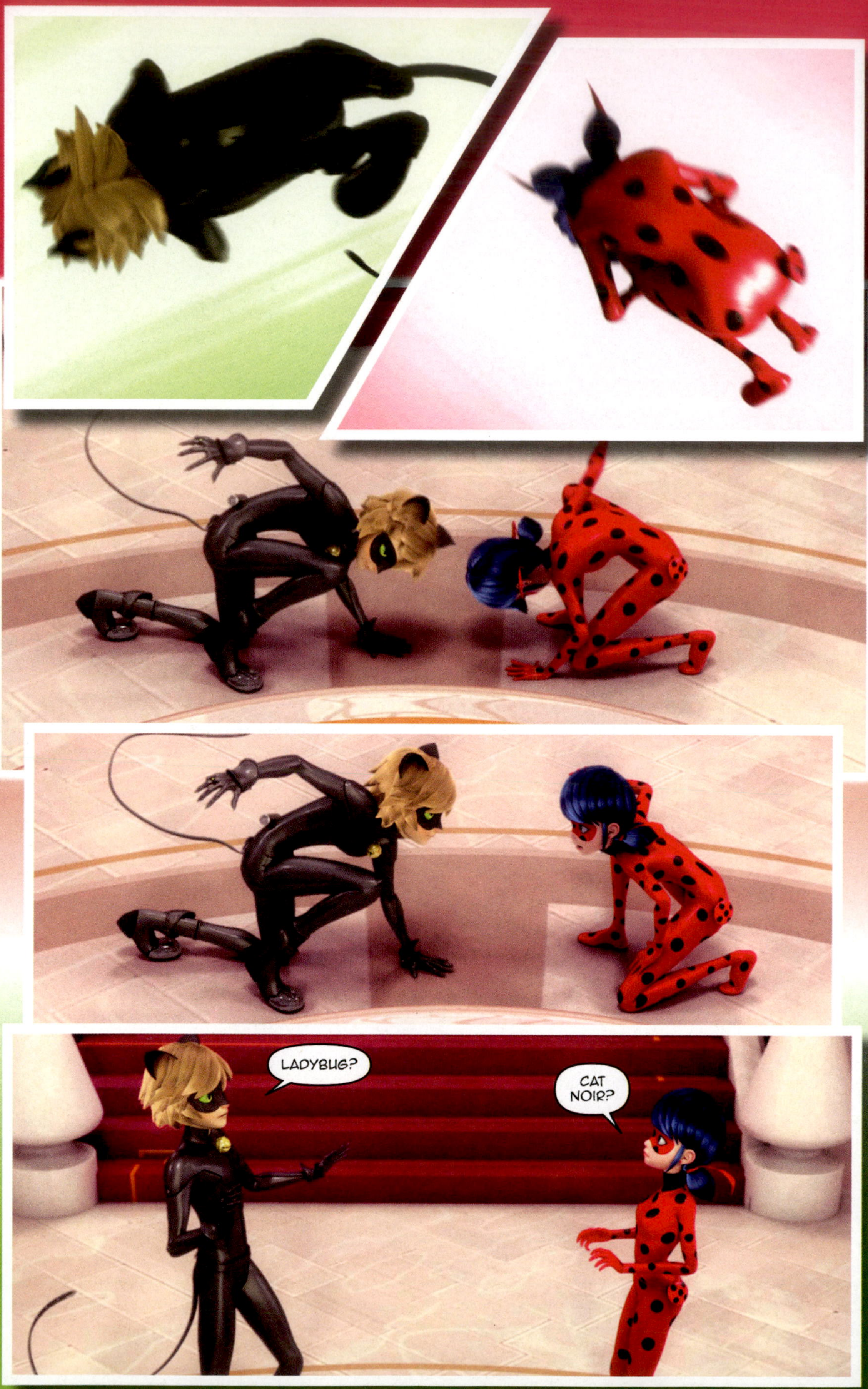
LADYBUG?
CAT NOIR?

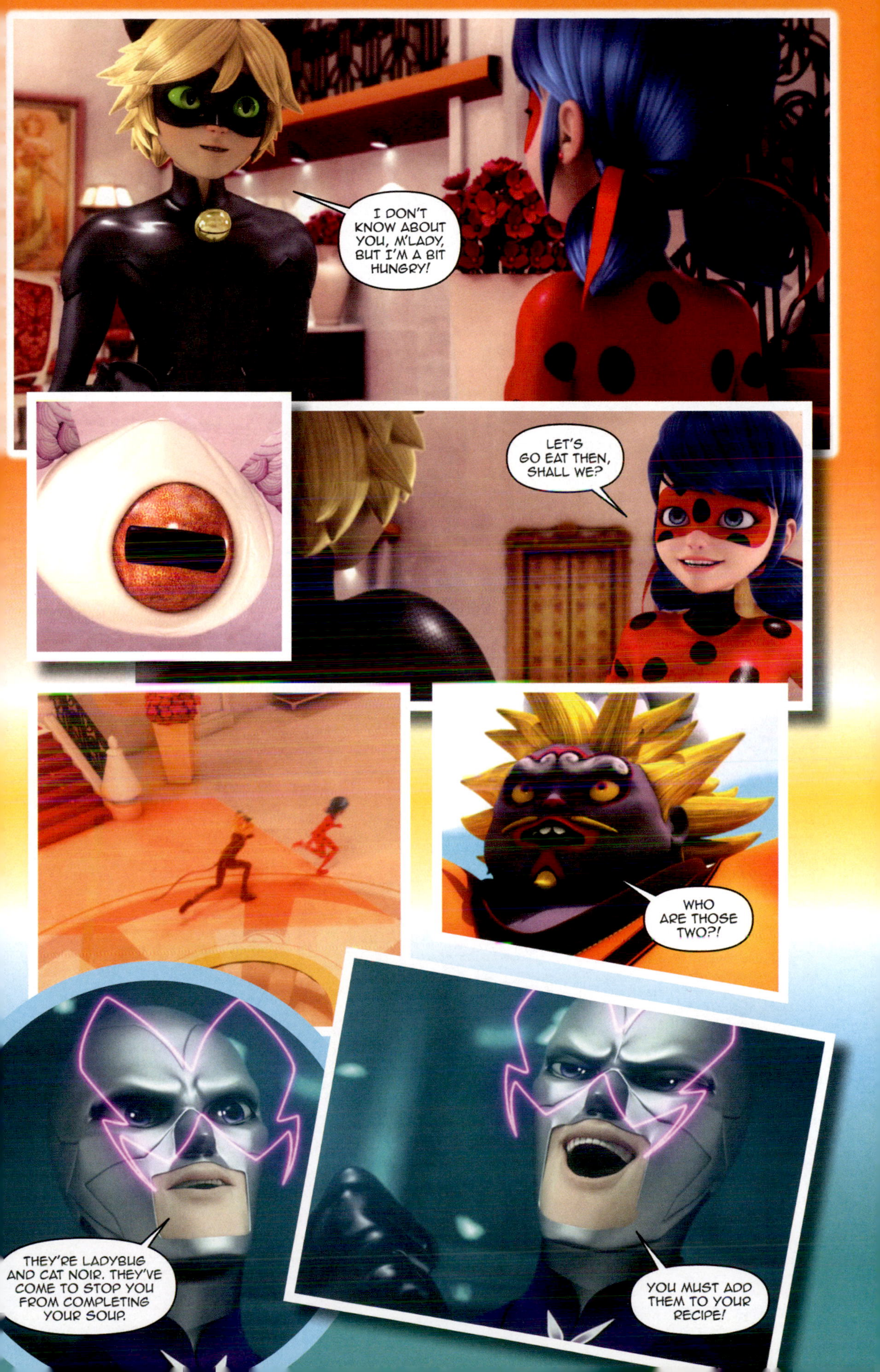
I DON'T KNOW ABOUT YOU, M'LADY, BUT I'M A BIT HUNGRY!
LET'S GO EAT THEN, SHALL WE?
WHO ARE THOSE TWO?!
THEY'RE LADYBUG AND CAT NOIR. THEY'VE COME TO STOP YOU FROM COMPLETING YOUR SOUP.
YOU MUST ADD THEM TO YOUR RECIPE!

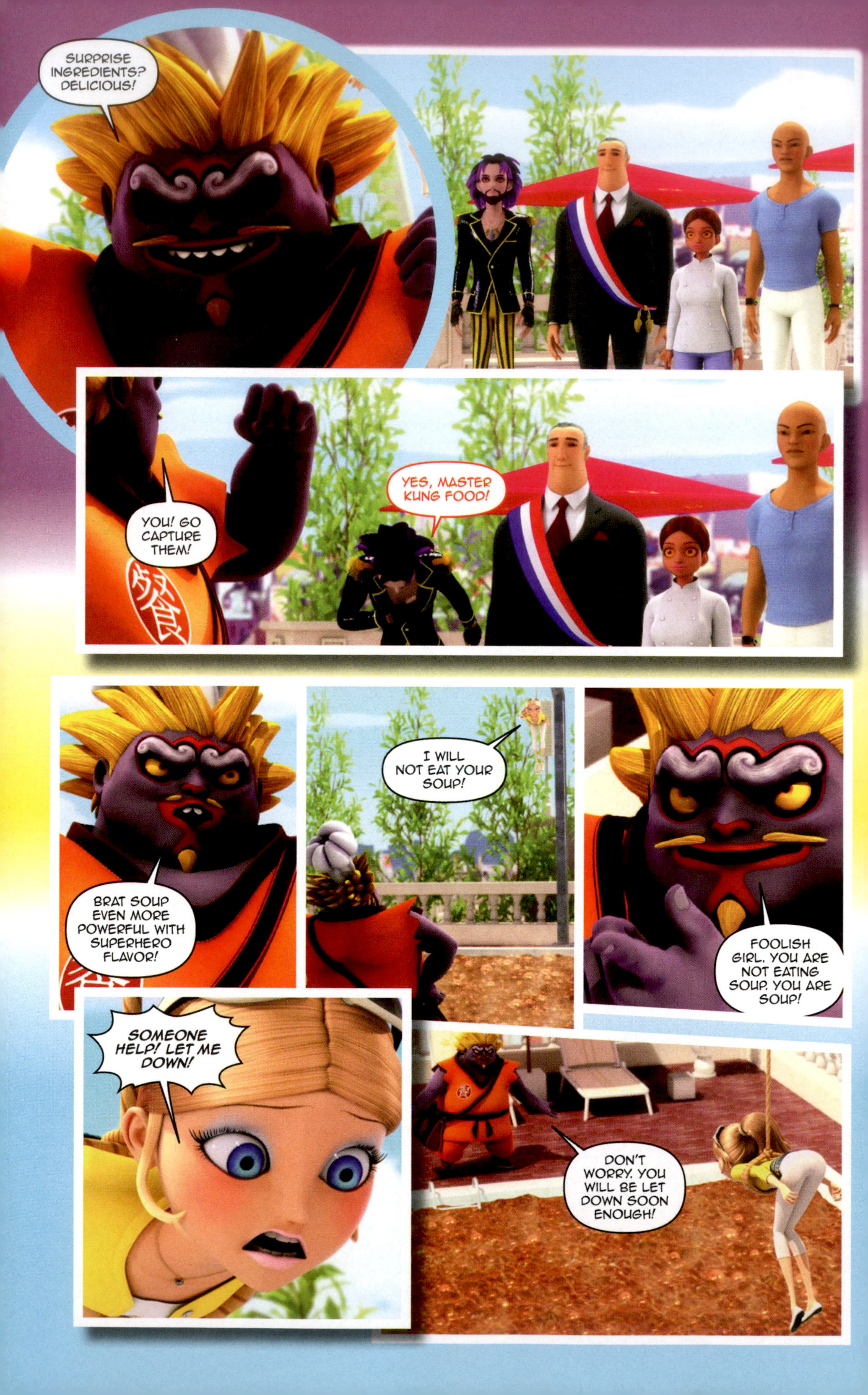
SURPRISE INGREDIENTS? DELICIOUS!
YOU! GO CAPTURE THEM!
YES, MASTER KUNG FOOD!
BRAT SOUP EVEN MORE POWERFUL WITH SUPERHERO FLAVOR!
I WILL NOT EAT YOUR SOUP!
FOOLISH GIRL. YOU ARE NOT EATING SOUP. YOU ARE SOUP!
SOMEONE HELP! LET ME DOWN!
DON'T WORRY. YOU WILL BE LET DOWN SOON ENOUGH!

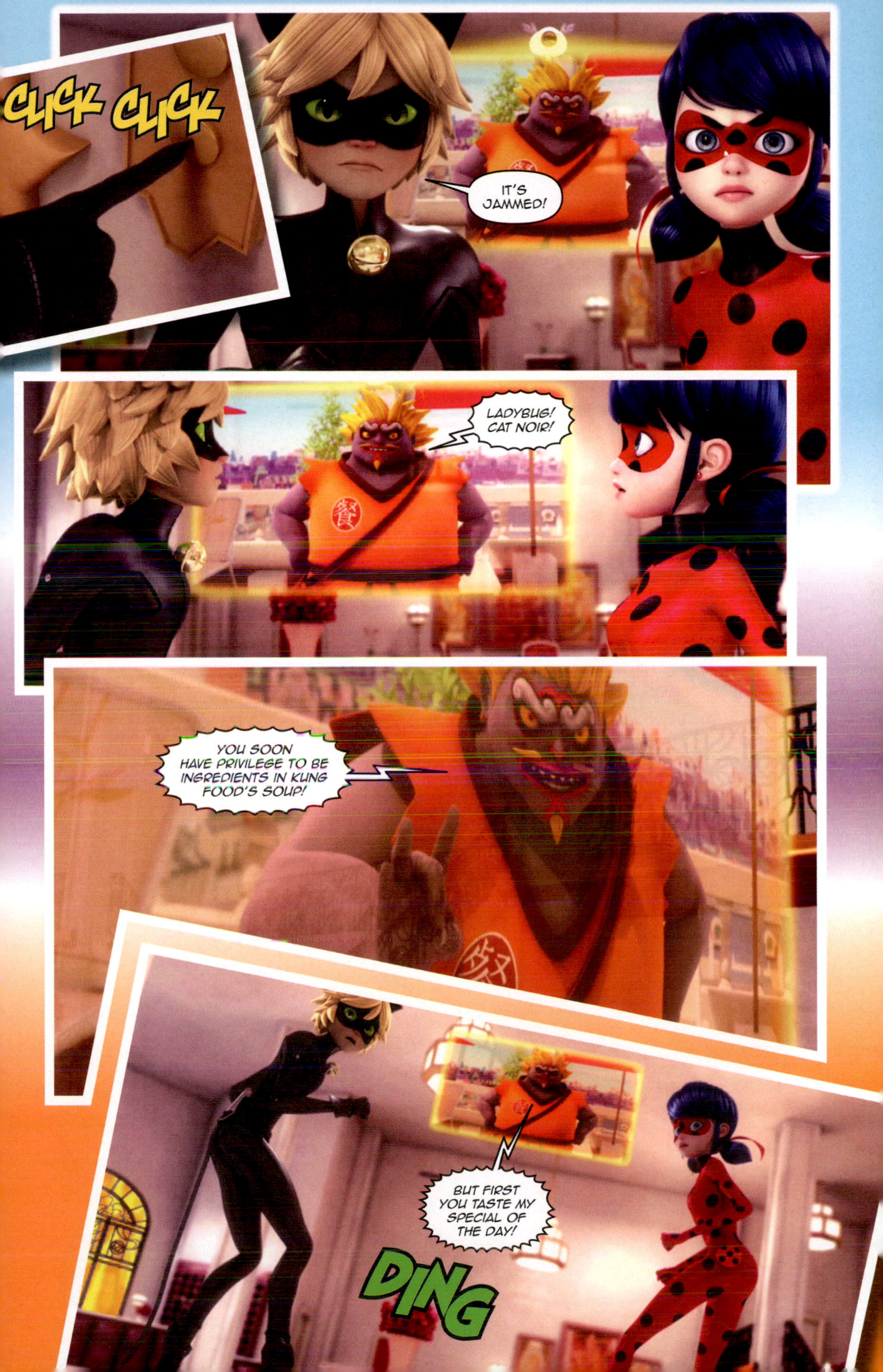
CLICK CLICK
IT'S JAMMED!
LADYBUG! CAT NOIR!
YOU SOON HAVE PRIVILEGE TO BE INGREDIENTS IN KUNG FOOD'S SOUP!
BUT FIRST YOU TASTE MY SPECIAL OF THE DAY!
DING

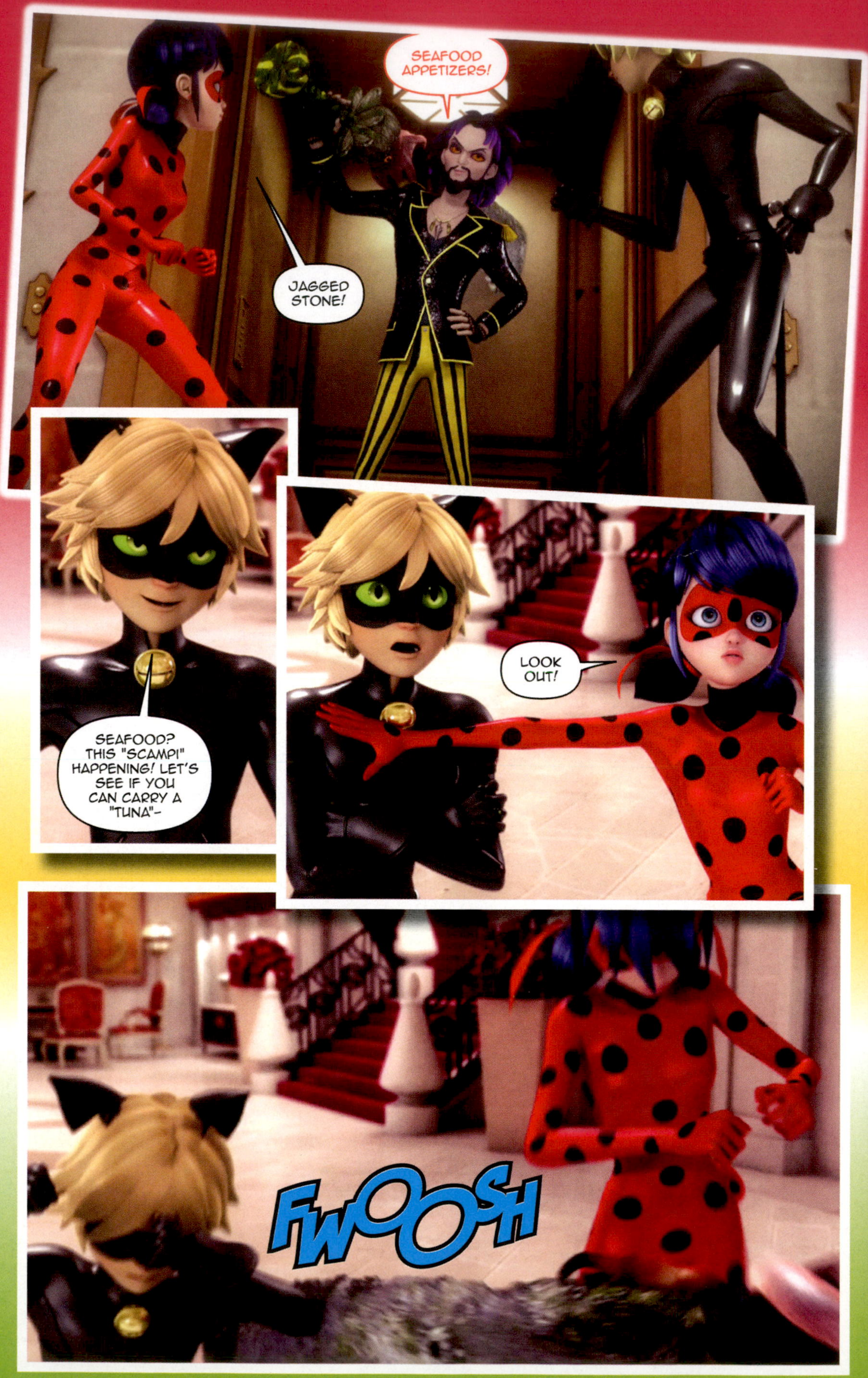
SEAFOOD APPETIZERS!
JAGGED STONE!
SEAFOOD? THIS "SCAMPI" HAPPENING! LET'S SEE IF YOU CAN CARRY A "TUNA"–
LOOK OUT!
FWOOSH

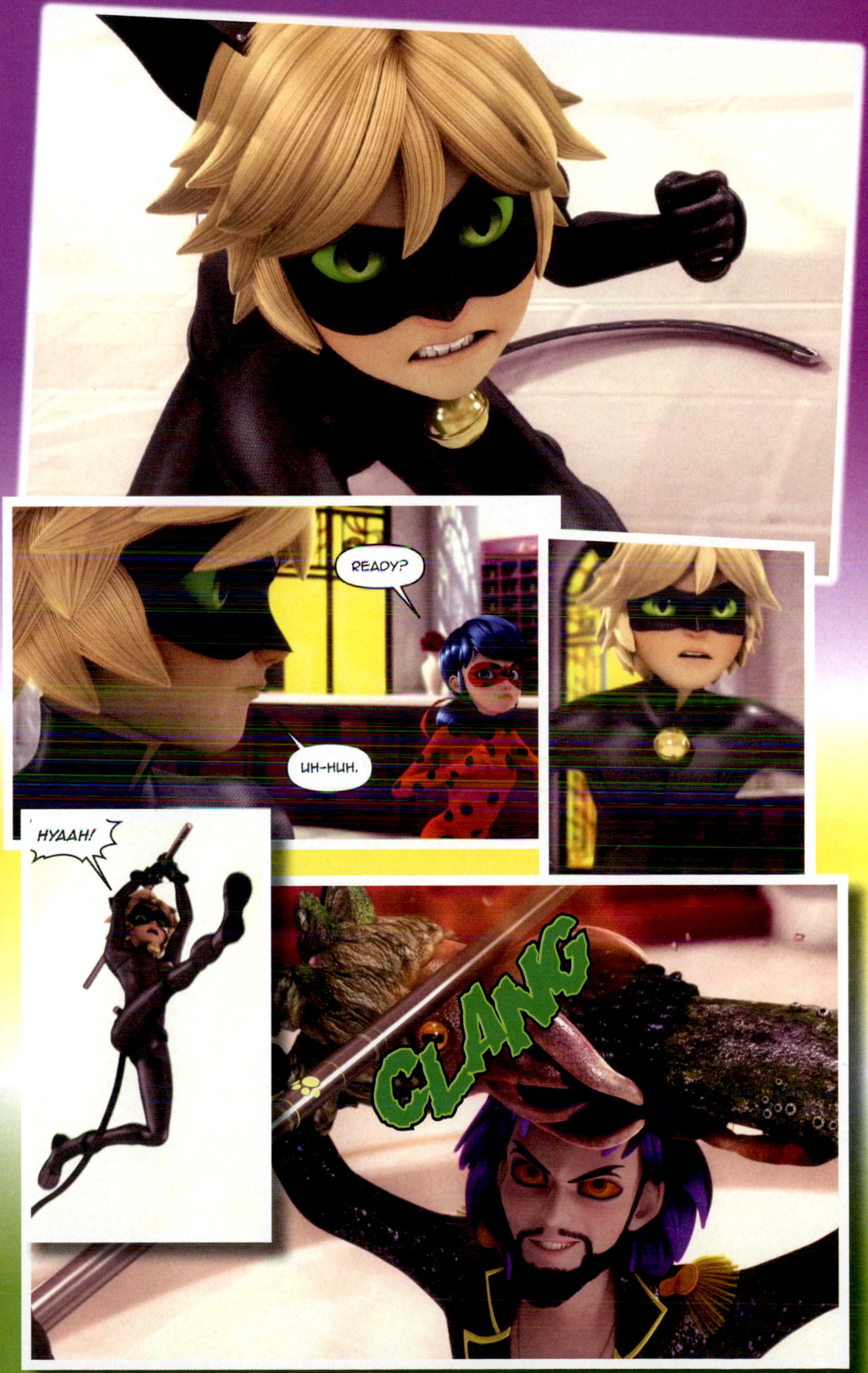
READY?
UH-HUH.
HYAAH!
CLANG

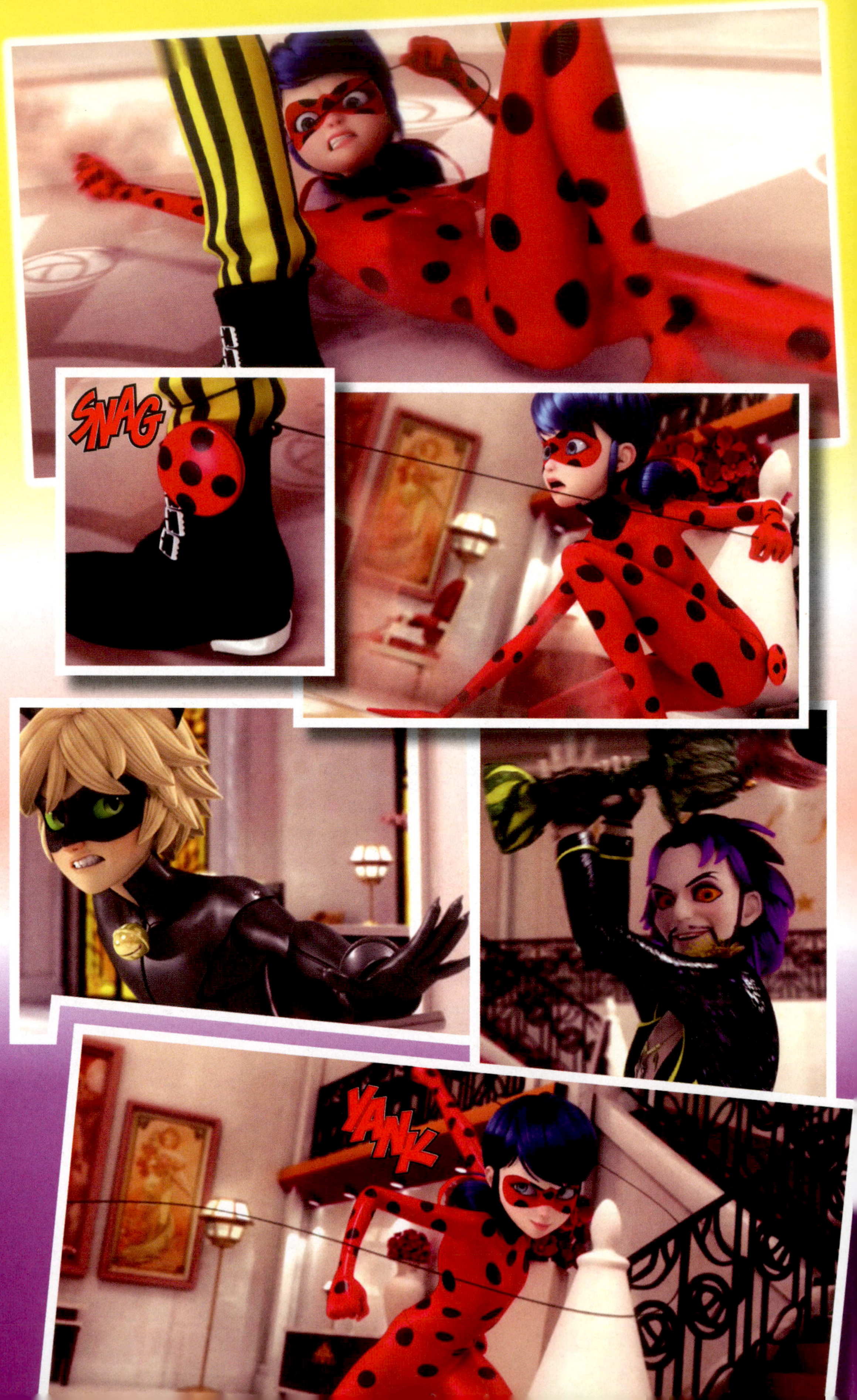
SNAG
YANK

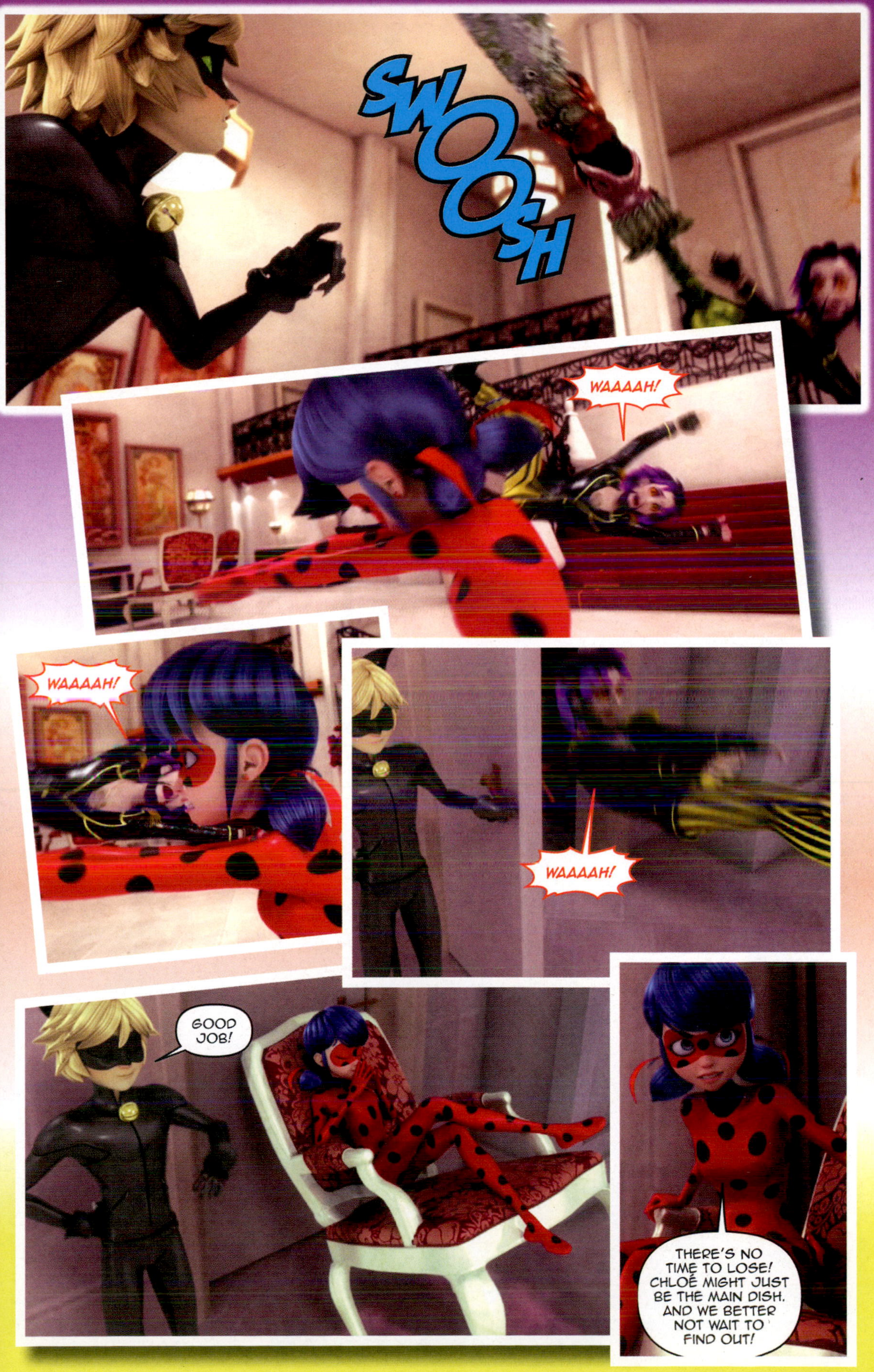
SWOOSH
WAAAAH!
WAAAAH!
WAAAAH!
GOOD JOB!
THERE'S NO TIME TO LOSE! CHLOÉ MIGHT JUST BE THE MAIN DISH. AND WE BETTER NOT WAIT TO FIND OUT!

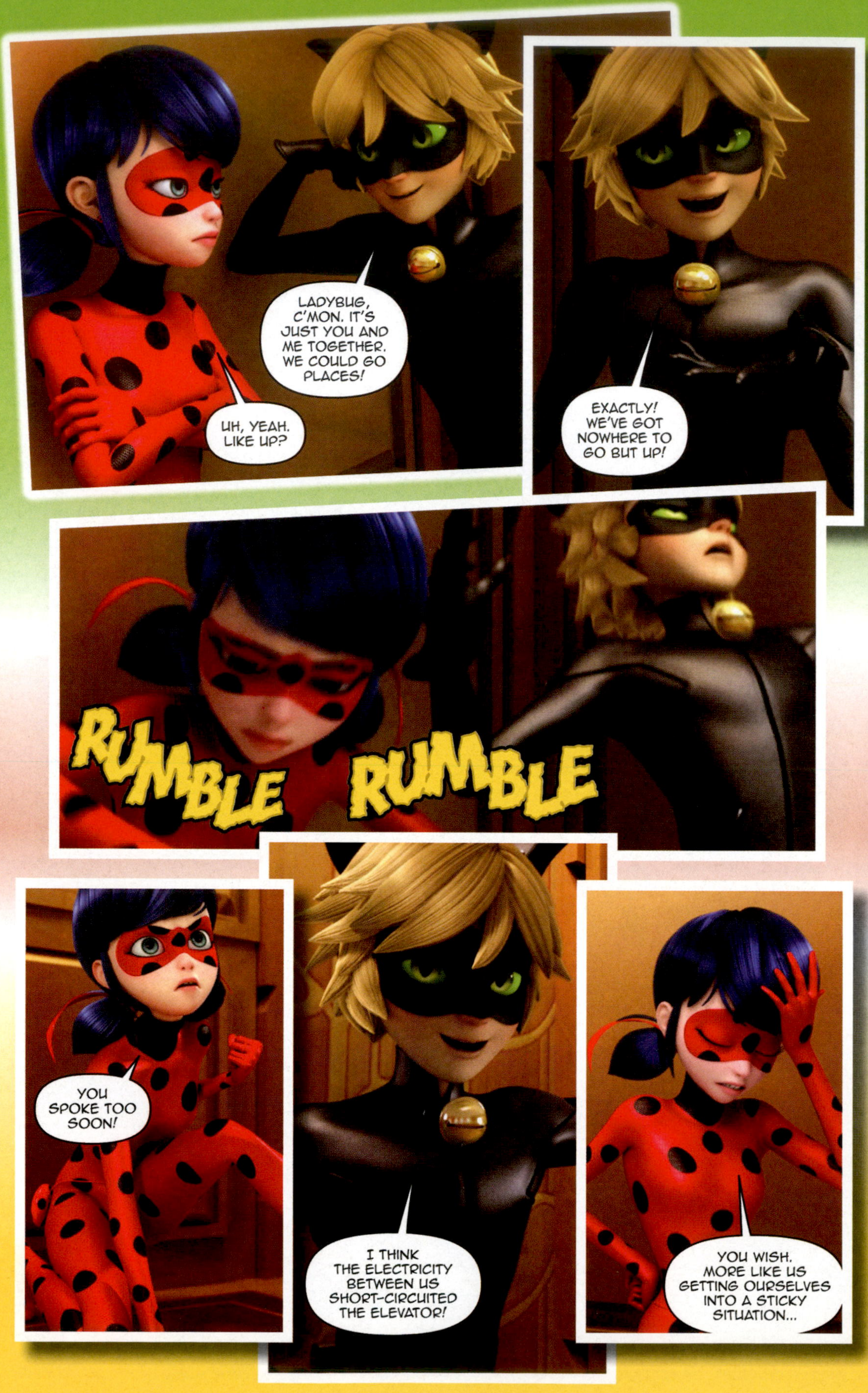
LADYBUG, C'MON. IT'S JUST YOU AND ME TOGETHER. WE COULD GO PLACES!
UH, YEAH. LIKE UP?
EXACTLY! WE'VE GOT NOWHERE TO GO BUT UP!
RUMBLE RUMBLE
YOU SPOKE TOO SOON!
I THINK THE ELECTRICITY BETWEEN US SHORT-CIRCUITED THE ELEVATOR!
YOU WISH. MORE LIKE US GETTING OURSELVES INTO A STICKY SITUATION...

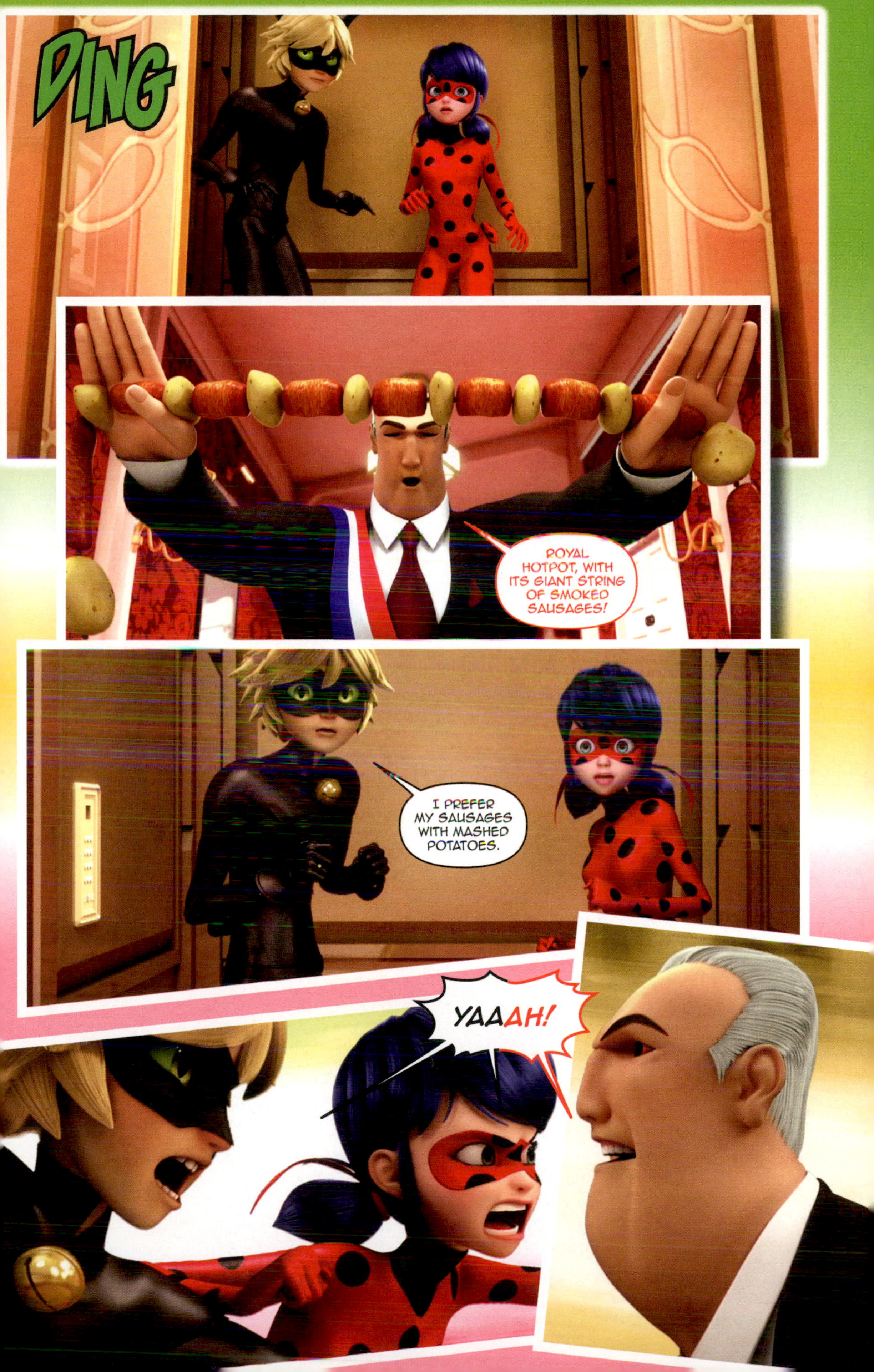
DING
ROYAL HOTPOT, WITH ITS GIANT STRING OF SMOKED SAUSAGES!
I PREFER MY SAUSAGES WITH MASHED POTATOES.
YAAAH!

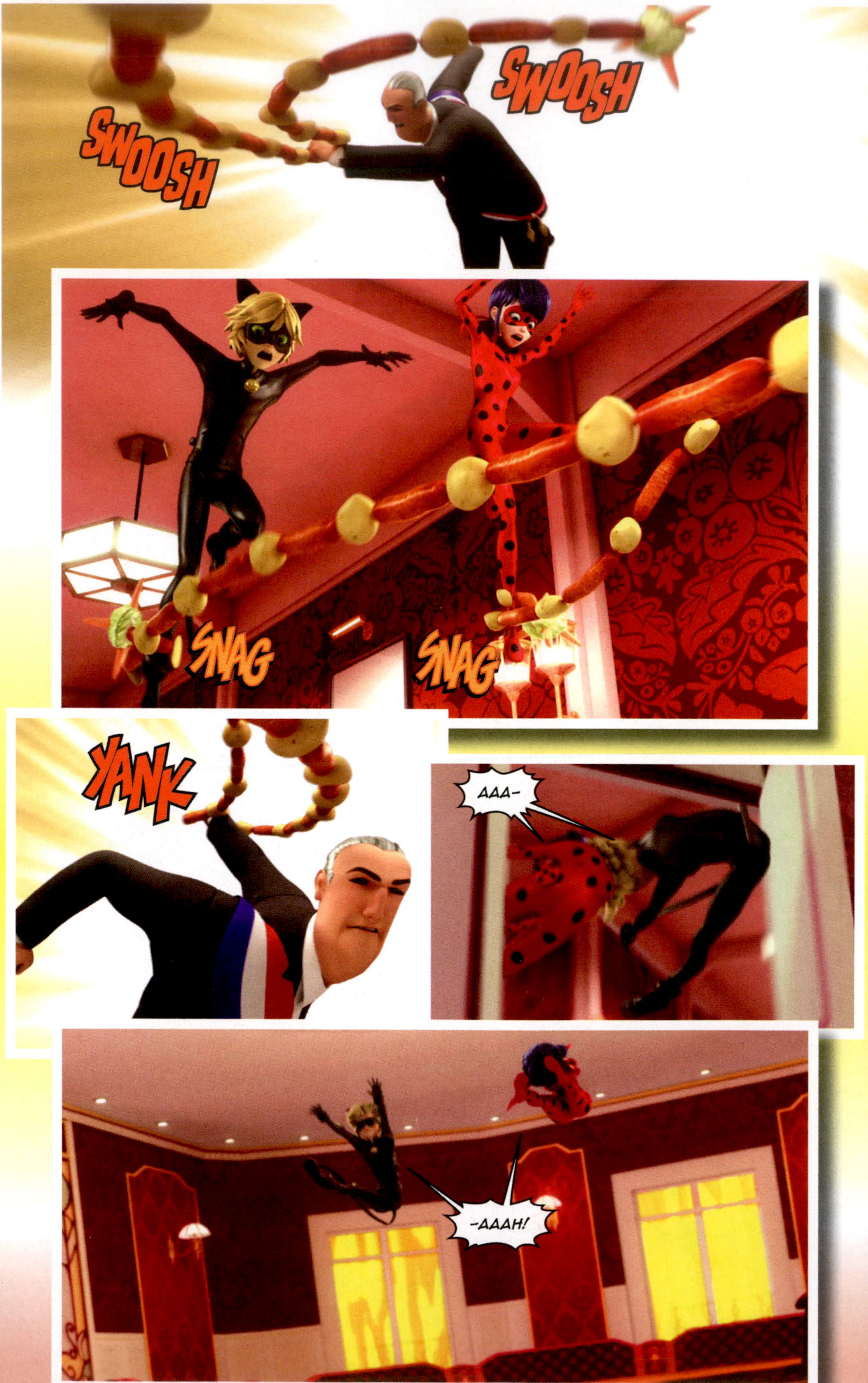
SWOOSH
SWOOSH
SNAG
SNAG
YANK
AAA-
-AAAH!

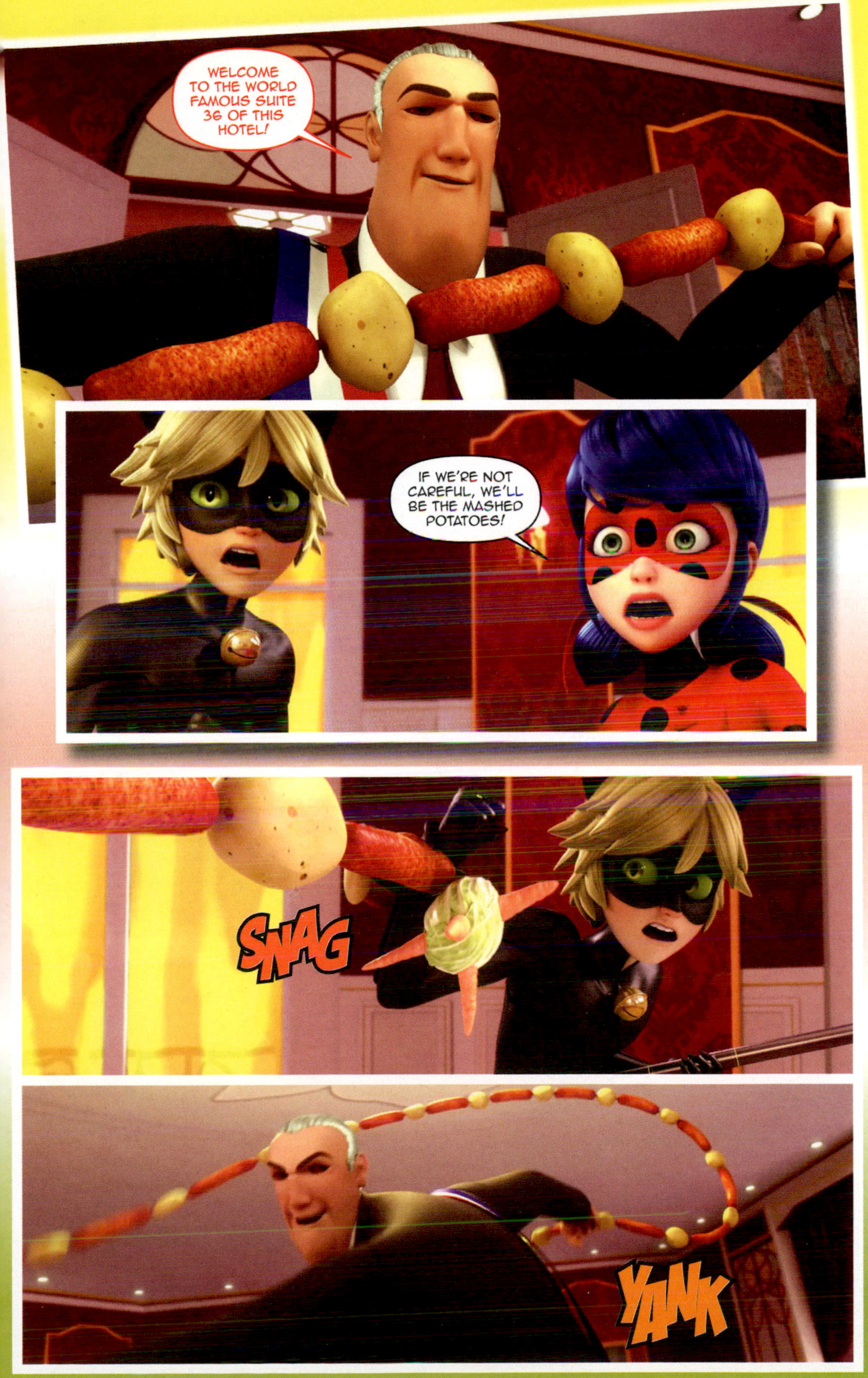
WELCOME TO THE WORLD FAMOUS SUITE 36 OF THIS HOTEL!
IF WE'RE NOT CAREFUL, WE'LL BE THE MASHED POTATOES!
SNAG
YANK

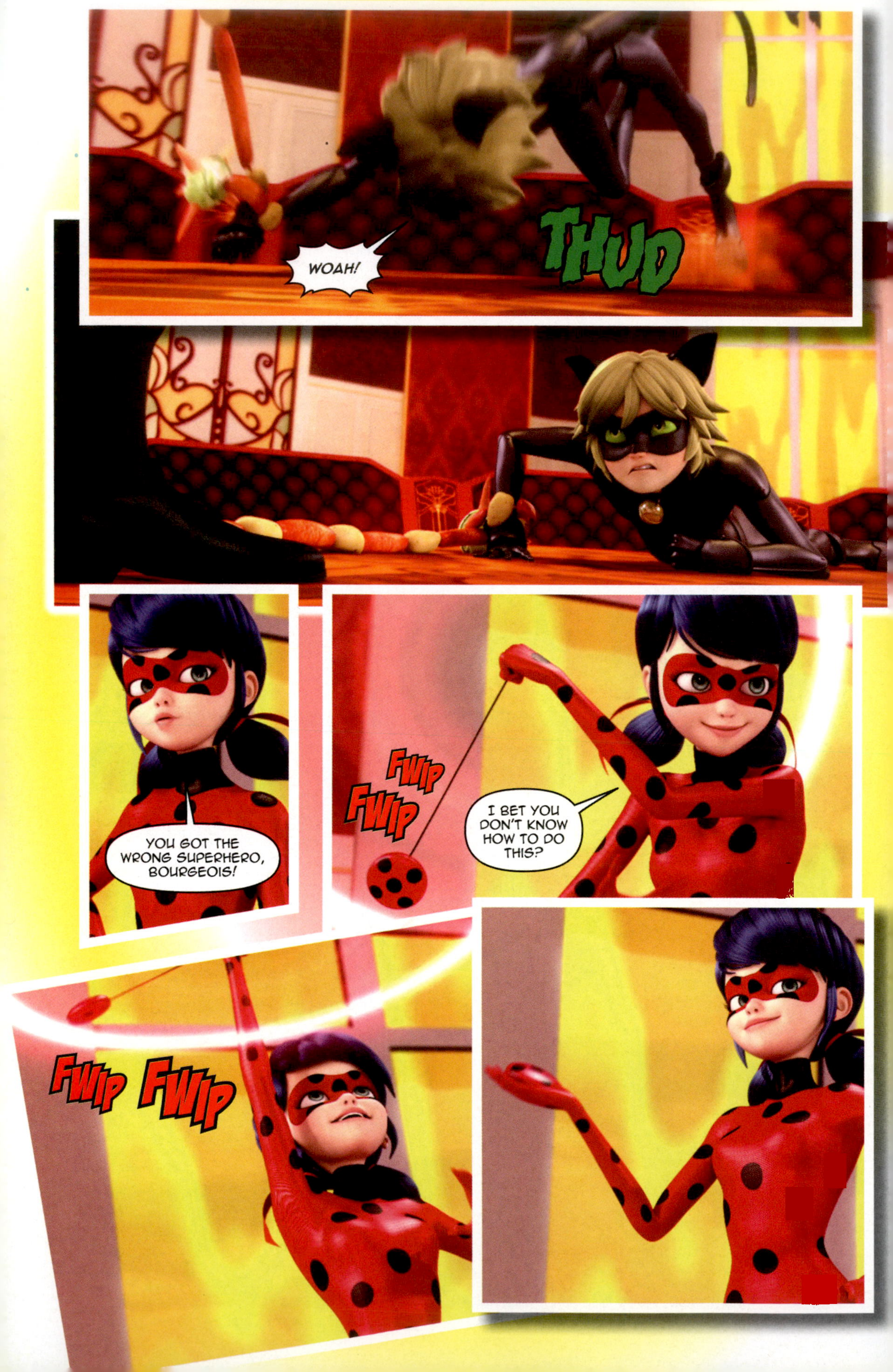
WOAH!
THUD
YOU GOT THE WRONG SUPERHERO, BOURGEOIS!
FWIP FWIP
I BET YOU DON'T KNOW HOW TO DO THIS?
FWIP FWIP

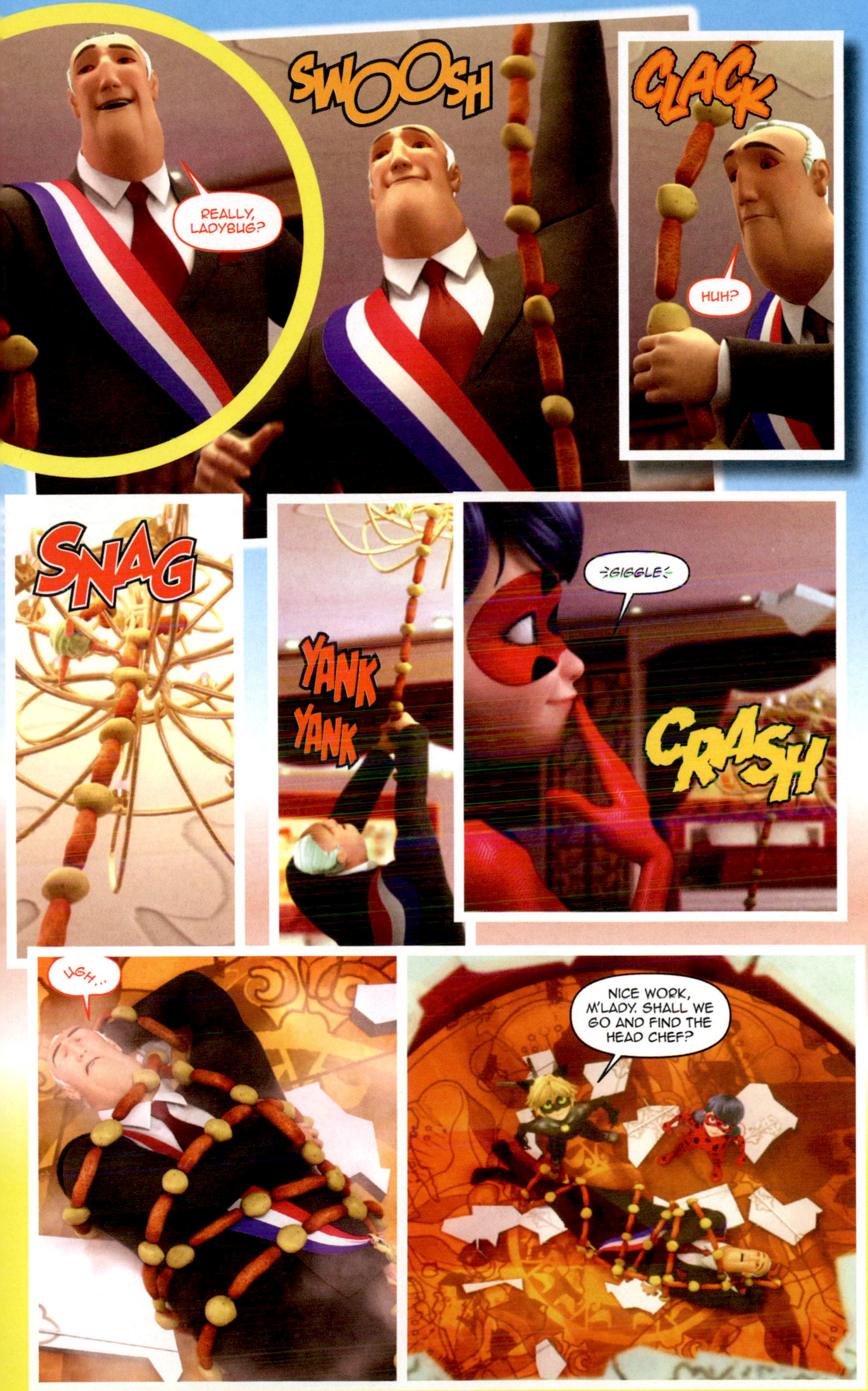

REALLY, LADYBUG?
SWOOSH
CLACK
HUH?
SNAG
YANK
YANK
GIGGLE
CRASH
UGH...
NICE WORK, M'LADY. SHALL WE GO AND FIND THE HEAD CHEF?

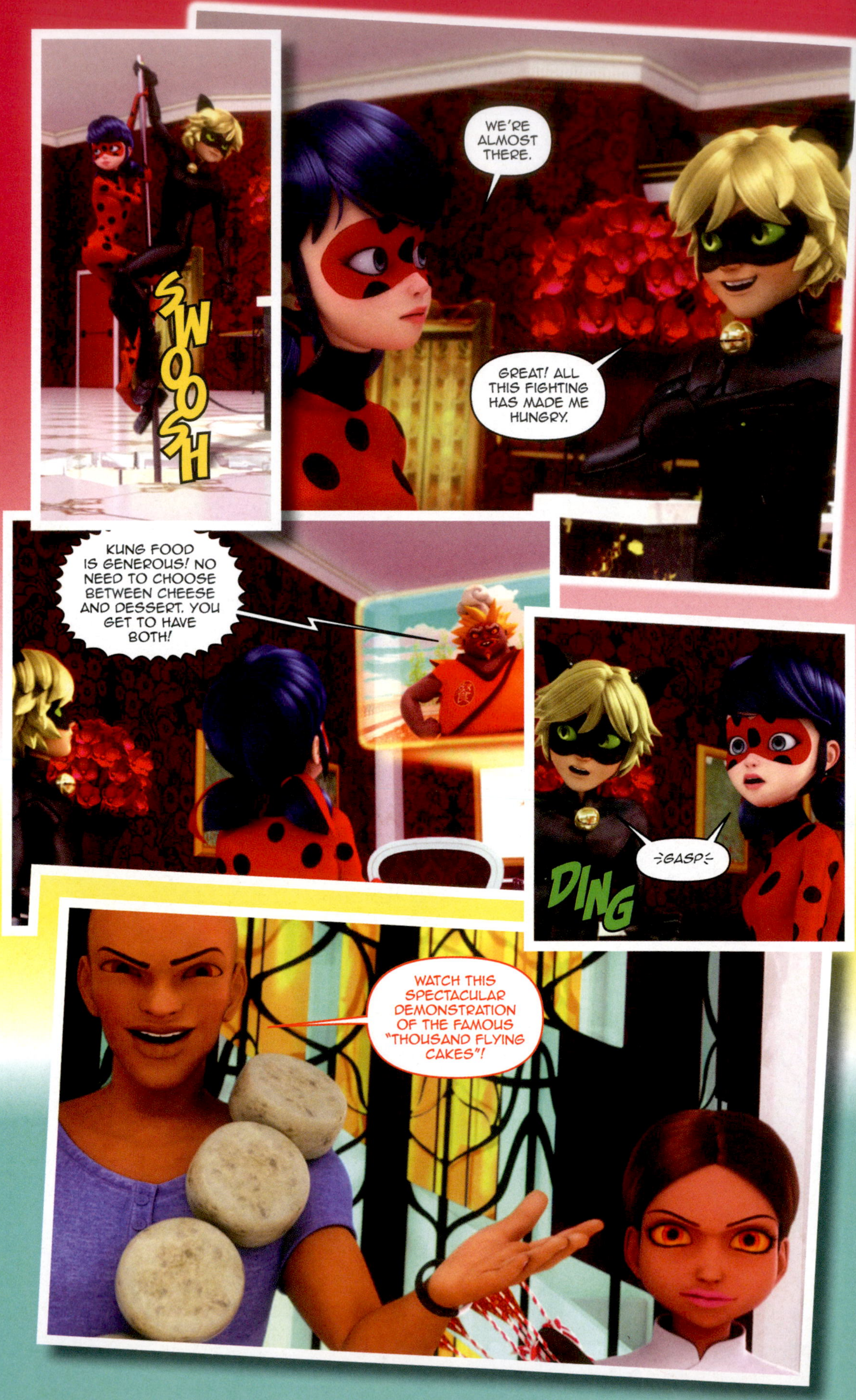
SWOOSH
WE'RE ALMOST THERE.
GREAT! ALL THIS FIGHTING HAS MADE ME HUNGRY.
KUNG FOOD IS GENEROUS! NO NEED TO CHOOSE BETWEEN CHEESE AND DESSERT. YOU GET TO HAVE BOTH!
DING
GASP
WATCH THIS SPECTACULAR DEMONSTRATION OF THE FAMOUS "THOUSAND FLYING CAKES"!

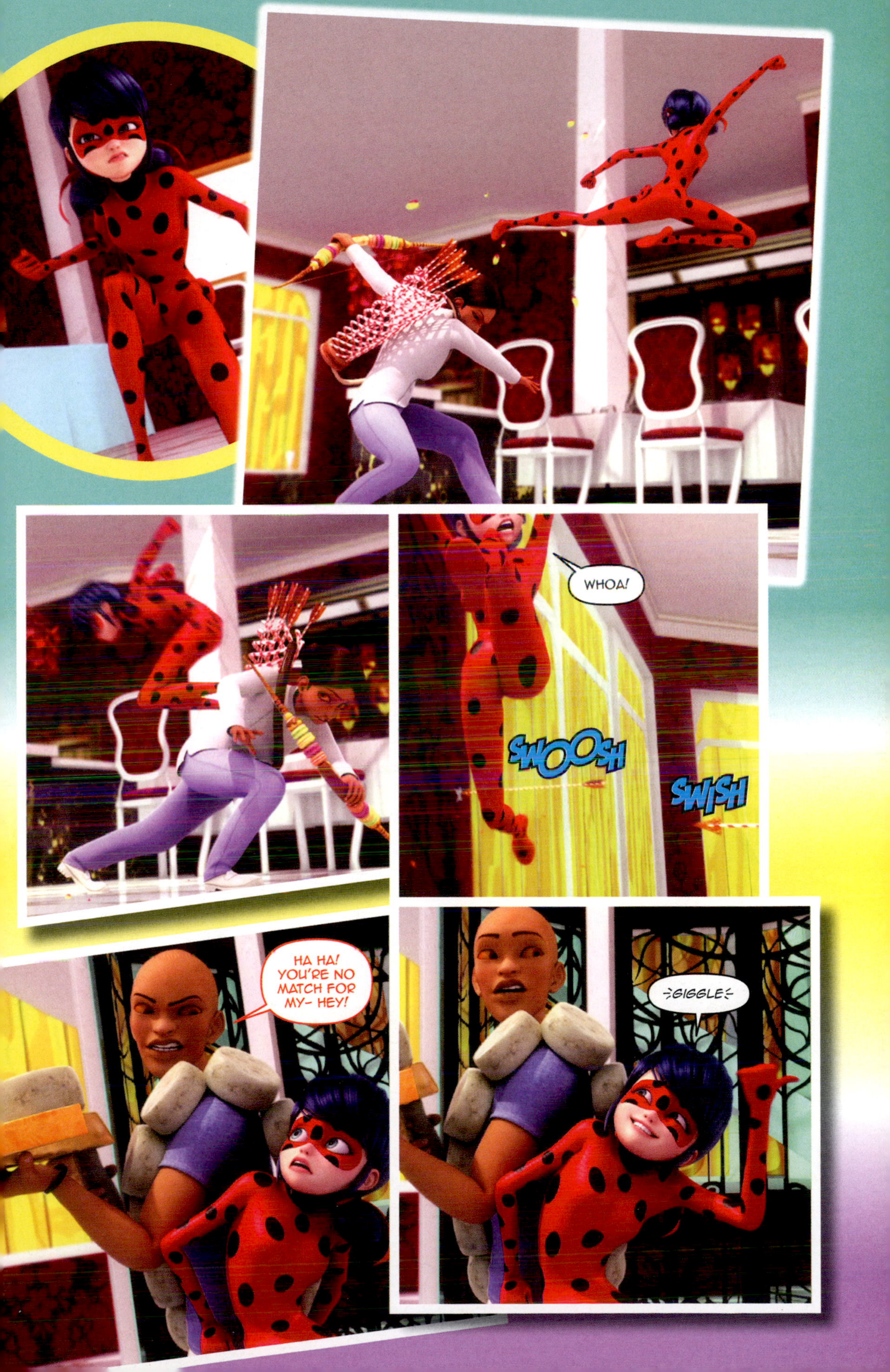
WHOA!
SWOOSH
SWISH
HA HA! YOU'RE NO MATCH FOR MY- HEY!
GIGGLE

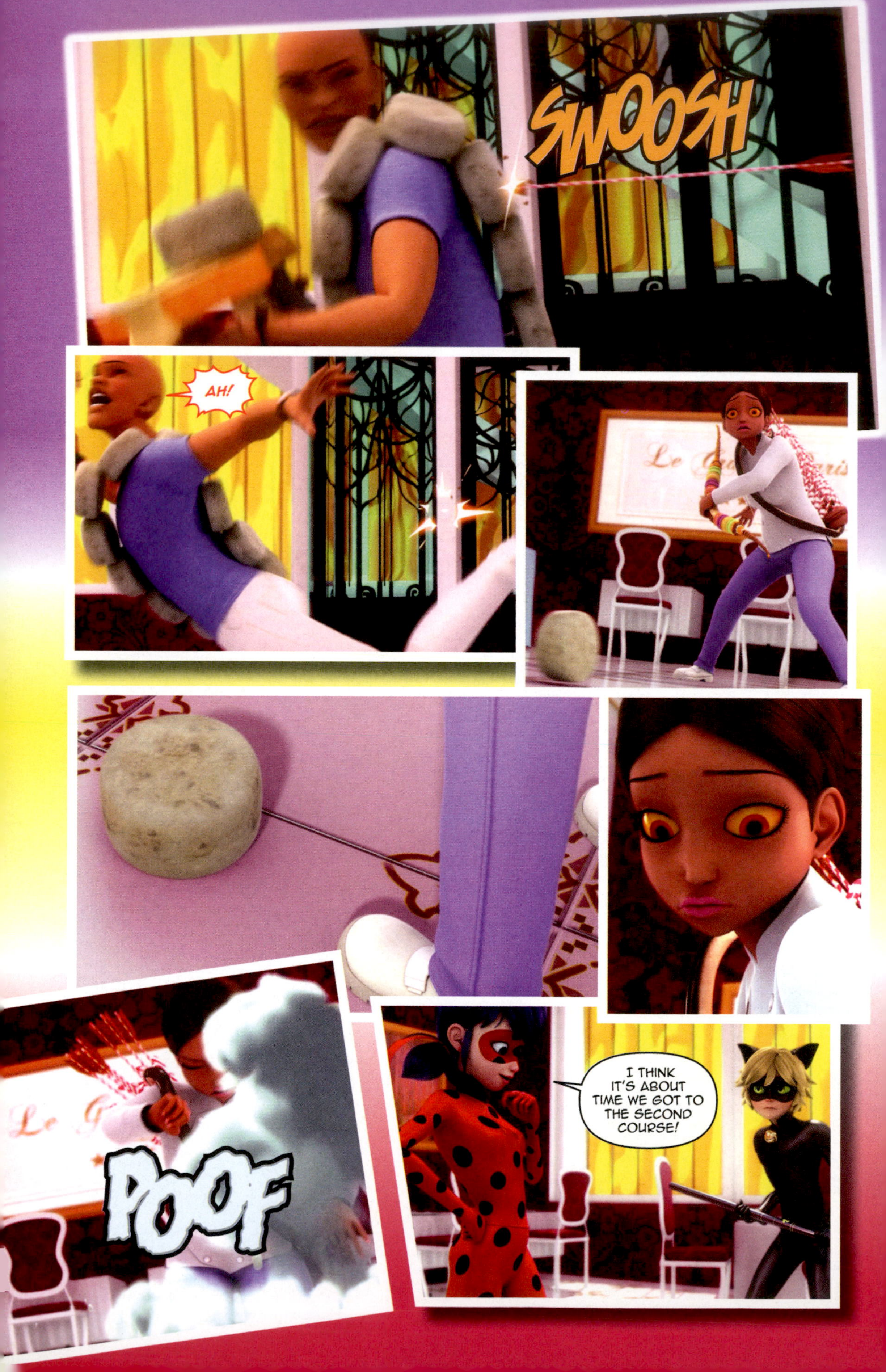
SWOOSH
AH!
POOF
I THINK IT'S ABOUT TIME WE GOT TO THE SECOND COURSE!

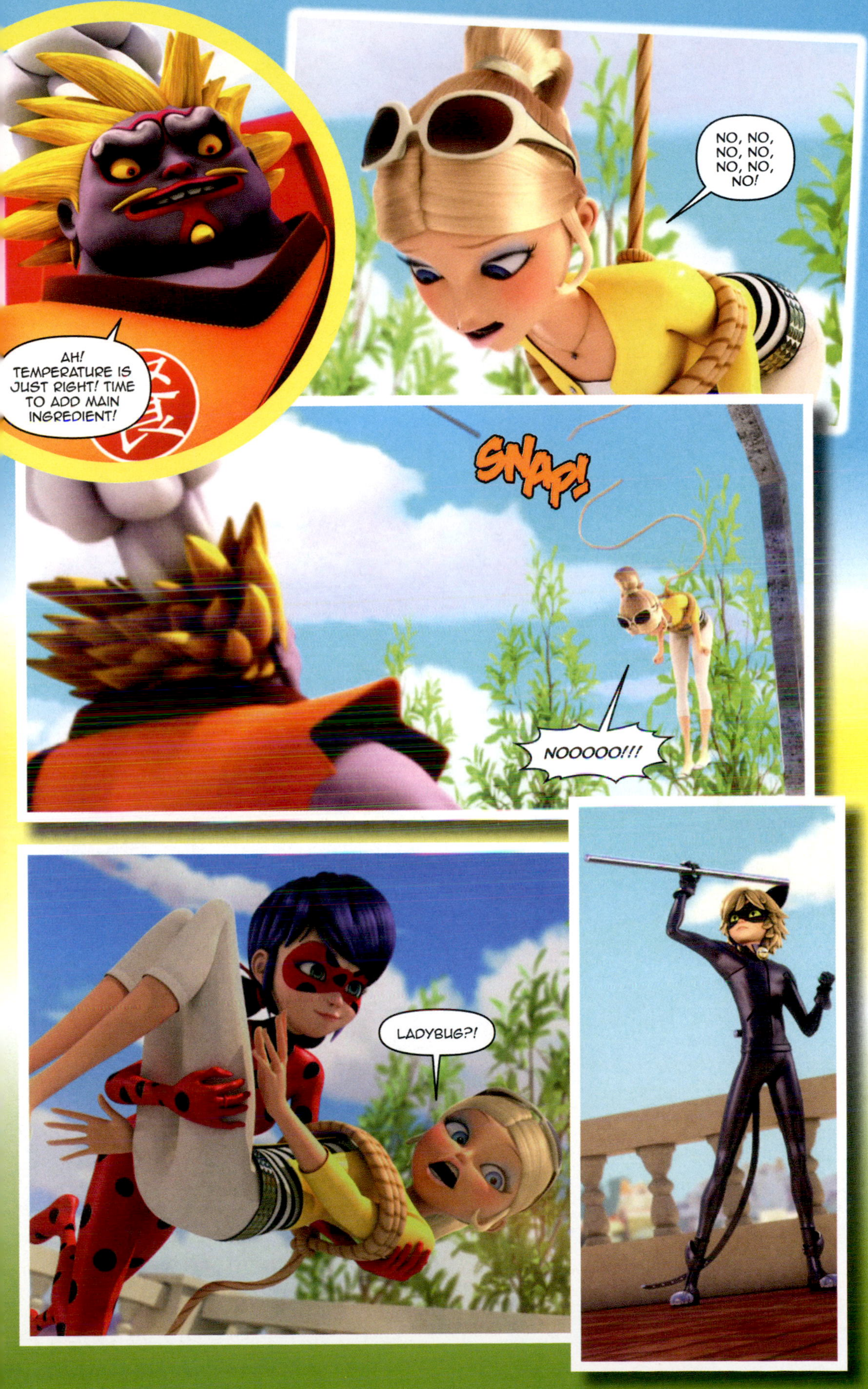
AH! TEMPERATURE IS JUST RIGHT! TIME TO ADD MAIN INGREDIENT!
NO, NO, NO, NO, NO, NO, NO!
SNAP!
NOOOOO!!!
LADYBUG?!

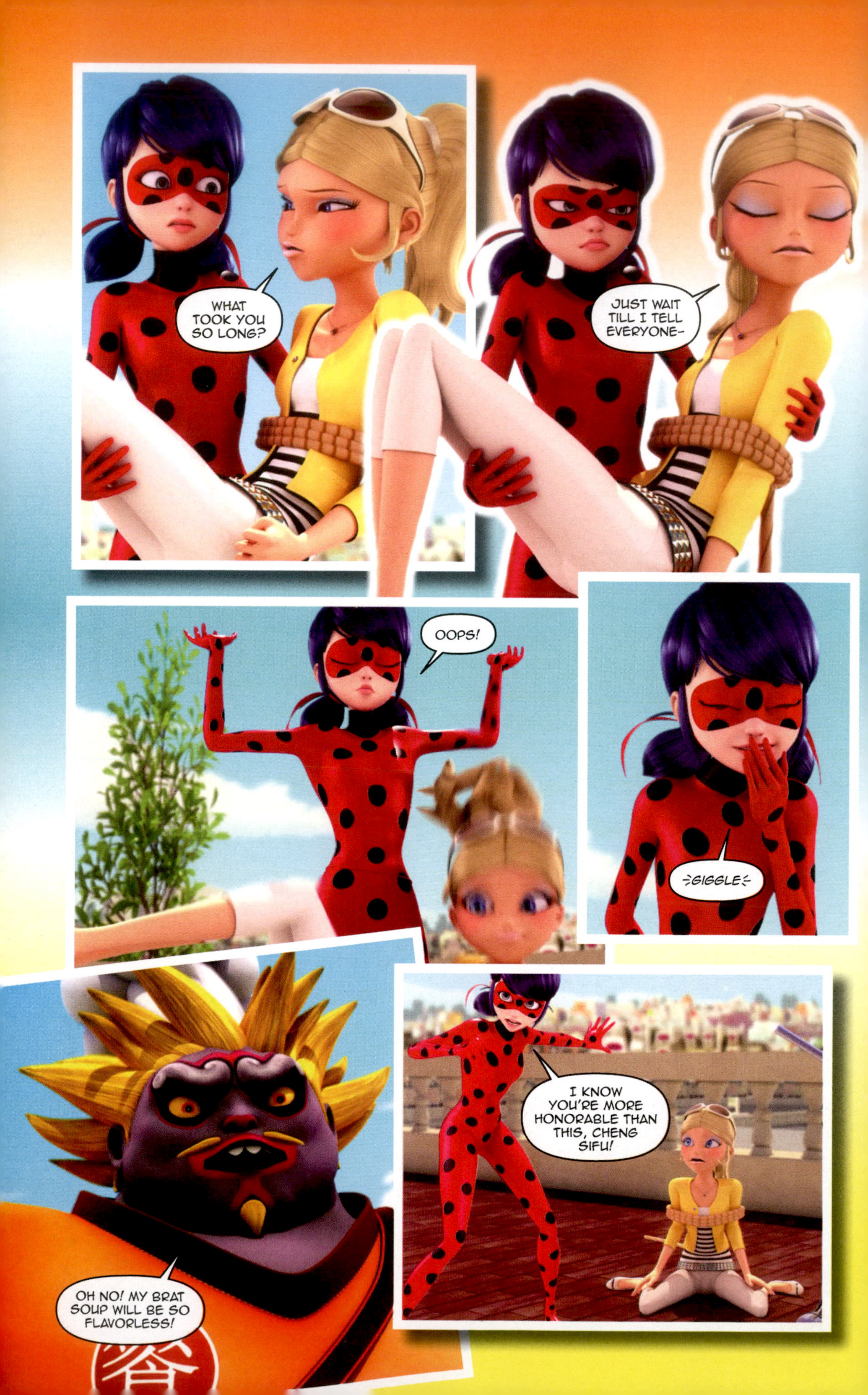
WHAT TOOK YOU SO LONG?
JUST WAIT TILL I TELL EVERYONE-
OOPS!
GIGGLE
OH NO! MY BRAT SOUP WILL BE SO FLAVORLESS!
I KNOW YOU'RE MORE HONORABLE THAN THIS, CHENG SIFU!

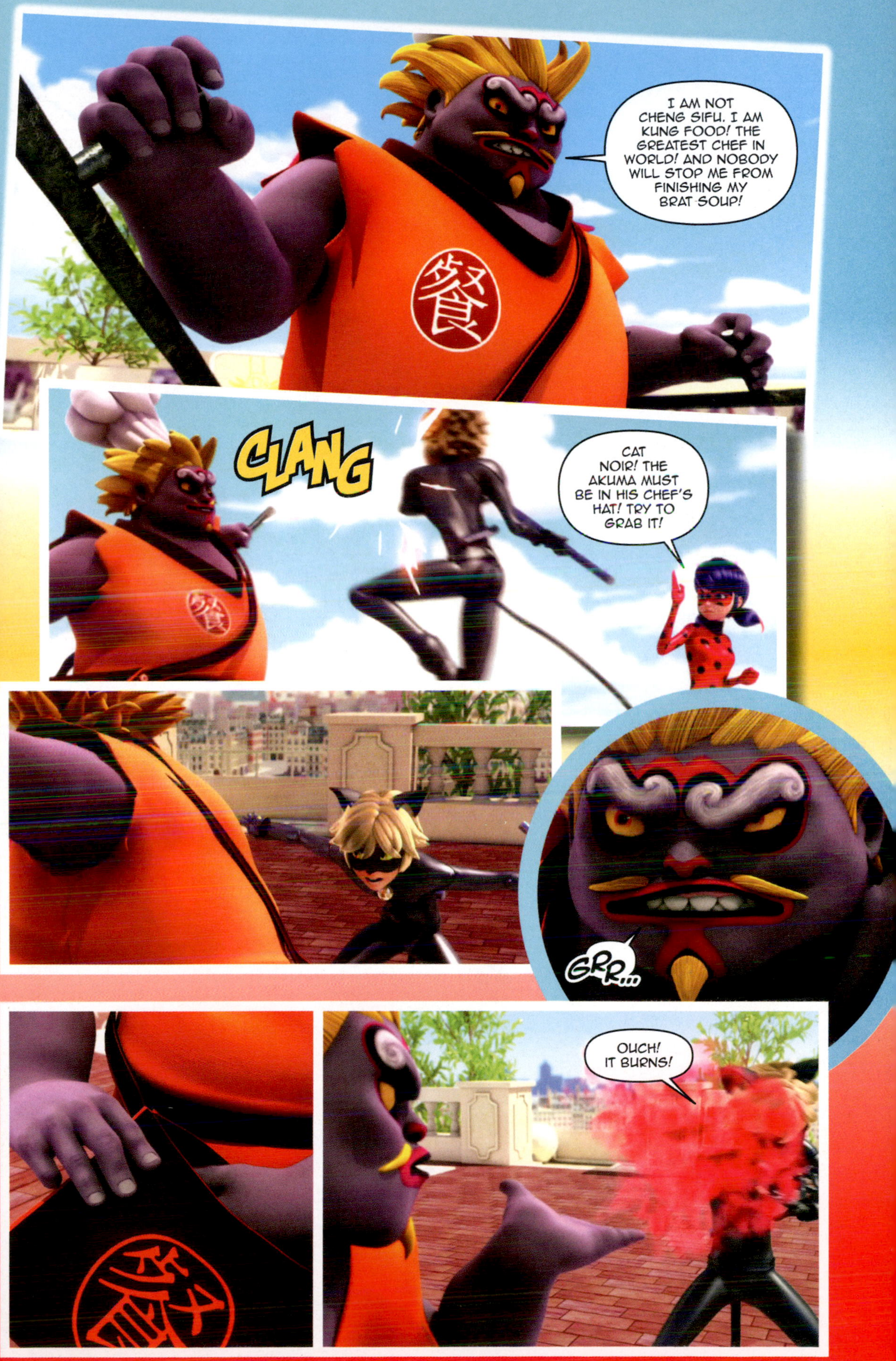
I AM NOT CHENG SIFU. I AM KUNG FOOD! THE GREATEST CHEF IN WORLD! AND NOBODY WILL STOP ME FROM FINISHING MY BRAT SOUP!
CLANG
CAT NOIR! THE AKUMA MUST BE IN HIS CHEF'S HAT! TRY TO GRAB IT!
GRR...
OUCH! IT BURNS!

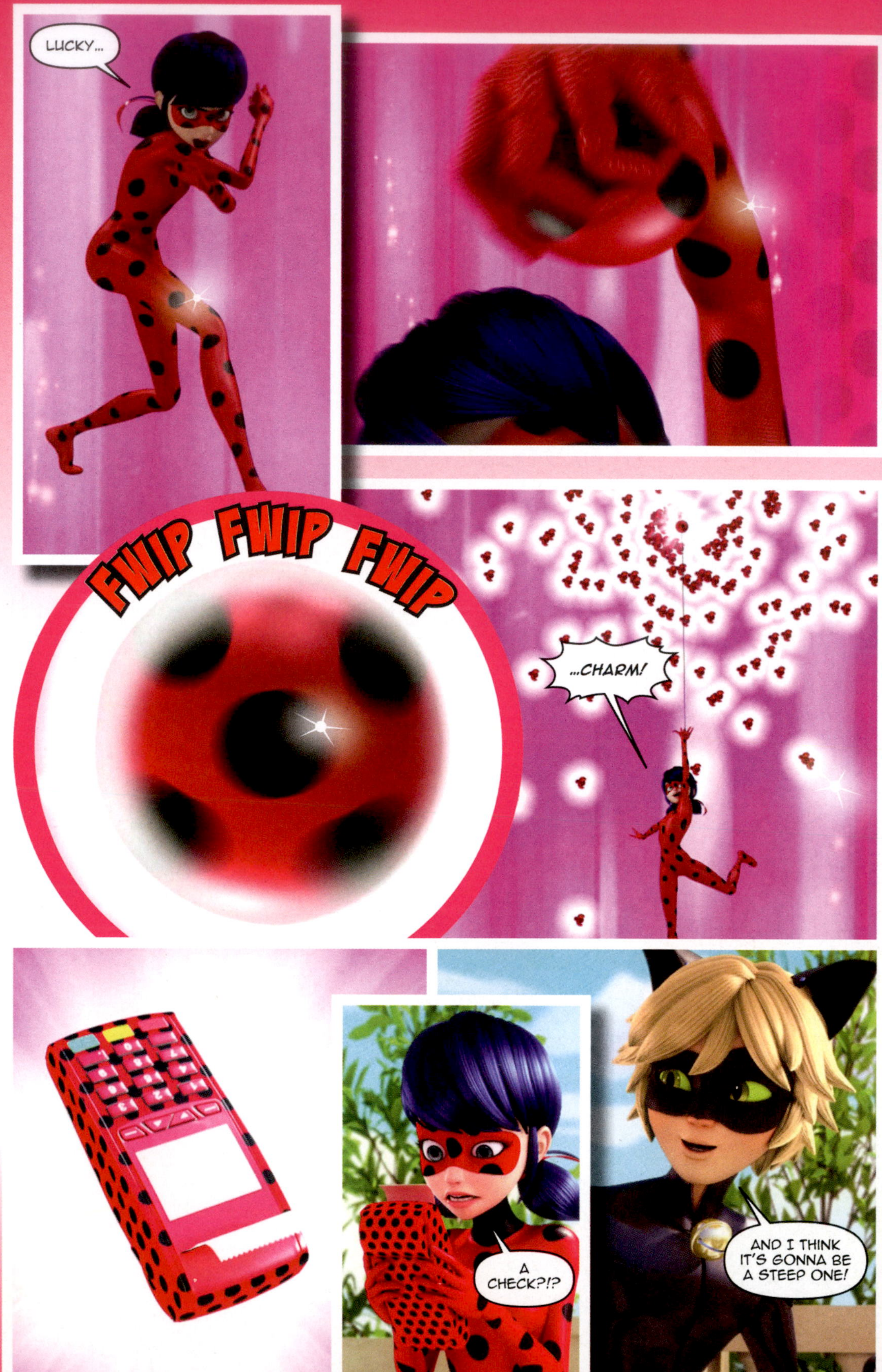
LUCKY...
FWIP FWIP FWIP
...CHARM!
A CHECK?!?
AND I THINK IT'S GONNA BE A STEEP ONE!

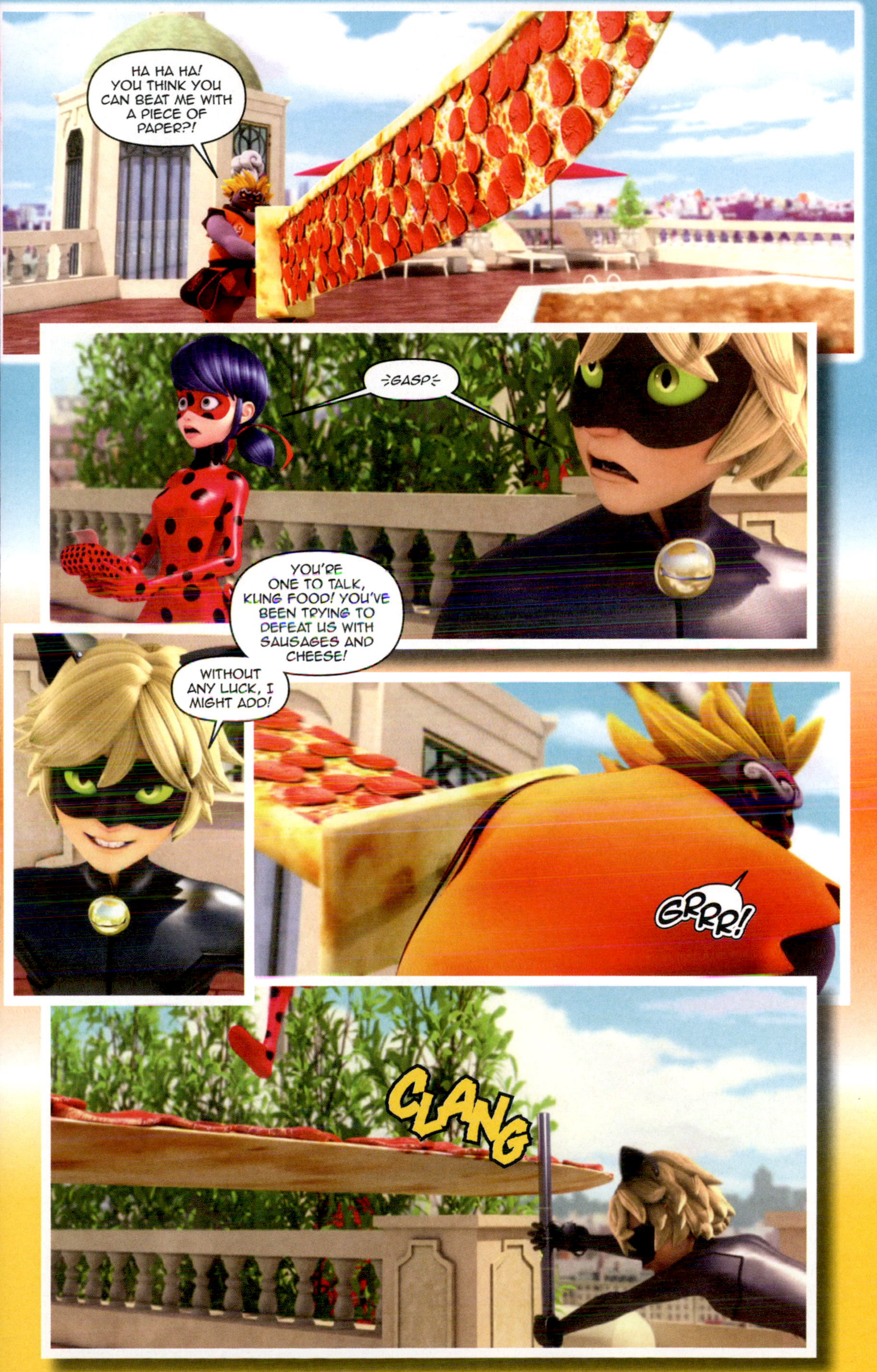
HA HA HA! YOU THINK YOU CAN BEAT ME WITH A PIECE OF PAPER?!
GASP
YOU'RE ONE TO TALK, KUNG FOOD! YOU'VE BEEN TRYING TO DEFEAT US WITH SAUSAGES AND CHEESE!
WITHOUT ANY LUCK, I MIGHT ADD!
GRRR!
CLANG

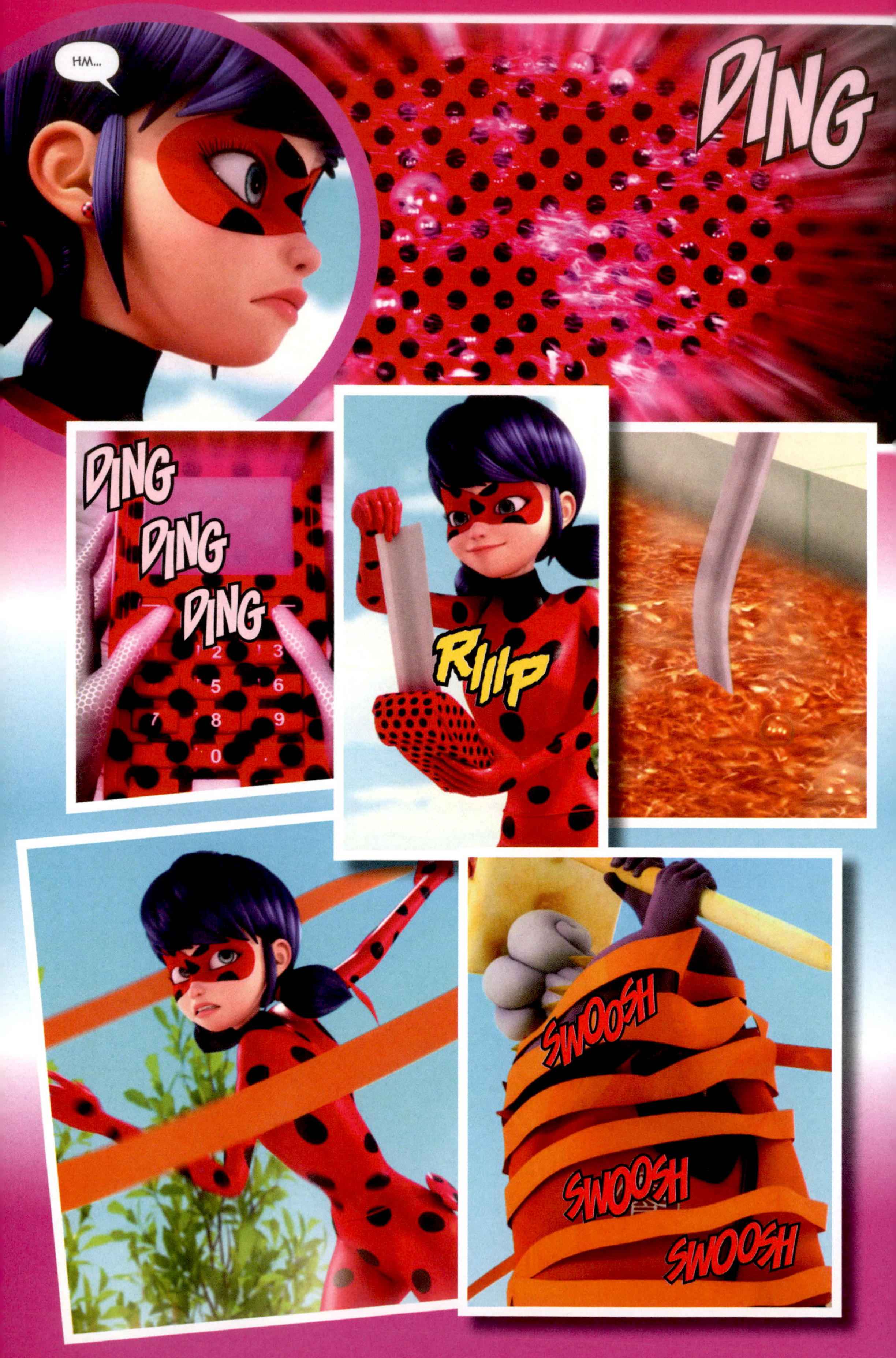
HM...
DING
DING
DING
DING
RIIIP
SWOOSH
SWOOSH
SWOOSH

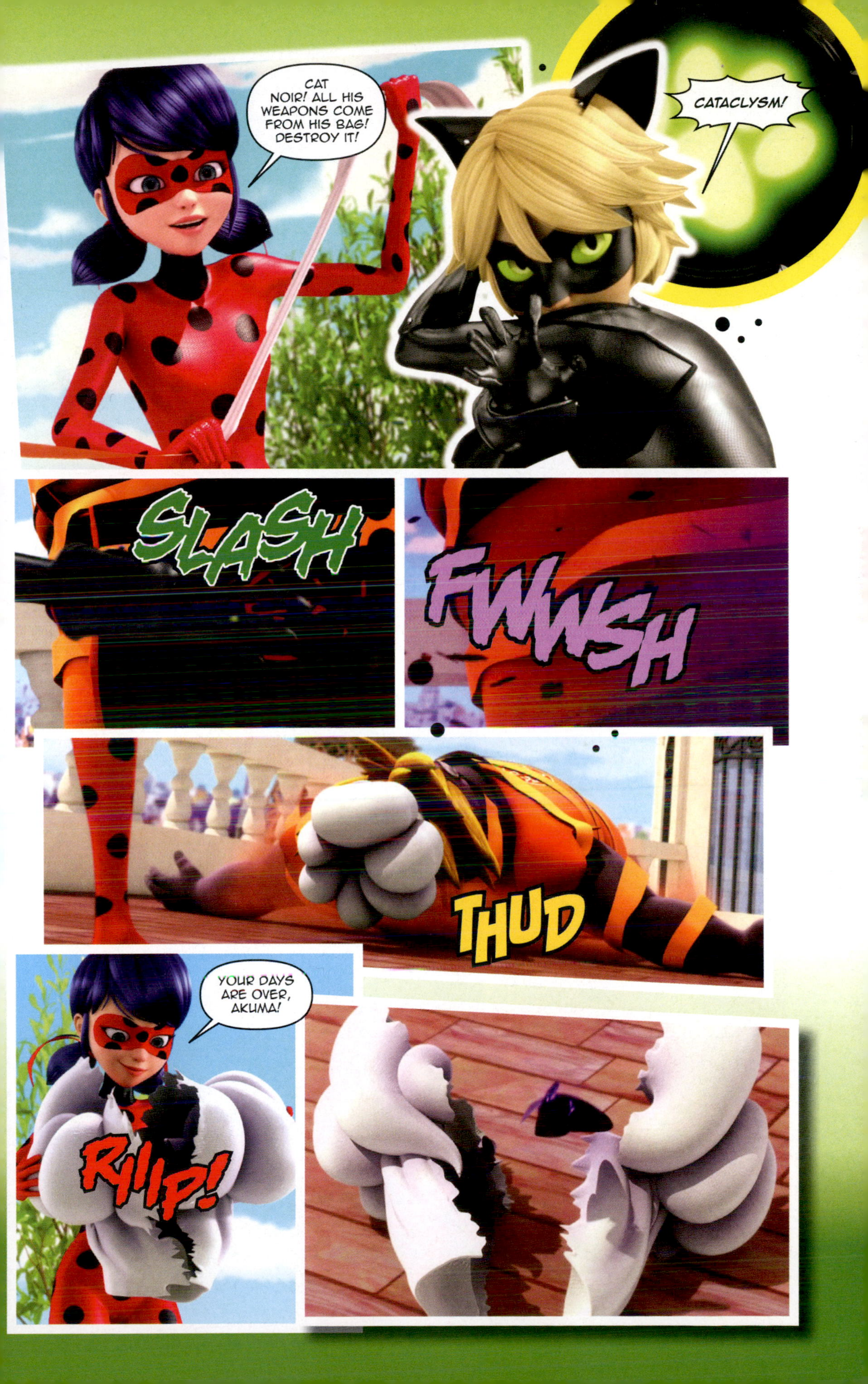
CAT NOIR! ALL HIS WEAPONS COME FROM HIS BAG! DESTROY IT!
CATACLYSM!
SLASH
FWWSH
THUD
YOUR DAYS ARE OVER, AKUMA!
RIIIP!

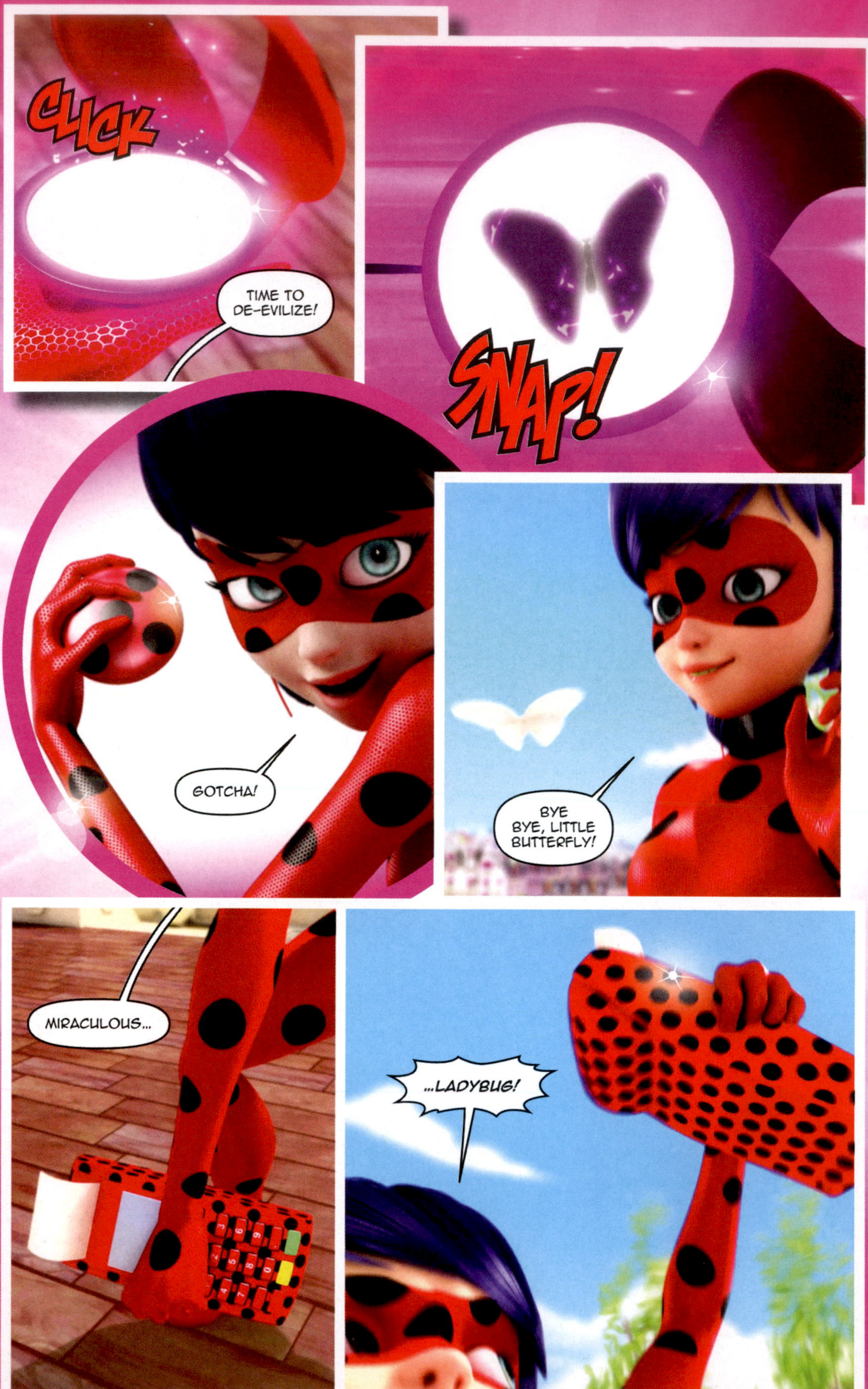
CLICK
TIME TO DE-EVILIZE!
SNAP!
GOTCHA!
BYE BYE, LITTLE BUTTERFLY!
MIRACULOUS...
...LADYBUG!

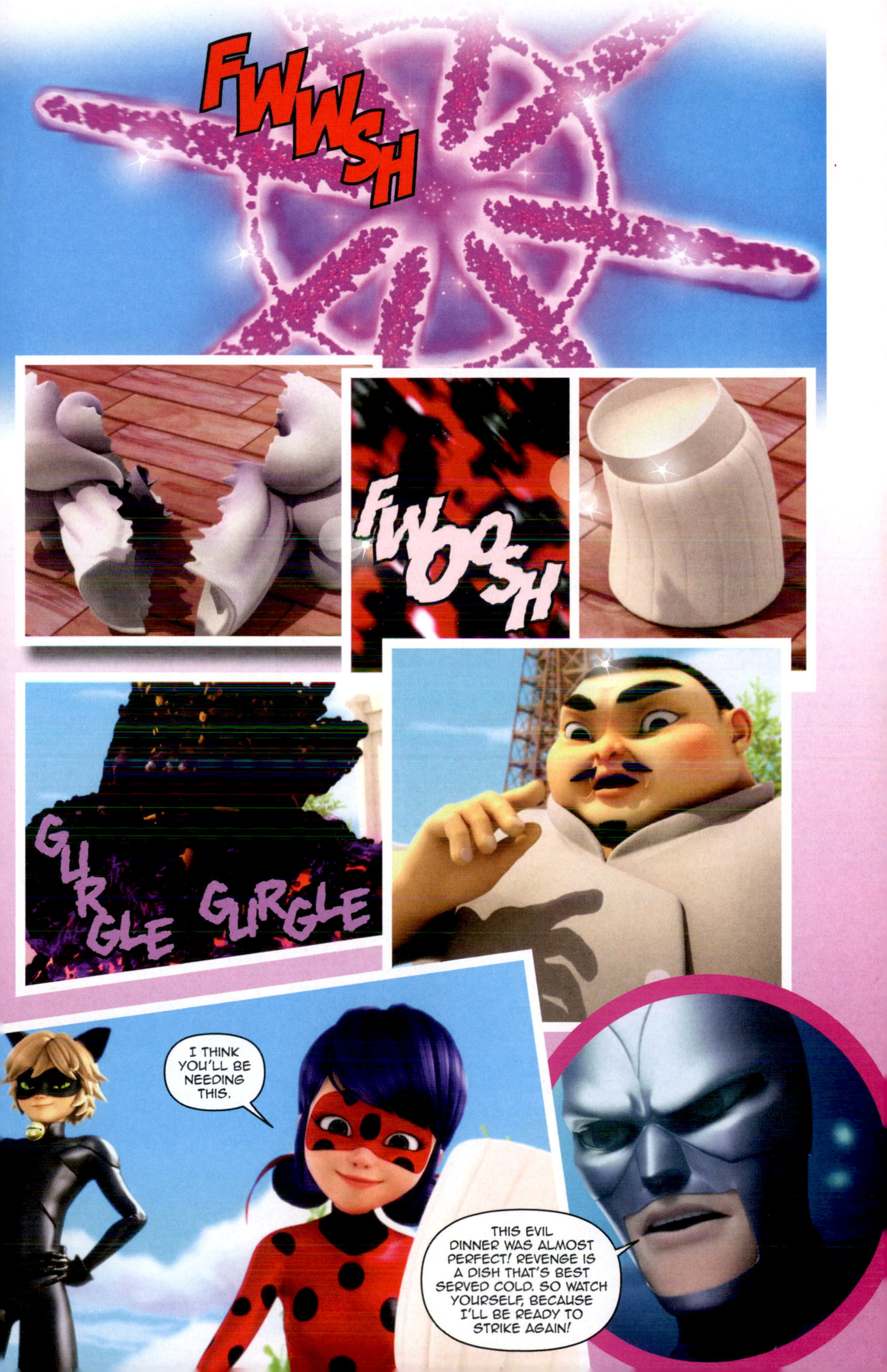
FWWSH
FWOOSH
GURGLE GURGLE
I THINK YOU'LL BE NEEDING THIS.
THIS EVIL DINNER WAS ALMOST PERFECT! REVENGE IS A DISH THAT'S BEST SERVED COLD. SO WATCH YOURSELF, BECAUSE I'LL BE READY TO STRIKE AGAIN!

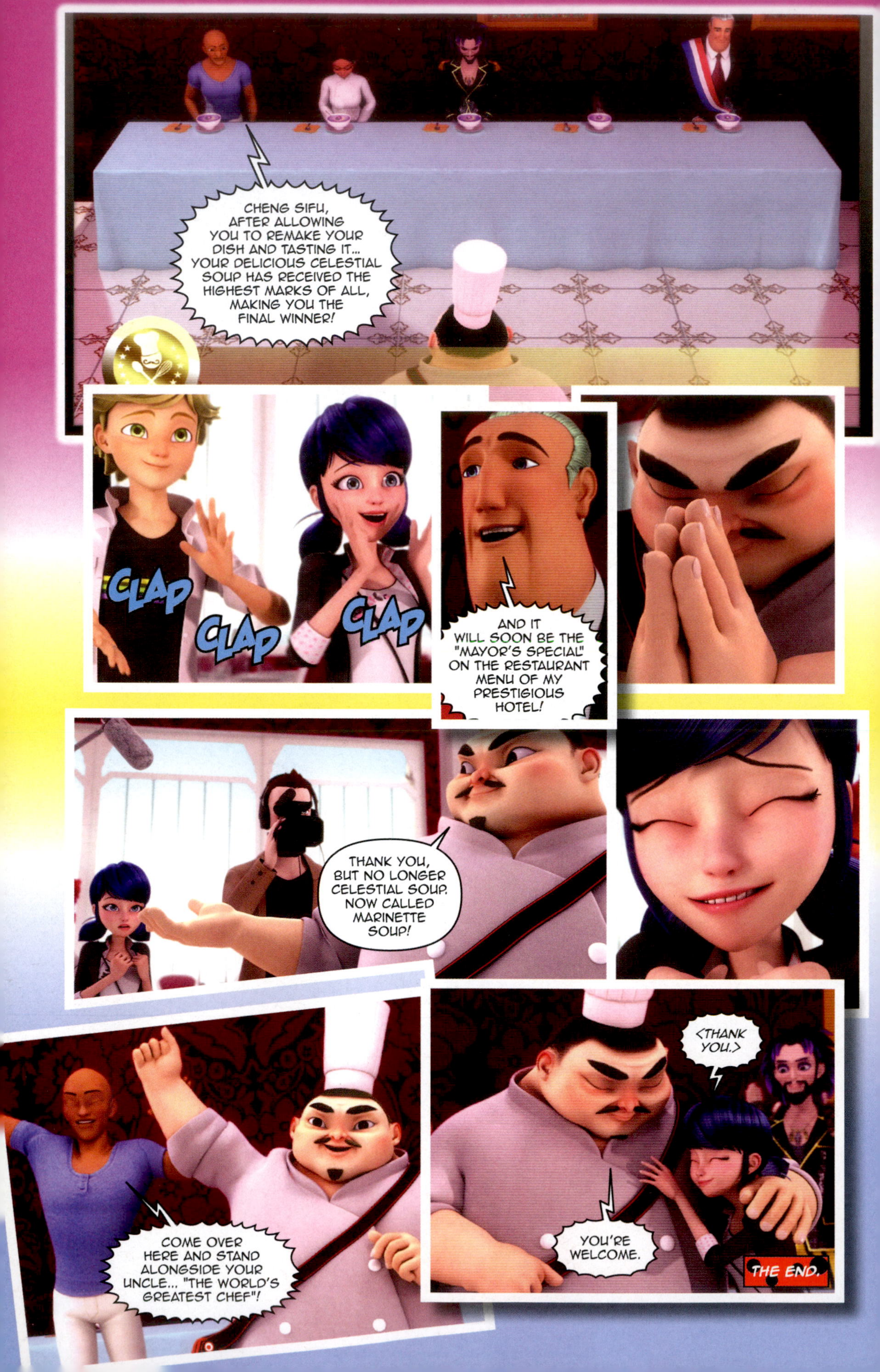
CHENG SIFU, AFTER ALLOWING YOU TO REMAKE YOUR DISH AND TASTING IT... YOUR DELICIOUS CELESTIAL SOUP HAS RECEIVED THE HIGHEST MARKS OF ALL, MAKING YOU THE FINAL WINNER!
CLAP
CLAP
CLAP
AND IT WILL SOON BE THE "MAYOR'S SPECIAL" ON THE RESTAURANT MENU OF MY PRESTIGIOUS HOTEL!
THANK YOU, BUT NO LONGER CELESTIAL SOUP. NOW CALLED MARINETTE SOUP!
COME OVER HERE AND STAND ALONGSIDE YOUR UNCLE... "THE WORLD'S GREATEST CHEF"!
<THANK YOU.>
YOU'RE WELCOME.
THE END.

Gamer

Created by: Thomas Astruc
Comics adaptation by: Nicole D'Andria
Written by: Guillaume Mautalent &
Sébastien Oursel
Art arranged by: Cheryl Black
Lettered by: Justin Birch

Bryan Seaton: Publisher/ CEO
Shawn Gabborin: Editor In Chief
Jason Martin: Publisher-Danger Zone
Nicole D'Andria: Marketing Director/Editor
Danielle Davison: Executive Administrator
Chad Cicconi: Akumatized
Shawn Pryor: President of Creator Relations

Dear diary,
Guess what? I was two spots away from transforming back and revealing my true identity to Cat Noir.

HEY, MARINETTE? WEREN'T YOU MEETING ALYA BACK AT SCHOOL THIS AFTERNOON TO RESEARCH YOUR TERM PAPER?

OH NO!

I'M LATE... AGAIN!

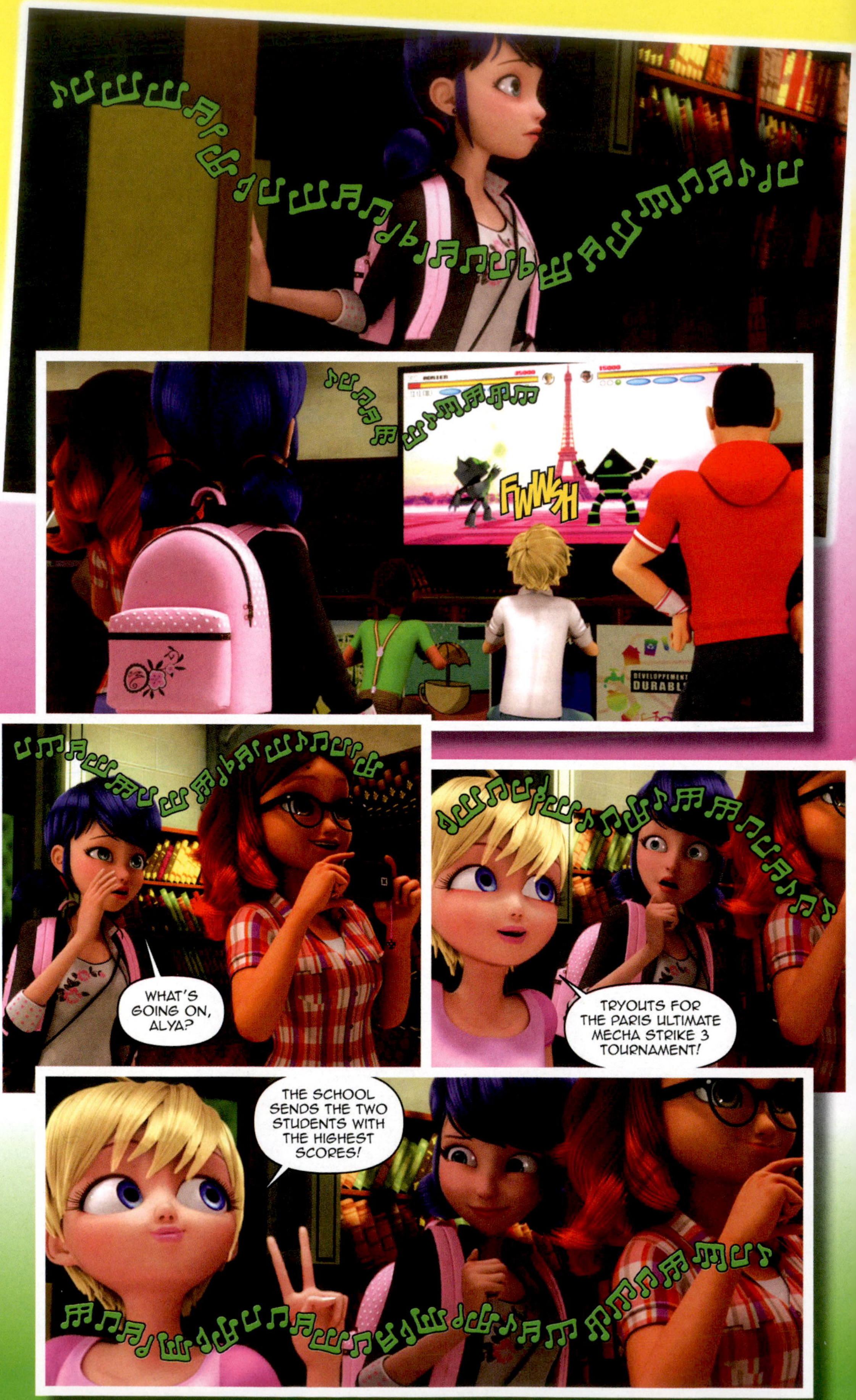
FWWSH
WHAT'S GOING ON, ALYA?
TRYOUTS FOR THE PARIS ULTIMATE MECHA STRIKE 3 TOURNAMENT!
THE SCHOOL SENDS THE TWO STUDENTS WITH THE HIGHEST SCORES!

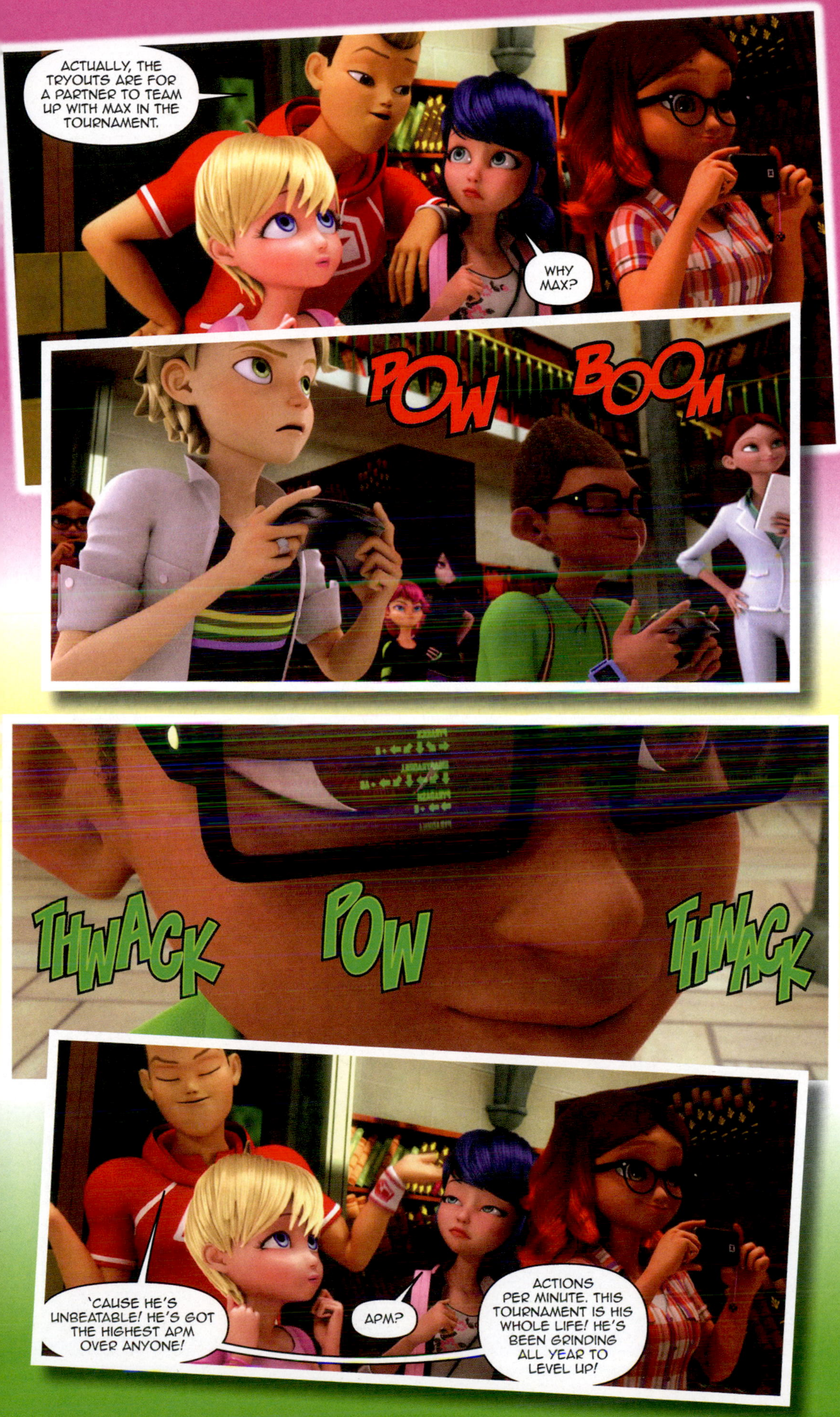

ACTUALLY, THE TRYOUTS ARE FOR A PARTNER TO TEAM UP WITH MAX IN THE TOURNAMENT.
WHY MAX?
POW
BOOM
THWACK
POW
THWACK
'CAUSE HE'S UNBEATABLE! HE'S GOT THE HIGHEST APM OVER ANYONE!
APM?
ACTIONS PER MINUTE. THIS TOURNAMENT IS HIS WHOLE LIFE! HE'S BEEN GRINDING ALL YEAR TO LEVEL UP!

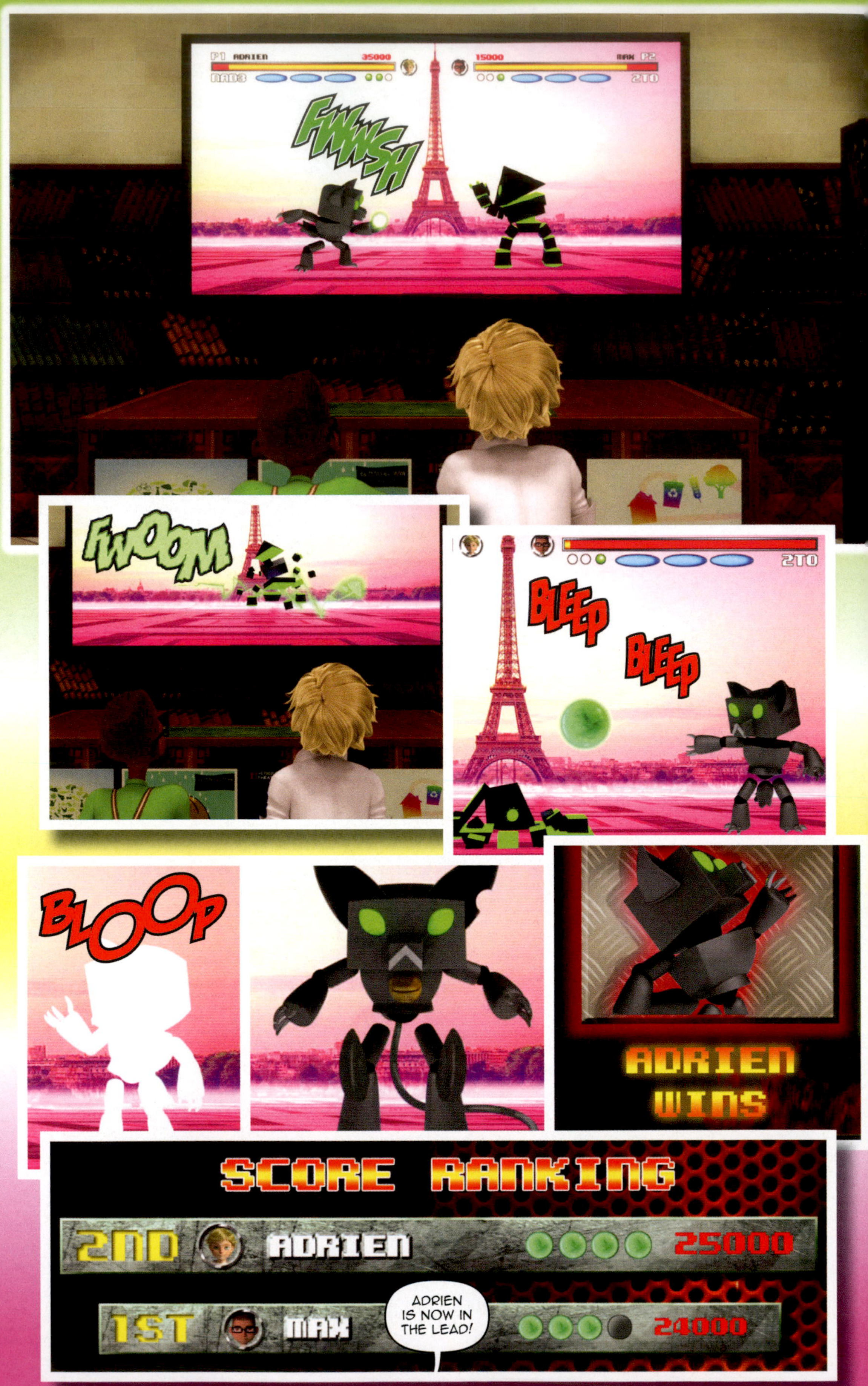

P1 ADRIEN 35000
15000 MAX P2
FWWSH
FWOOM
BLEEP
BLEEP
BLOOP
ADRIEN WINS
SCORE RANKING
2ND ADRIEN 25000
1ST MAX 24000
ADRIEN IS NOW IN THE LEAD!

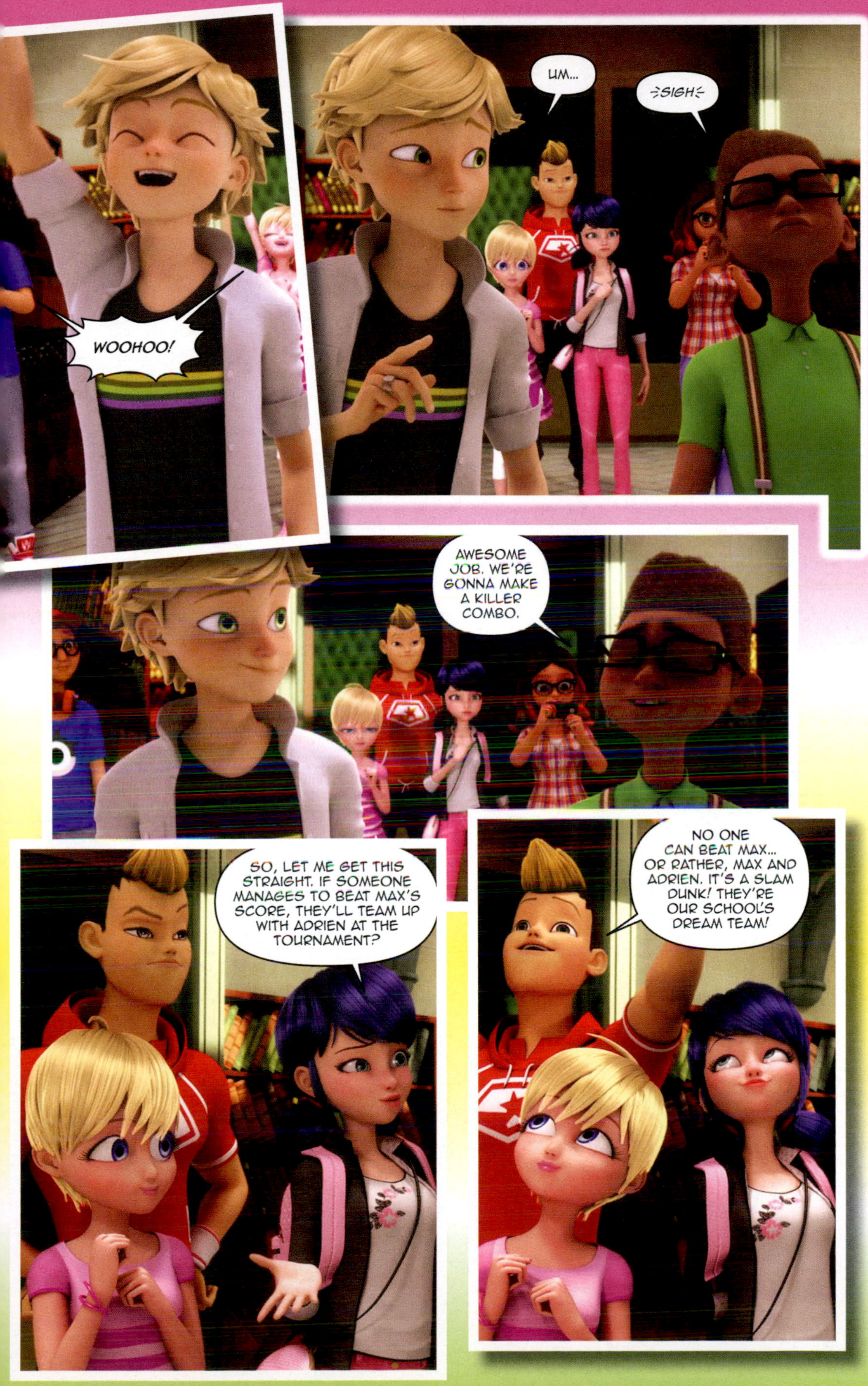
WOOHOO!
UM...
≈SIGH≈
AWESOME JOB. WE'RE GONNA MAKE A KILLER COMBO.
SO, LET ME GET THIS STRAIGHT. IF SOMEONE MANAGES TO BEAT MAX'S SCORE, THEY'LL TEAM UP WITH ADRIEN AT THE TOURNAMENT?
NO ONE CAN BEAT MAX... OR RATHER, MAX AND ADRIEN. IT'S A SLAM DUNK! THEY'RE OUR SCHOOL'S DREAM TEAM!

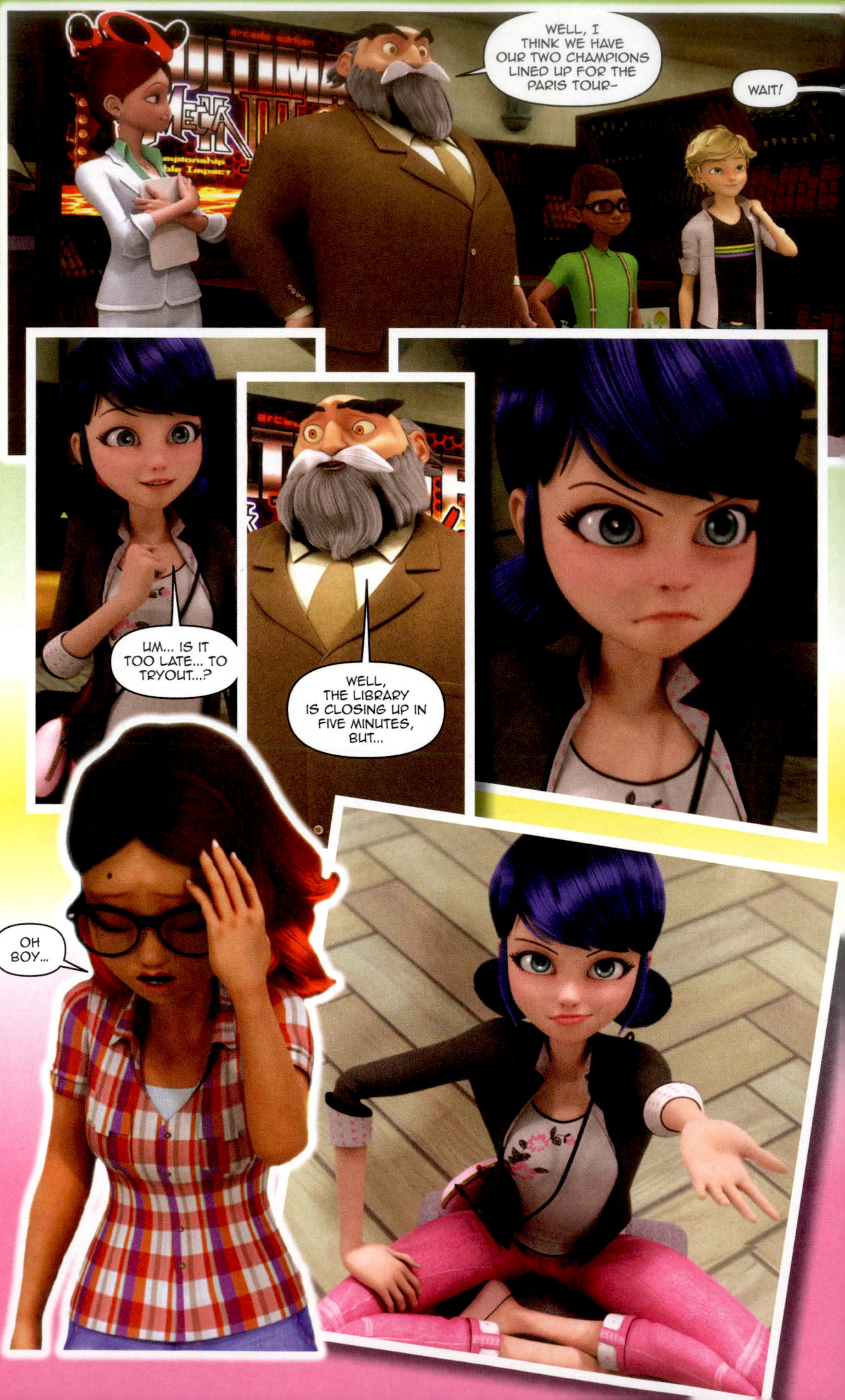
WELL, I THINK WE HAVE OUR TWO CHAMPIONS LINED UP FOR THE PARIS TOUR-
WAIT!
UM... IS IT TOO LATE... TO TRYOUT...?
WELL, THE LIBRARY IS CLOSING UP IN FIVE MINUTES, BUT...
OH BOY...

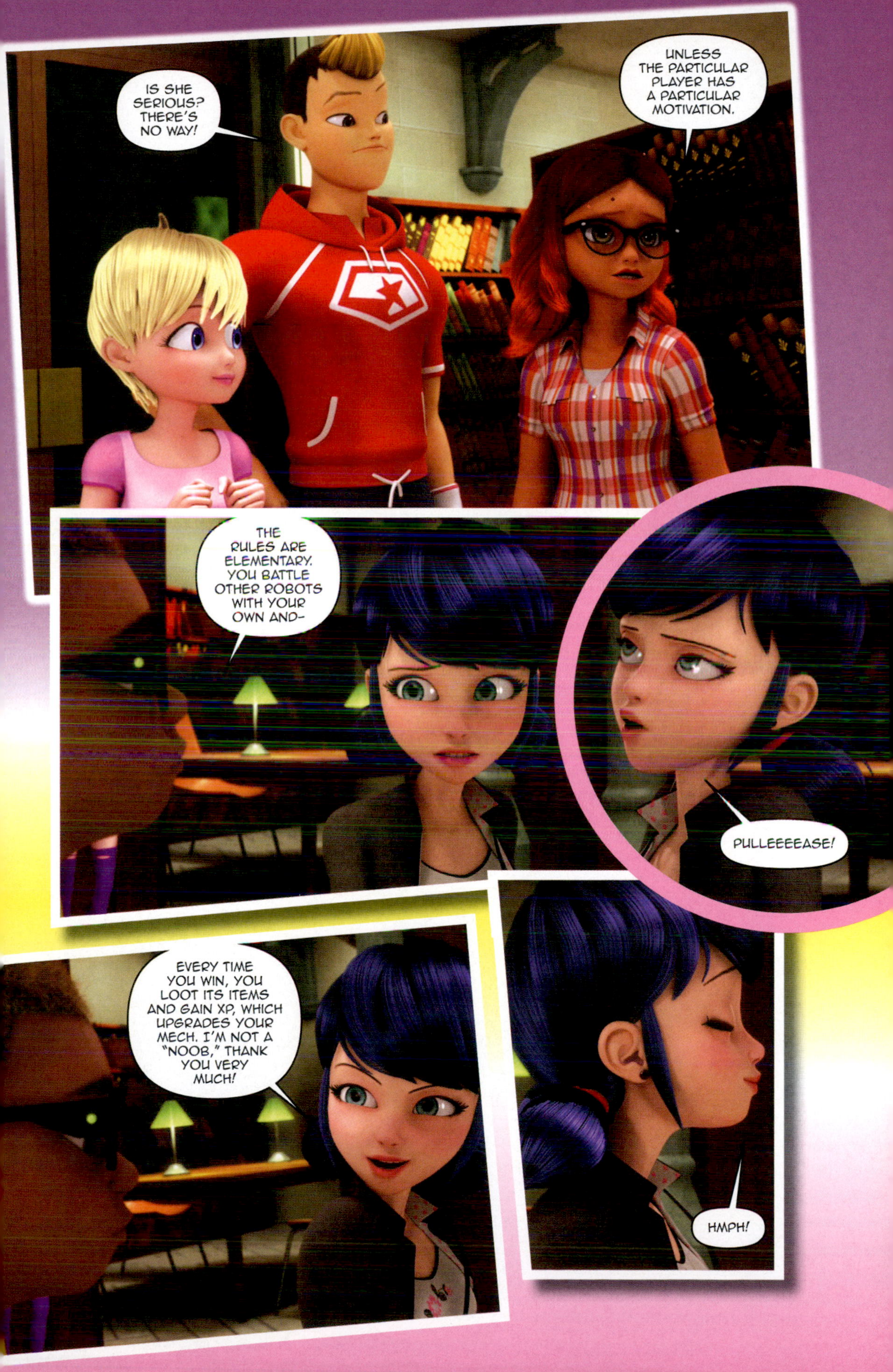
IS SHE SERIOUS? THERE'S NO WAY!
UNLESS THE PARTICULAR PLAYER HAS A PARTICULAR MOTIVATION.
THE RULES ARE ELEMENTARY. YOU BATTLE OTHER ROBOTS WITH YOUR OWN AND-
PULLEEEEASE!
EVERY TIME YOU WIN, YOU LOOT ITS ITEMS AND GAIN XP, WHICH UPGRADES YOUR MECH. I'M NOT A "NOOB," THANK YOU VERY MUCH!
HMPH!

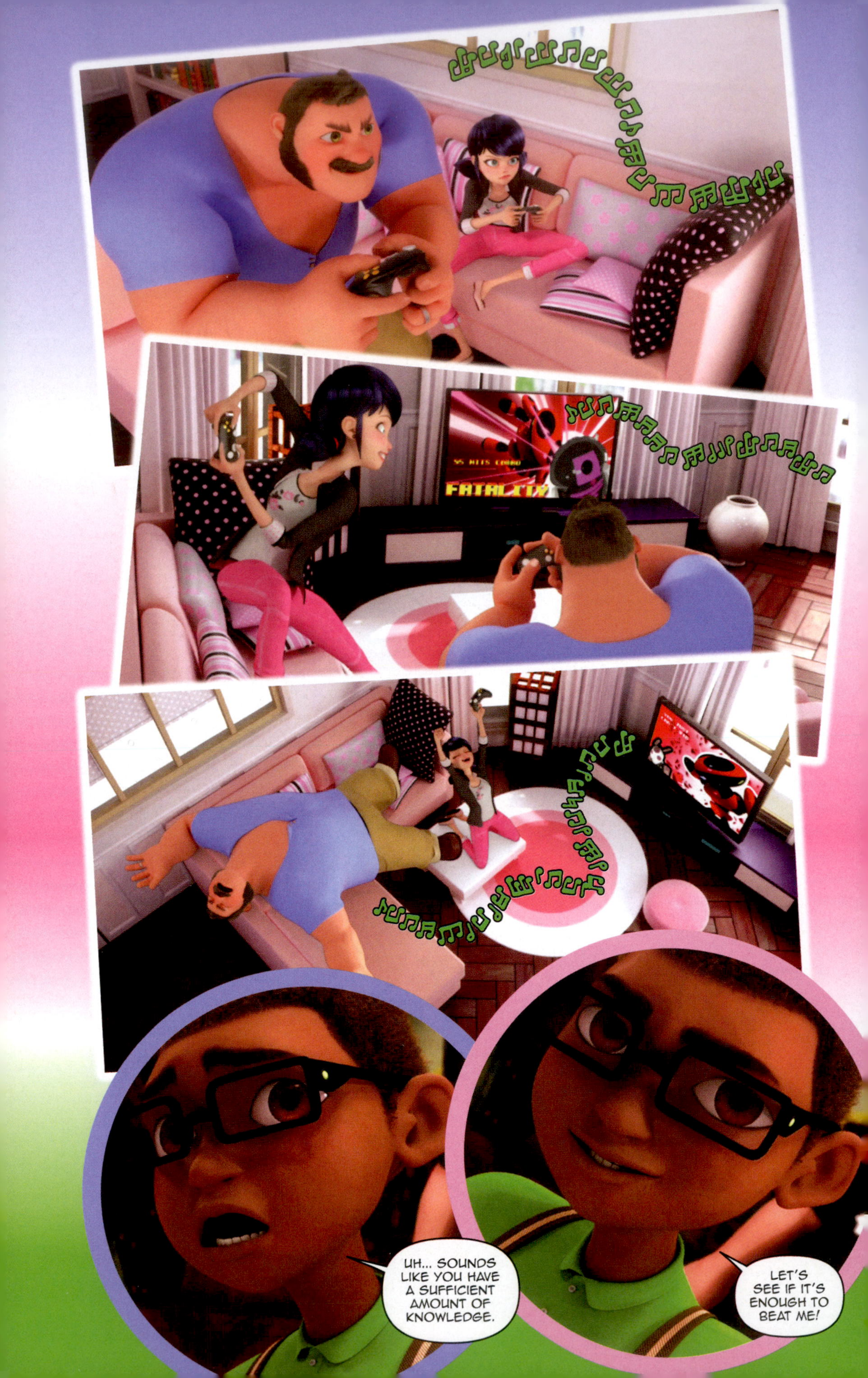
UH... SOUNDS LIKE YOU HAVE A SUFFICIENT AMOUNT OF KNOWLEDGE.
LET'S SEE IF IT'S ENOUGH TO BEAT ME!

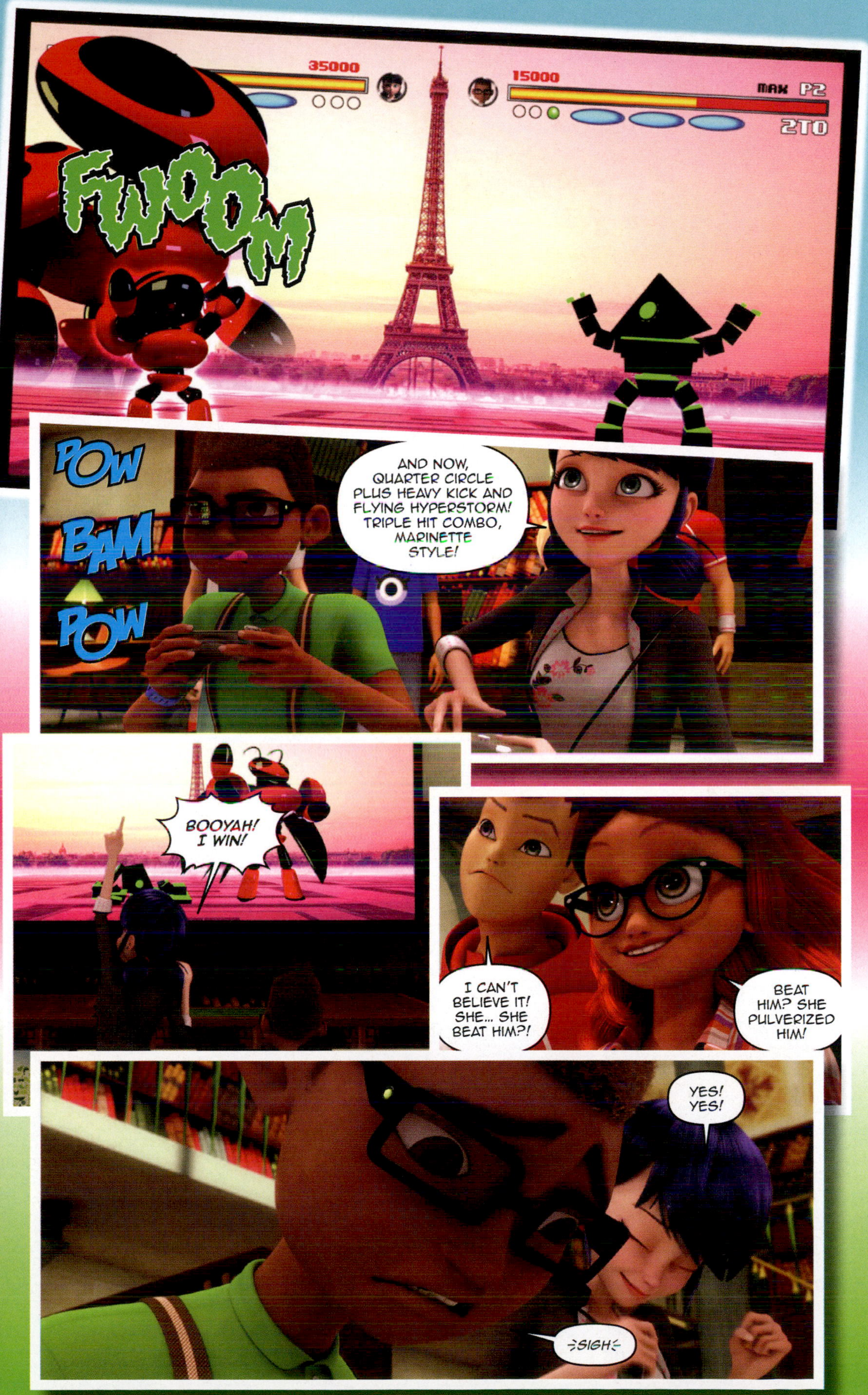
35000
15000
MAX P2
2TO
FWOOM
POW
BAM
POW
AND NOW, QUARTER CIRCLE PLUS HEAVY KICK AND FLYING HYPERSTORM! TRIPLE HIT COMBO, MARINETTE STYLE!
BOOYAH! I WIN!
I CAN'T BELIEVE IT! SHE... SHE BEAT HIM?!
BEAT HIM? SHE PULVERIZED HIM!
YES! YES!
SIGH

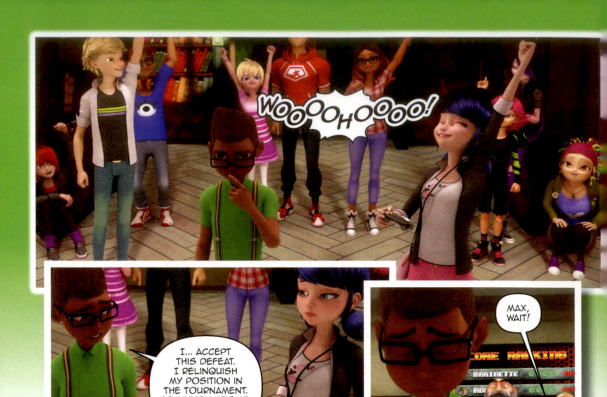

WOOOOHOOOO!

I... ACCEPT THIS DEFEAT. I RELINQUISH MY POSITION IN THE TOURNAMENT. CONGRATULATIONS, MARINETTE. AND ADRIEN.

MAX, WAIT!

LOOK, I'M FINE. BUT IF YOU DON'T MIND, I'D LIKE A LITTLE SOLITUDE.

SO, MARINETTE DUPAIN-CHENG AND ADRIEN AGRESTE WILL REPRESENT FRANÇOISE DUPONT HIGH SCHOOL AT THE PARIS ULTIMATE MECHA STRIKE 3 TOURNAMENT. GOOD LUCK TO BOTH OF YOU!

WELL, I GUESS I'LL BE COMING OVER TO PRACTICE... WITH MY NEW PARTNER! SEE YOU LATER.

SEE... YA...

NOW YOU GOTTA WIN, M. YOU'RE GONNA BE REPRESENTING THE SCHOOL, NOT JUST HANGING OUT WITH ADRIEN!

OH, ADRIEN...

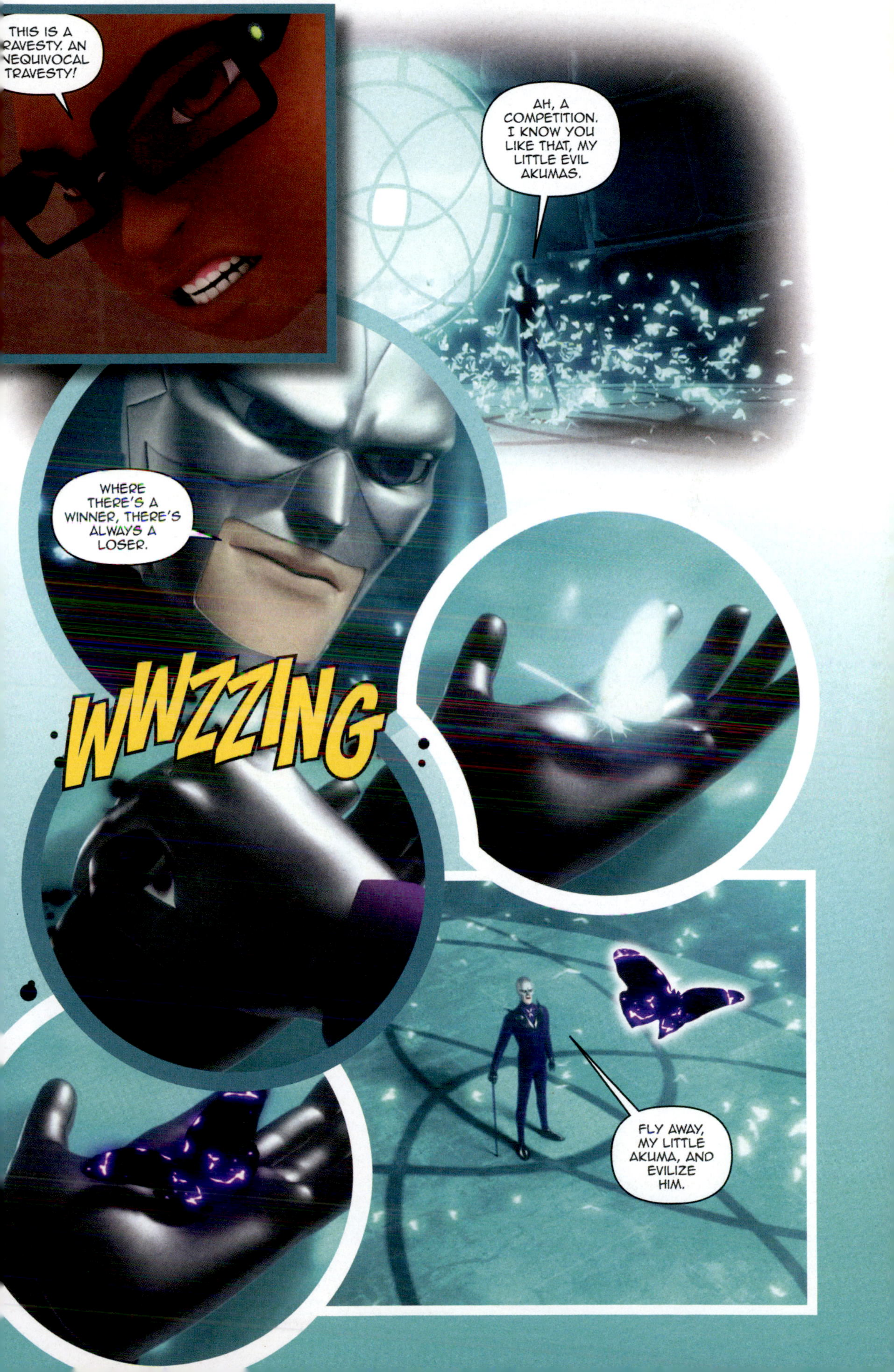
THIS IS A TRAVESTY. AN UNEQUIVOCAL TRAVESTY!
AH, A COMPETITION. I KNOW YOU LIKE THAT, MY LITTLE EVIL AKUMAS.
WHERE THERE'S A WINNER, THERE'S ALWAYS A LOSER.
WWZZING
FLY AWAY, MY LITTLE AKUMA, AND EVILIZE HIM.

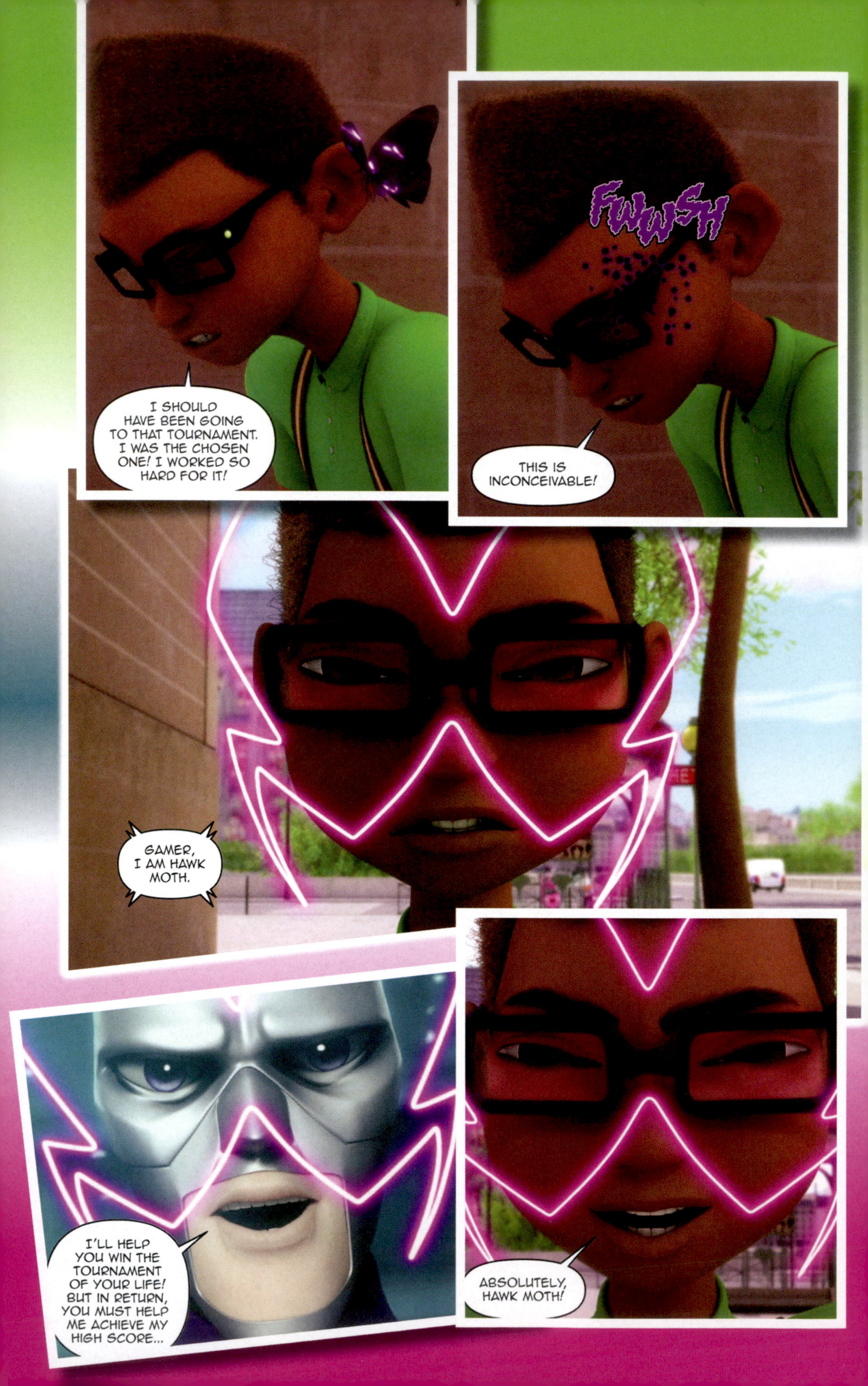

I SHOULD HAVE BEEN GOING TO THAT TOURNAMENT. I WAS THE CHOSEN ONE! I WORKED SO HARD FOR IT!
FWWSH
THIS IS INCONCEIVABLE!
GAMER, I AM HAWK MOTH.
I'LL HELP YOU WIN THE TOURNAMENT OF YOUR LIFE! BUT IN RETURN, YOU MUST HELP ME ACHIEVE MY HIGH SCORE...
ABSOLUTELY, HAWK MOTH!

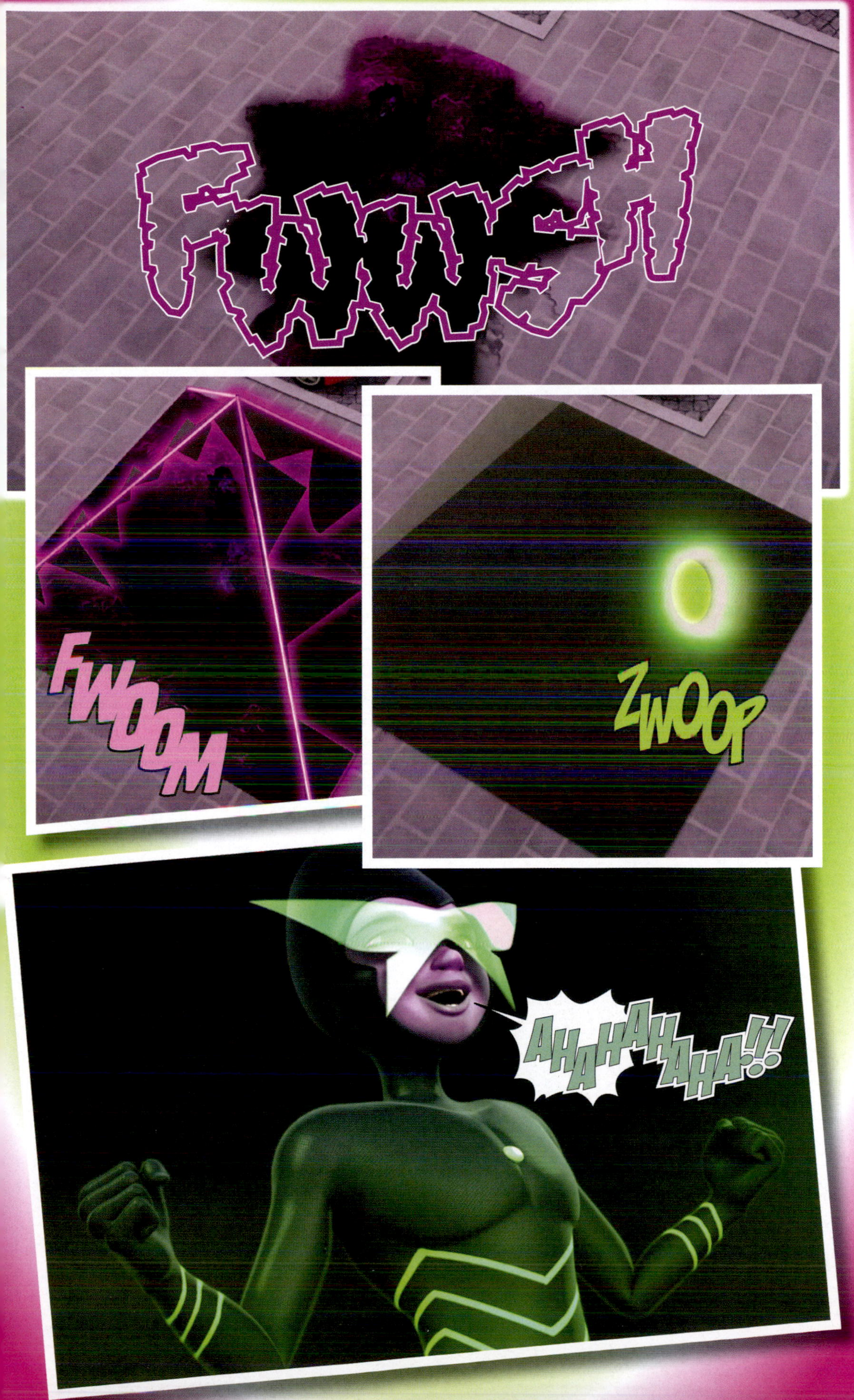
FWOOSH
FWOOM
ZWOOP
AHAHAHAHAHA!!!

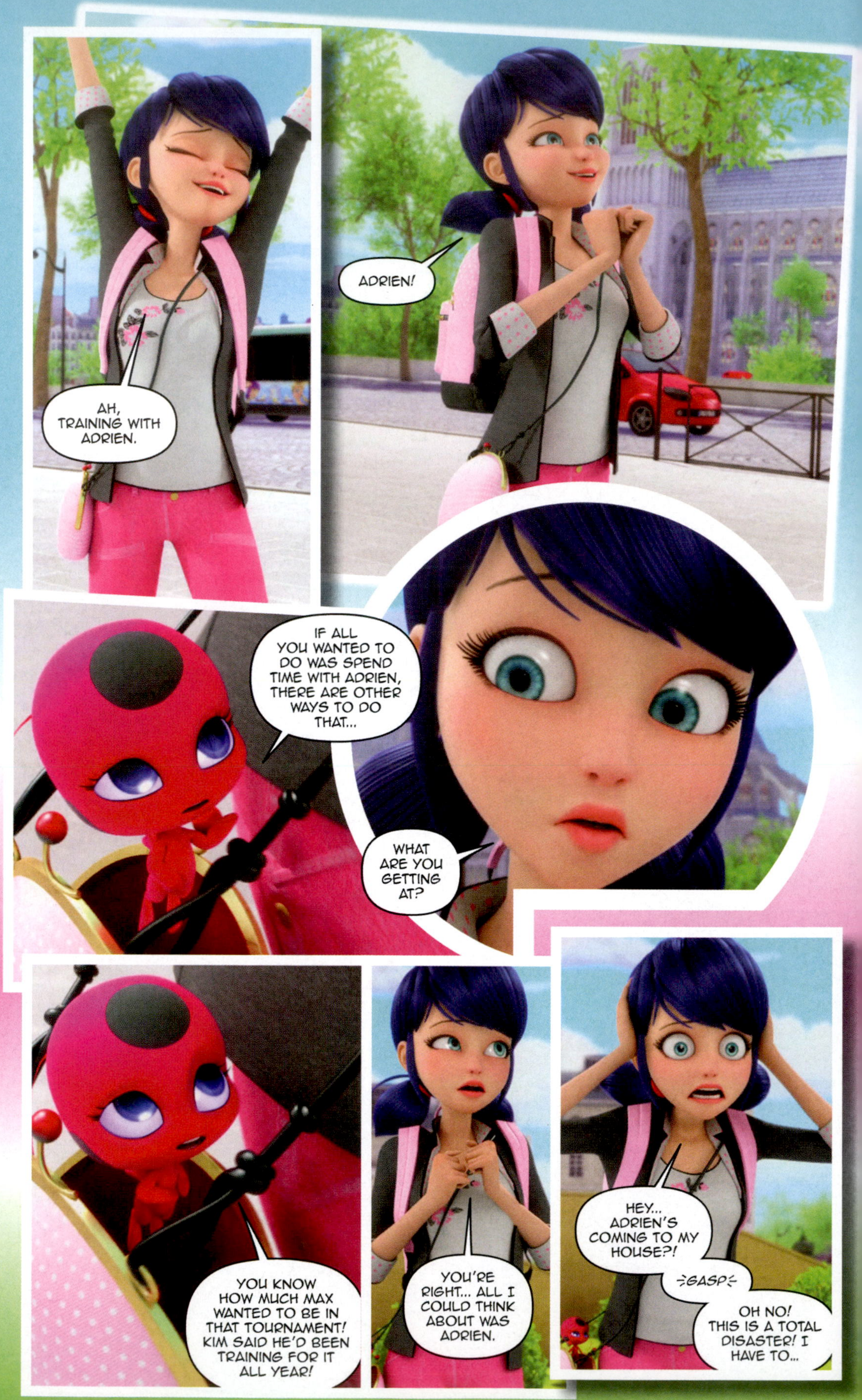
AH, TRAINING WITH ADRIEN.
ADRIEN!
IF ALL YOU WANTED TO DO WAS SPEND TIME WITH ADRIEN, THERE ARE OTHER WAYS TO DO THAT...
WHAT ARE YOU GETTING AT?
YOU KNOW HOW MUCH MAX WANTED TO BE IN THAT TOURNAMENT! KIM SAID HE'D BEEN TRAINING FOR IT ALL YEAR!
YOU'RE RIGHT... ALL I COULD THINK ABOUT WAS ADRIEN.
HEY... ADRIEN'S COMING TO MY HOUSE?!
GASP
OH NO! THIS IS A TOTAL DISASTER! I HAVE TO...

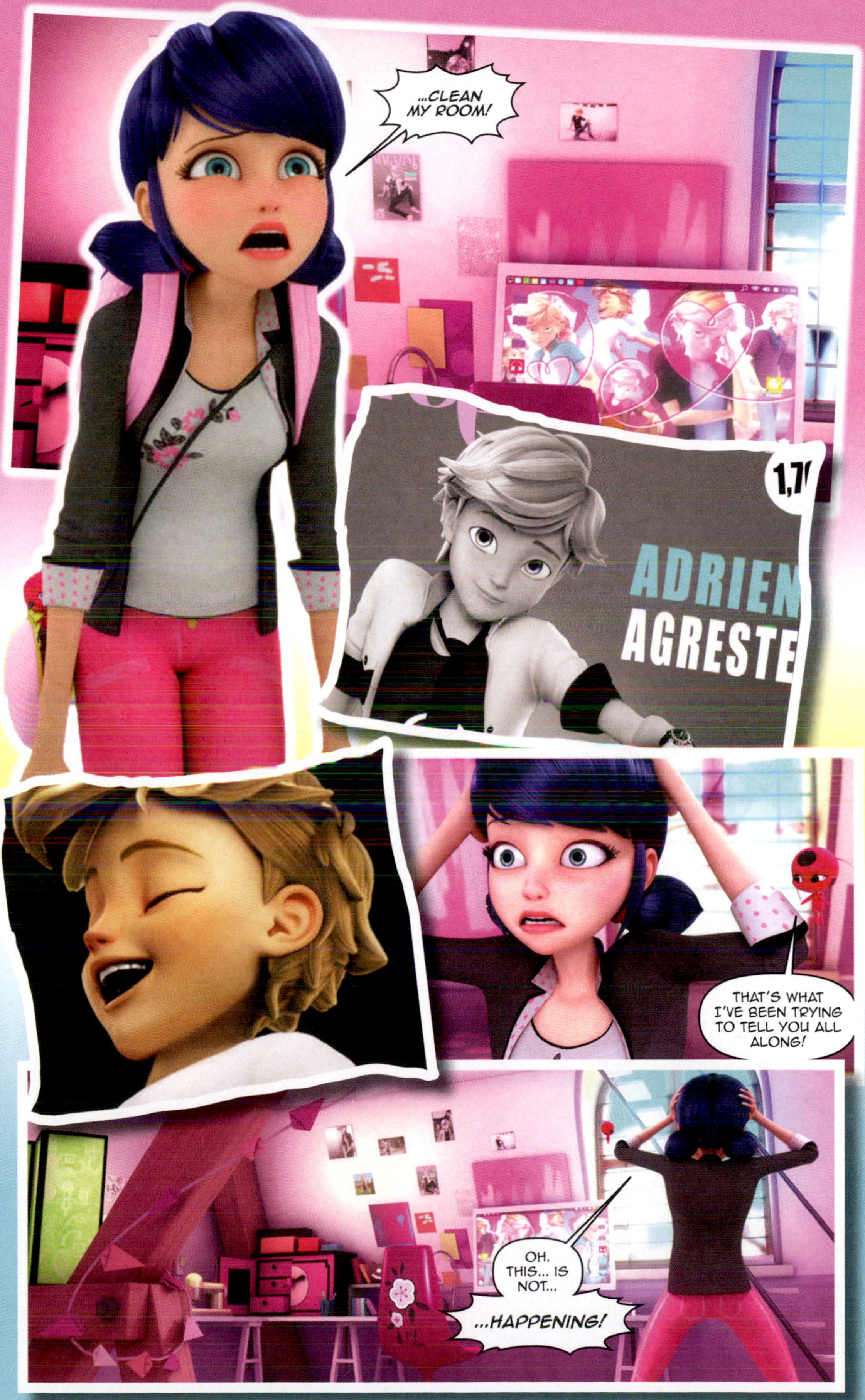
...CLEAN MY ROOM!
MAGAZINE
1,7
ADRIEN AGRESTE
THAT'S WHAT I'VE BEEN TRYING TO TELL YOU ALL ALONG!
OH, THIS... IS NOT...
...HAPPENING!

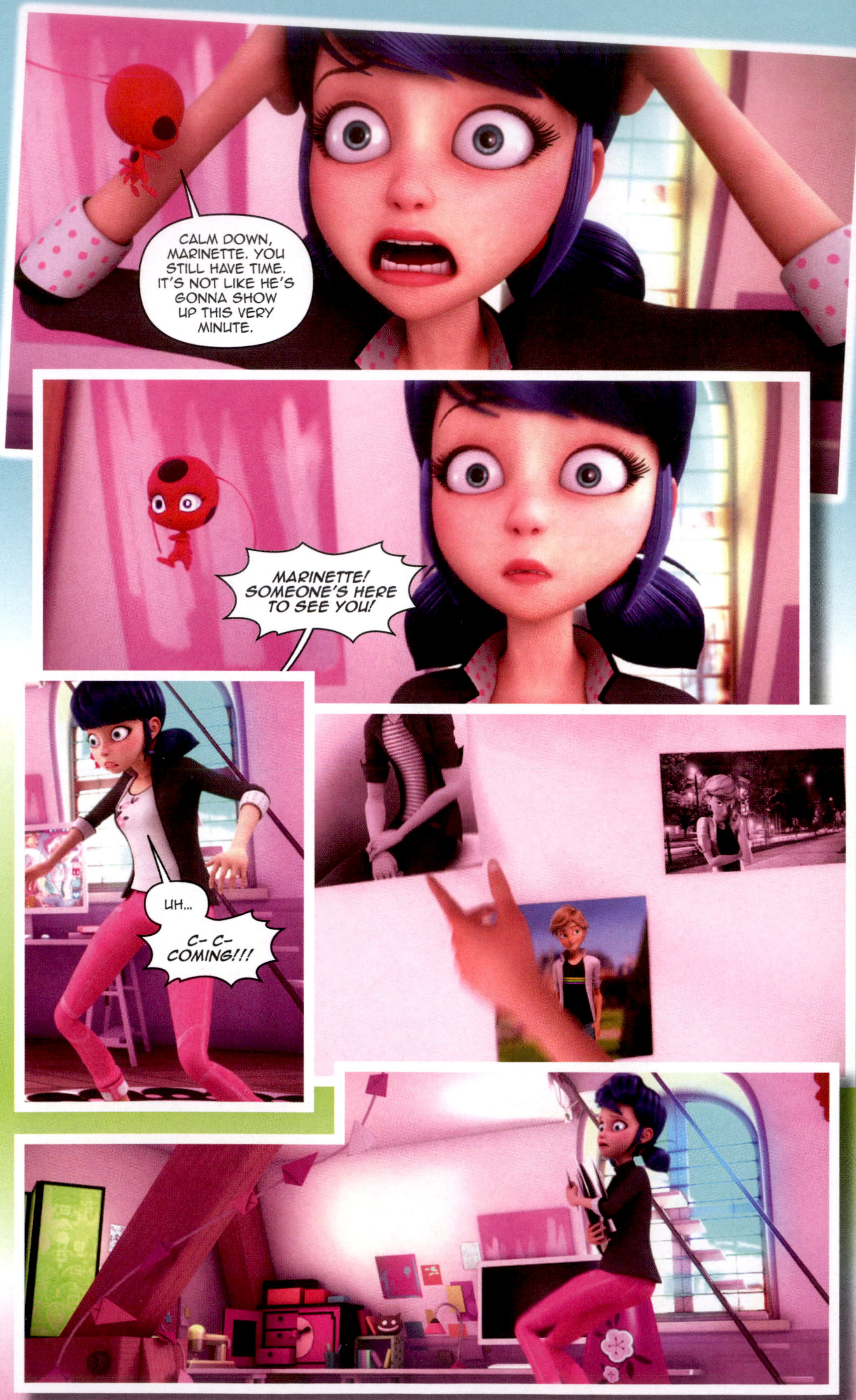
CALM DOWN, MARINETTE. YOU STILL HAVE TIME. IT'S NOT LIKE HE'S GONNA SHOW UP THIS VERY MINUTE.
MARINETTE! SOMEONE'S HERE TO SEE YOU!
UH...
C- C- COMING!!!

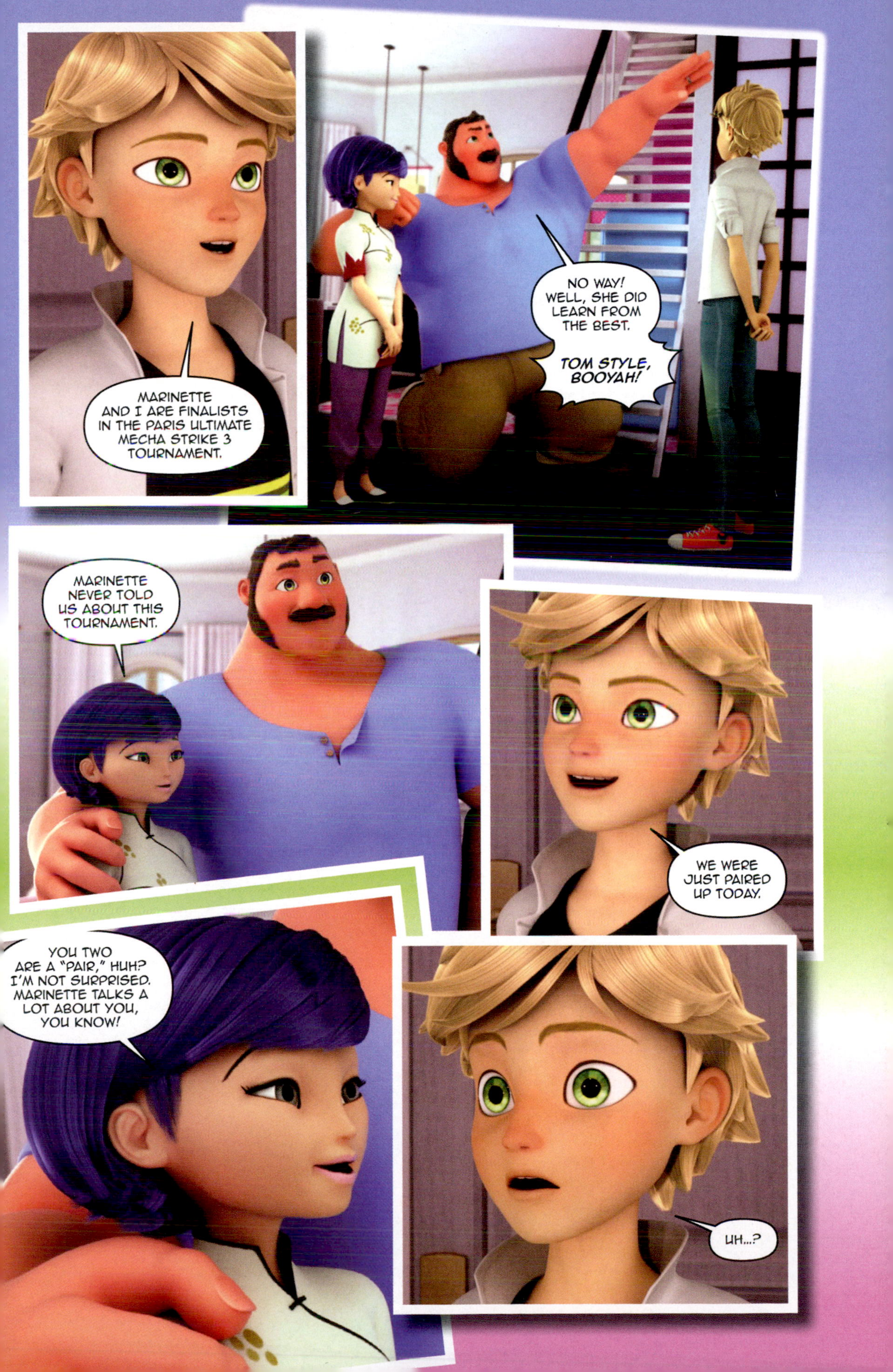
MARINETTE AND I ARE FINALISTS IN THE PARIS ULTIMATE MECHA STRIKE 3 TOURNAMENT.
NO WAY! WELL, SHE DID LEARN FROM THE BEST.
TOM STYLE, BOOYAH!
MARINETTE NEVER TOLD US ABOUT THIS TOURNAMENT.
WE WERE JUST PAIRED UP TODAY.
YOU TWO ARE A "PAIR," HUH? I'M NOT SURPRISED. MARINETTE TALKS A LOT ABOUT YOU, YOU KNOW!
UH...?

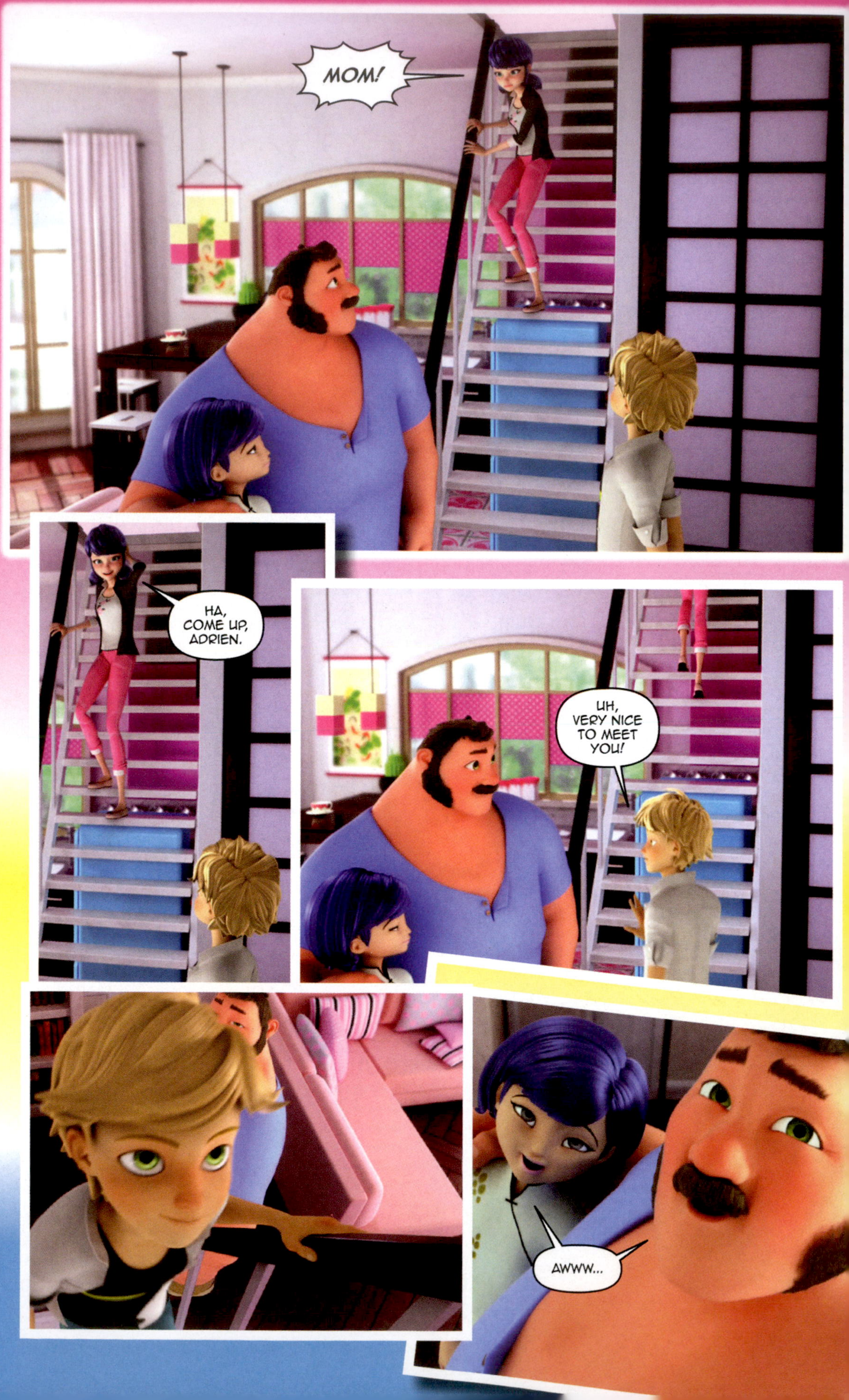
MOM!
HA, COME UP, ADRIEN.
UH, VERY NICE TO MEET YOU!
AWWW...

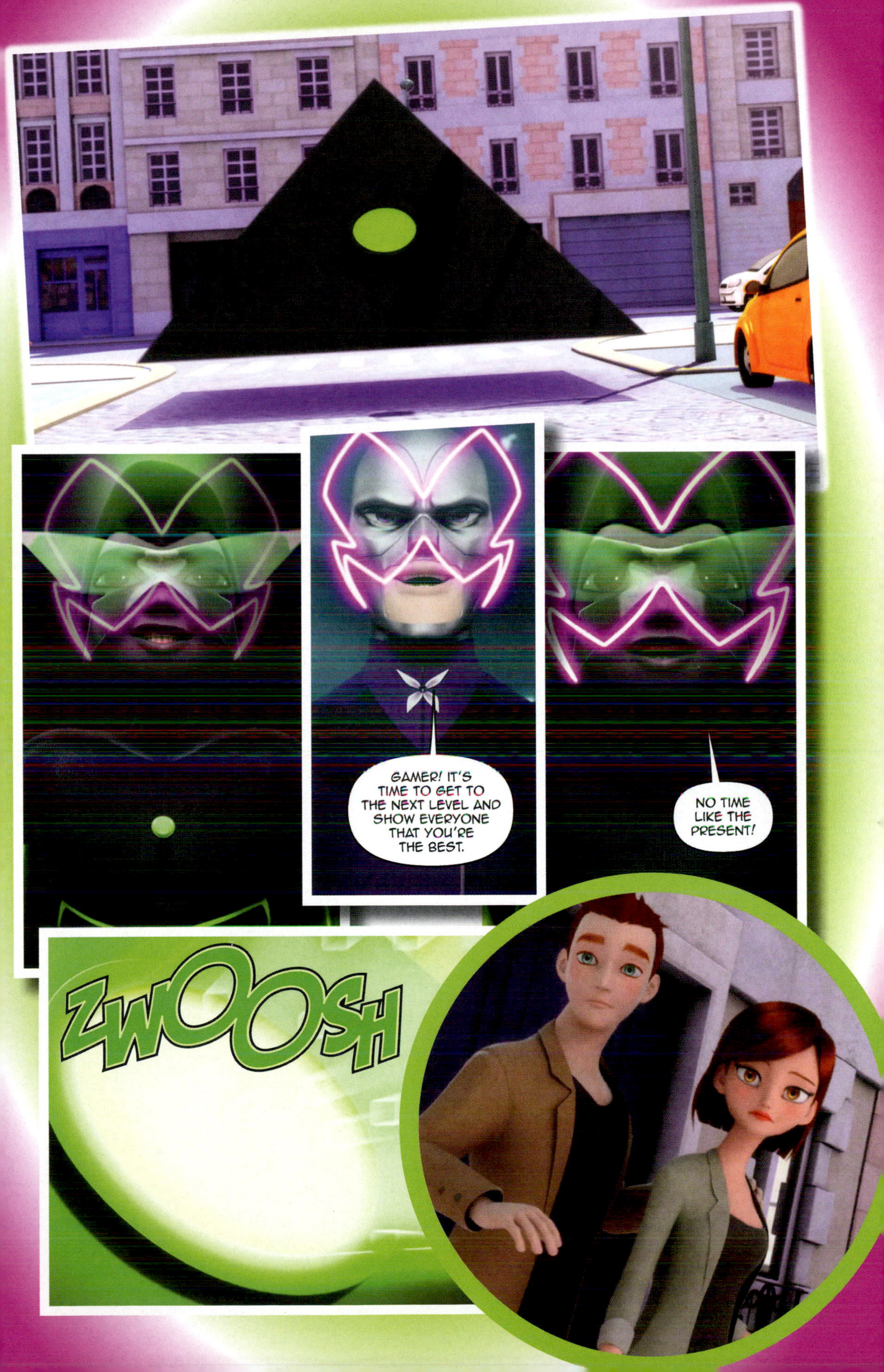
GAMER! IT'S TIME TO GET TO THE NEXT LEVEL AND SHOW EVERYONE THAT YOU'RE THE BEST.
NO TIME LIKE THE PRESENT!
ZWOOSH

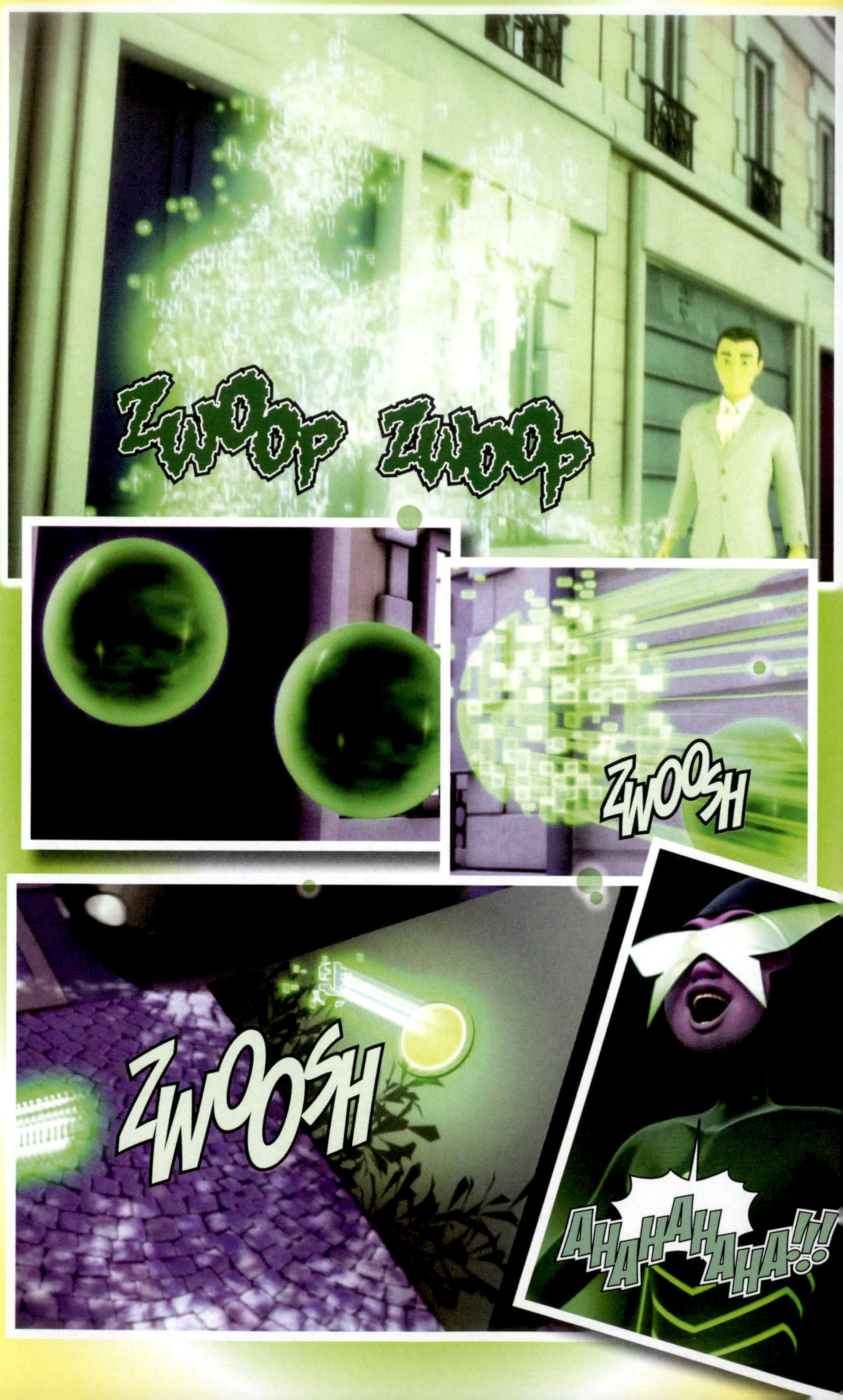
ZWOOP ZWOOP
ZWOOSH
ZWOOSH
AHAHAHAHAHA!!!

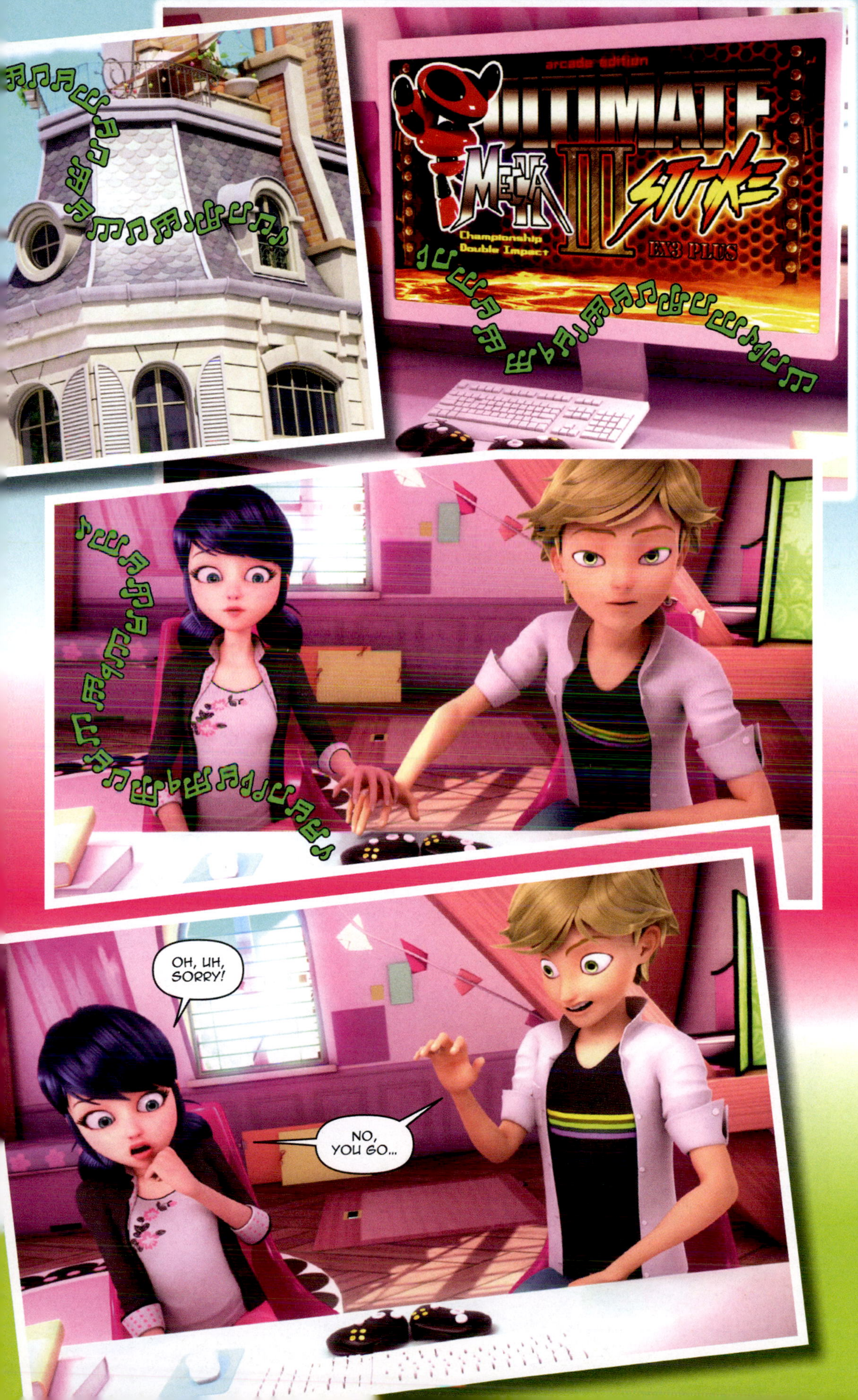
arcade edition
ULTIMATE
MEGA
III
STRIKE
Championship
Double Impact
EX3 PLUS
OH, UH, SORRY!
NO, YOU GO...

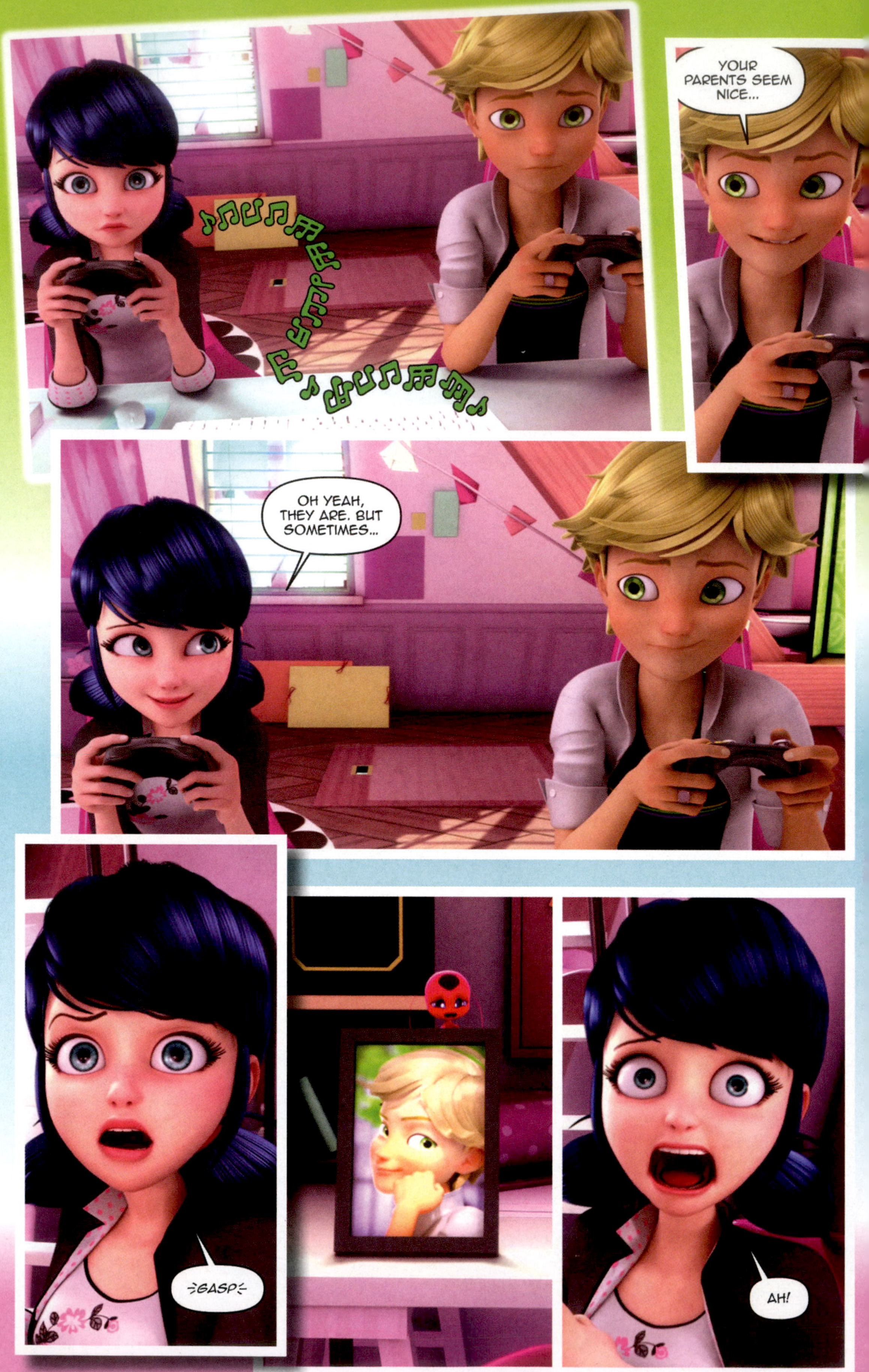
YOUR PARENTS SEEM NICE...
OH YEAH, THEY ARE. BUT SOMETIMES...
GASP
AH!

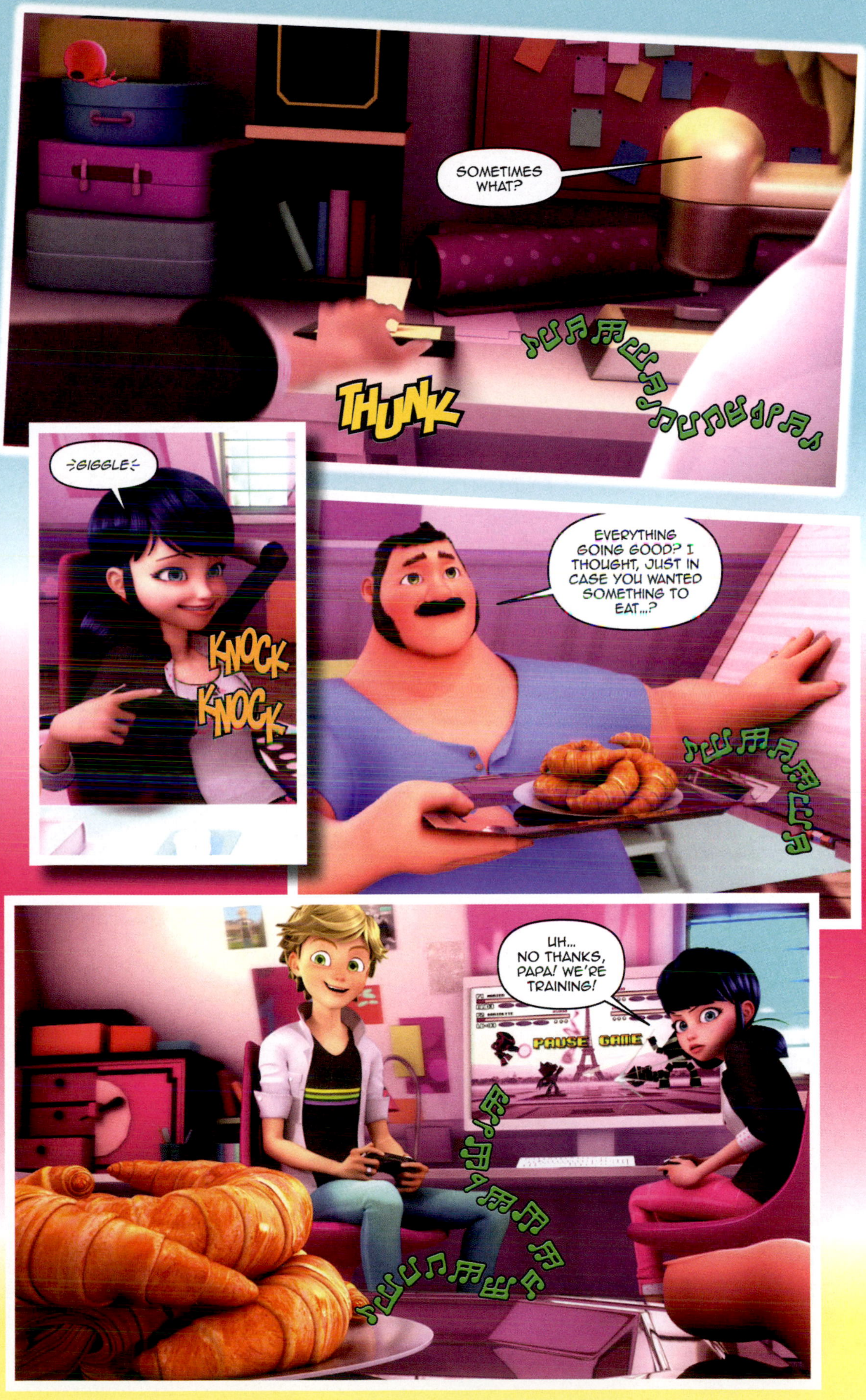
SOMETIMES WHAT?
THUNK
=GIGGLE=
KNOCK KNOCK
EVERYTHING GOING GOOD? I THOUGHT, JUST IN CASE YOU WANTED SOMETHING TO EAT...?
UH... NO THANKS, PAPA! WE'RE TRAINING!
PAUSE GAME

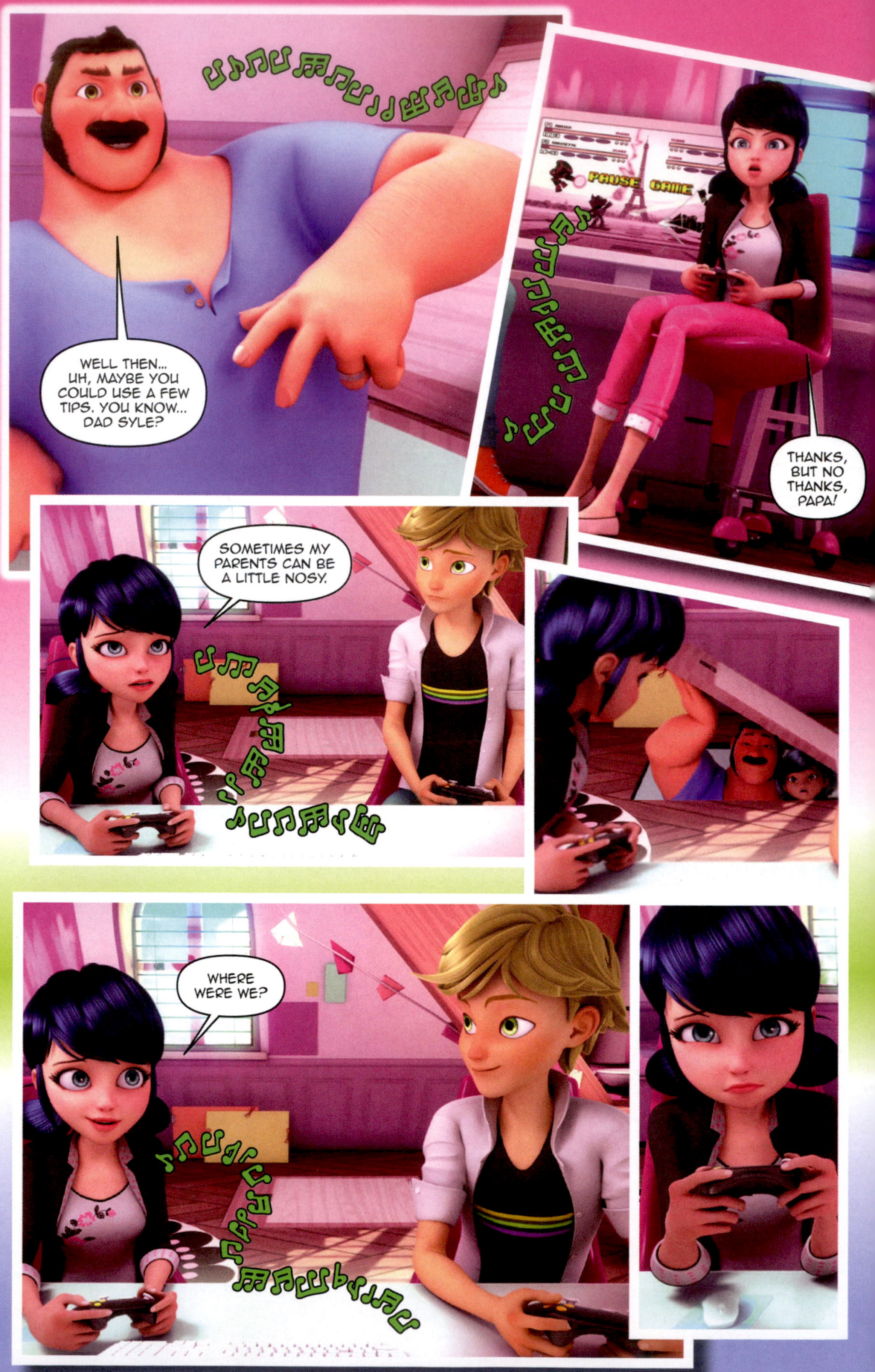
WELL THEN... UH, MAYBE YOU COULD USE A FEW TIPS. YOU KNOW... DAD SYLE?
PAUSE GAME
THANKS, BUT NO THANKS, PAPA!
SOMETIMES MY PARENTS CAN BE A LITTLE NOSY.
WHERE WERE WE?

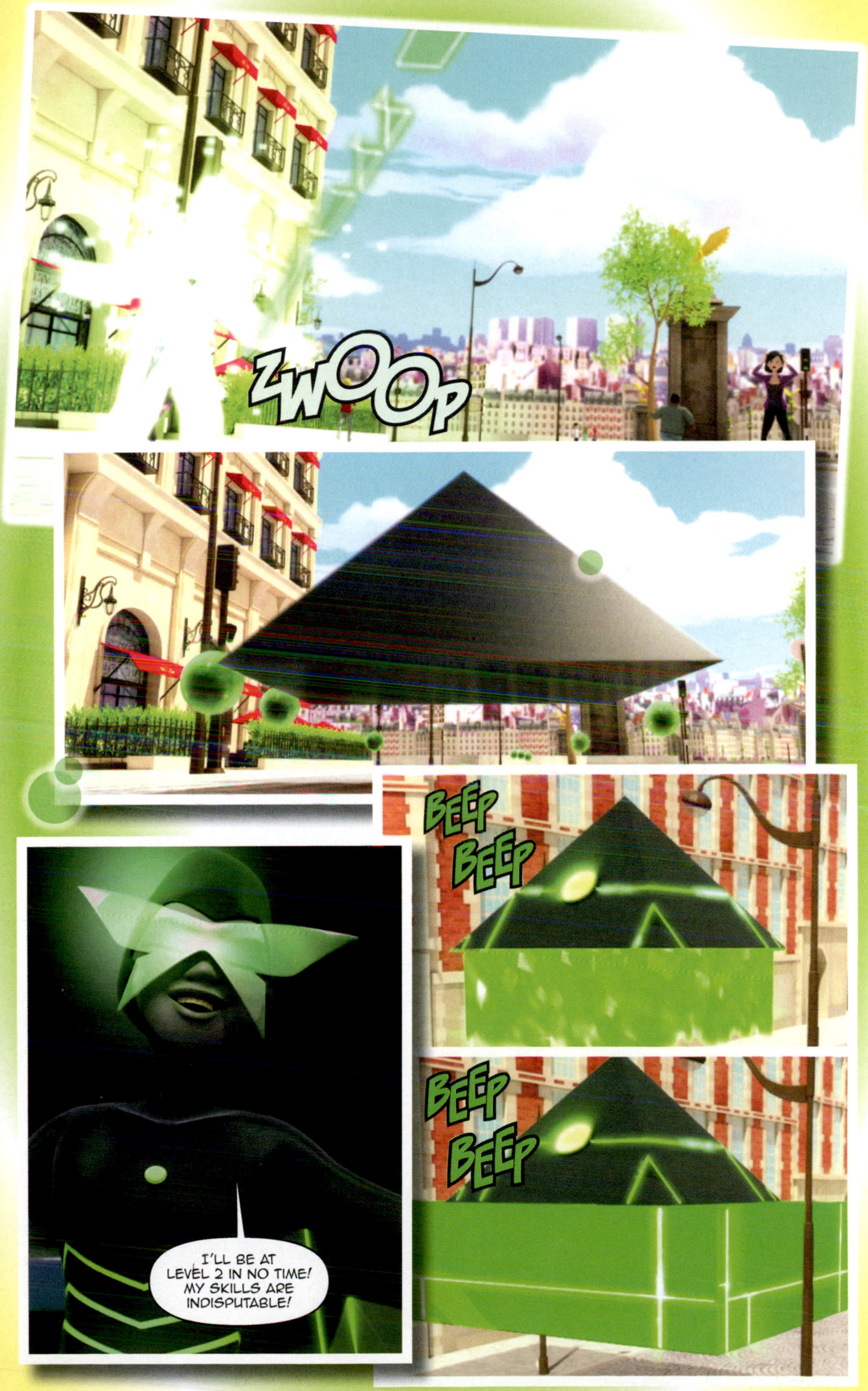
ZWOOP
BEEP BEEP
BEEP BEEP
I'LL BE AT LEVEL 2 IN NO TIME! MY SKILLS ARE INDISPUTABLE!

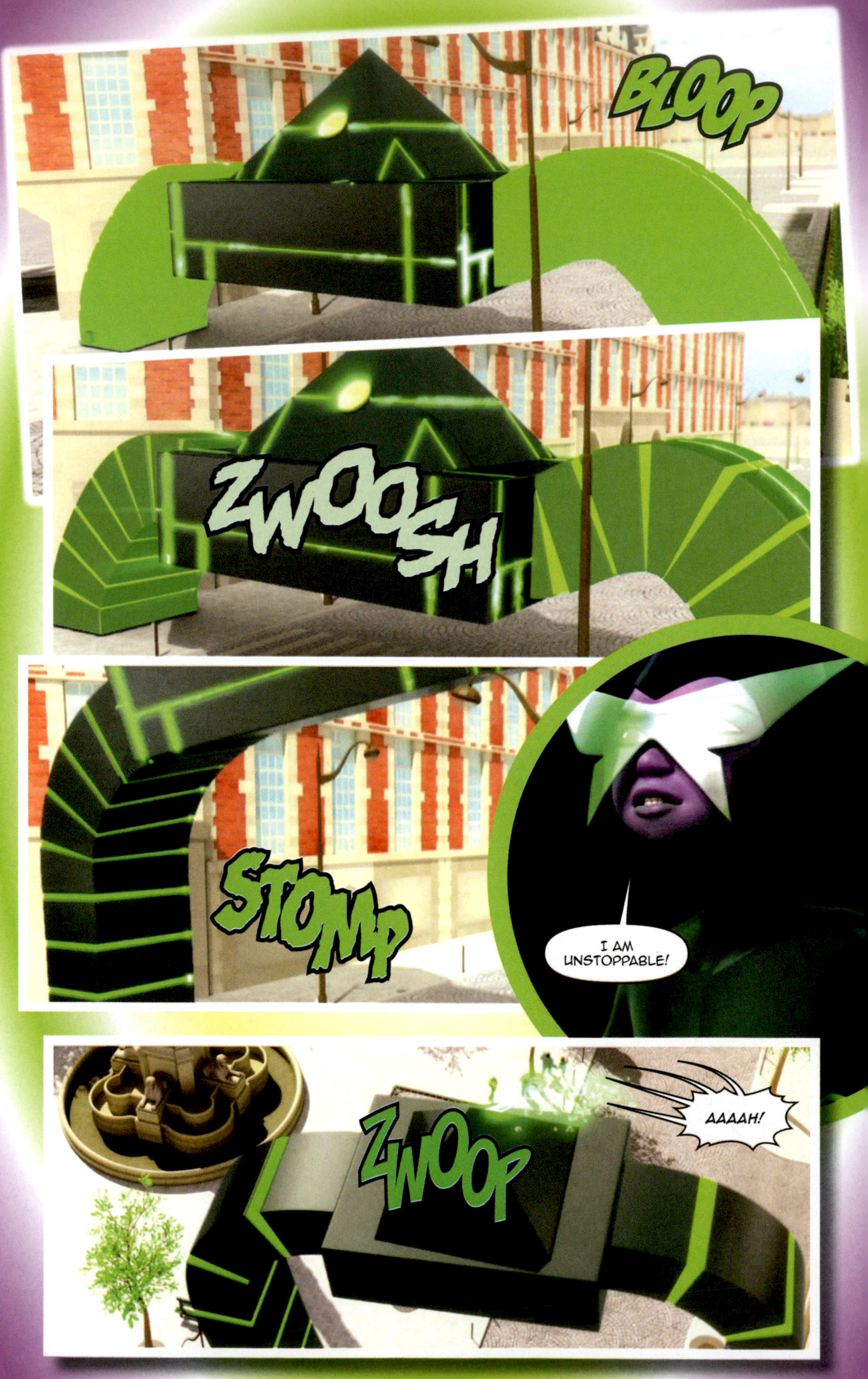
BLOOP
ZWOOSH
STOMP
I AM UNSTOPPABLE!
ZWOOP
AAAAH!

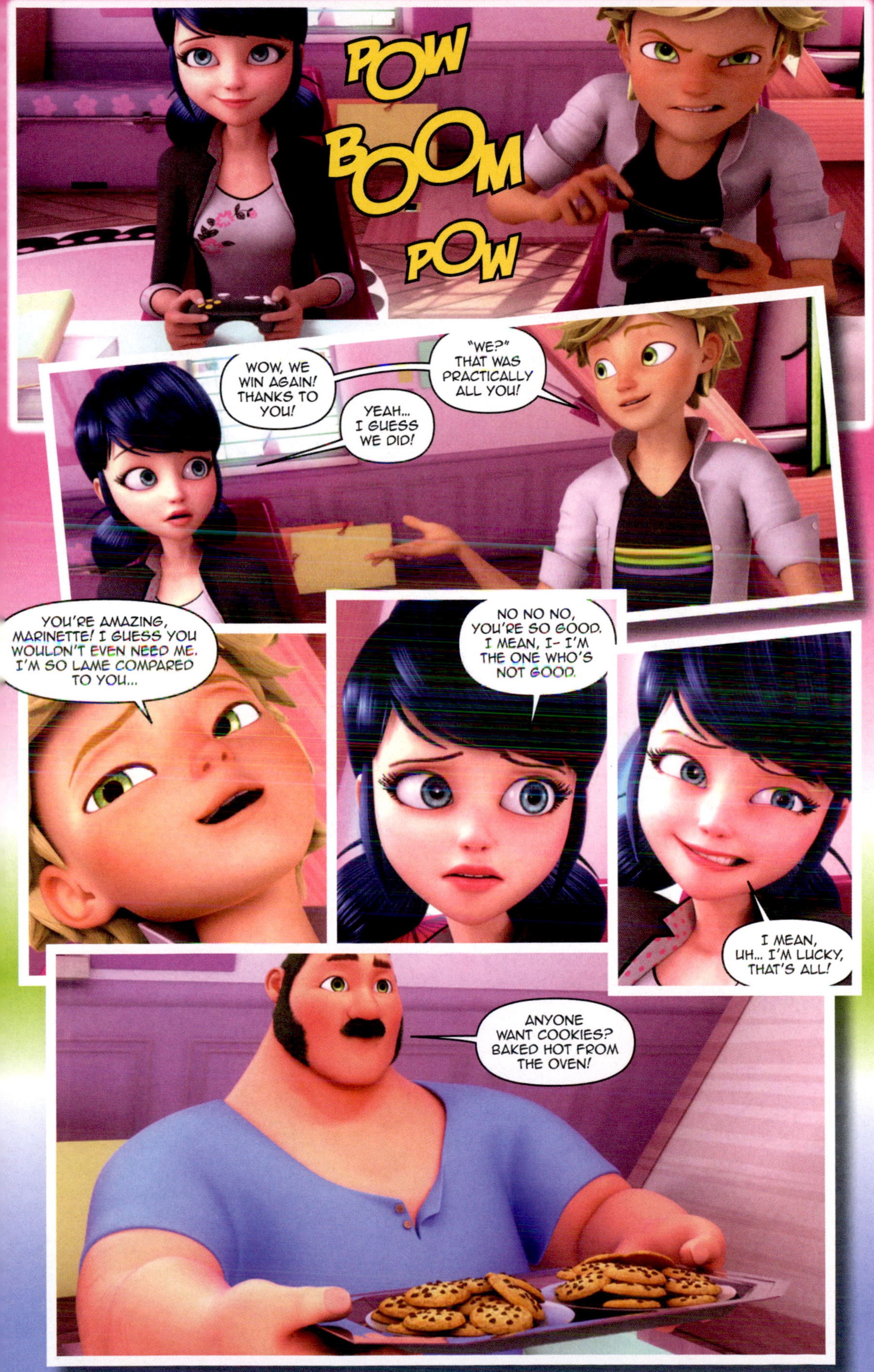
POW
BOOM
POW
WOW, WE WIN AGAIN! THANKS TO YOU!
YEAH... I GUESS WE DID!
"WE?" THAT WAS PRACTICALLY ALL YOU!
YOU'RE AMAZING, MARINETTE! I GUESS YOU WOULDN'T EVEN NEED ME. I'M SO LAME COMPARED TO YOU...
NO NO NO, YOU'RE SO GOOD. I MEAN, I- I'M THE ONE WHO'S NOT GOOD.
I MEAN, UH... I'M LUCKY, THAT'S ALL!
ANYONE WANT COOKIES? BAKED HOT FROM THE OVEN!

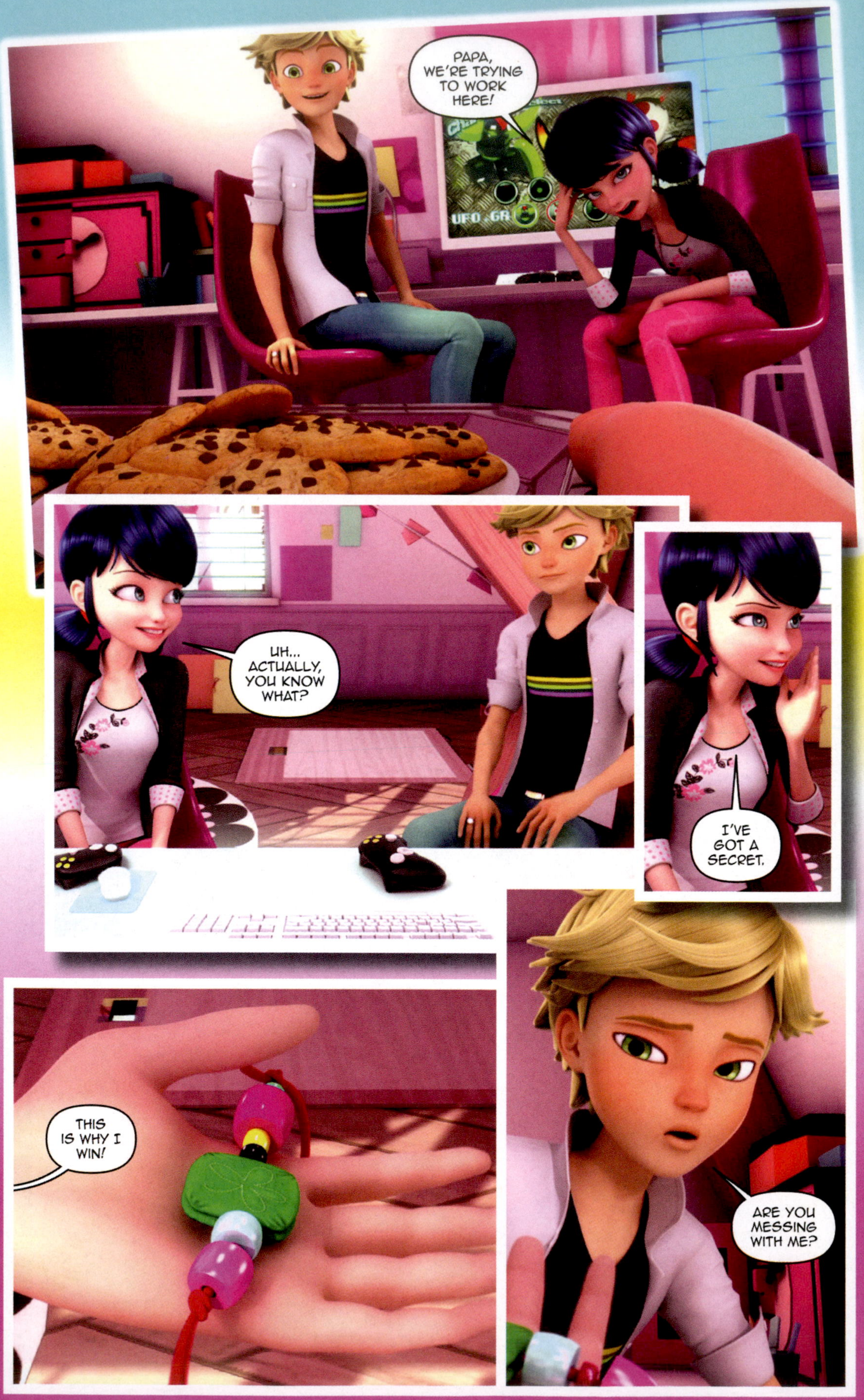
PAPA, WE'RE TRYING TO WORK HERE!
UH... ACTUALLY, YOU KNOW WHAT?
I'VE GOT A SECRET.
THIS IS WHY I WIN!
ARE YOU MESSING WITH ME?

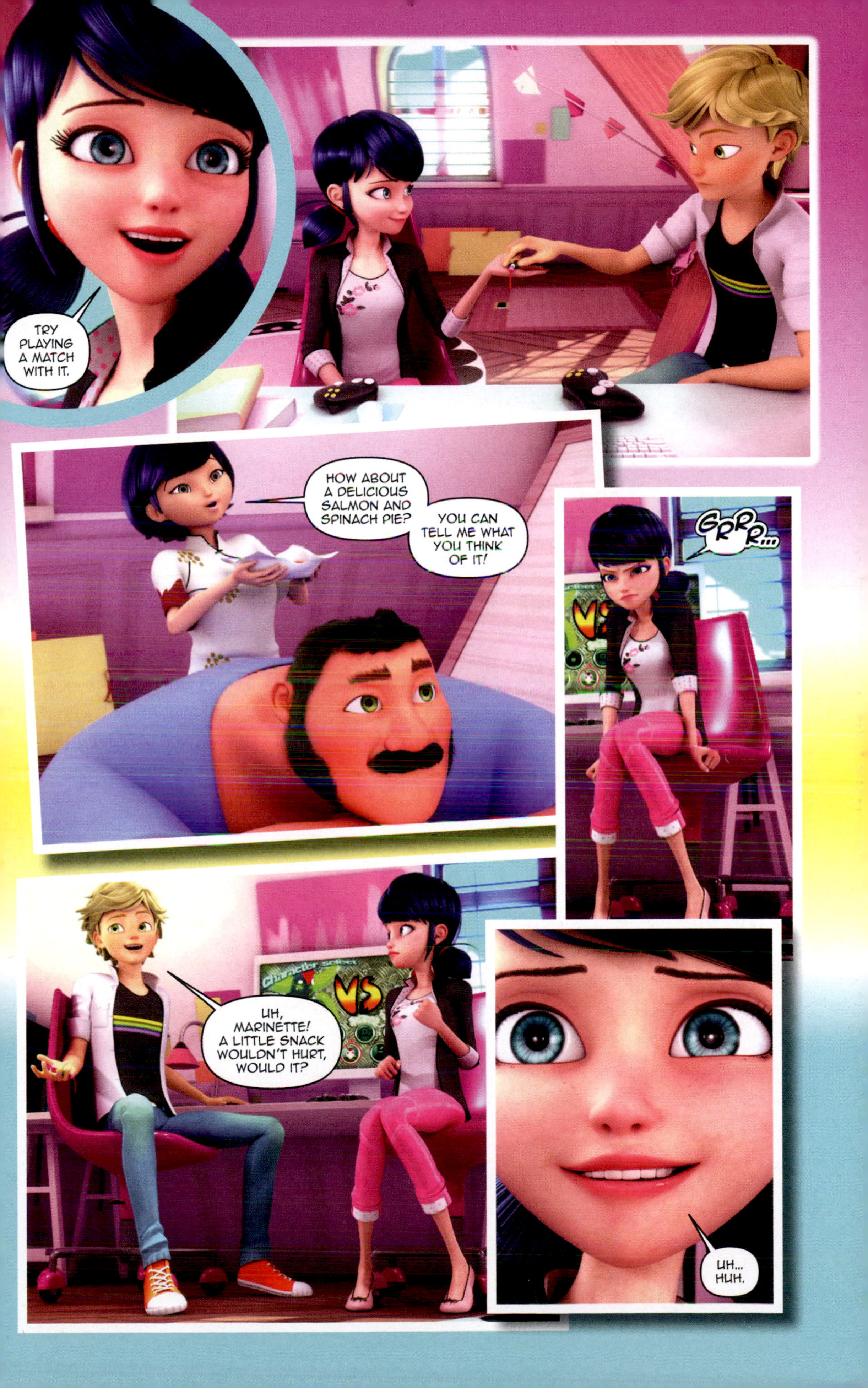
TRY PLAYING A MATCH WITH IT.
HOW ABOUT A DELICIOUS SALMON AND SPINACH PIE?
YOU CAN TELL ME WHAT YOU THINK OF IT!
GRRR...
UH, MARINETTE! A LITTLE SNACK WOULDN'T HURT, WOULD IT?
UH... HUH.

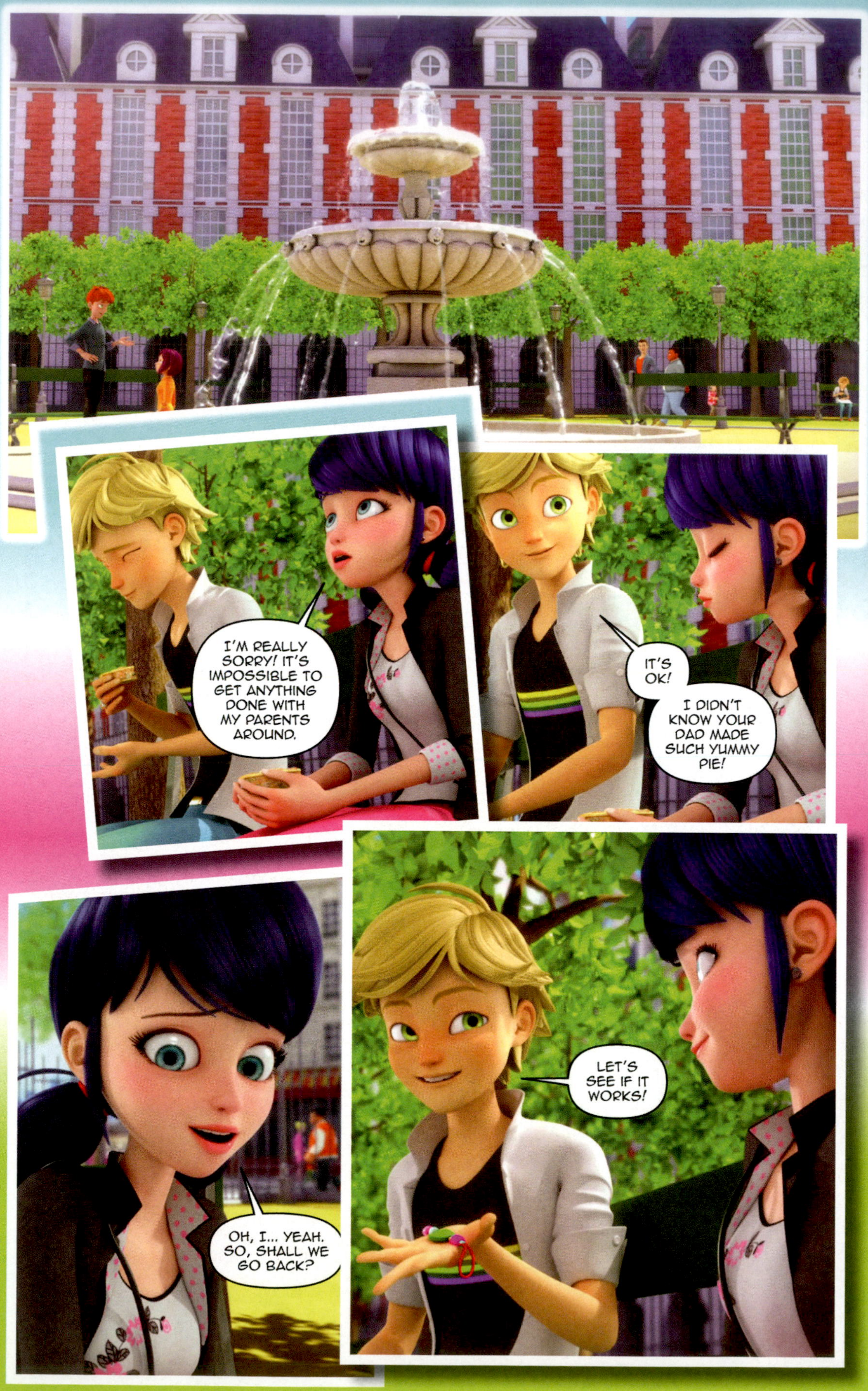

I'M REALLY SORRY! IT'S IMPOSSIBLE TO GET ANYTHING DONE WITH MY PARENTS AROUND.
IT'S OK!
I DIDN'T KNOW YOUR DAD MADE SUCH YUMMY PIE!
OH, I... YEAH. SO, SHALL WE GO BACK?
LET'S SEE IF IT WORKS!

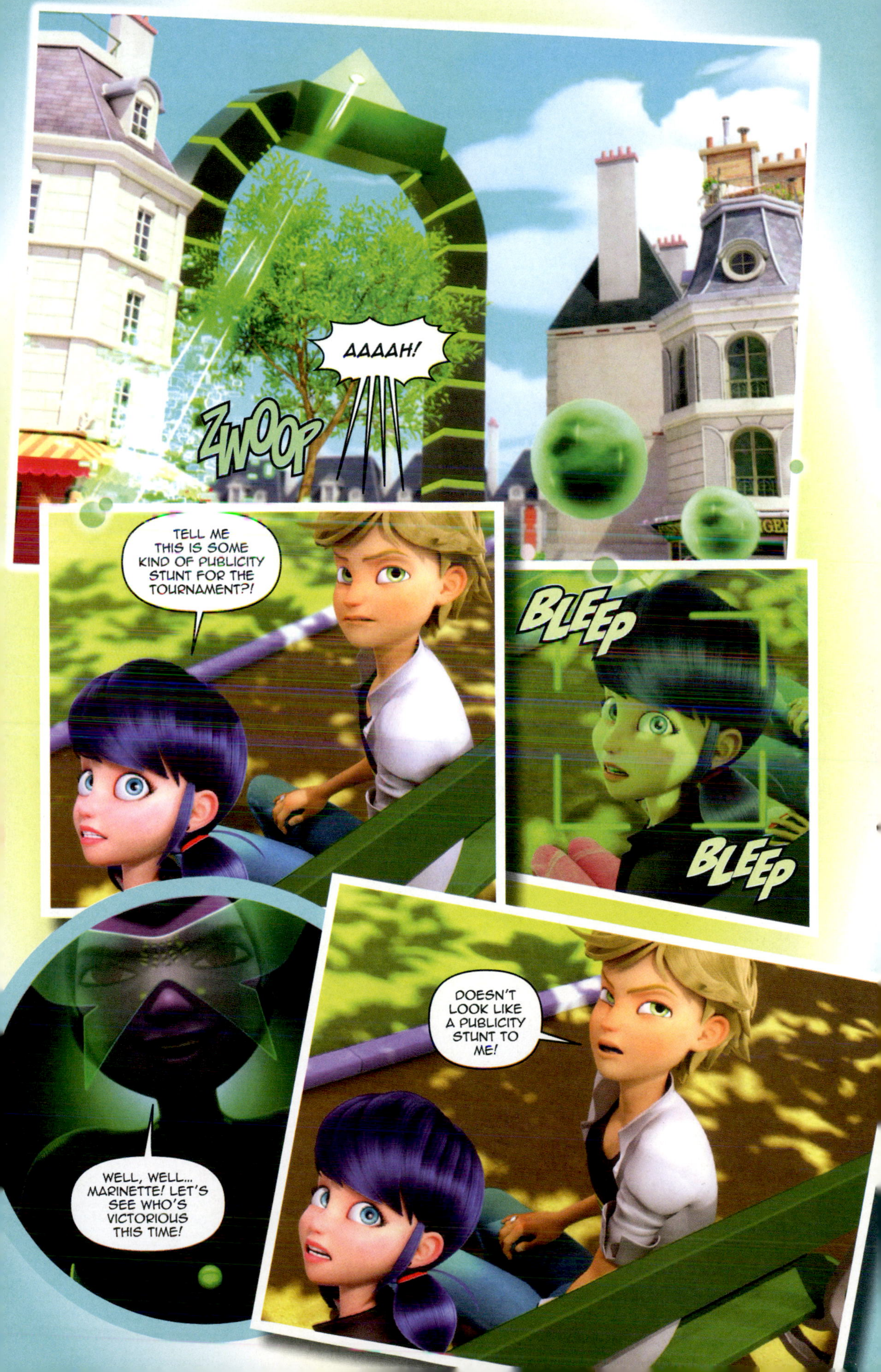
AAAAH!
ZWOOP
TELL ME THIS IS SOME KIND OF PUBLICITY STUNT FOR THE TOURNAMENT?!
BLEEP
BLEEP
WELL, WELL... MARINETTE! LET'S SEE WHO'S VICTORIOUS THIS TIME!
DOESN'T LOOK LIKE A PUBLICITY STUNT TO ME!

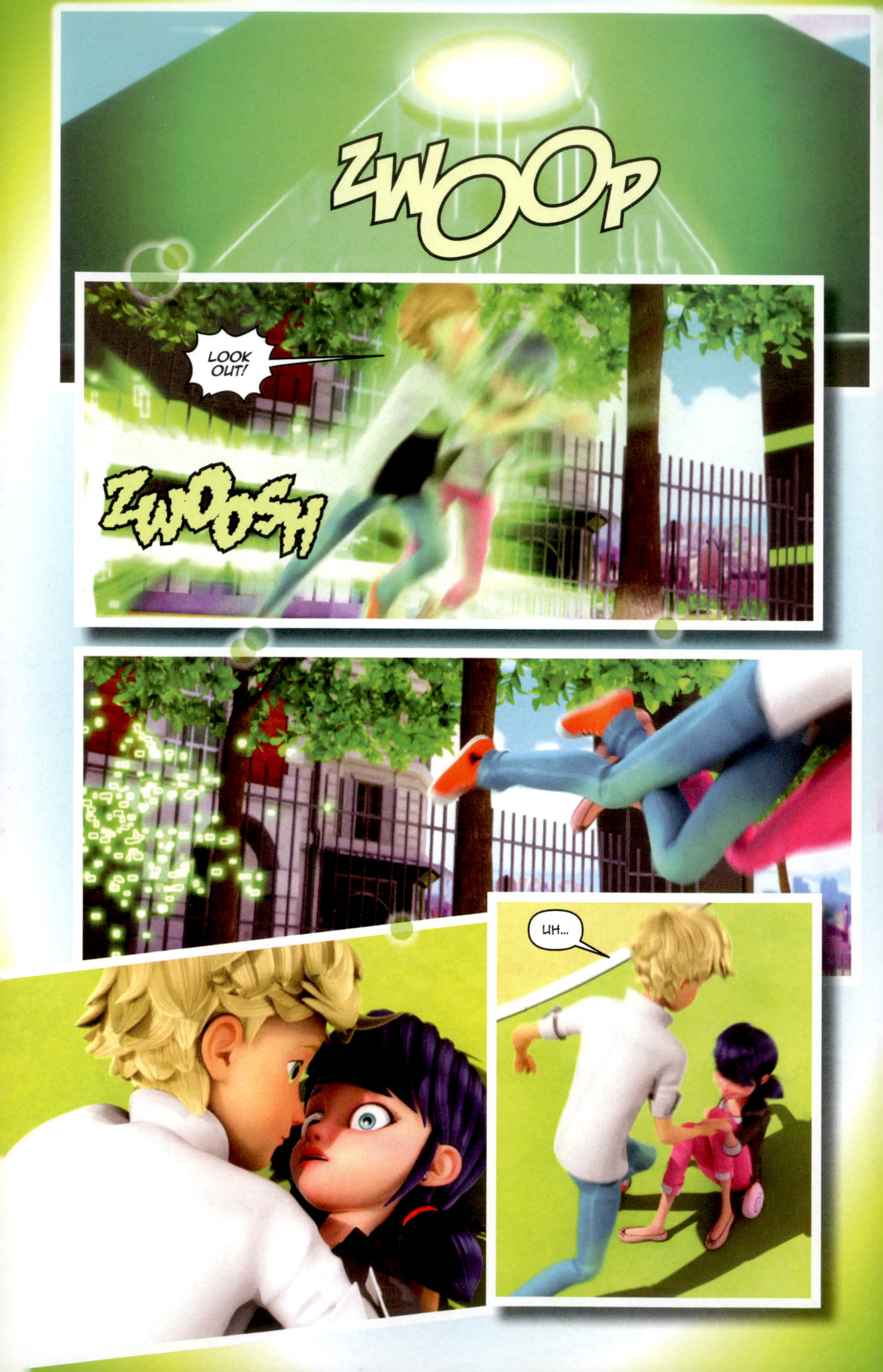

ZWOOP
LOOK OUT!
ZWOOSH
UH...

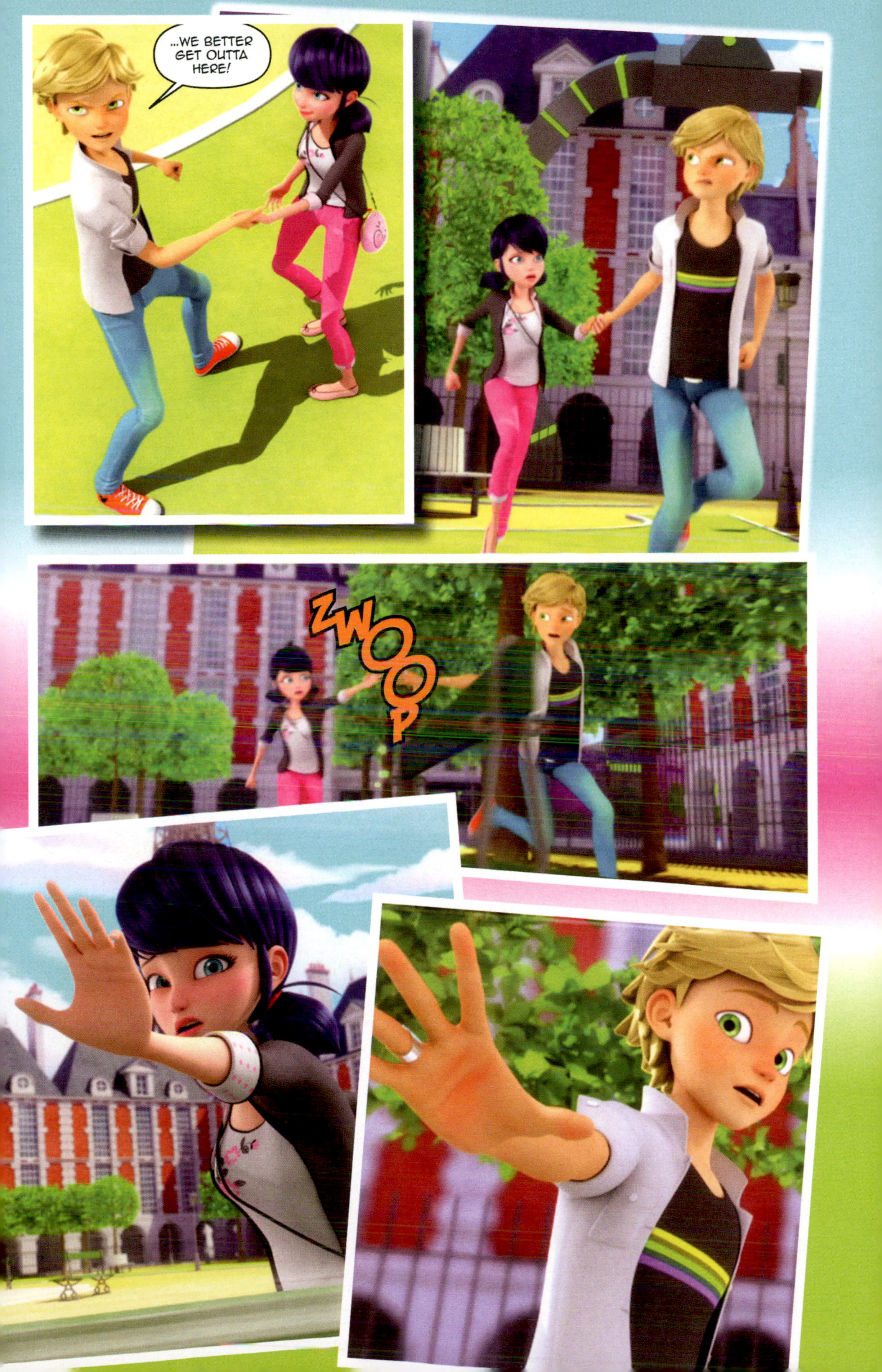
...WE BETTER GET OUTTA HERE!
ZWOOP

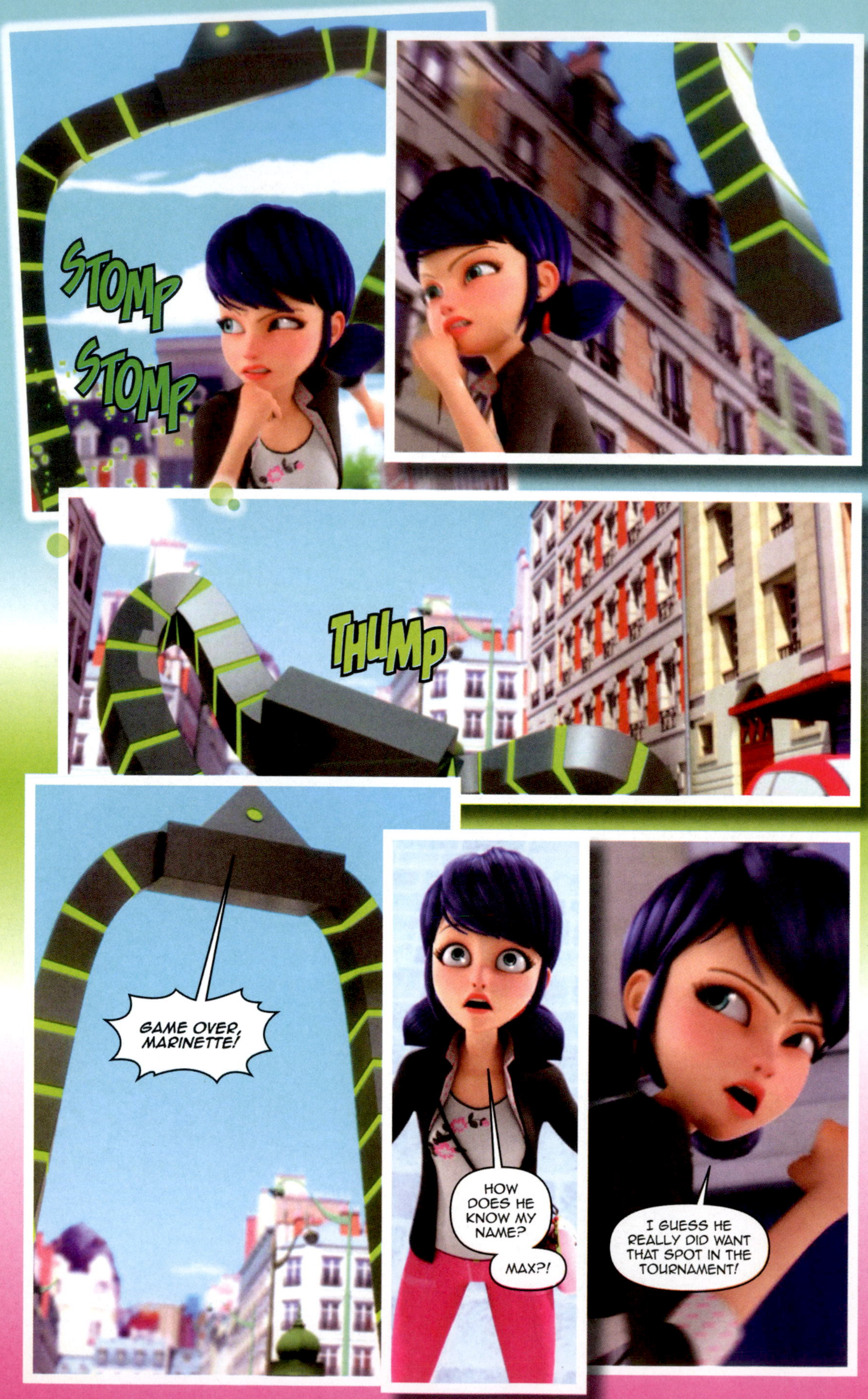
STOMP
STOMP
THUMP
GAME OVER, MARINETTE!
HOW DOES HE KNOW MY NAME?
MAX?!
I GUESS HE REALLY DID WANT THAT SPOT IN THE TOURNAMENT!

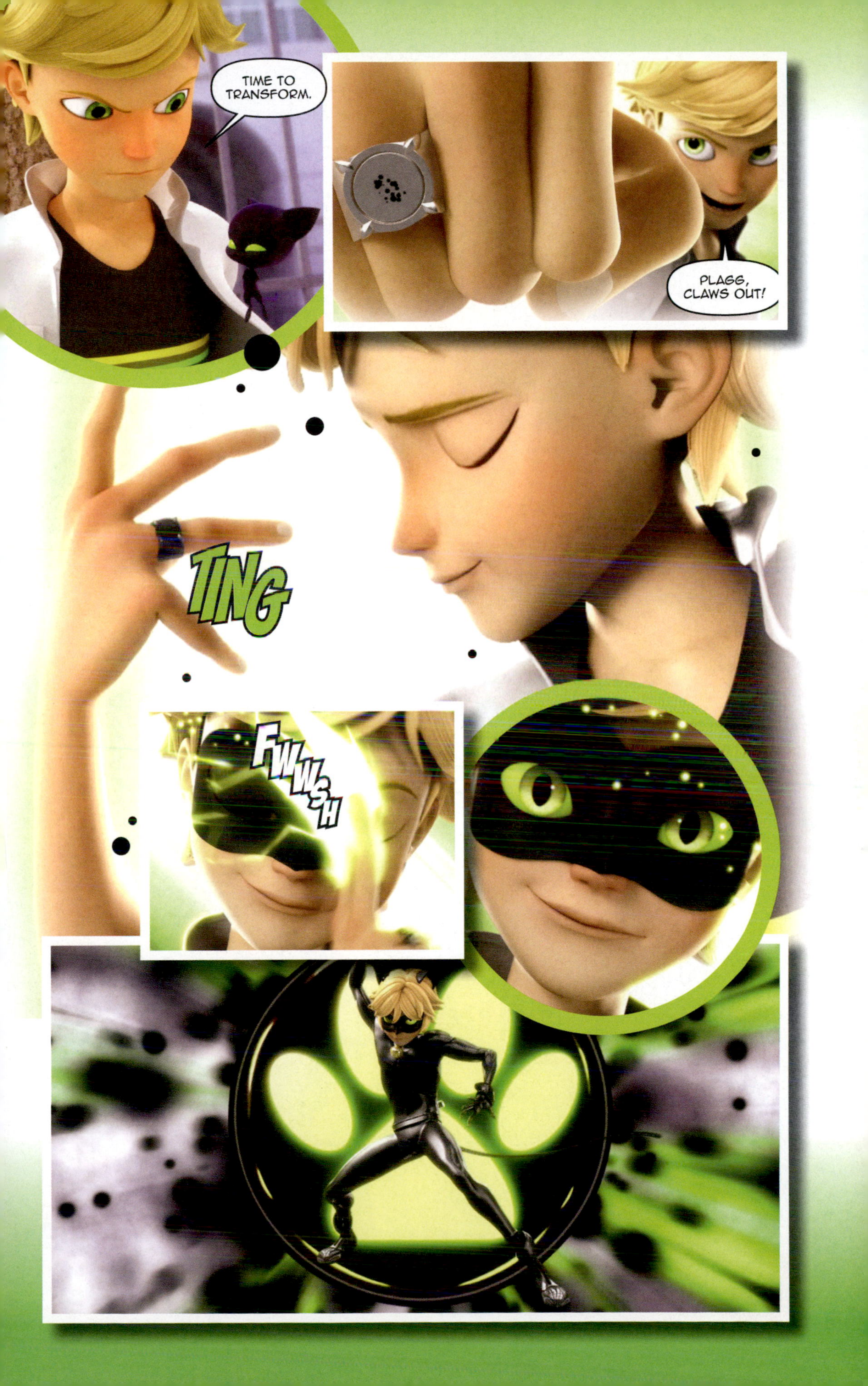
TIME TO TRANSFORM.
PLAGG, CLAWS OUT!
TING
FWWSH

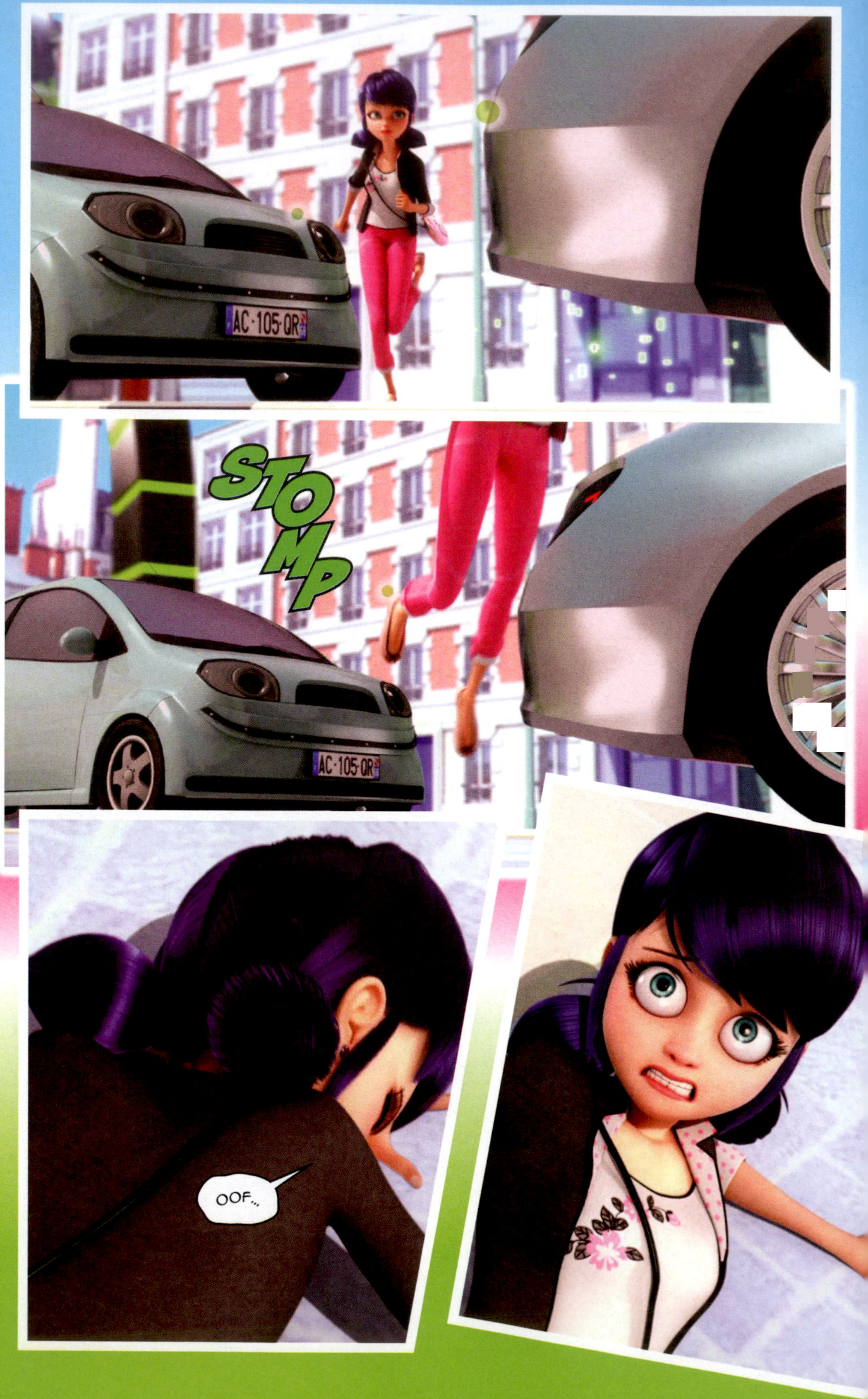
AC·105·QR
STOMP
AC·105·QR
OOF...

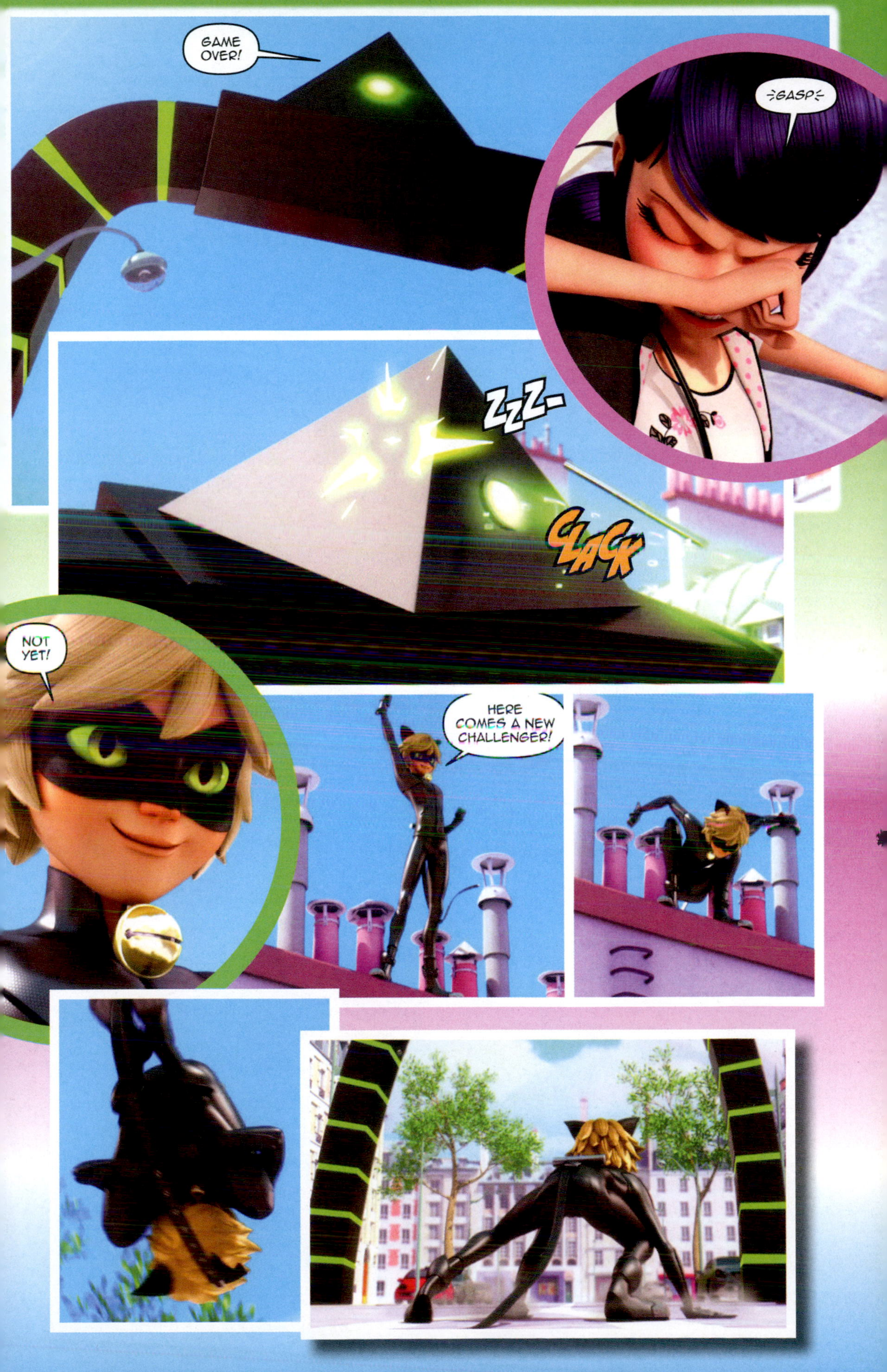
GAME OVER!
-GASP-
ZZZ-
CLACK
NOT YET!
HERE COMES A NEW CHALLENGER!

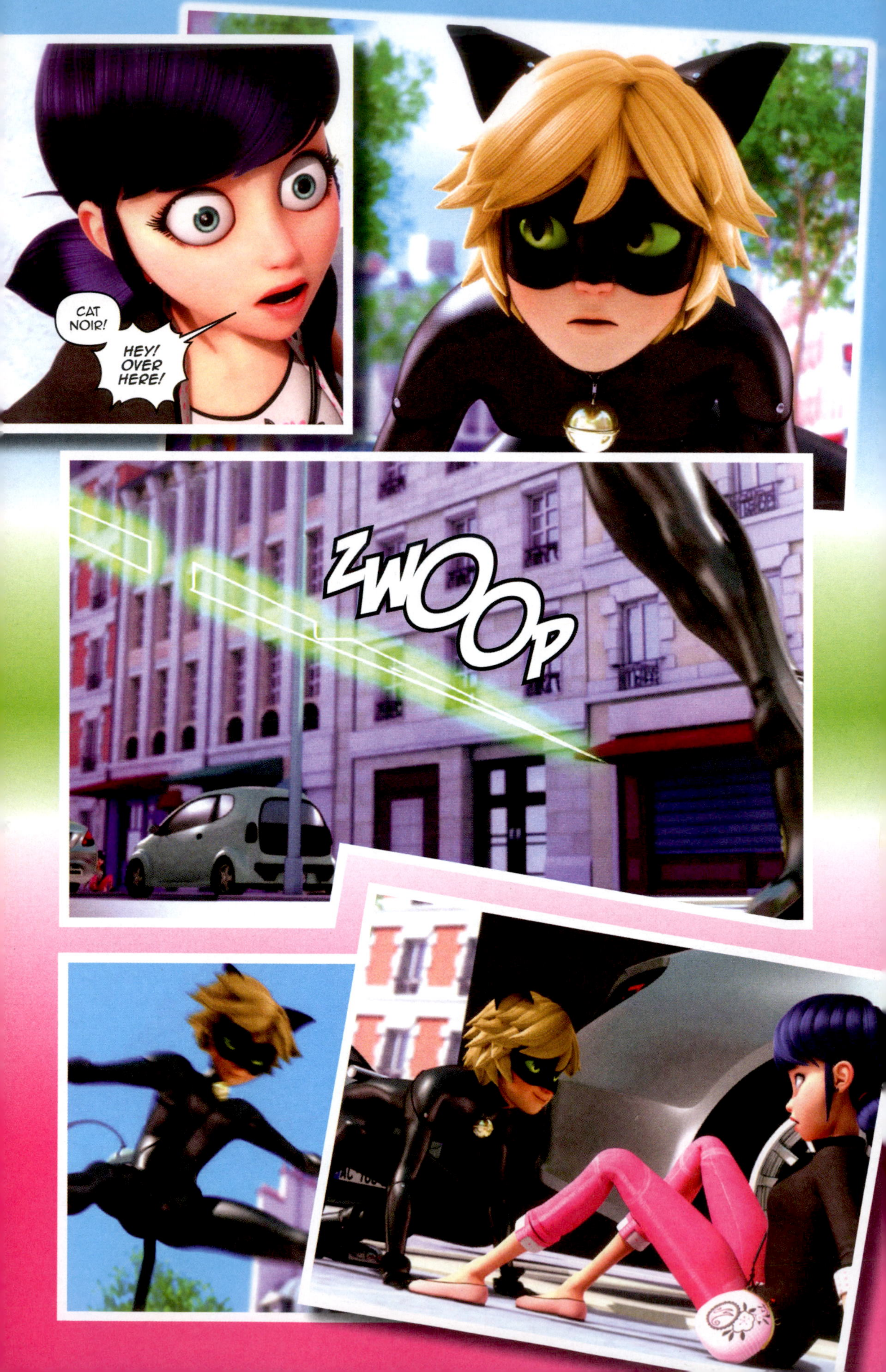
CAT NOIR!
HEY! OVER HERE!
ZWOOP

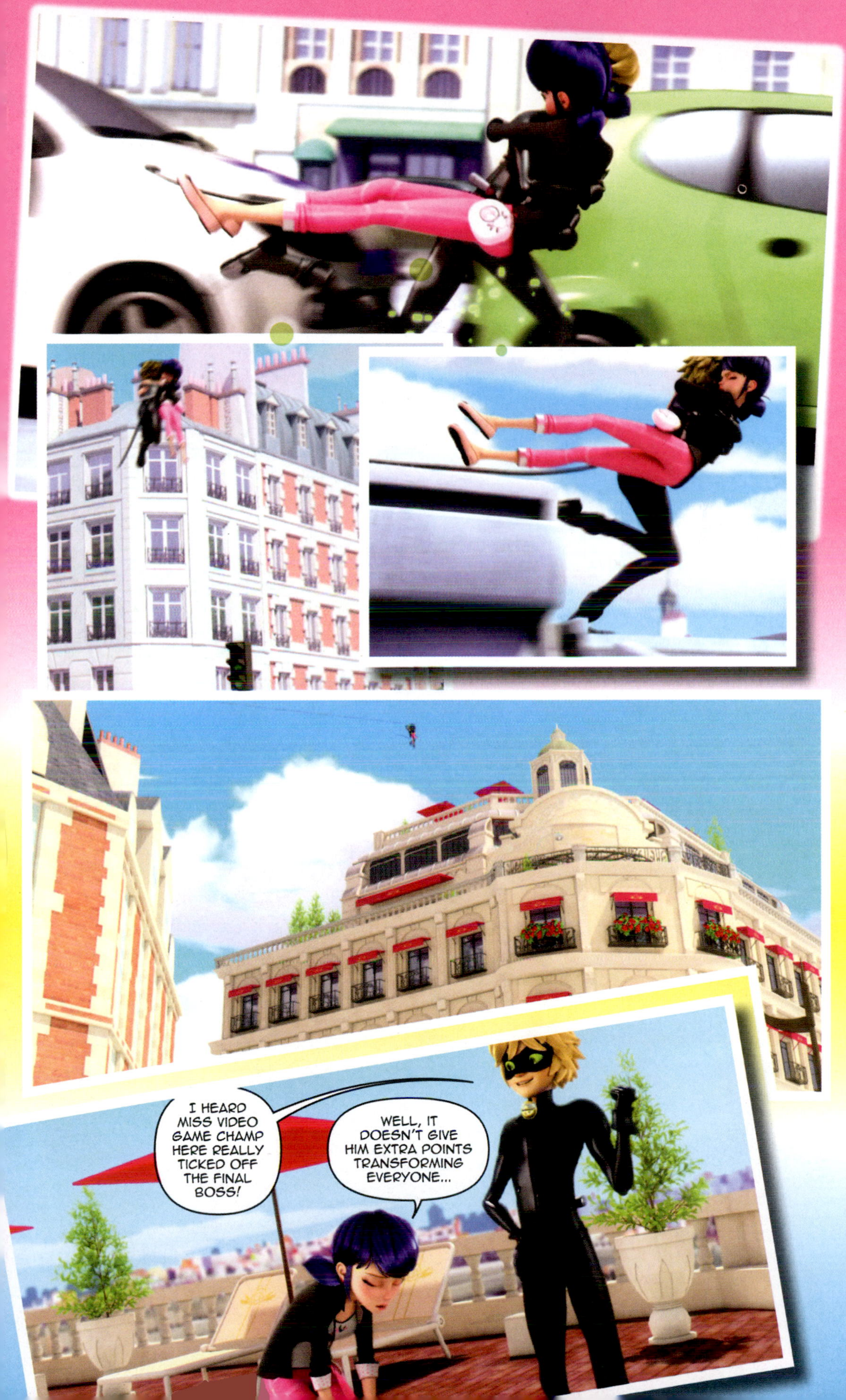
I HEARD MISS VIDEO GAME CHAMP HERE REALLY TICKED OFF THE FINAL BOSS!
WELL, IT DOESN'T GIVE HIM EXTRA POINTS TRANSFORMING EVERYONE...

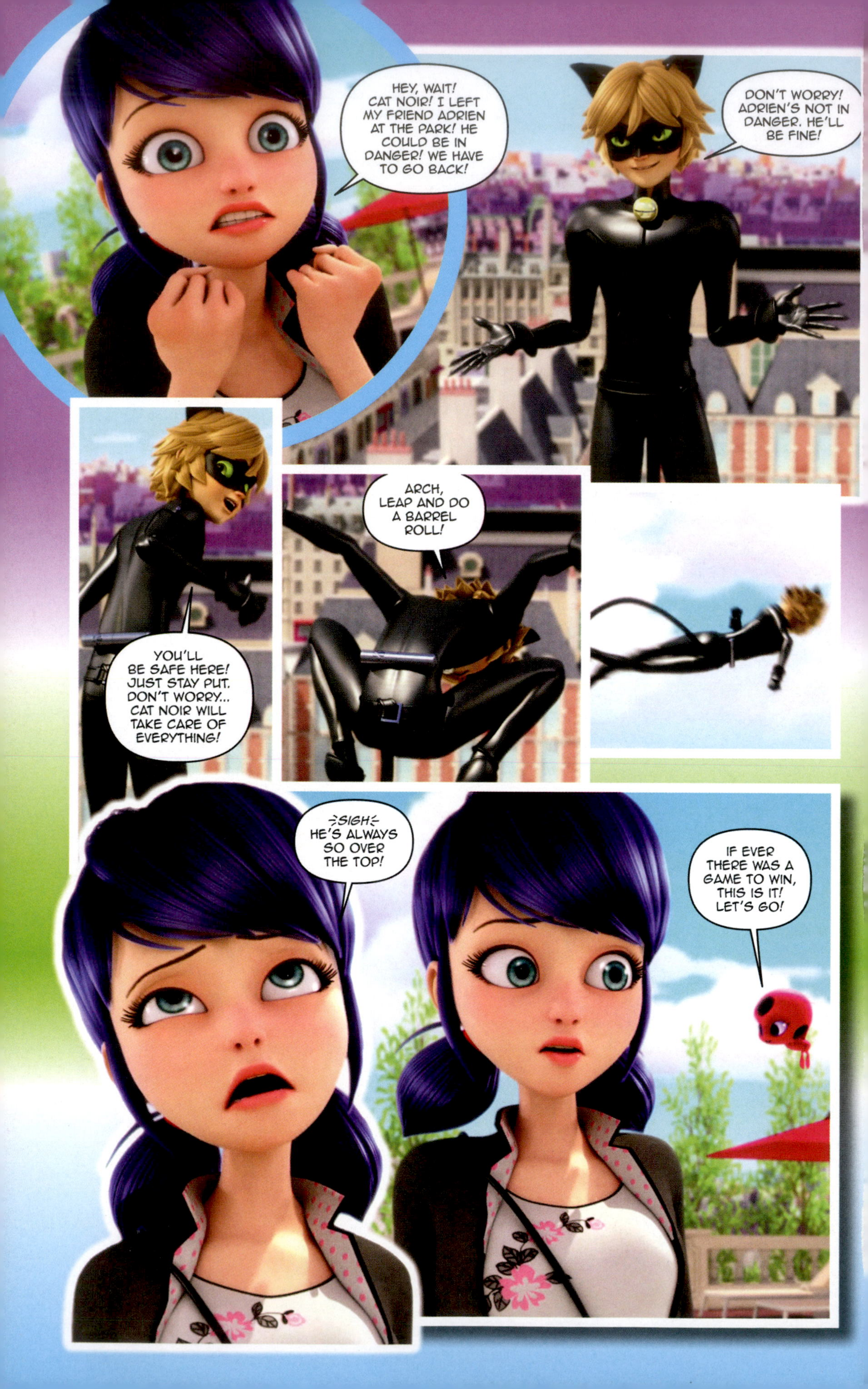

HEY, WAIT! CAT NOIR! I LEFT MY FRIEND ADRIEN AT THE PARK! HE COULD BE IN DANGER! WE HAVE TO GO BACK!
DON'T WORRY! ADRIEN'S NOT IN DANGER. HE'LL BE FINE!
YOU'LL BE SAFE HERE! JUST STAY PUT. DON'T WORRY... CAT NOIR WILL TAKE CARE OF EVERYTHING!
ARCH, LEAP AND DO A BARREL ROLL!
SIGH HE'S ALWAYS SO OVER THE TOP!
IF EVER THERE WAS A GAME TO WIN, THIS IS IT! LET'S GO!

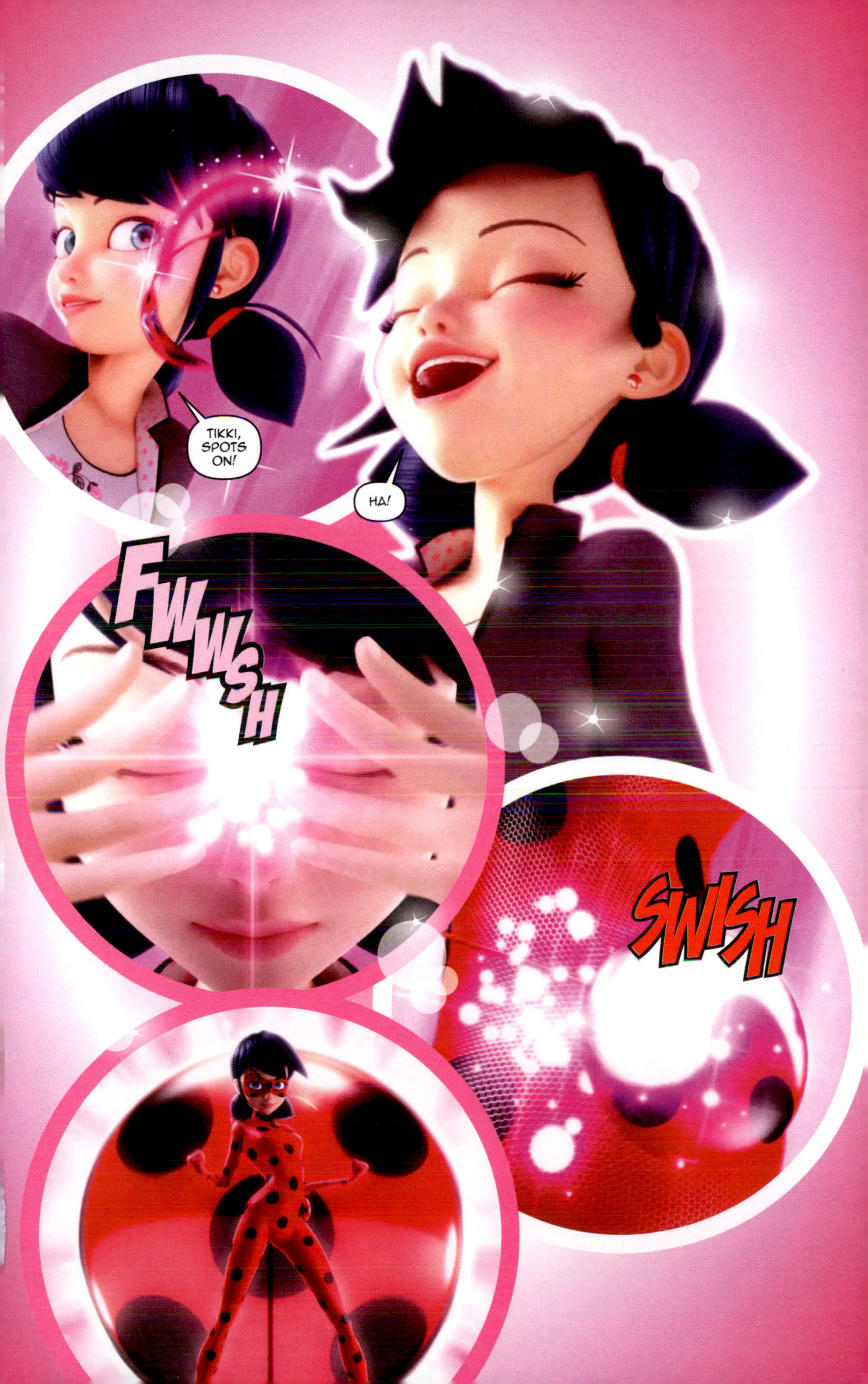
TIKKI, SPOTS ON!
HA!
FWWISH
SWISH

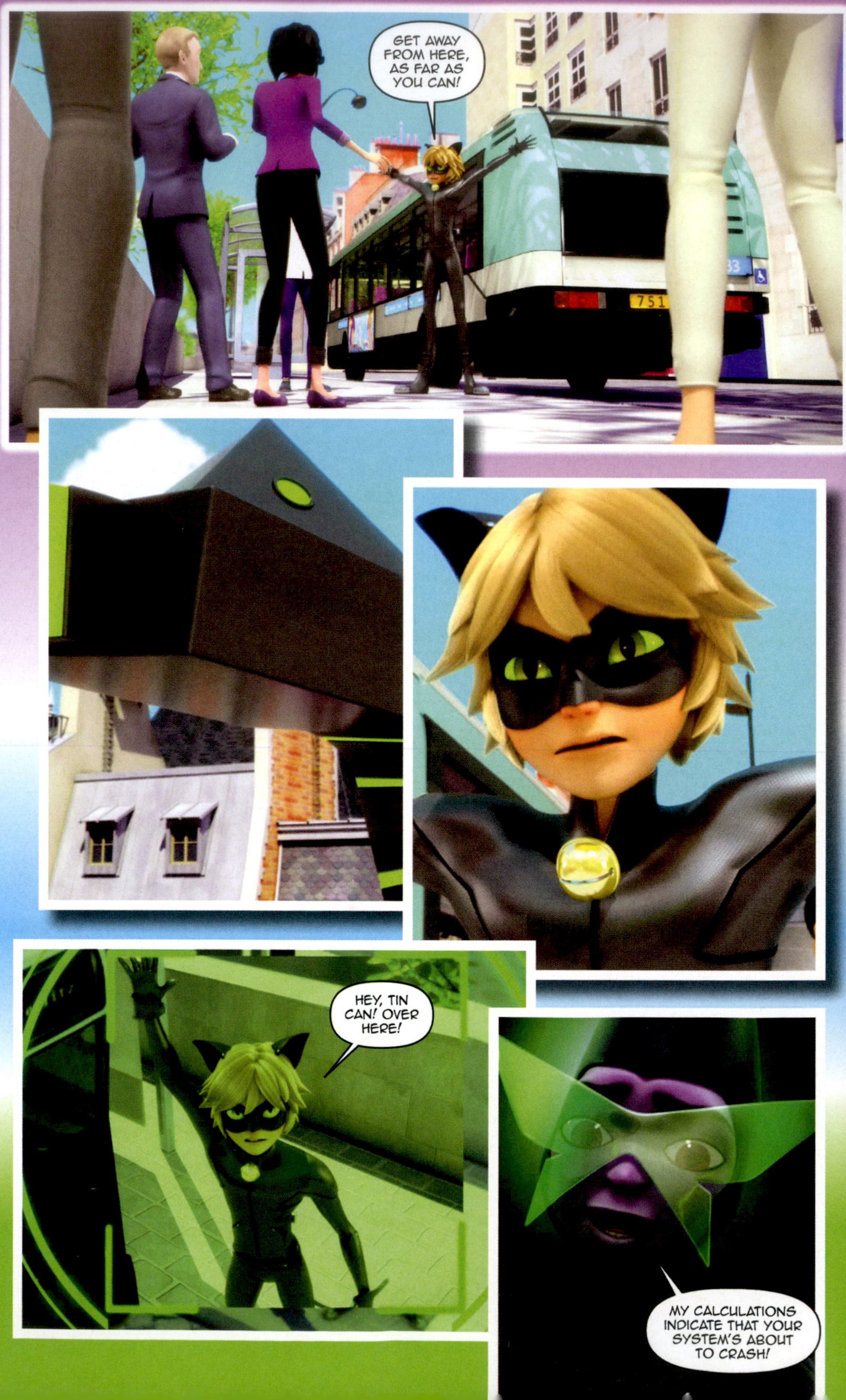
GET AWAY FROM HERE, AS FAR AS YOU CAN!
HEY, TIN CAN! OVER HERE!
MY CALCULATIONS INDICATE THAT YOUR SYSTEM'S ABOUT TO CRASH!

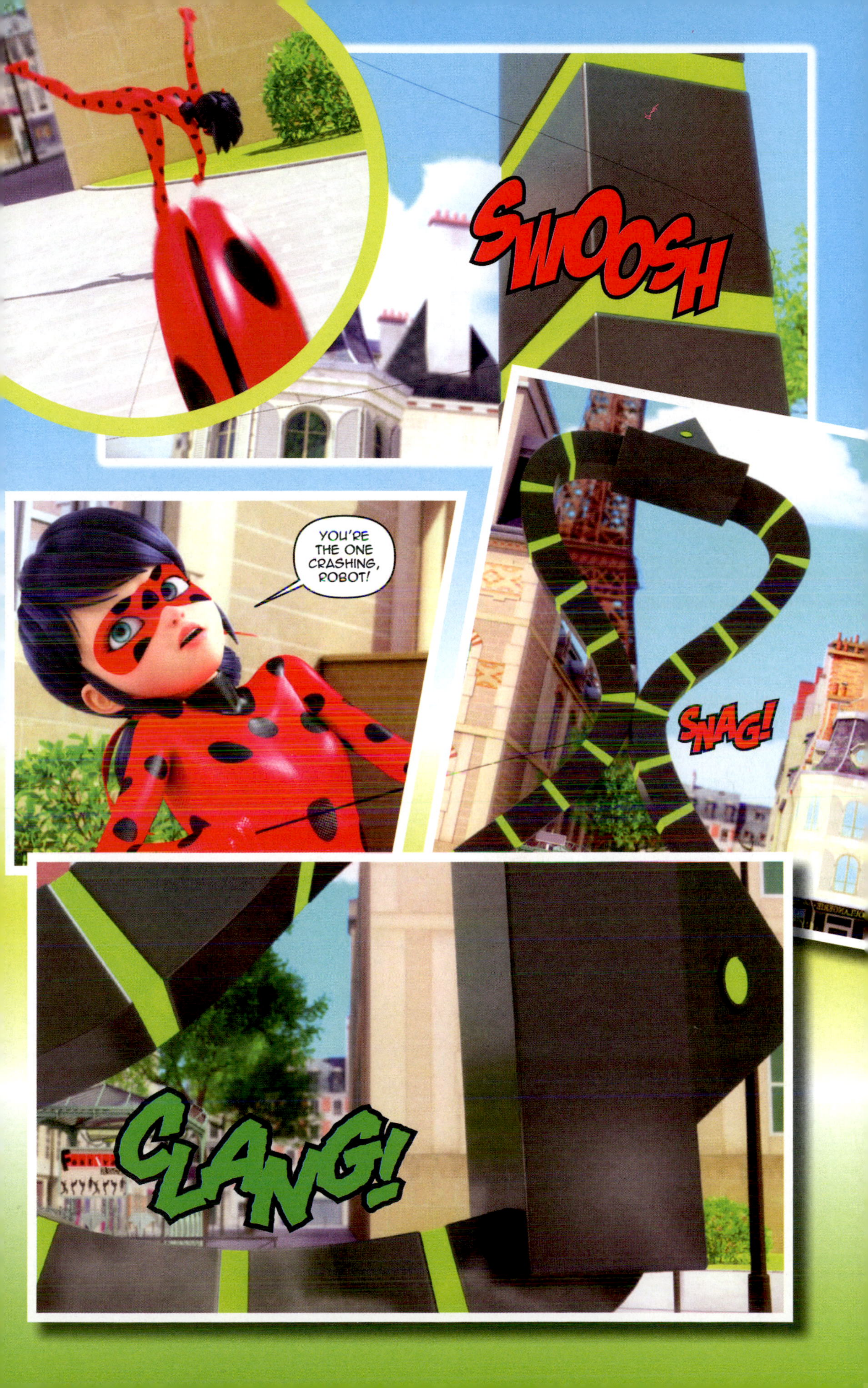
SWOOSH
YOU'RE THE ONE CRASHING, ROBOT!
SNAG!
CLANG!

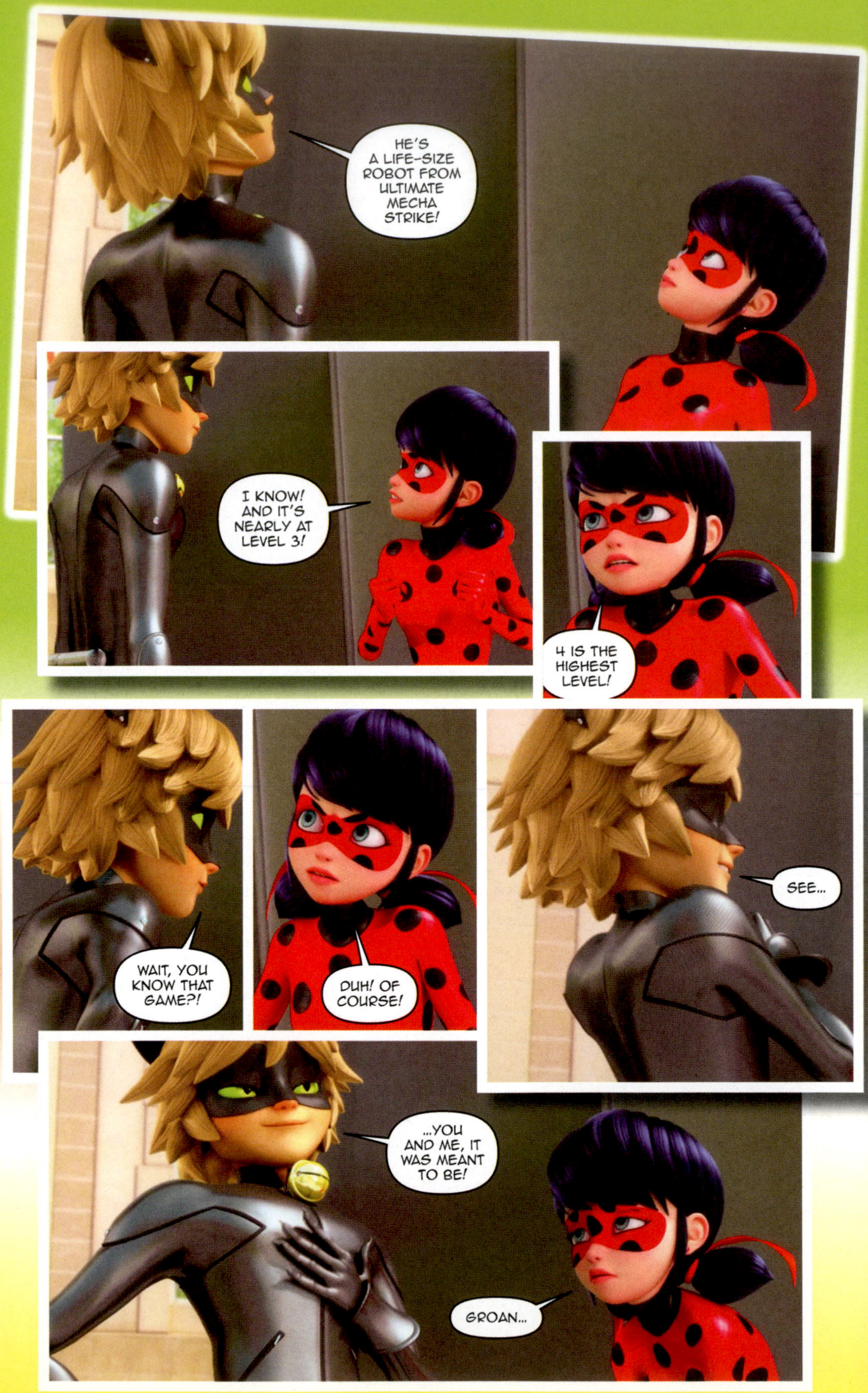
HE'S A LIFE-SIZE ROBOT FROM ULTIMATE MECHA STRIKE!
I KNOW! AND IT'S NEARLY AT LEVEL 3!
4 IS THE HIGHEST LEVEL!
WAIT, YOU KNOW THAT GAME?!
DUH! OF COURSE!
SEE...
...YOU AND ME, IT WAS MEANT TO BE!
GROAN...

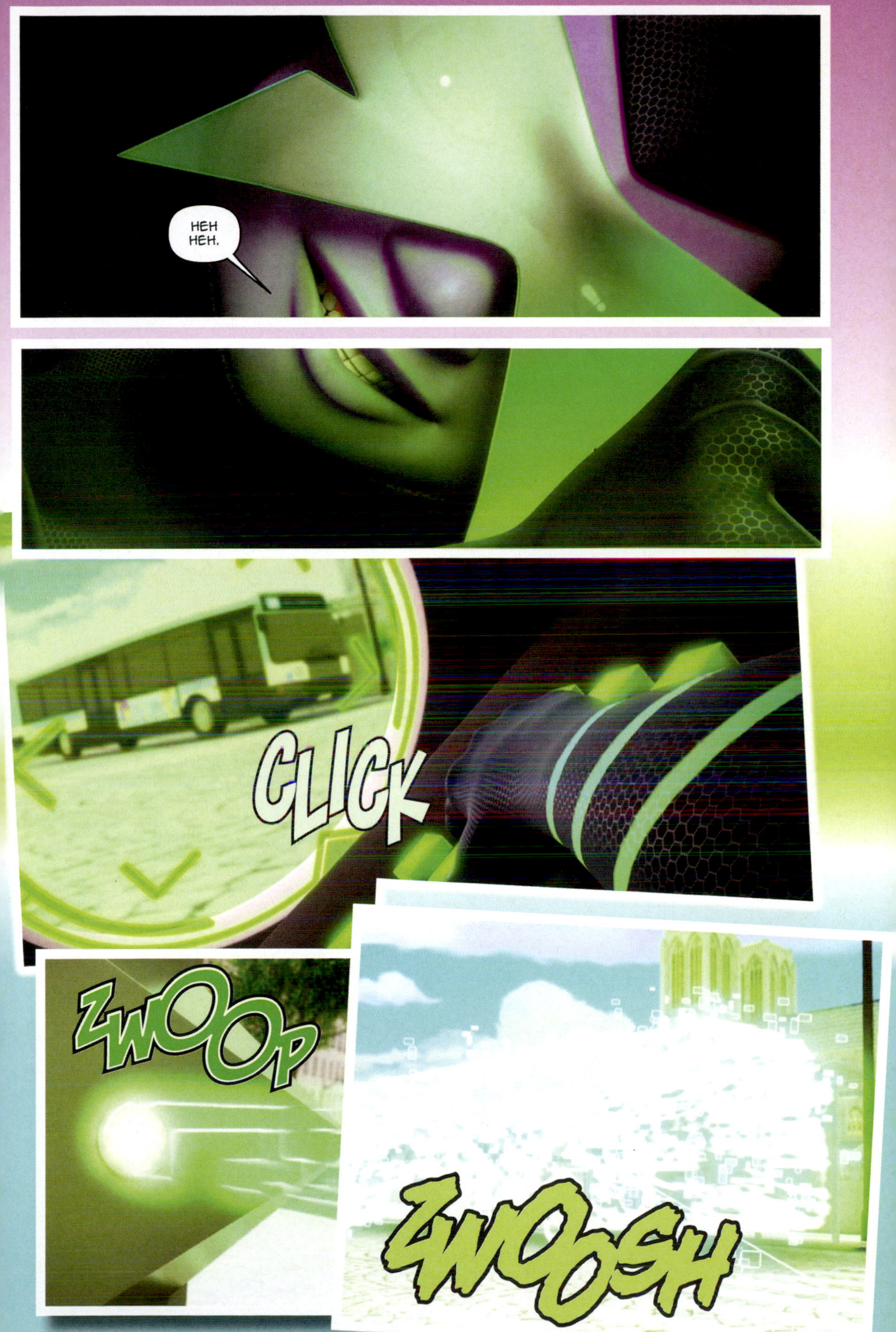
HEH HEH.
CLICK
ZWOOP
ZWOOSH

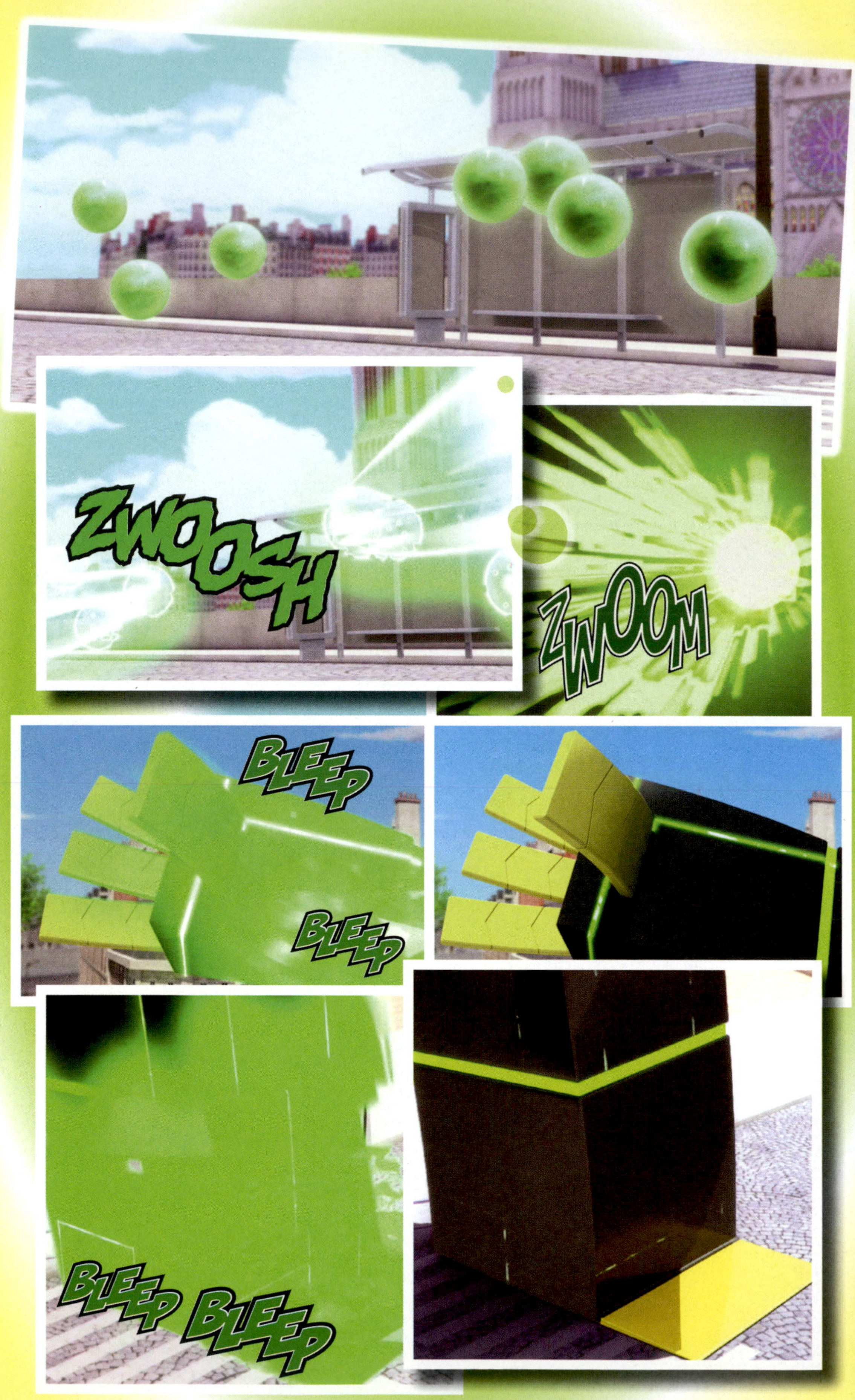
ZWOOSH
ZWOOM
BLEEP
BLEEP
BLEEP BLEEP

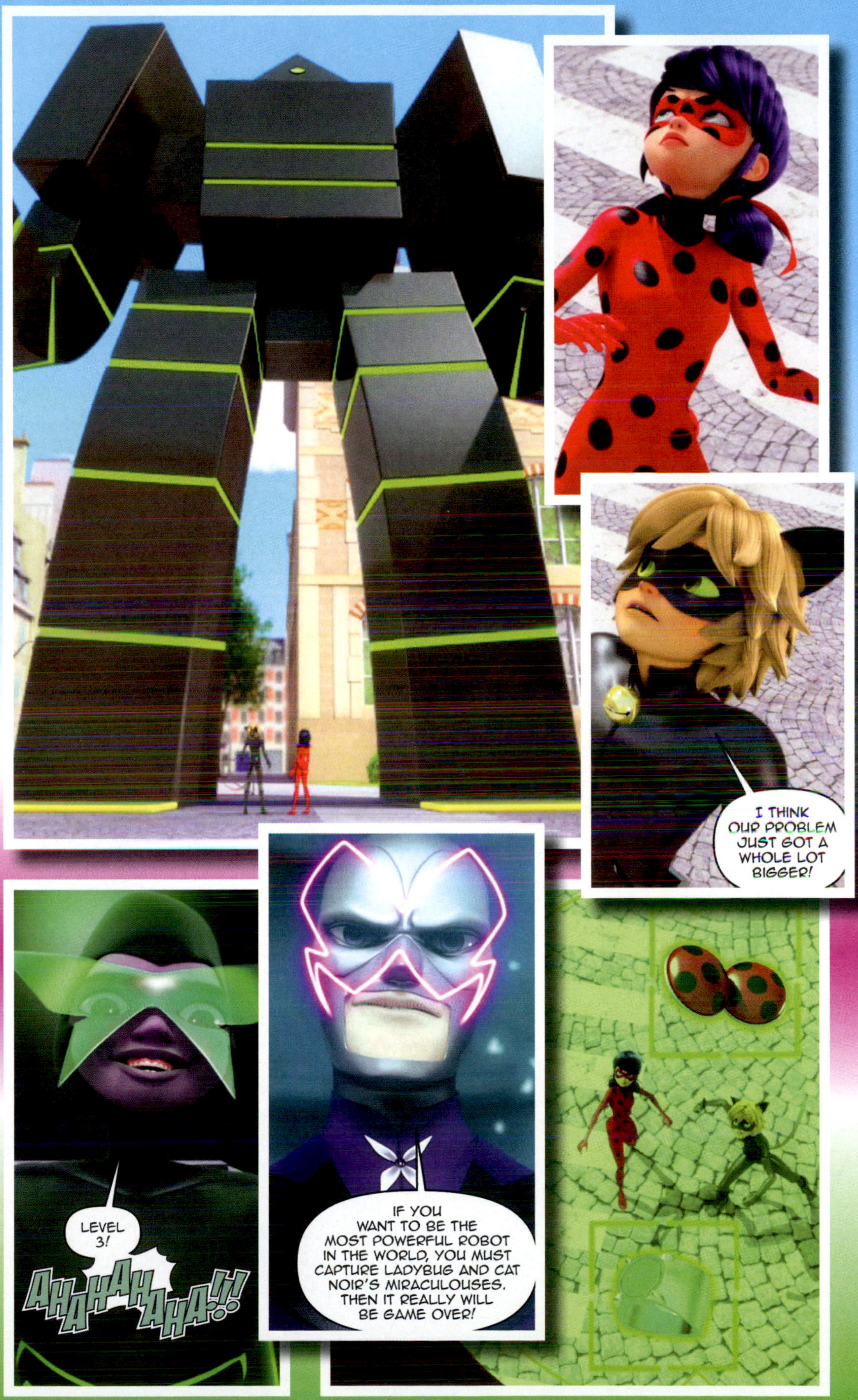
I THINK OUR PROBLEM JUST GOT A WHOLE LOT BIGGER!
LEVEL 3!
AHAHAHAHAHA!!!
IF YOU WANT TO BE THE MOST POWERFUL ROBOT IN THE WORLD, YOU MUST CAPTURE LADYBUG AND CAT NOIR'S MIRACULOUSES. THEN IT REALLY WILL BE GAME OVER!

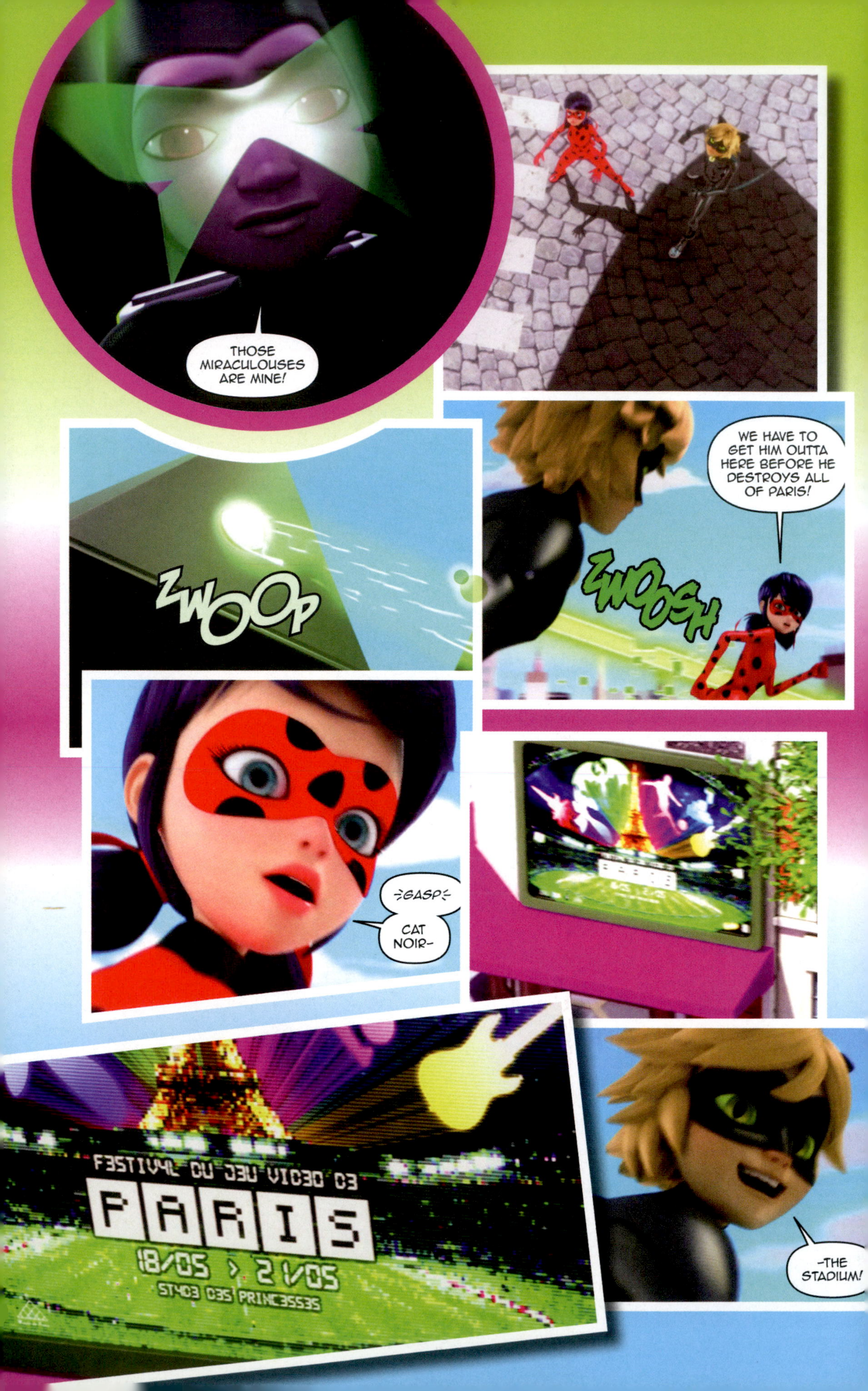

THOSE MIRACULOUSES ARE MINE!
ZWOOP
WE HAVE TO GET HIM OUTTA HERE BEFORE HE DESTROYS ALL OF PARIS!
ZWOOSH
GASP
CAT NOIR-
F3STIV4L DU J3U VID3O D3
PARIS
18/05 > 21/05
ST4D3 D3S PRINC3SS3S
-THE STADIUM!

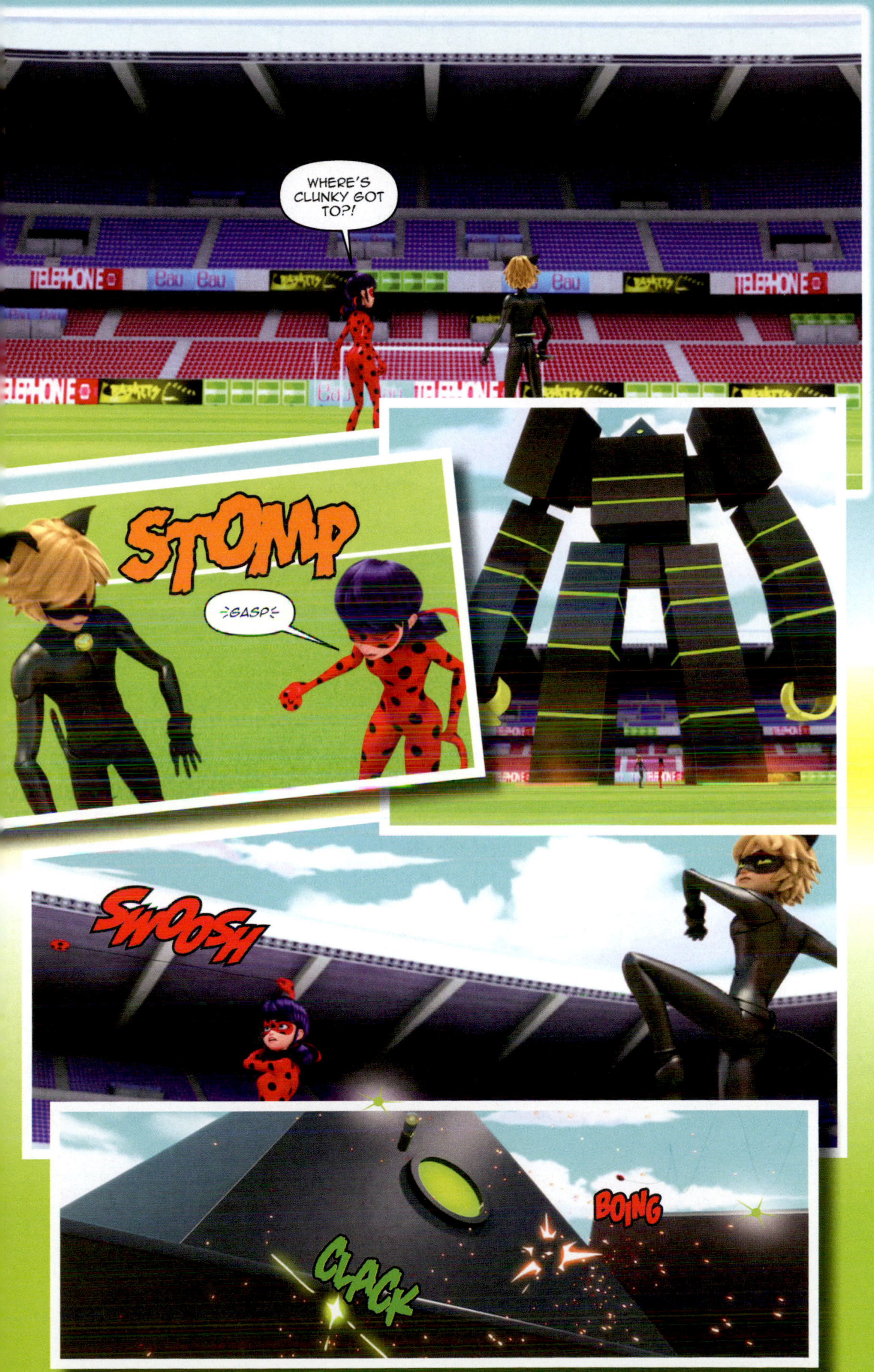
WHERE'S CLUNKY GOT TO?!
STOMP
GASP
SWOOSH
BOING
CLACK

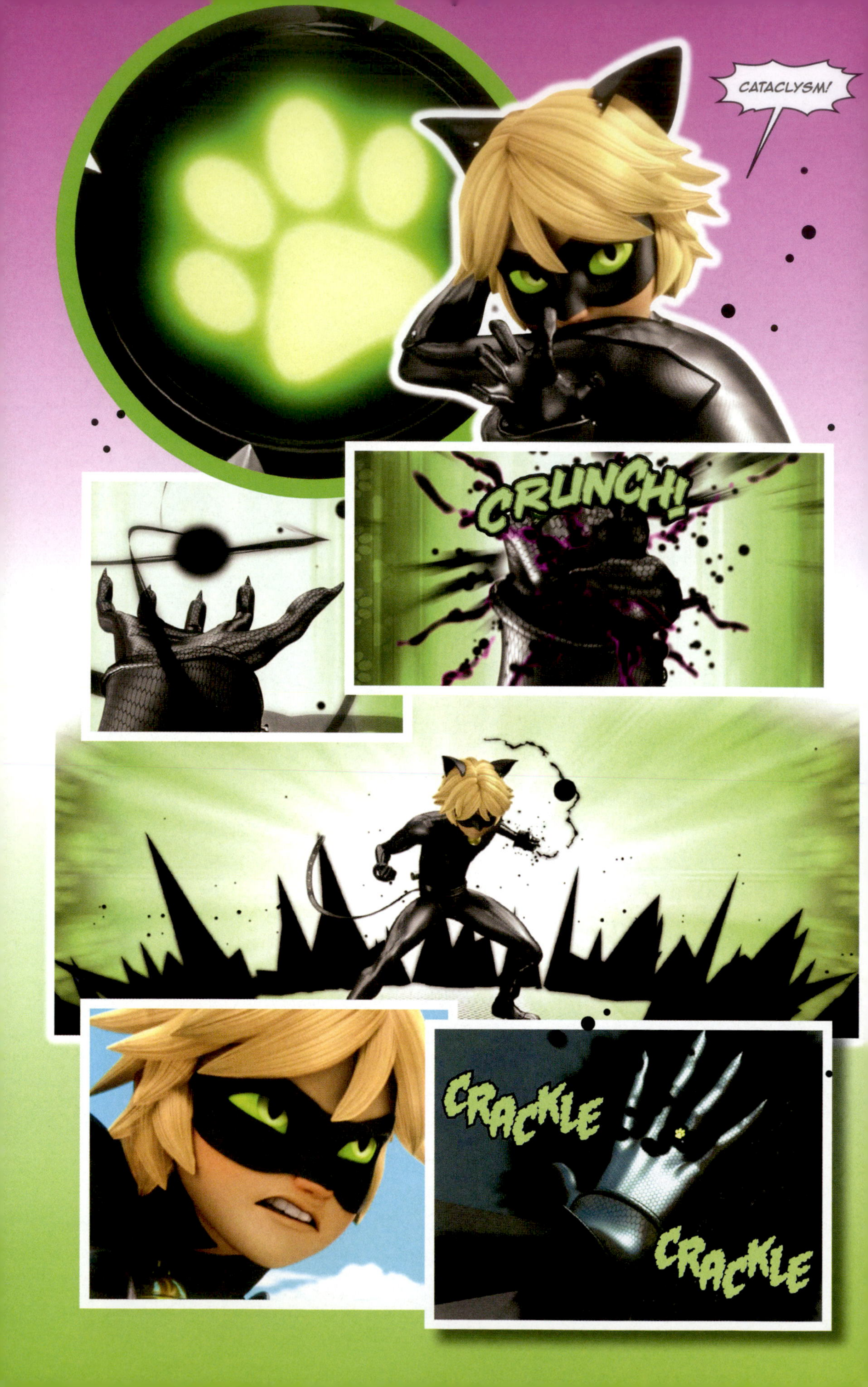
CATACLYSM!
CRUNCH!
CRACKLE
CRACKLE

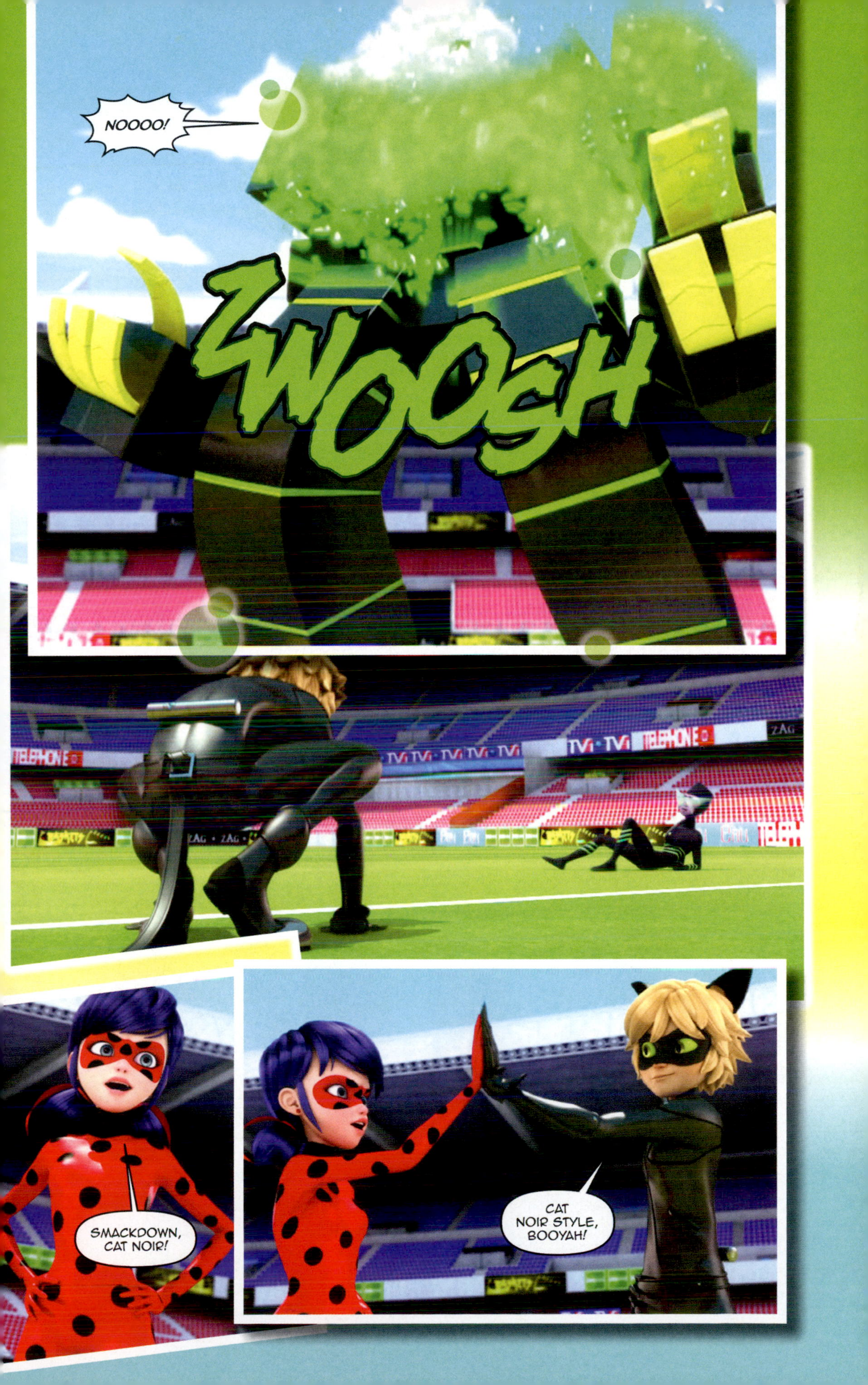
NOOOO!
ZWOOSH
SMACKDOWN, CAT NOIR!
CAT NOIR STYLE, BOOYAH!

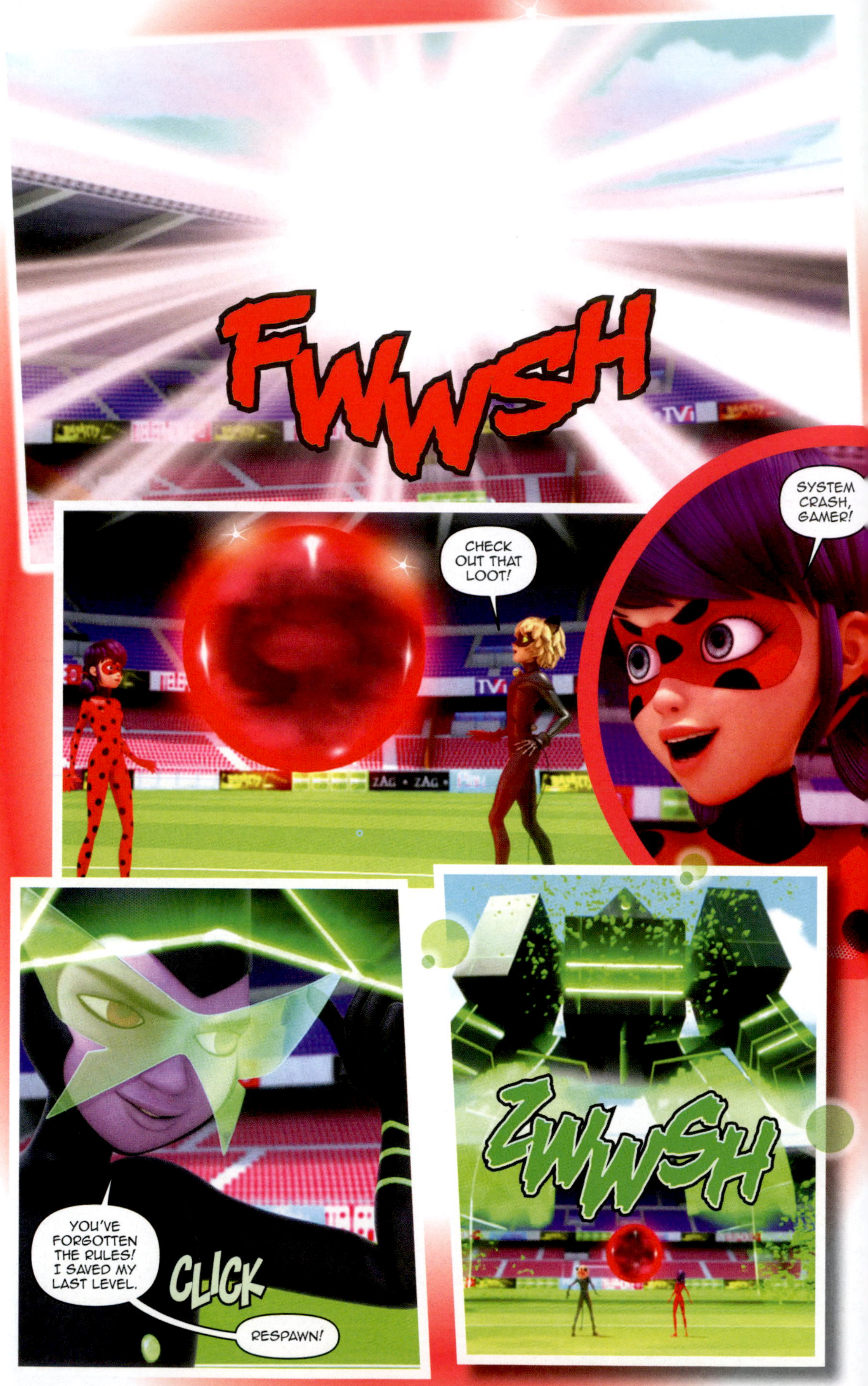

FWWSH
CHECK OUT THAT LOOT!
SYSTEM CRASH, GAMER!
YOU'VE FORGOTTEN THE RULES! I SAVED MY LAST LEVEL.
CLICK
RESPAWN!
ZWWSH

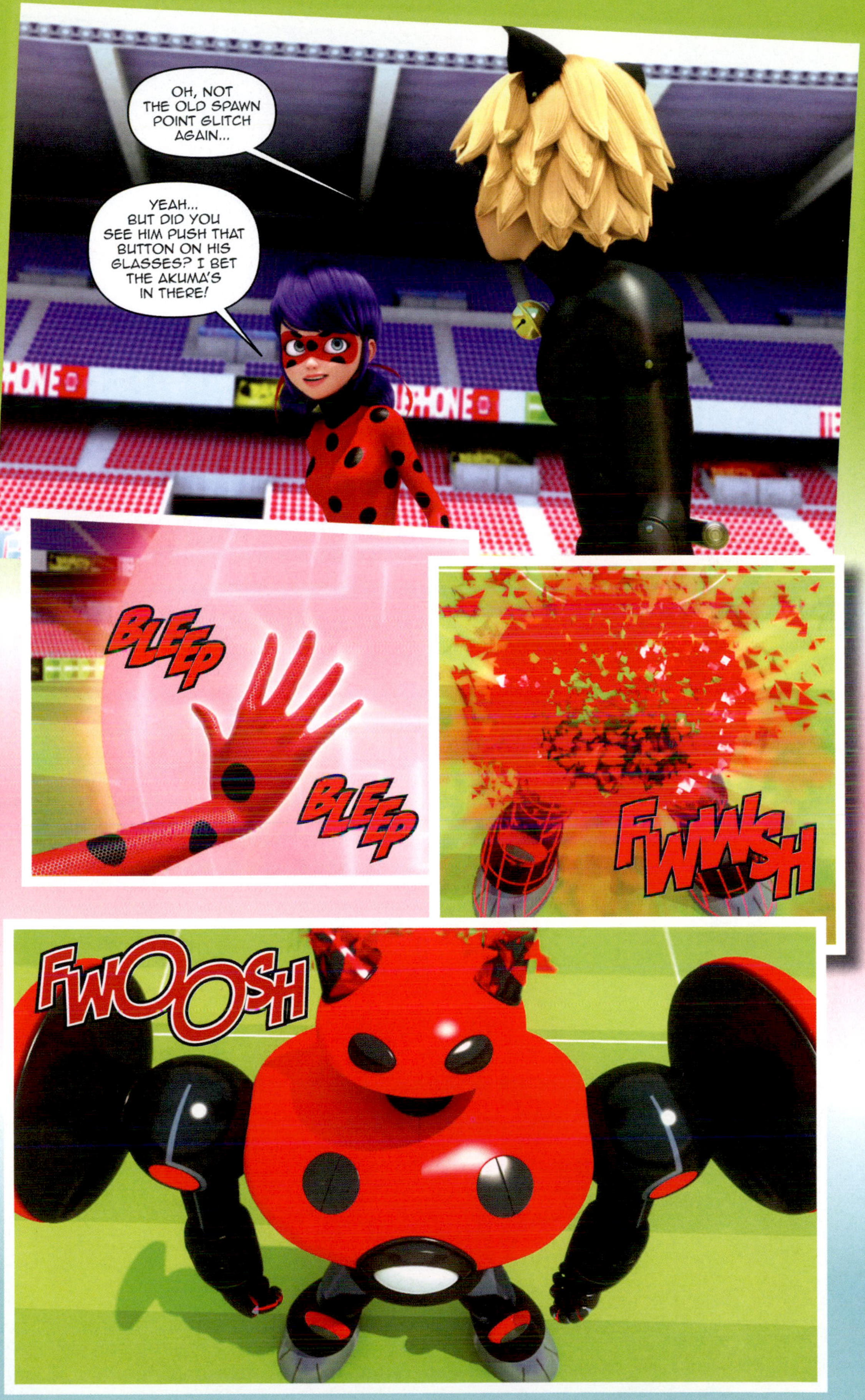
OH, NOT THE OLD SPAWN POINT GLITCH AGAIN...
YEAH... BUT DID YOU SEE HIM PUSH THAT BUTTON ON HIS GLASSES? I BET THE AKUMA'S IN THERE!
BLEEP
BLEEP
FWWSH
FWOOSH

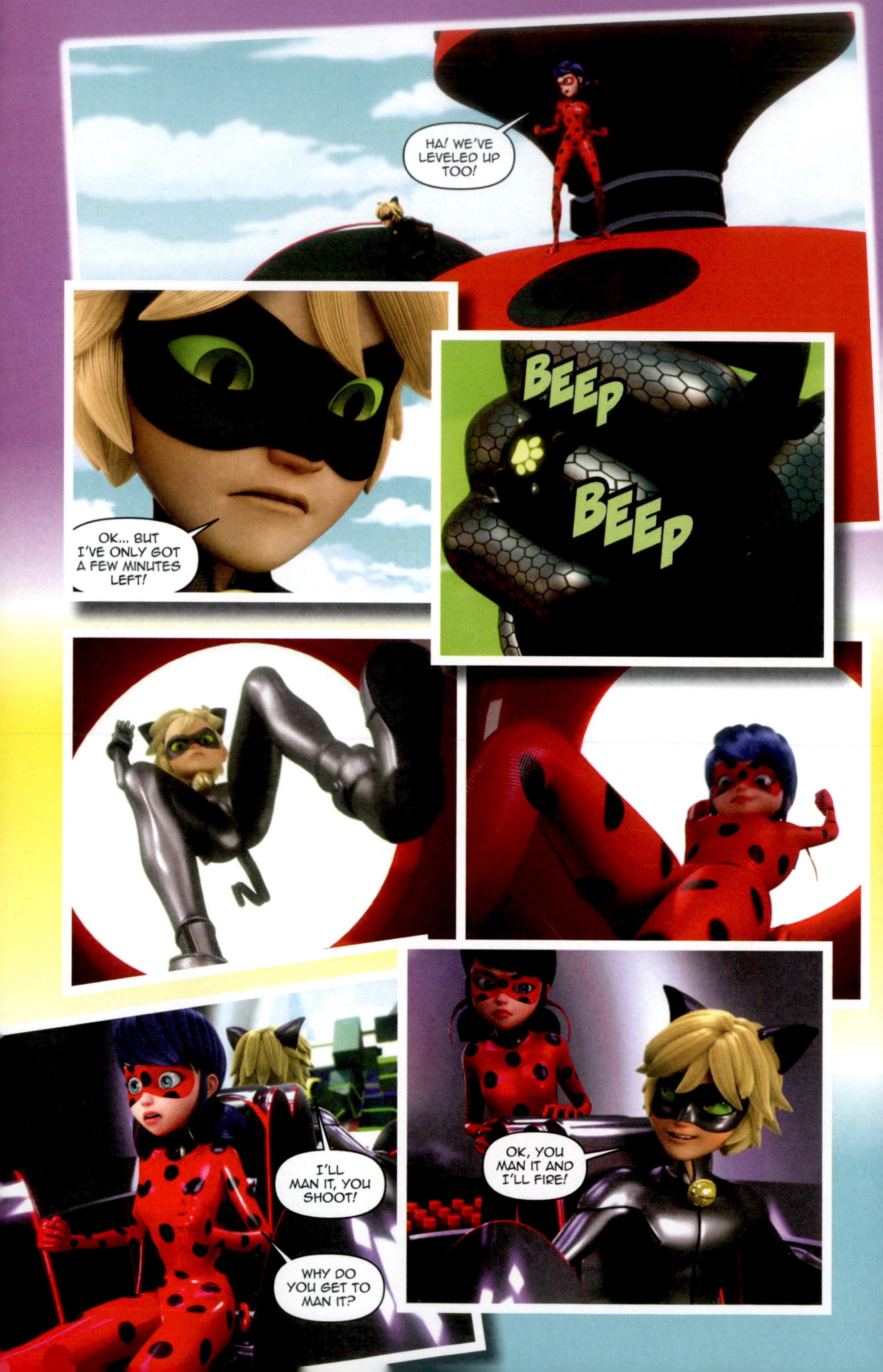
HA! WE'VE LEVELED UP TOO!
OK... BUT I'VE ONLY GOT A FEW MINUTES LEFT!
BEEP
BEEP
I'LL MAN IT, YOU SHOOT!
WHY DO YOU GET TO MAN IT?
OK, YOU MAN IT AND I'LL FIRE!

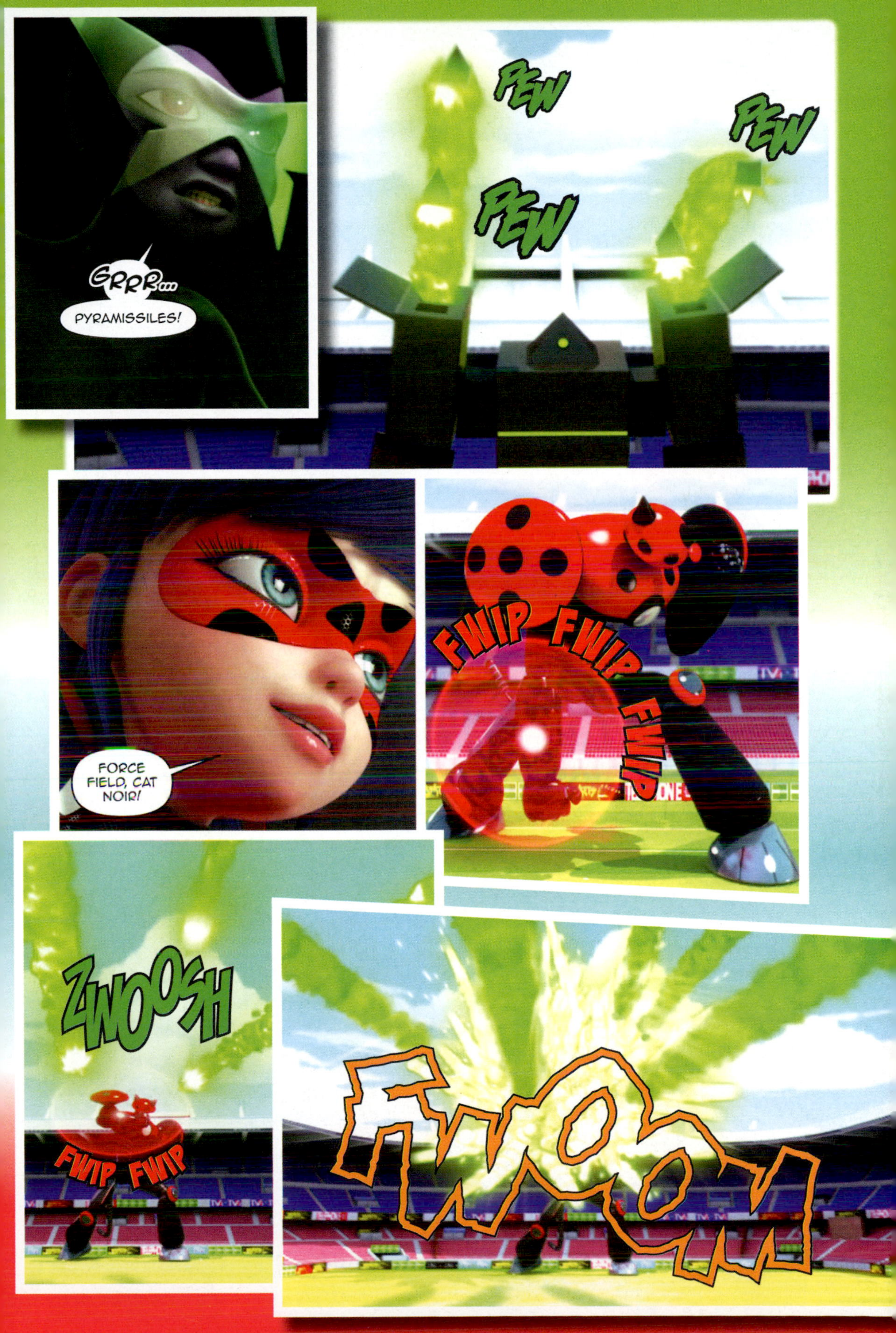
GRRR...
PYRAMISSILES!
PEW
PEW
PEW
FORCE FIELD, CAT NOIR!
FWIP FWIP FWIP FWIP
ZWOOSH
FWIP FWIP
FWOOM

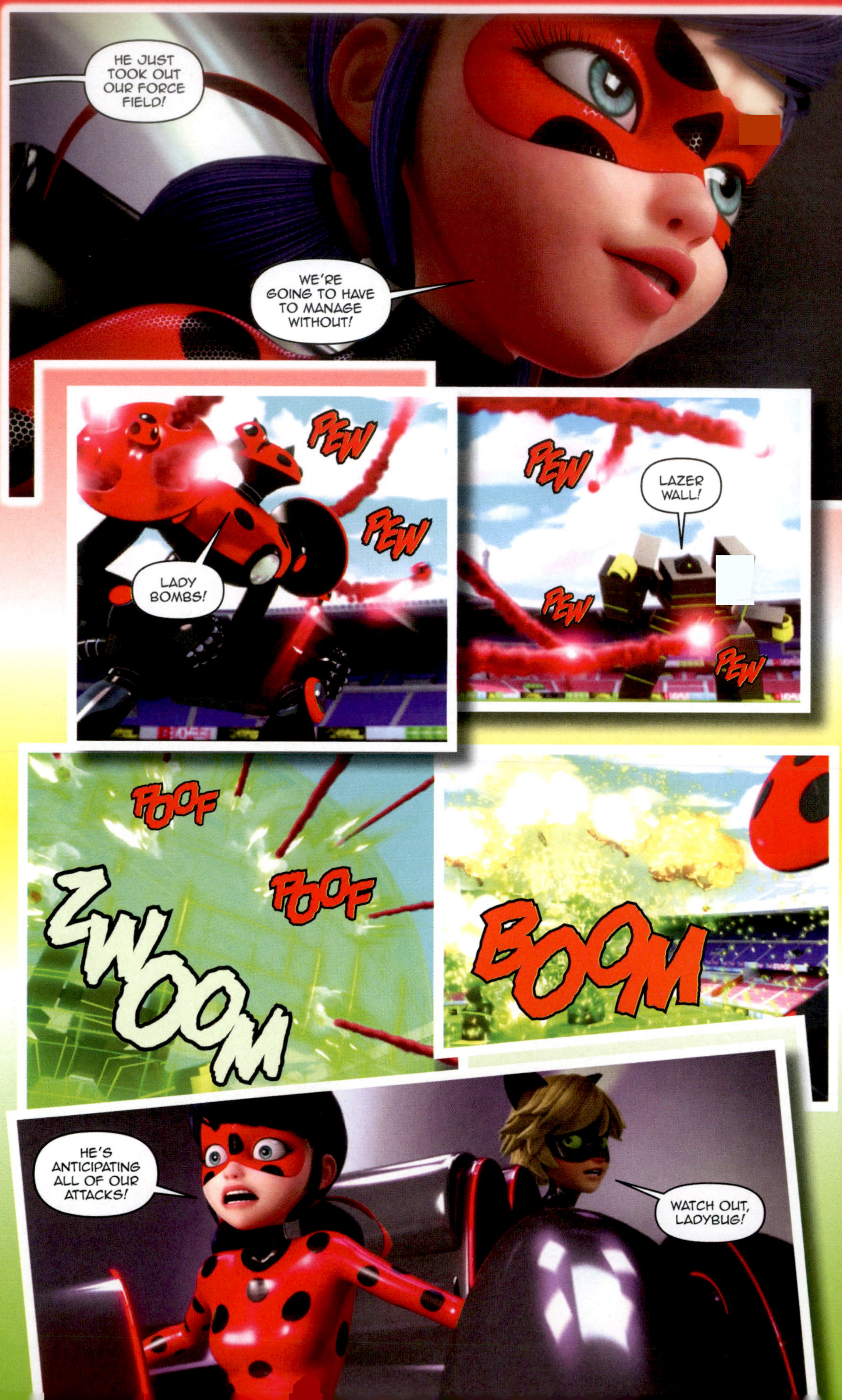
HE JUST TOOK OUT OUR FORCE FIELD!
WE'RE GOING TO HAVE TO MANAGE WITHOUT!
PEW
PEW
LADY BOMBS!
PEW
LAZER WALL!
PEW
PEW
POOF
POOF
ZWOOM
BOOM
HE'S ANTICIPATING ALL OF OUR ATTACKS!
WATCH OUT, LADYBUG!

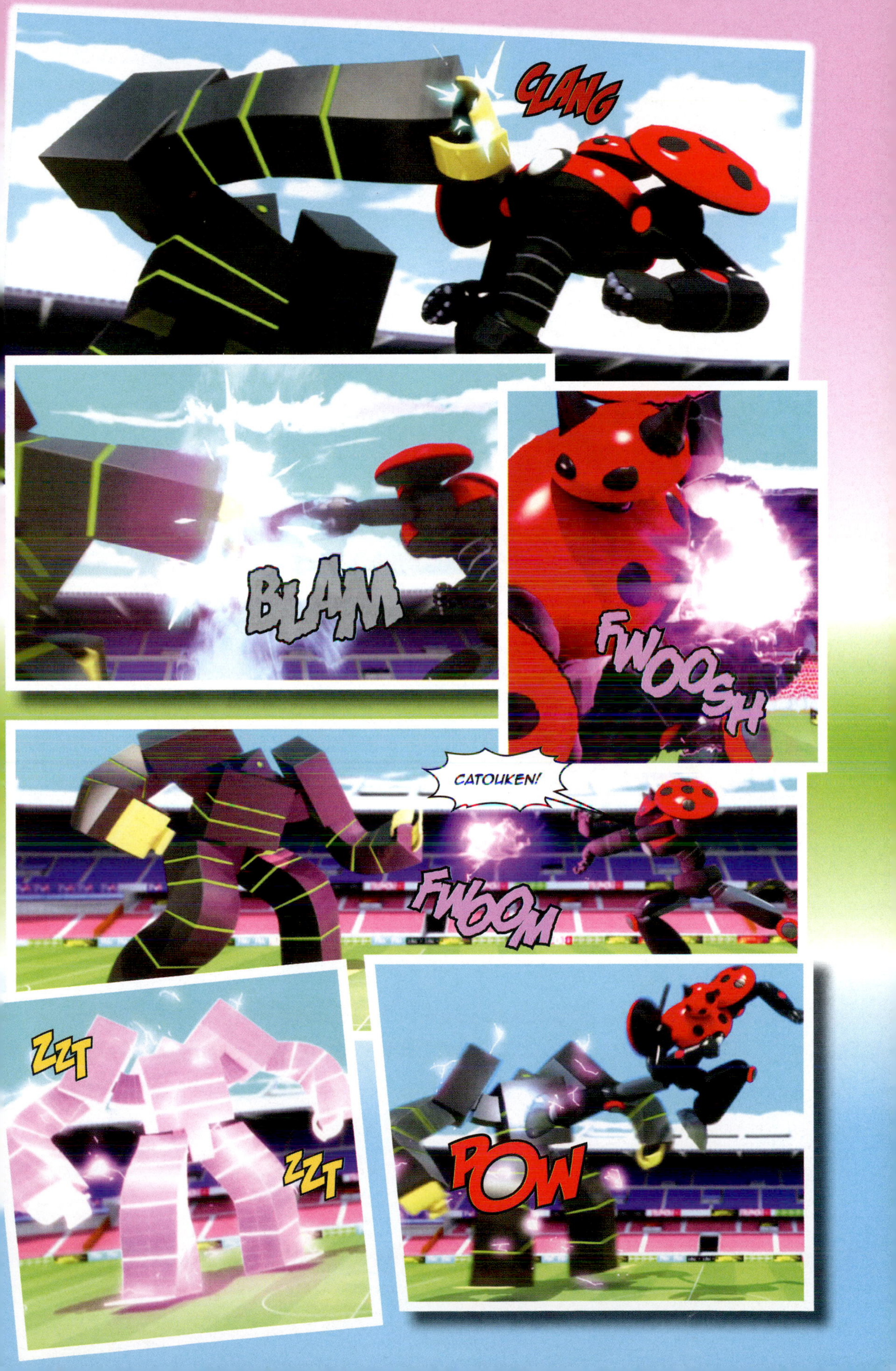
CLANG
BLAM
FWOOSH
CATOUKEN!
FWOOM
ZZT
ZZT
POW

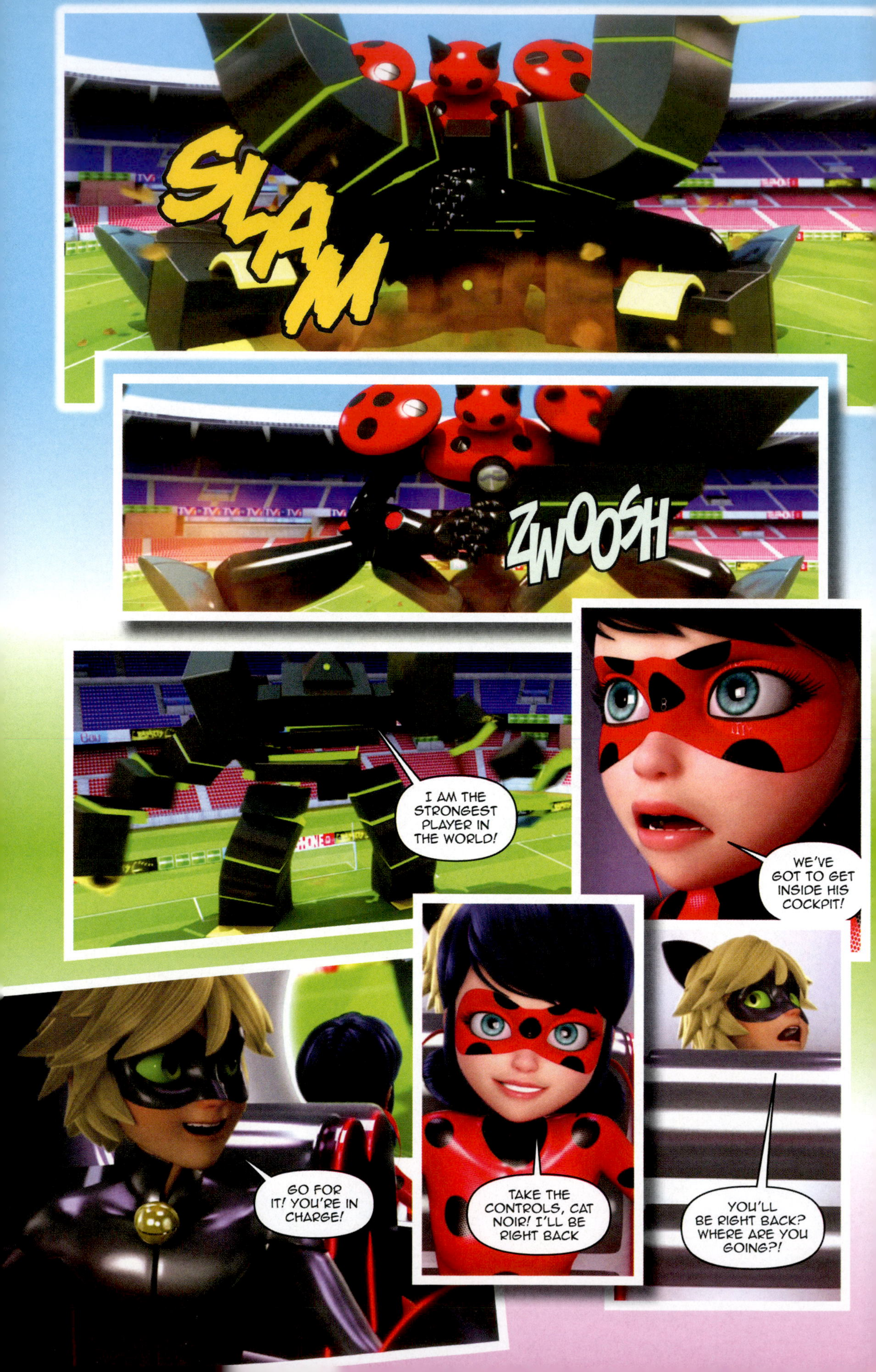
SLAM
ZWOOSH
I AM THE STRONGEST PLAYER IN THE WORLD!
WE'VE GOT TO GET INSIDE HIS COCKPIT!
GO FOR IT! YOU'RE IN CHARGE!
TAKE THE CONTROLS, CAT NOIR! I'LL BE RIGHT BACK
YOU'LL BE RIGHT BACK? WHERE ARE YOU GOING?!

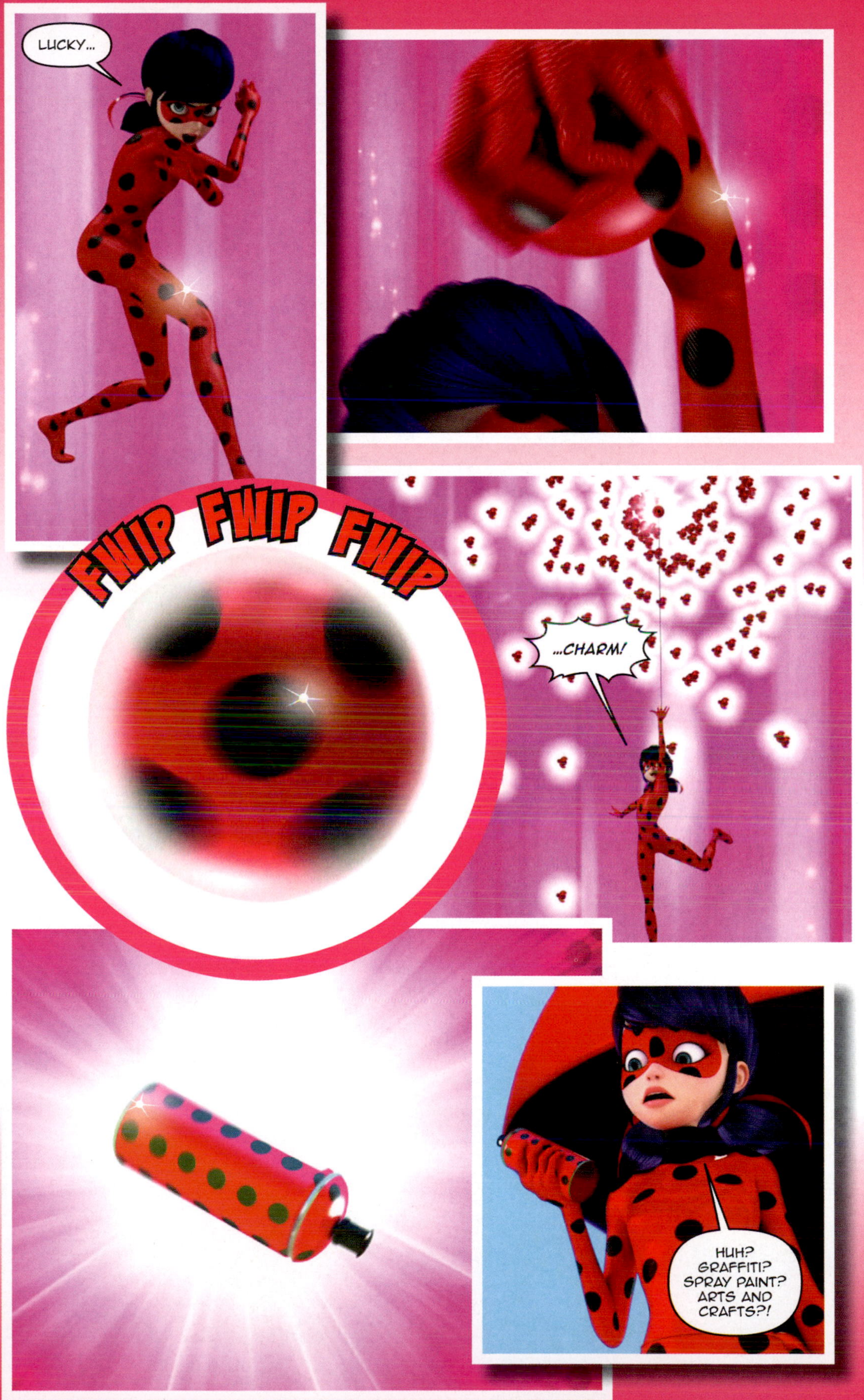
LUCKY...
FWIP FWIP FWIP
...CHARM!
HUH? GRAFFITI? SPRAY PAINT? ARTS AND CRAFTS?!

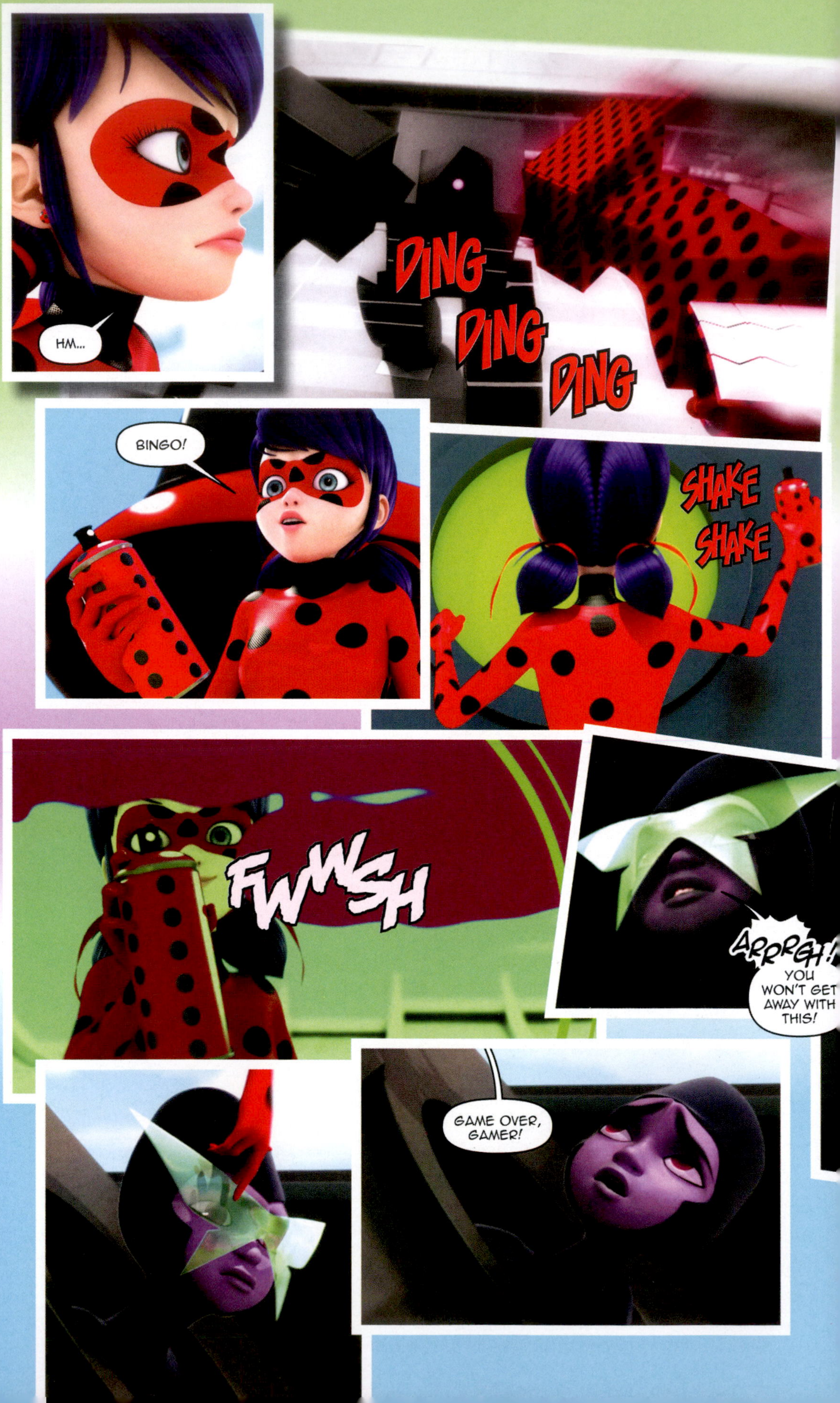
HM...
DING
DING
DING
BINGO!
SHAKE
SHAKE
FWWSH
ARRRGH! YOU WON'T GET AWAY WITH THIS!
GAME OVER, GAMER!

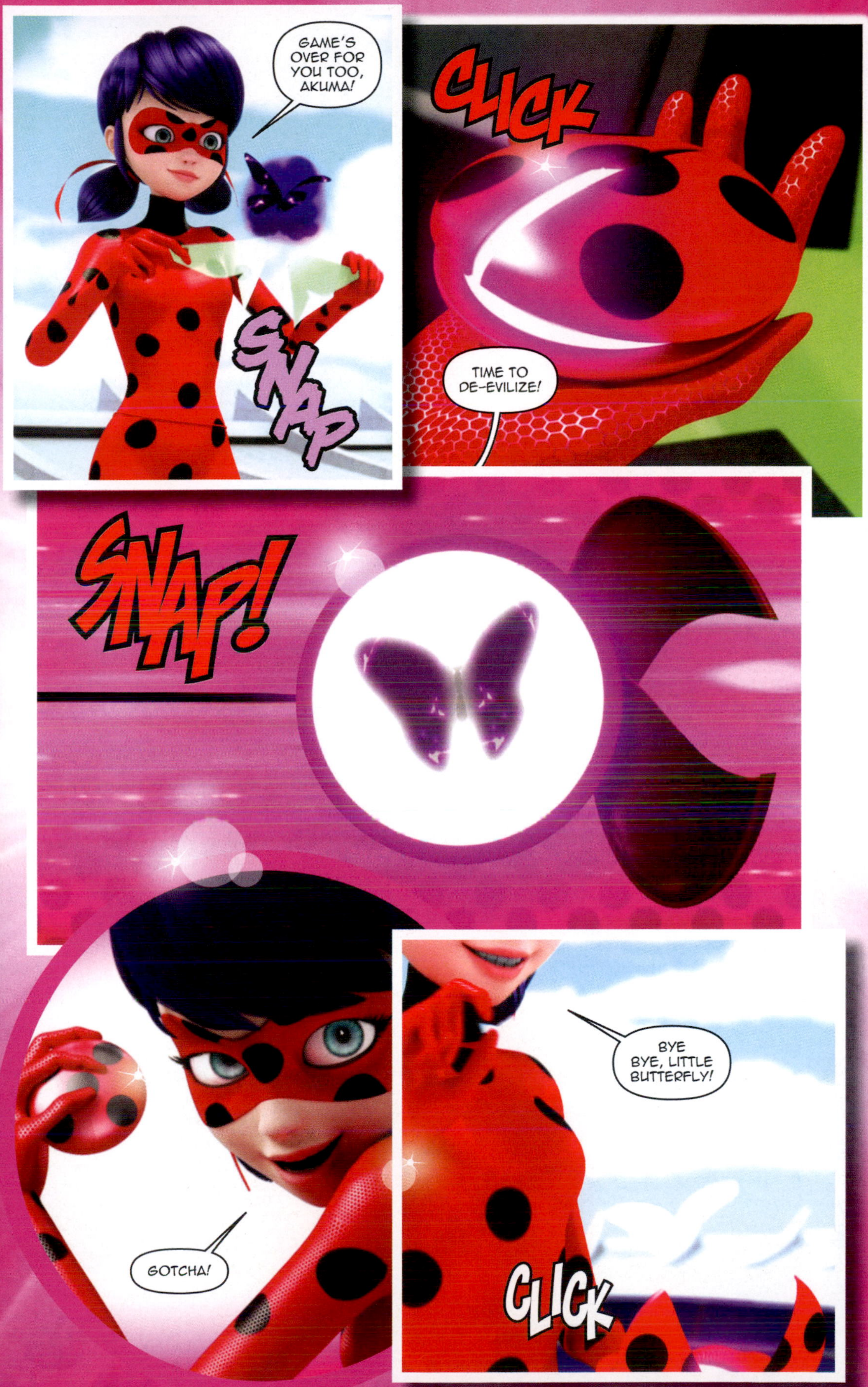
GAME'S OVER FOR YOU TOO, AKUMA!
SNAP
CLICK
TIME TO DE-EVILIZE!
SNAP!
GOTCHA!
BYE BYE, LITTLE BUTTERFLY!
CLICK

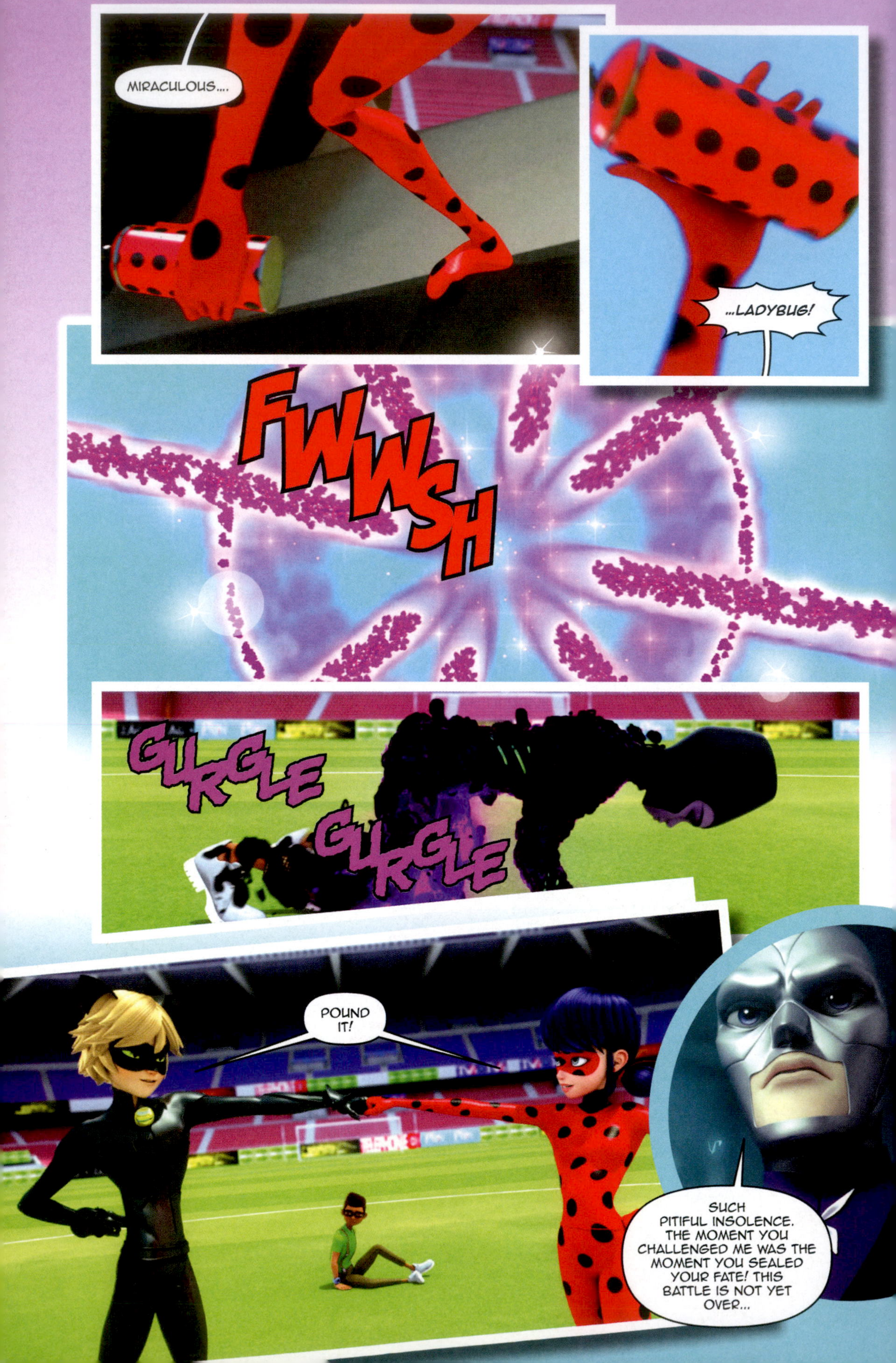
MIRACULOUS....
...LADYBUG!
FWWSH
GURGLE
GURGLE
POUND IT!
SUCH PITIFUL INSOLENCE. THE MOMENT YOU CHALLENGED ME WAS THE MOMENT YOU SEALED YOUR FATE! THIS BATTLE IS NOT YET OVER...

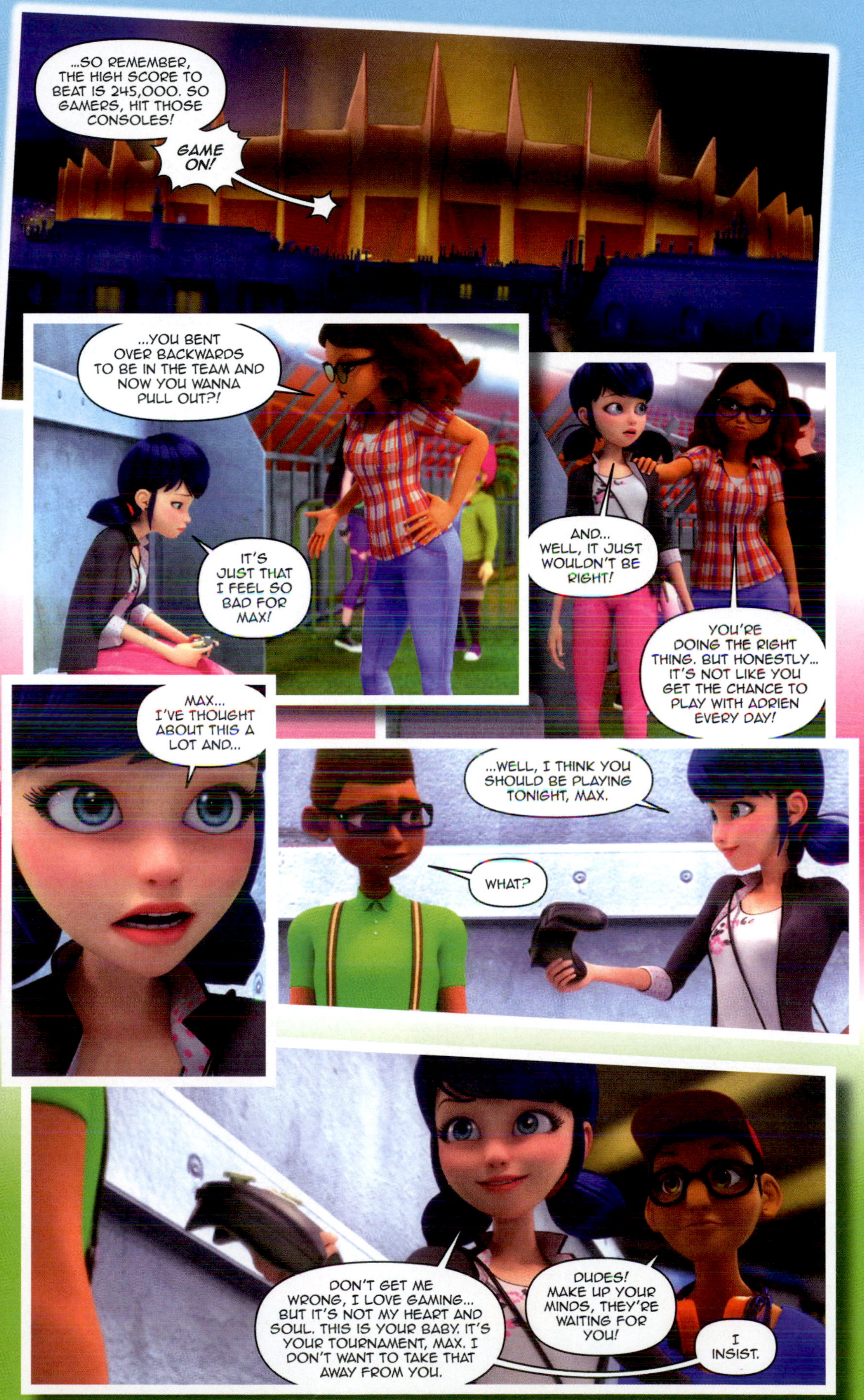
...SO REMEMBER, THE HIGH SCORE TO BEAT IS 245,000. SO GAMERS, HIT THOSE CONSOLES!
GAME ON!
...YOU BENT OVER BACKWARDS TO BE IN THE TEAM AND NOW YOU WANNA PULL OUT?!
IT'S JUST THAT I FEEL SO BAD FOR MAX!
AND... WELL, IT JUST WOULDN'T BE RIGHT!
YOU'RE DOING THE RIGHT THING. BUT HONESTLY... IT'S NOT LIKE YOU GET THE CHANCE TO PLAY WITH ADRIEN EVERY DAY!
MAX... I'VE THOUGHT ABOUT THIS A LOT AND...
...WELL, I THINK YOU SHOULD BE PLAYING TONIGHT, MAX.
WHAT?
DON'T GET ME WRONG, I LOVE GAMING... BUT IT'S NOT MY HEART AND SOUL. THIS IS YOUR BABY. IT'S YOUR TOURNAMENT, MAX. I DON'T WANT TO TAKE THAT AWAY FROM YOU.
DUDES! MAKE UP YOUR MINDS, THEY'RE WAITING FOR YOU!
I INSIST.

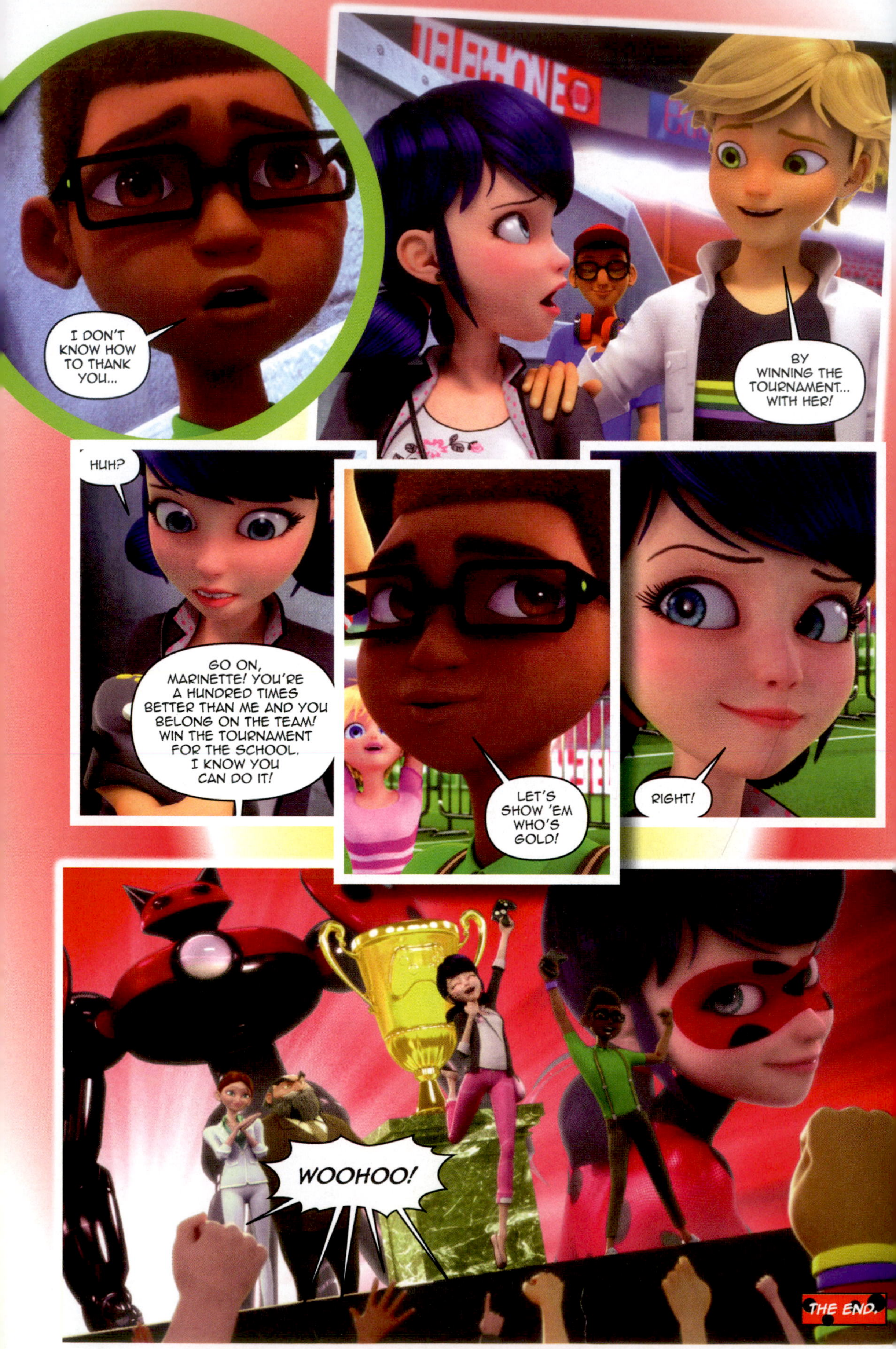
I DON'T KNOW HOW TO THANK YOU...
BY WINNING THE TOURNAMENT... WITH HER!
HUH?
GO ON, MARINETTE! YOU'RE A HUNDRED TIMES BETTER THAN ME AND YOU BELONG ON THE TEAM! WIN THE TOURNAMENT FOR THE SCHOOL. I KNOW YOU CAN DO IT!
LET'S SHOW 'EM WHO'S GOLD!
RIGHT!
WOOHOO!
THE END.

Reflekta

Created by: Thomas Astruc
Comics adaptation by: Nicole D'Andria
Written by: Sophie Lodwitz & Eve Pisler
Art arranged by: Cheryl Black
Lettered by: Justin Birch

Bryan Seaton: Publisher/ CEO
Shawn Gabborin: Editor In Chief
Jason Martin: Publisher-Danger Zone
Nicole D'Andria: Marketing Director/Editor
Danielle Davison: Executive Administrator
Chad Cicconi: Akumatized
Shawn Pryor: President of Creator Relations

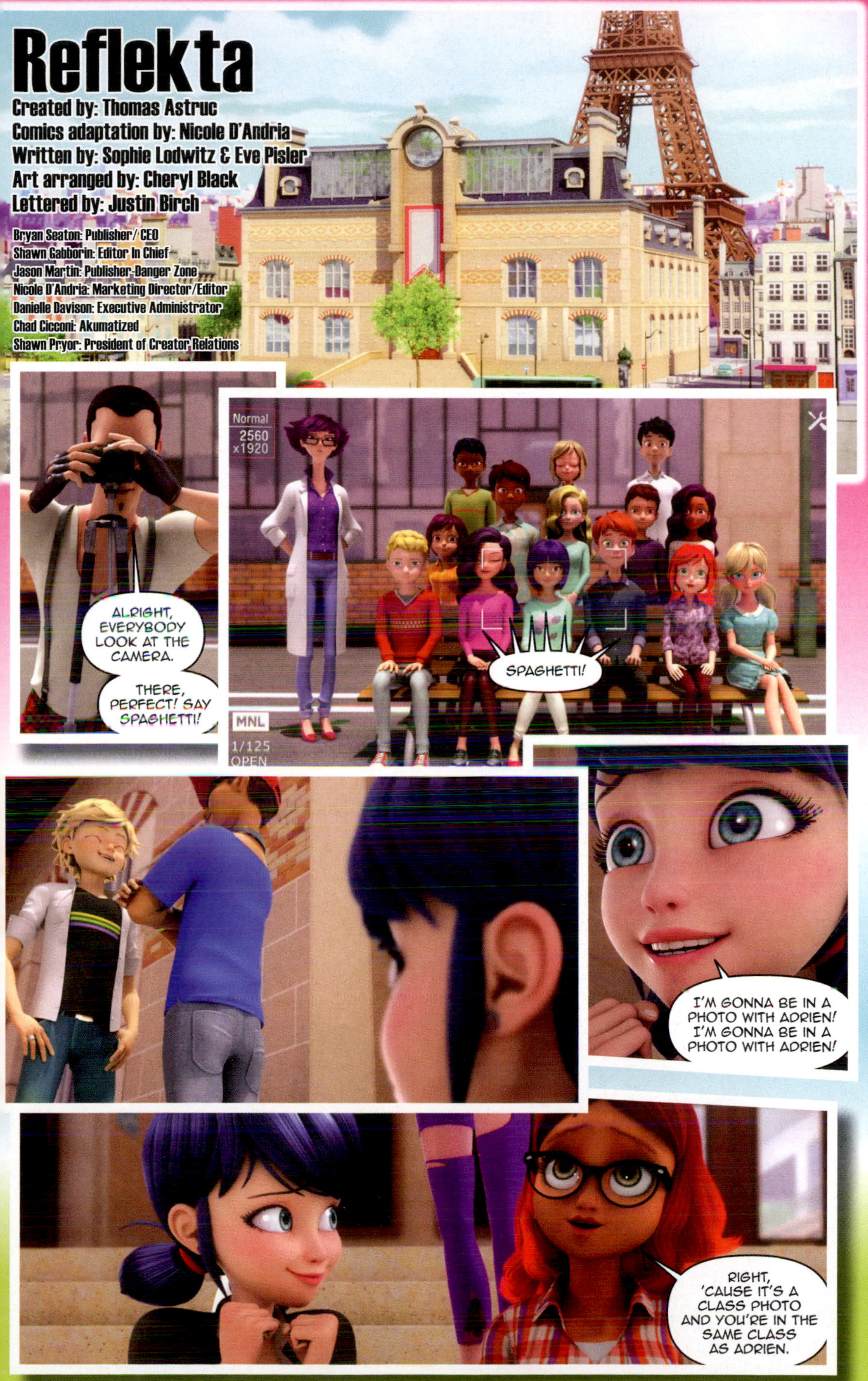

ALRIGHT, EVERYBODY LOOK AT THE CAMERA.
THERE, PERFECT! SAY SPAGHETTI!
Normal
2560 x1920
MNL
1/125
OPEN
SPAGHETTI!
I'M GONNA BE IN A PHOTO WITH ADRIEN! I'M GONNA BE IN A PHOTO WITH ADRIEN!
RIGHT, 'CAUSE IT'S A CLASS PHOTO AND YOU'RE IN THE SAME CLASS AS ADRIEN.

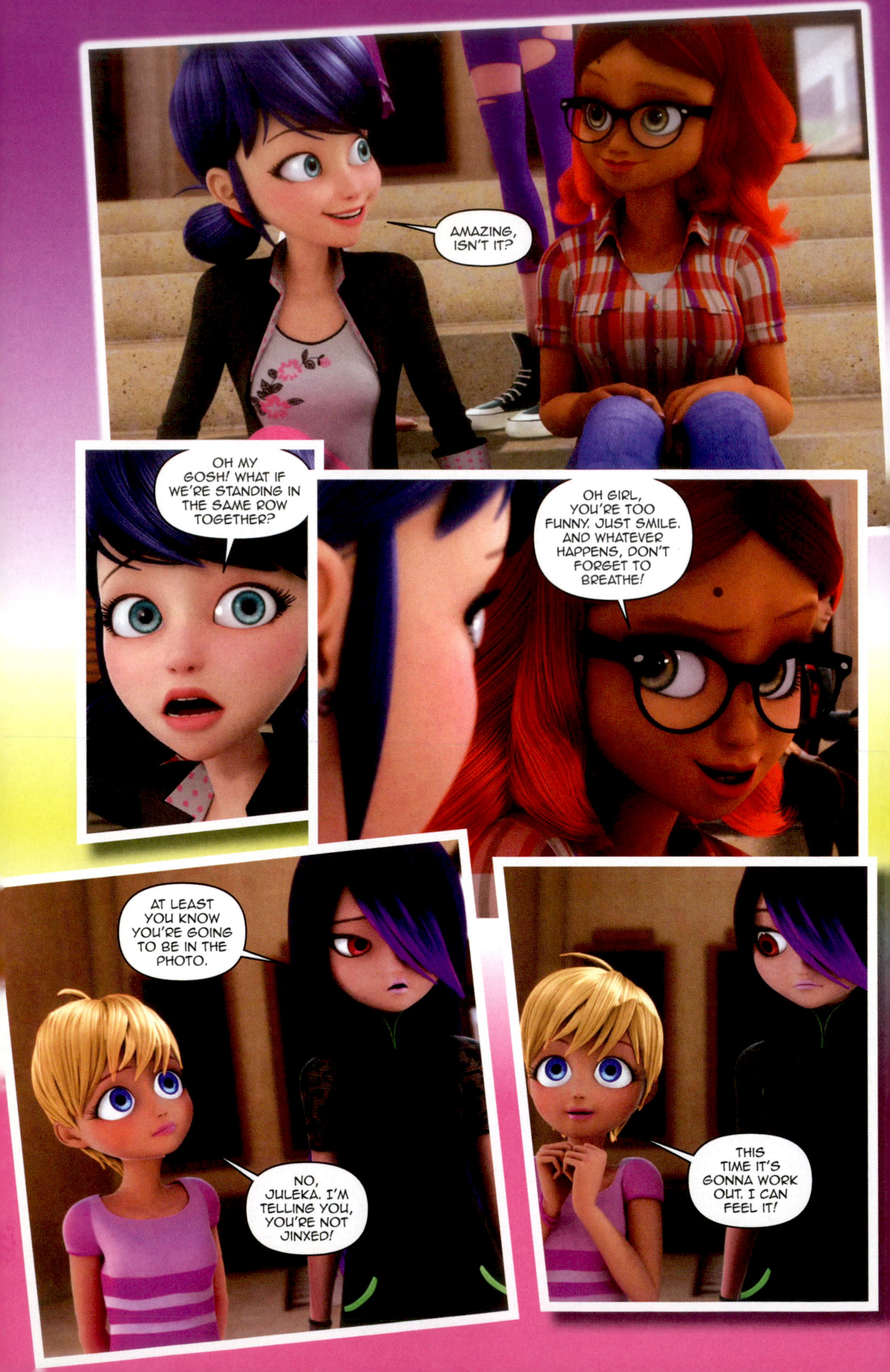
AMAZING, ISN'T IT?
OH MY GOSH! WHAT IF WE'RE STANDING IN THE SAME ROW TOGETHER?
OH GIRL, YOU'RE TOO FUNNY. JUST SMILE. AND WHATEVER HAPPENS, DON'T FORGET TO BREATHE!
AT LEAST YOU KNOW YOU'RE GOING TO BE IN THE PHOTO.
NO, JULEKA. I'M TELLING YOU, YOU'RE NOT JINXED!
THIS TIME IT'S GONNA WORK OUT. I CAN FEEL IT!

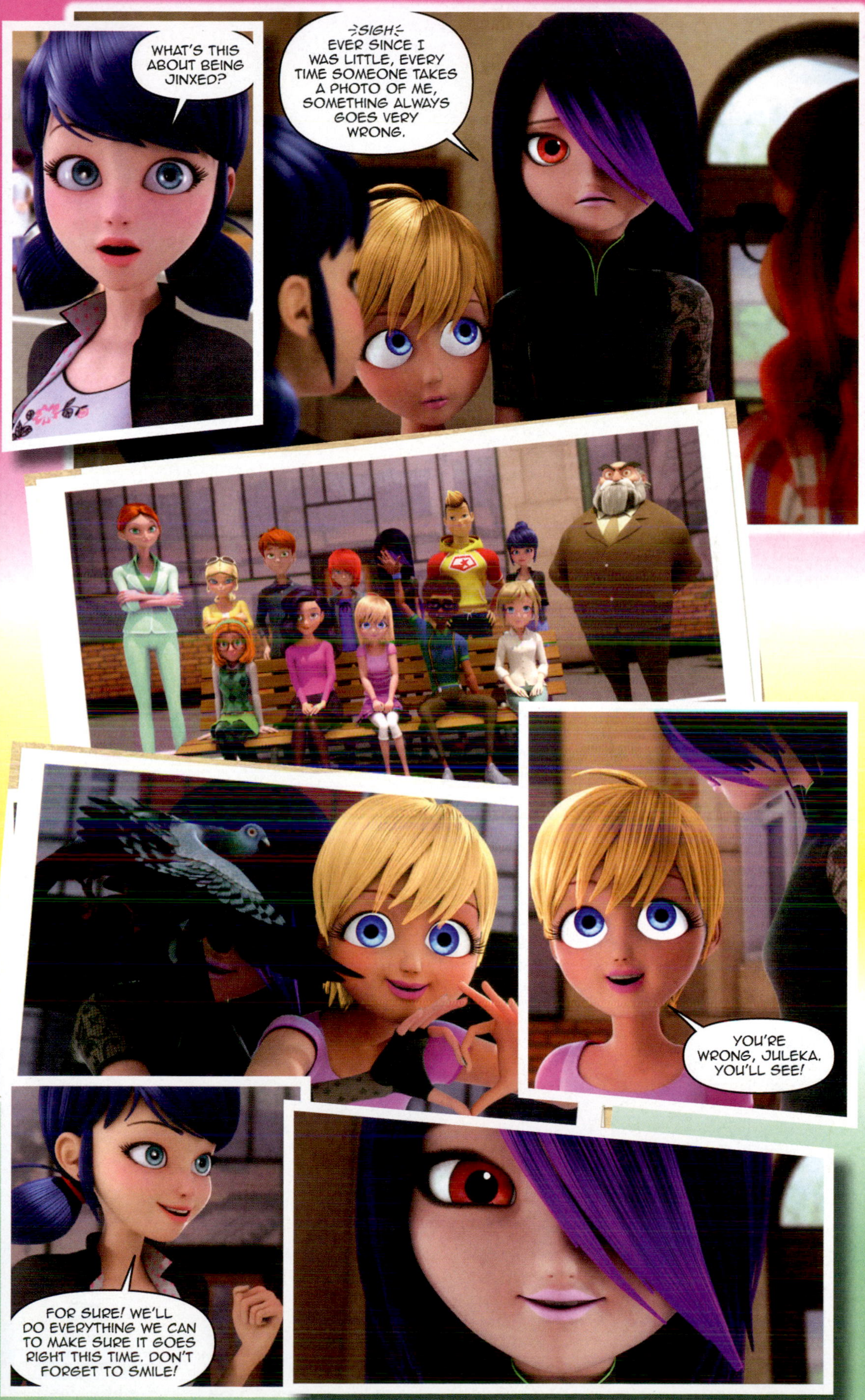
WHAT'S THIS ABOUT BEING JINXED?
SIGH
EVER SINCE I WAS LITTLE, EVERY TIME SOMEONE TAKES A PHOTO OF ME, SOMETHING ALWAYS GOES VERY WRONG.
YOU'RE WRONG, JULEKA. YOU'LL SEE!
FOR SURE! WE'LL DO EVERYTHING WE CAN TO MAKE SURE IT GOES RIGHT THIS TIME. DON'T FORGET TO SMILE!

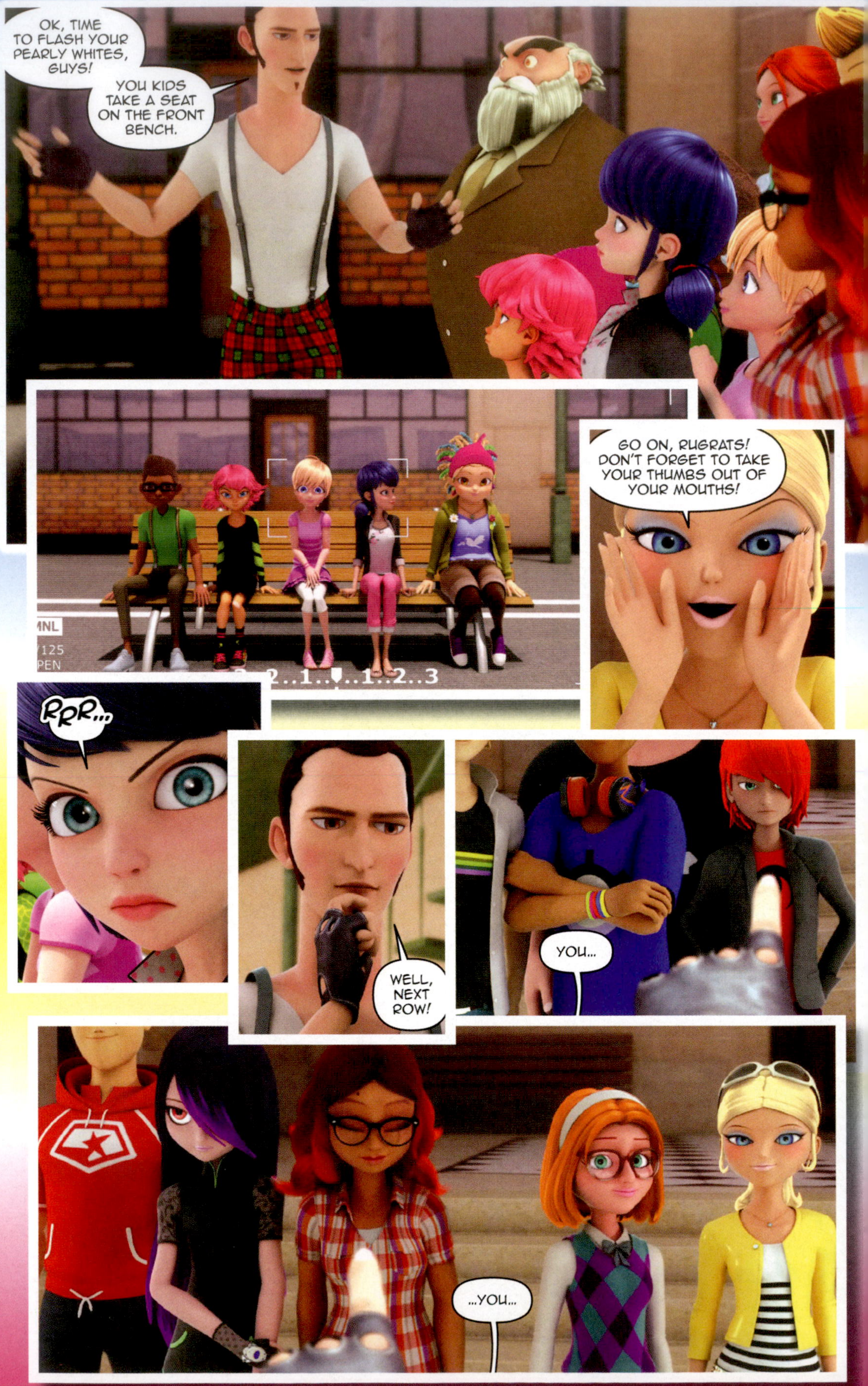
OK, TIME TO FLASH YOUR PEARLY WHITES, GUYS!
YOU KIDS TAKE A SEAT ON THE FRONT BENCH.
GO ON, RUGRATS! DON'T FORGET TO TAKE YOUR THUMBS OUT OF YOUR MOUTHS!
RRR...
WELL, NEXT ROW!
YOU...
...YOU...

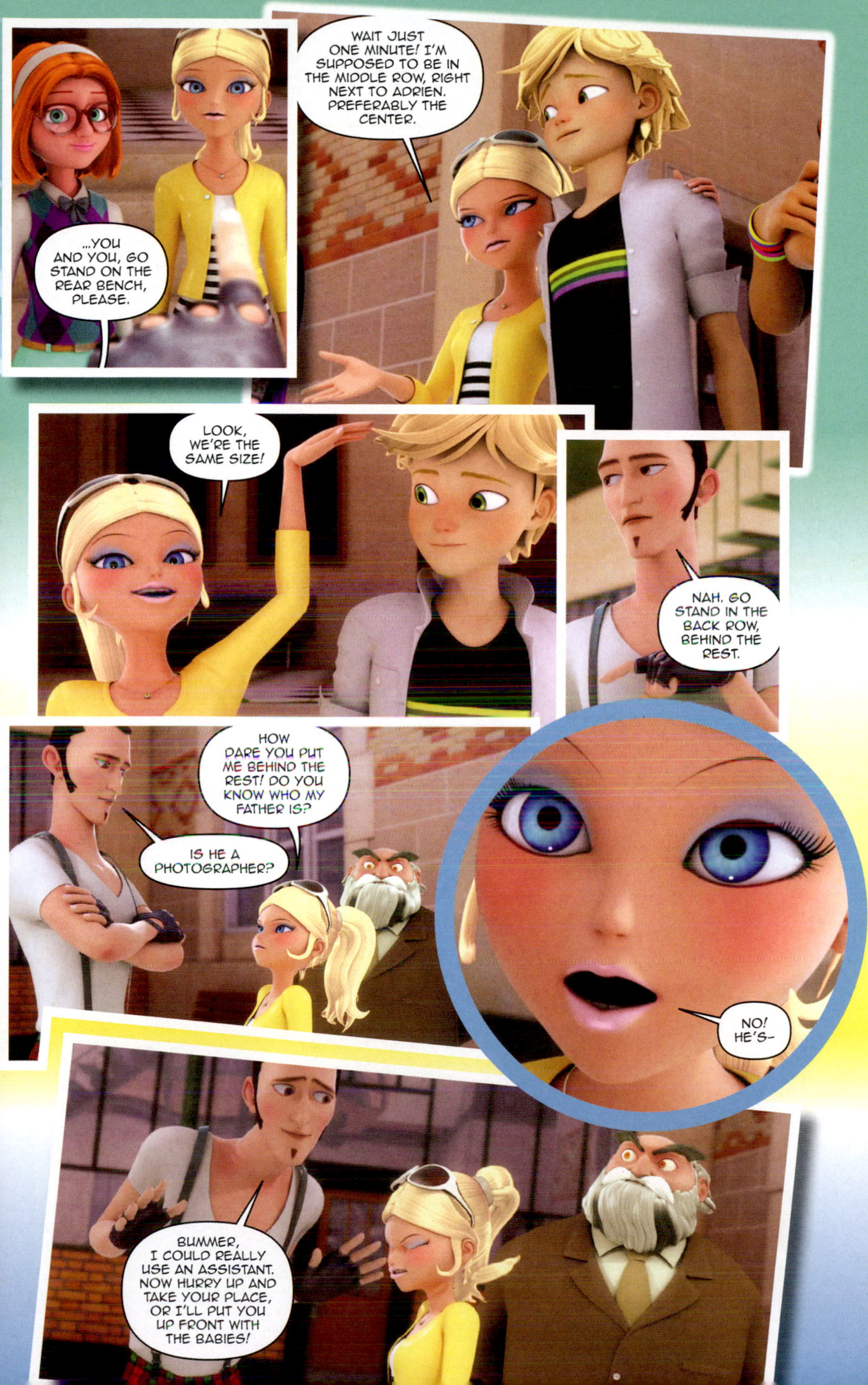
...YOU AND YOU, GO STAND ON THE REAR BENCH, PLEASE.
WAIT JUST ONE MINUTE! I'M SUPPOSED TO BE IN THE MIDDLE ROW, RIGHT NEXT TO ADRIEN. PREFERABLY THE CENTER.
LOOK, WE'RE THE SAME SIZE!
NAH. GO STAND IN THE BACK ROW, BEHIND THE REST.
HOW DARE YOU PUT ME BEHIND THE REST! DO YOU KNOW WHO MY FATHER IS?
IS HE A PHOTOGRAPHER?
NO! HE'S-
BUMMER, I COULD REALLY USE AN ASSISTANT. NOW HURRY UP AND TAKE YOUR PLACE, OR I'LL PUT YOU UP FRONT WITH THE BABIES!

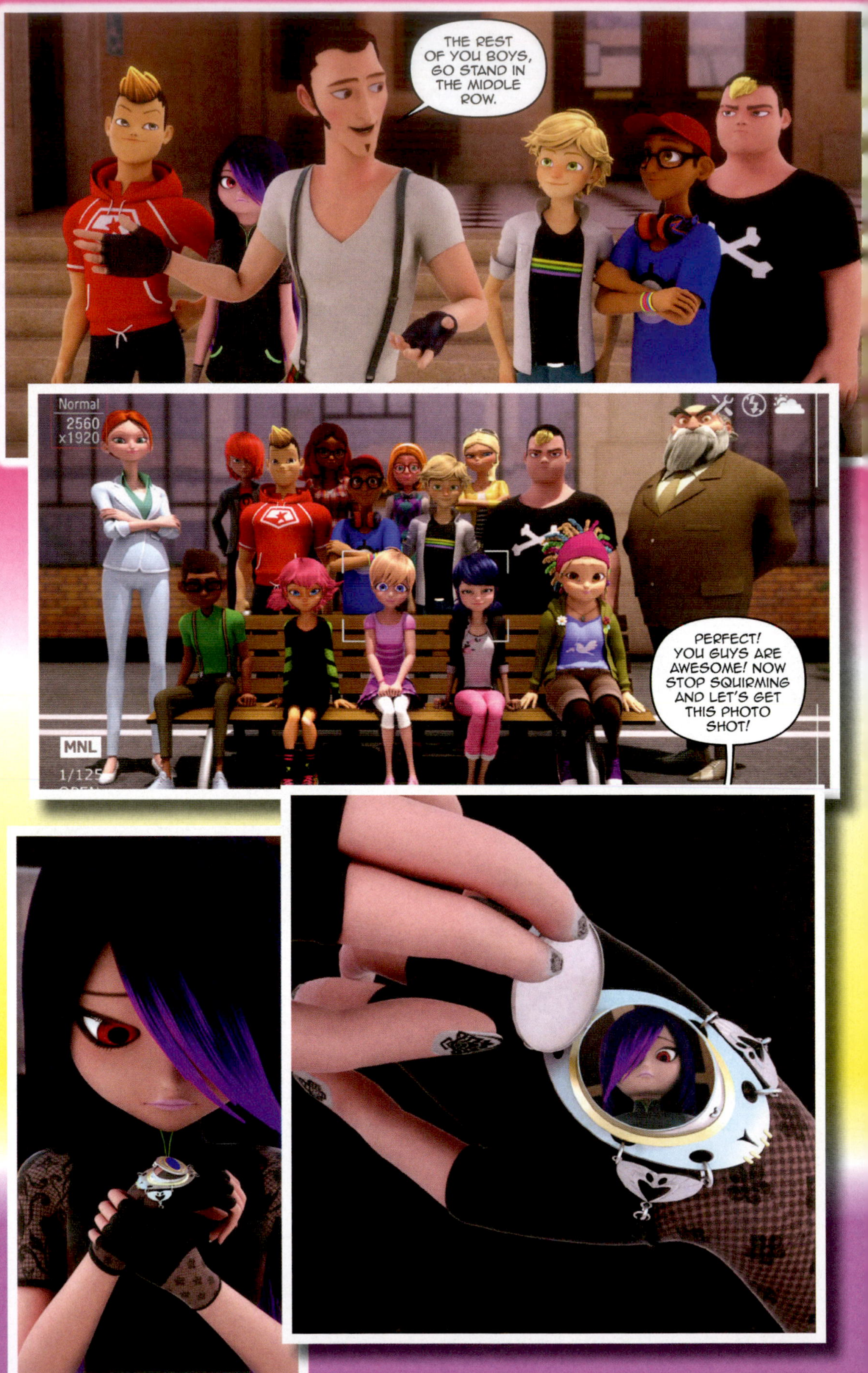
THE REST OF YOU BOYS, GO STAND IN THE MIDDLE ROW.
Normal
2560
x1920
MNL
PERFECT! YOU GUYS ARE AWESOME! NOW STOP SQUIRMING AND LET'S GET THIS PHOTO SHOT!

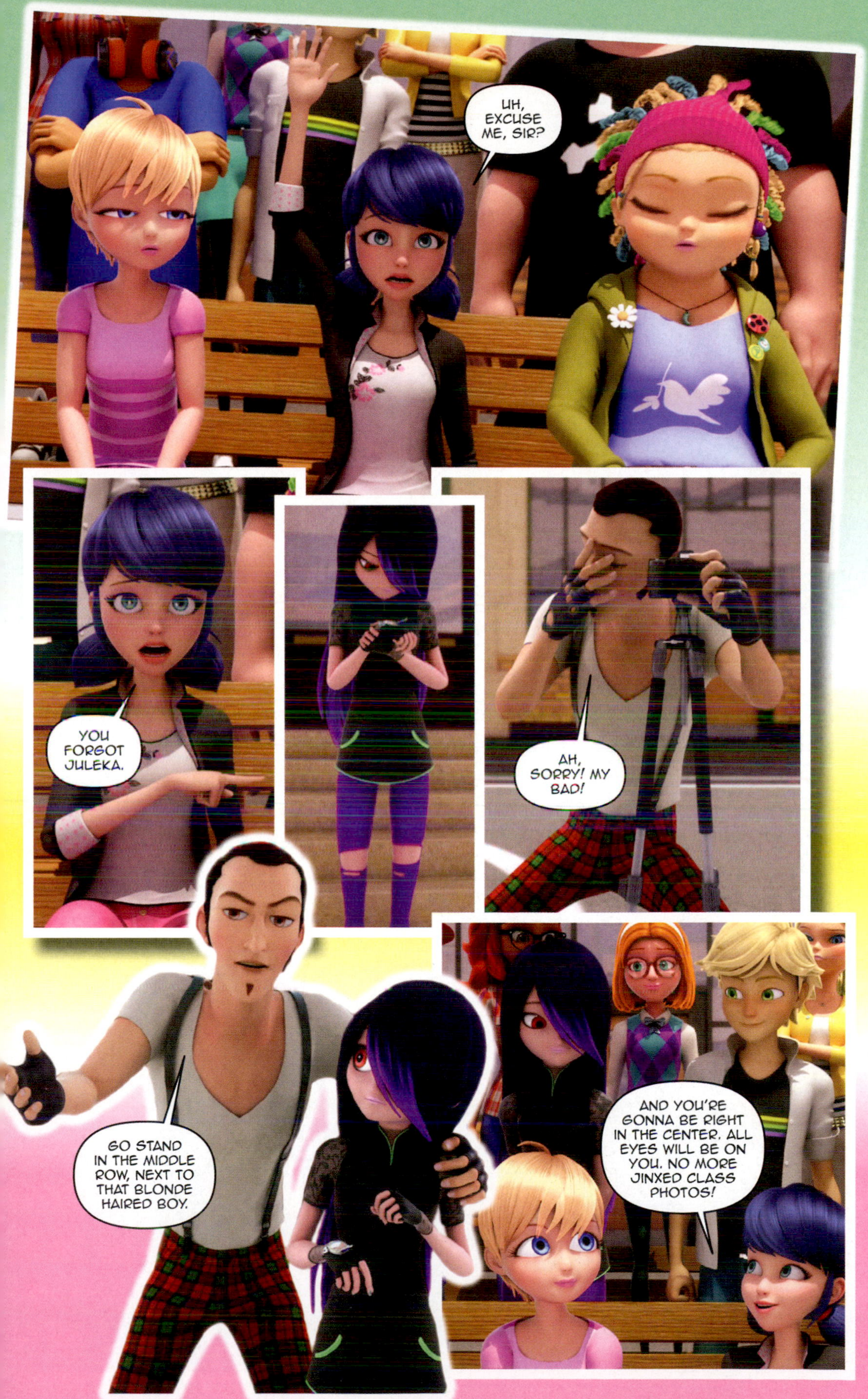
UH, EXCUSE ME, SIR?
YOU FORGOT JULEKA.
AH, SORRY! MY BAD!
GO STAND IN THE MIDDLE ROW, NEXT TO THAT BLONDE HAIRED BOY.
AND YOU'RE GONNA BE RIGHT IN THE CENTER. ALL EYES WILL BE ON YOU. NO MORE JINXED CLASS PHOTOS!

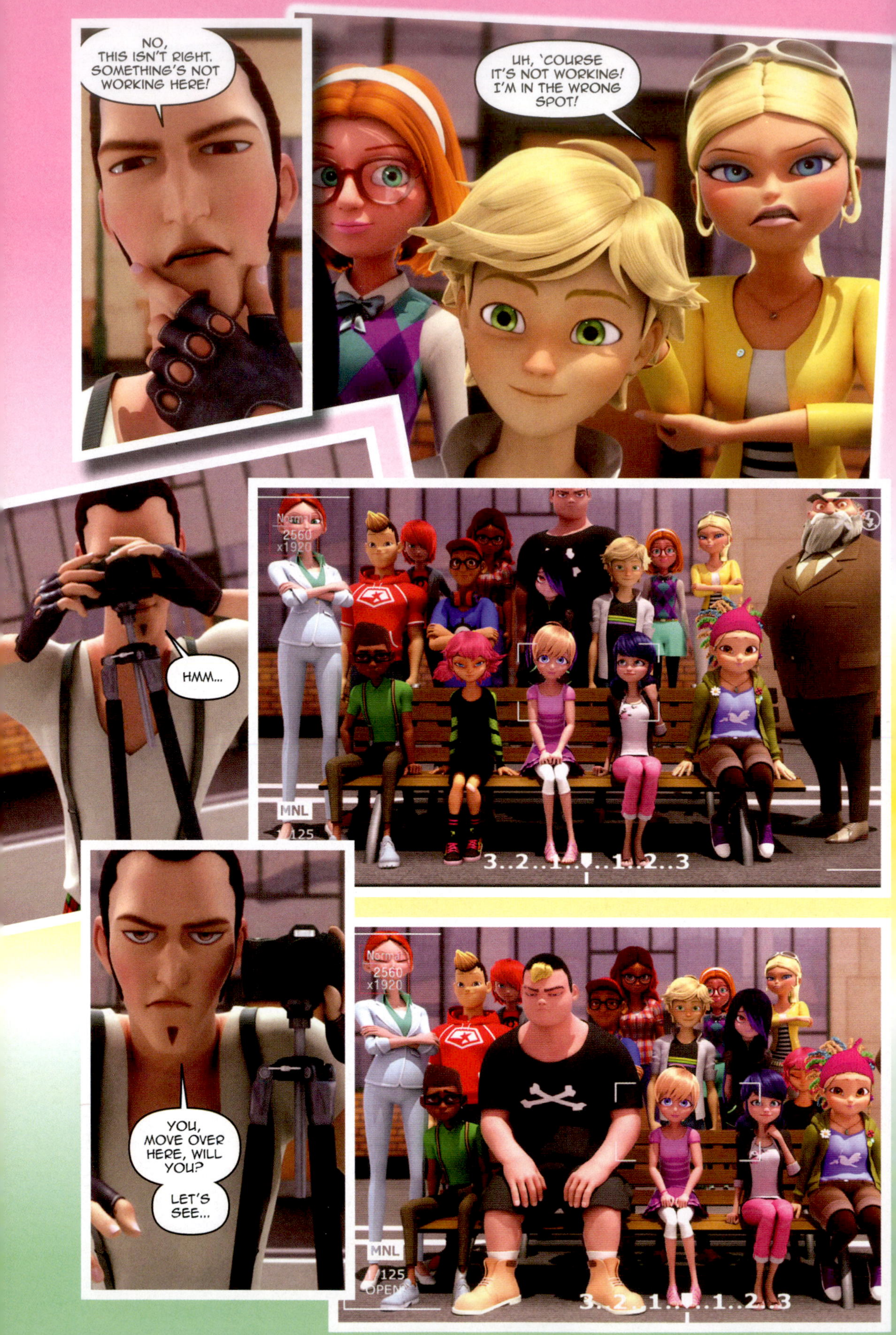
NO, THIS ISN'T RIGHT. SOMETHING'S NOT WORKING HERE!
UH, 'COURSE IT'S NOT WORKING! I'M IN THE WRONG SPOT!
HMM...
YOU, MOVE OVER HERE, WILL YOU?
LET'S SEE...

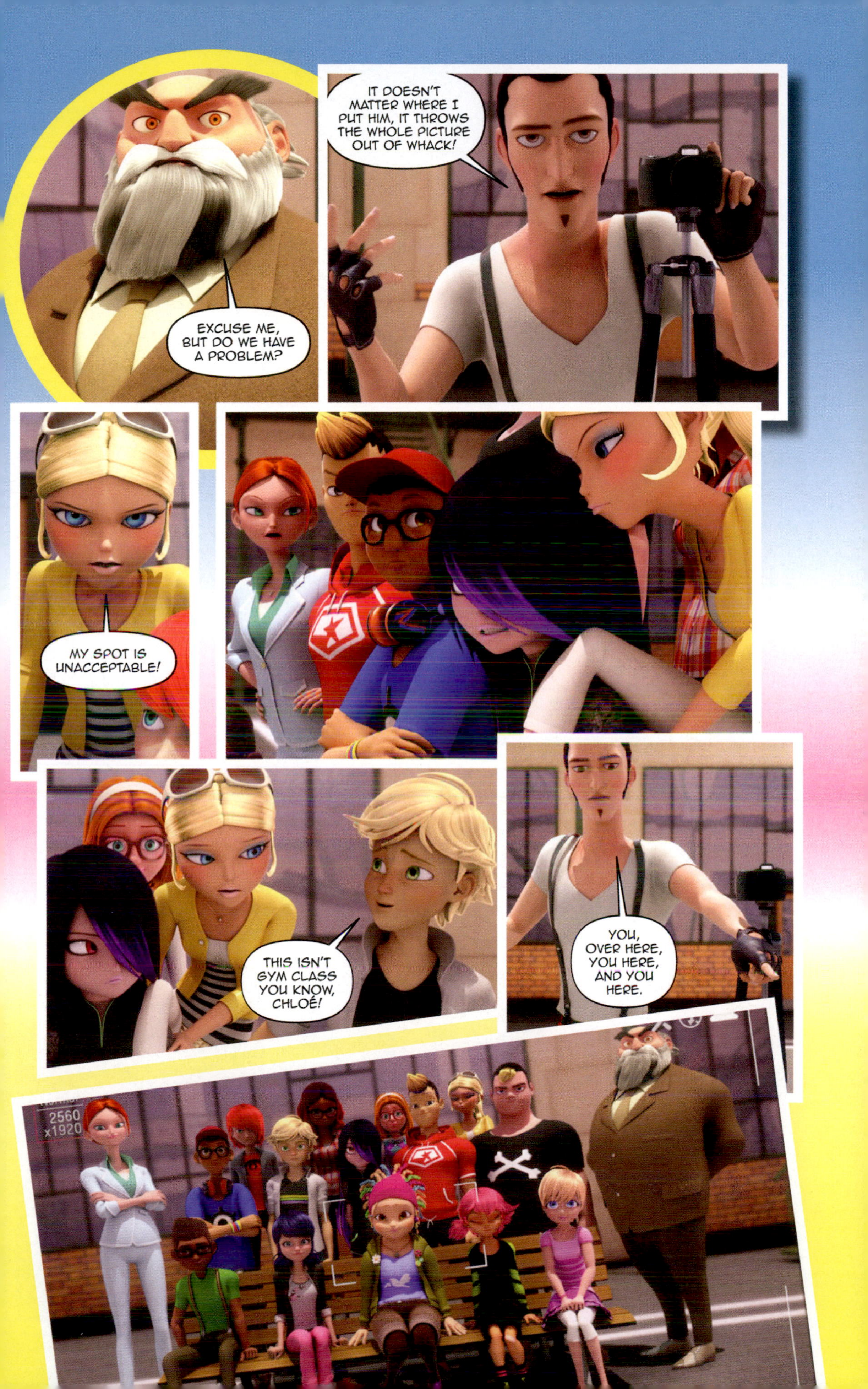
EXCUSE ME, BUT DO WE HAVE A PROBLEM?
IT DOESN'T MATTER WHERE I PUT HIM, IT THROWS THE WHOLE PICTURE OUT OF WHACK!
MY SPOT IS UNACCEPTABLE!
THIS ISN'T GYM CLASS YOU KNOW, CHLOÉ!
YOU, OVER HERE, YOU HERE, AND YOU HERE.
2560 x1920

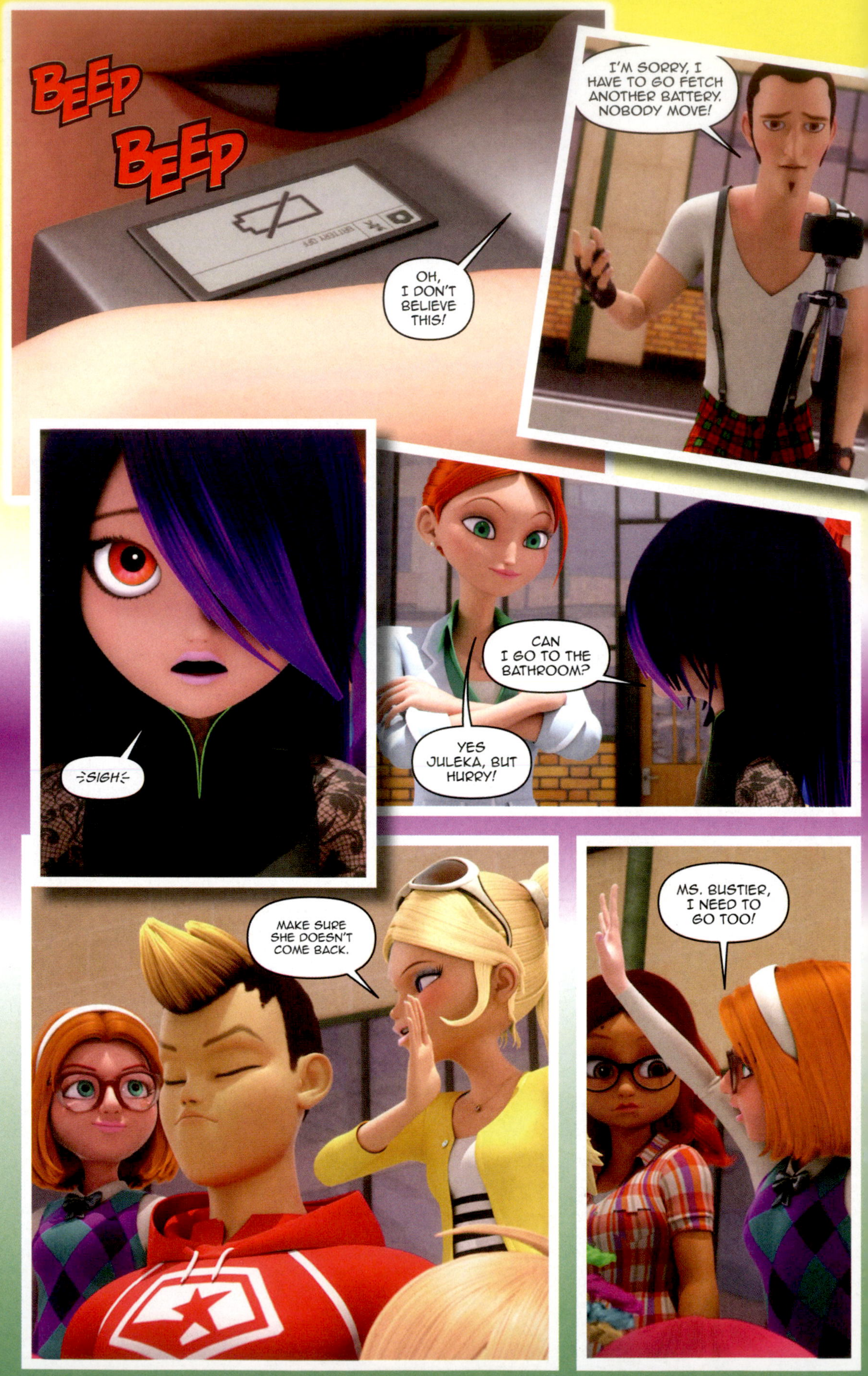
BEEP BEEP
BATTERY OFF
OH, I DON'T BELIEVE THIS!
I'M SORRY, I HAVE TO GO FETCH ANOTHER BATTERY. NOBODY MOVE!
SIGH
CAN I GO TO THE BATHROOM?
YES JULEKA, BUT HURRY!
MAKE SURE SHE DOESN'T COME BACK.
MS. BUSTIER, I NEED TO GO TOO!

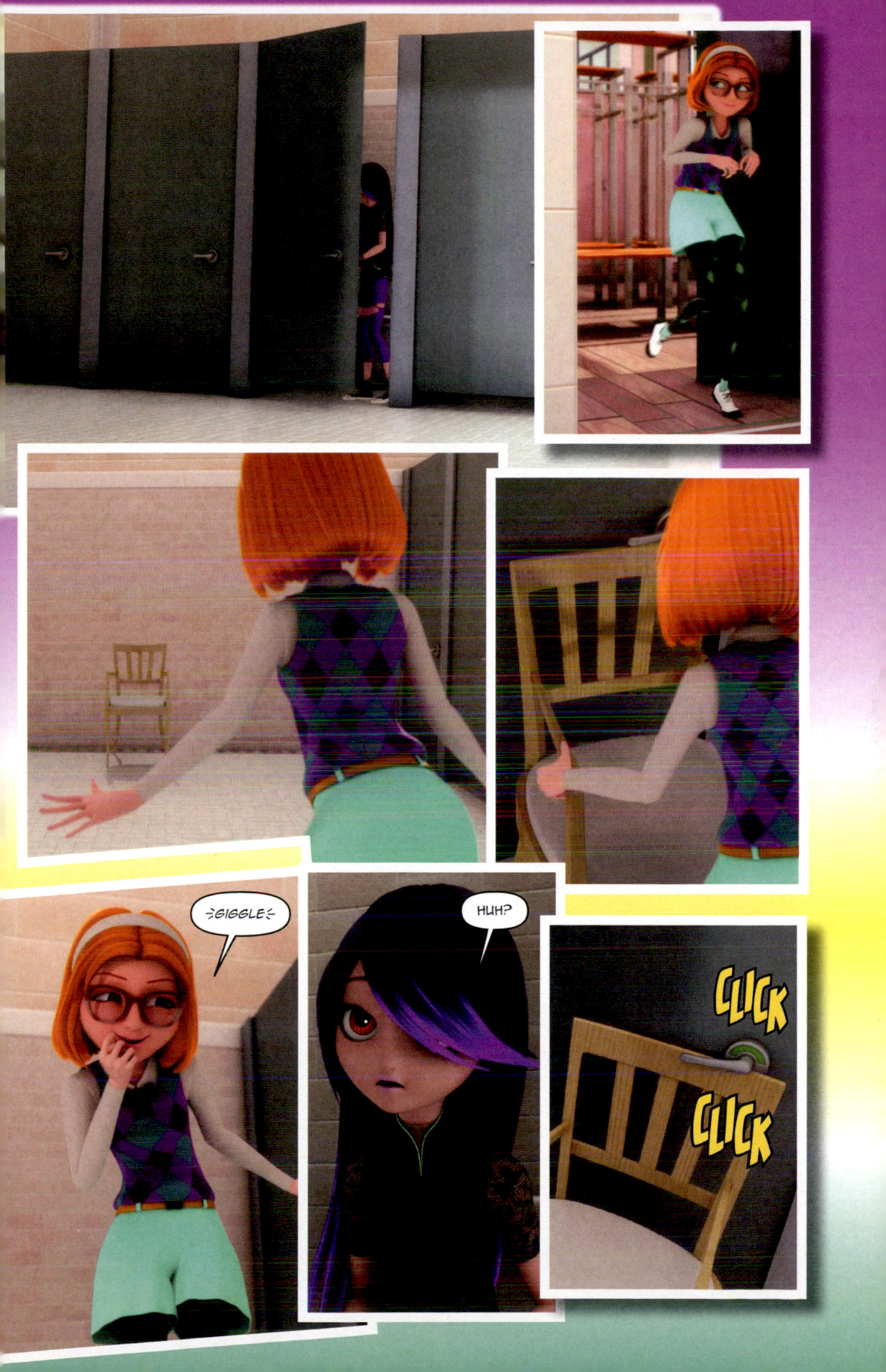

GIGGLE
HUH?
CLICK
CLICK

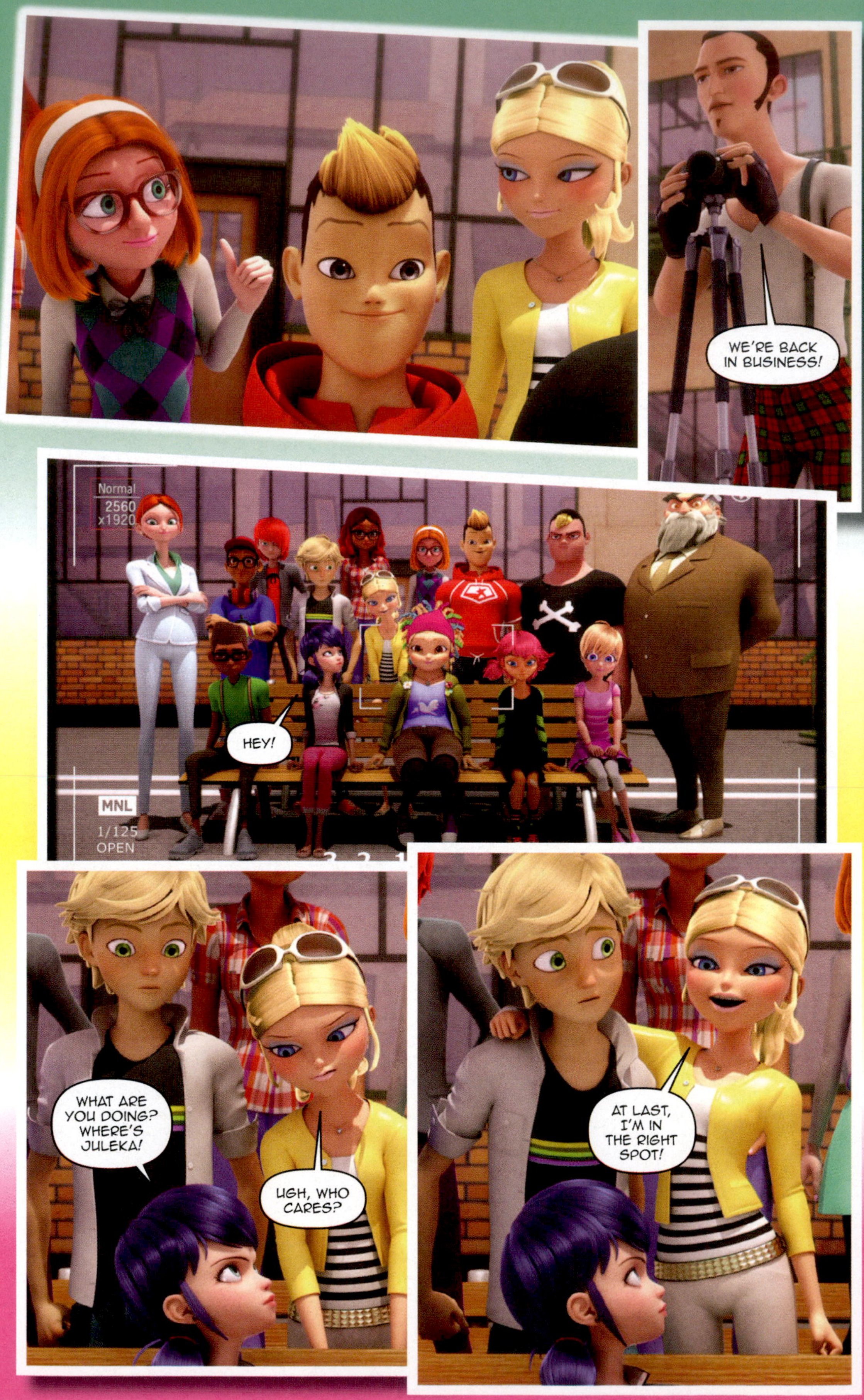
WE'RE BACK IN BUSINESS!
Normal
2560 x1920
HEY!
MNL
1/125
OPEN
WHAT ARE YOU DOING? WHERE'S JULEKA?
UGH, WHO CARES?
AT LAST, I'M IN THE RIGHT SPOT!

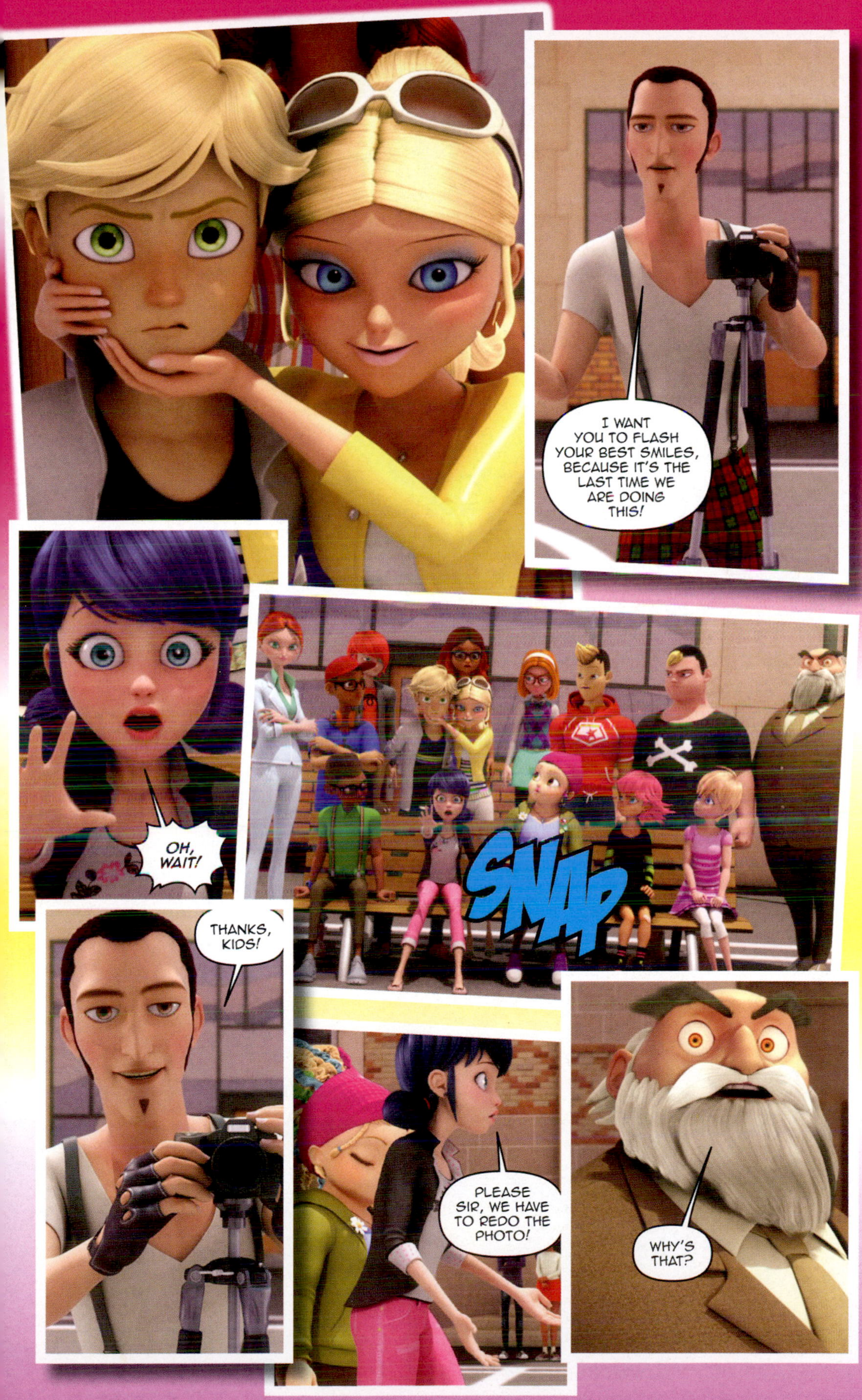
I WANT YOU TO FLASH YOUR BEST SMILES, BECAUSE IT'S THE LAST TIME WE ARE DOING THIS!
OH, WAIT!
SNAP
THANKS, KIDS!
PLEASE SIR, WE HAVE TO REDO THE PHOTO!
WHY'S THAT?

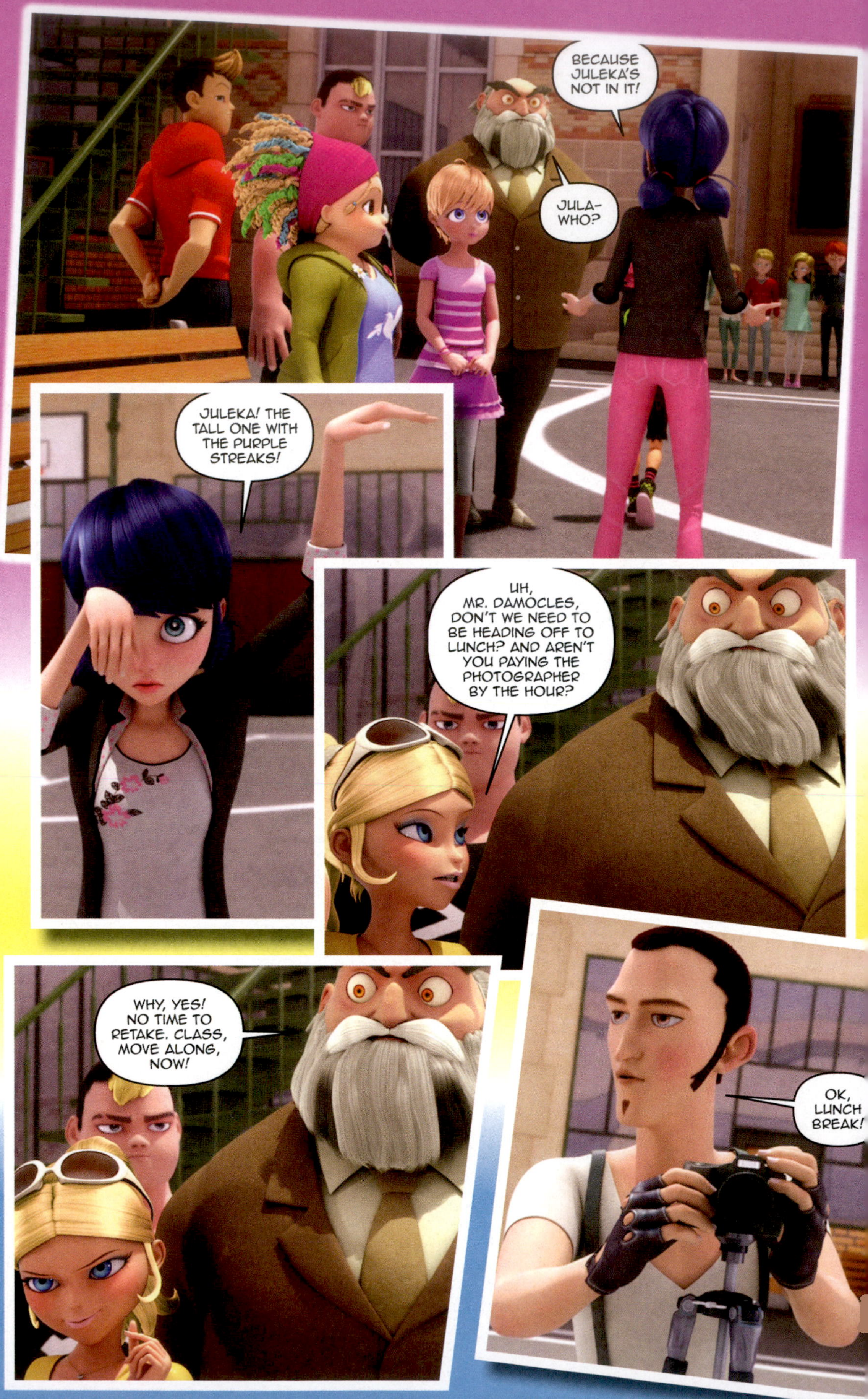

BECAUSE JULEKA'S NOT IN IT!
JULA-WHO?
JULEKA! THE TALL ONE WITH THE PURPLE STREAKS!
UH, MR. DAMOCLES, DON'T WE NEED TO BE HEADING OFF TO LUNCH? AND AREN'T YOU PAYING THE PHOTOGRAPHER BY THE HOUR?
WHY, YES! NO TIME TO RETAKE. CLASS, MOVE ALONG, NOW!
OK, LUNCH BREAK!

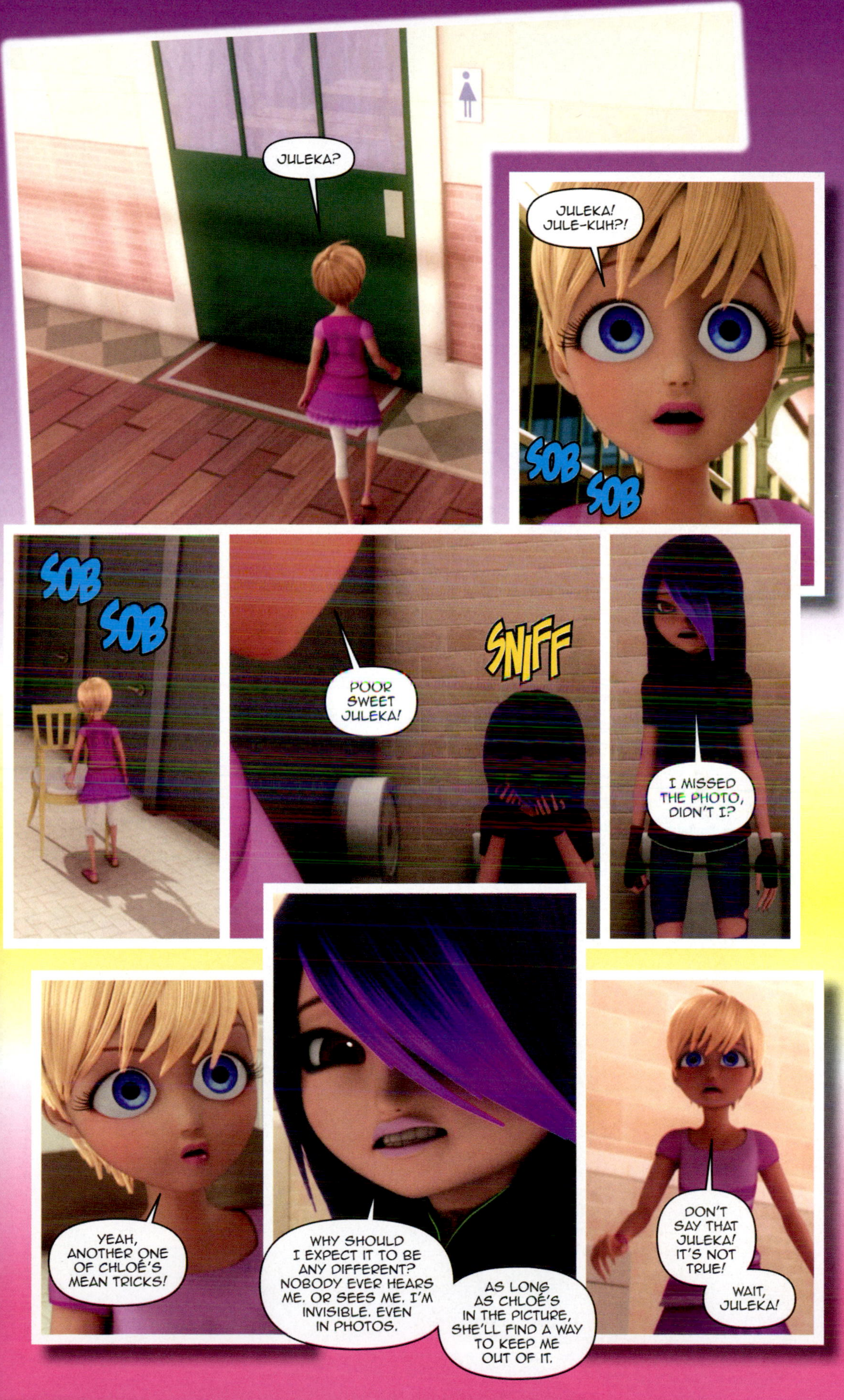
JULEKA?
JULEKA! JULE-KUH?!
SOB
SOB
SOB
SOB
POOR SWEET JULEKA!
SNIFF
I MISSED THE PHOTO, DIDN'T I?
YEAH, ANOTHER ONE OF CHLOÉ'S MEAN TRICKS!
WHY SHOULD I EXPECT IT TO BE ANY DIFFERENT? NOBODY EVER HEARS ME. OR SEES ME. I'M INVISIBLE. EVEN IN PHOTOS.
AS LONG AS CHLOÉ'S IN THE PICTURE, SHE'LL FIND A WAY TO KEEP ME OUT OF IT.
DON'T SAY THAT JULEKA! IT'S NOT TRUE!
WAIT, JULEKA!

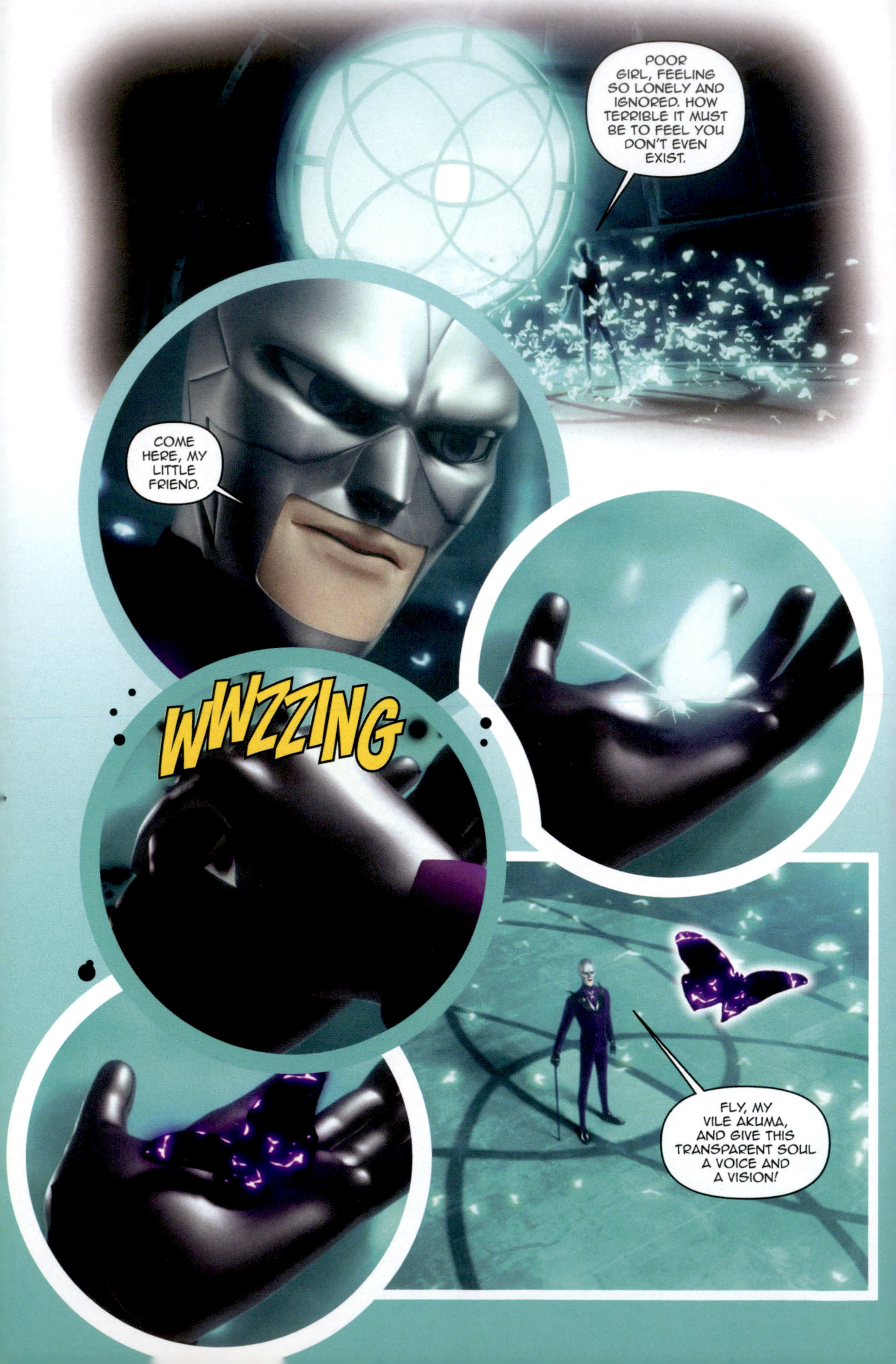
POOR GIRL, FEELING SO LONELY AND IGNORED. HOW TERRIBLE IT MUST BE TO FEEL YOU DON'T EVEN EXIST.
COME HERE, MY LITTLE FRIEND.
WWZZING
FLY, MY VILE AKUMA, AND GIVE THIS TRANSPARENT SOUL A VOICE AND A VISION!

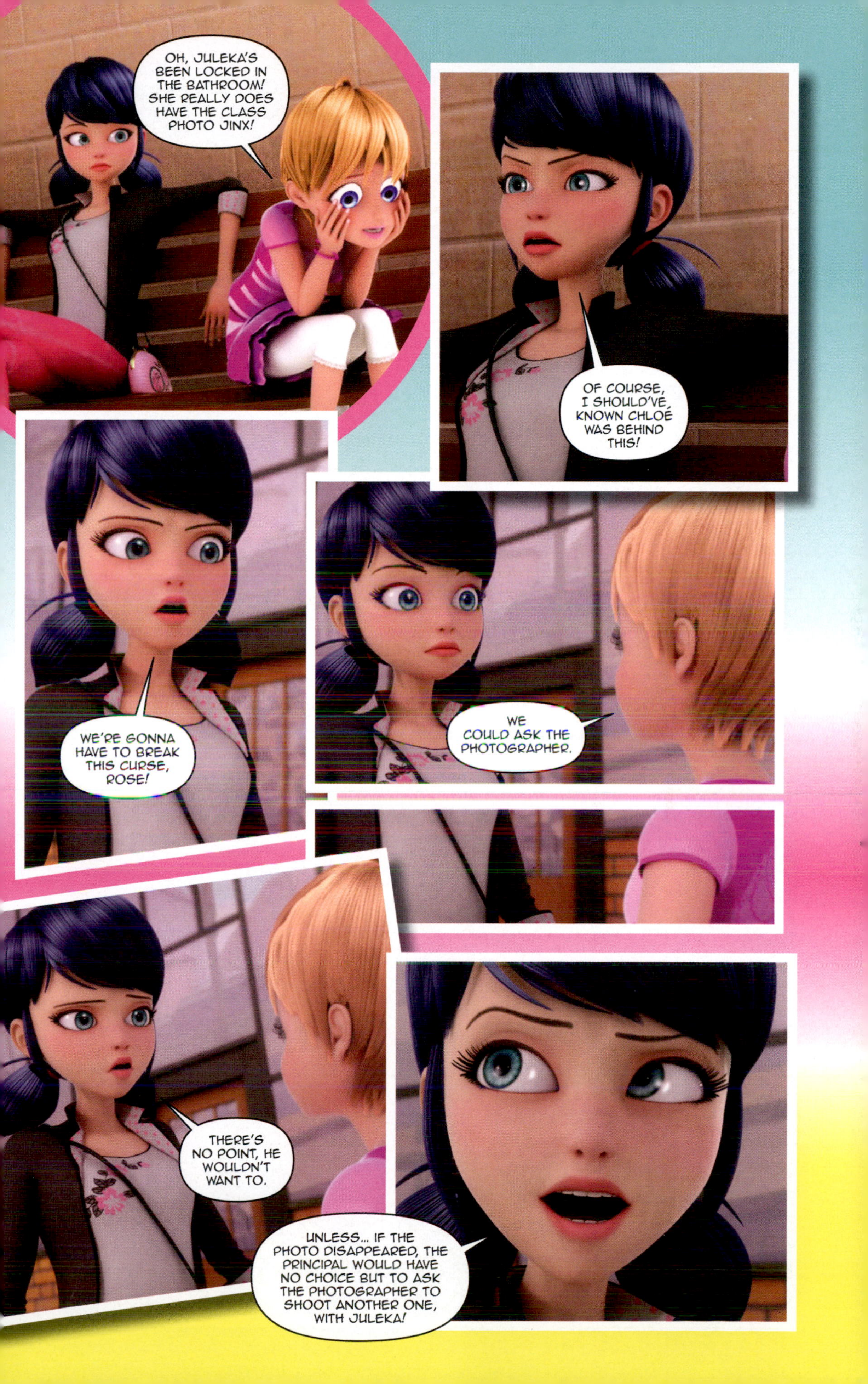
OH, JULEKA'S BEEN LOCKED IN THE BATHROOM! SHE REALLY DOES HAVE THE CLASS PHOTO JINX!
OF COURSE, I SHOULD'VE KNOWN CHLOÉ WAS BEHIND THIS!
WE'RE GONNA HAVE TO BREAK THIS CURSE, ROSE!
WE COULD ASK THE PHOTOGRAPHER.
THERE'S NO POINT, HE WOULDN'T WANT TO.
UNLESS... IF THE PHOTO DISAPPEARED, THE PRINCIPAL WOULD HAVE NO CHOICE BUT TO ASK THE PHOTOGRAPHER TO SHOOT ANOTHER ONE, WITH JULEKA!

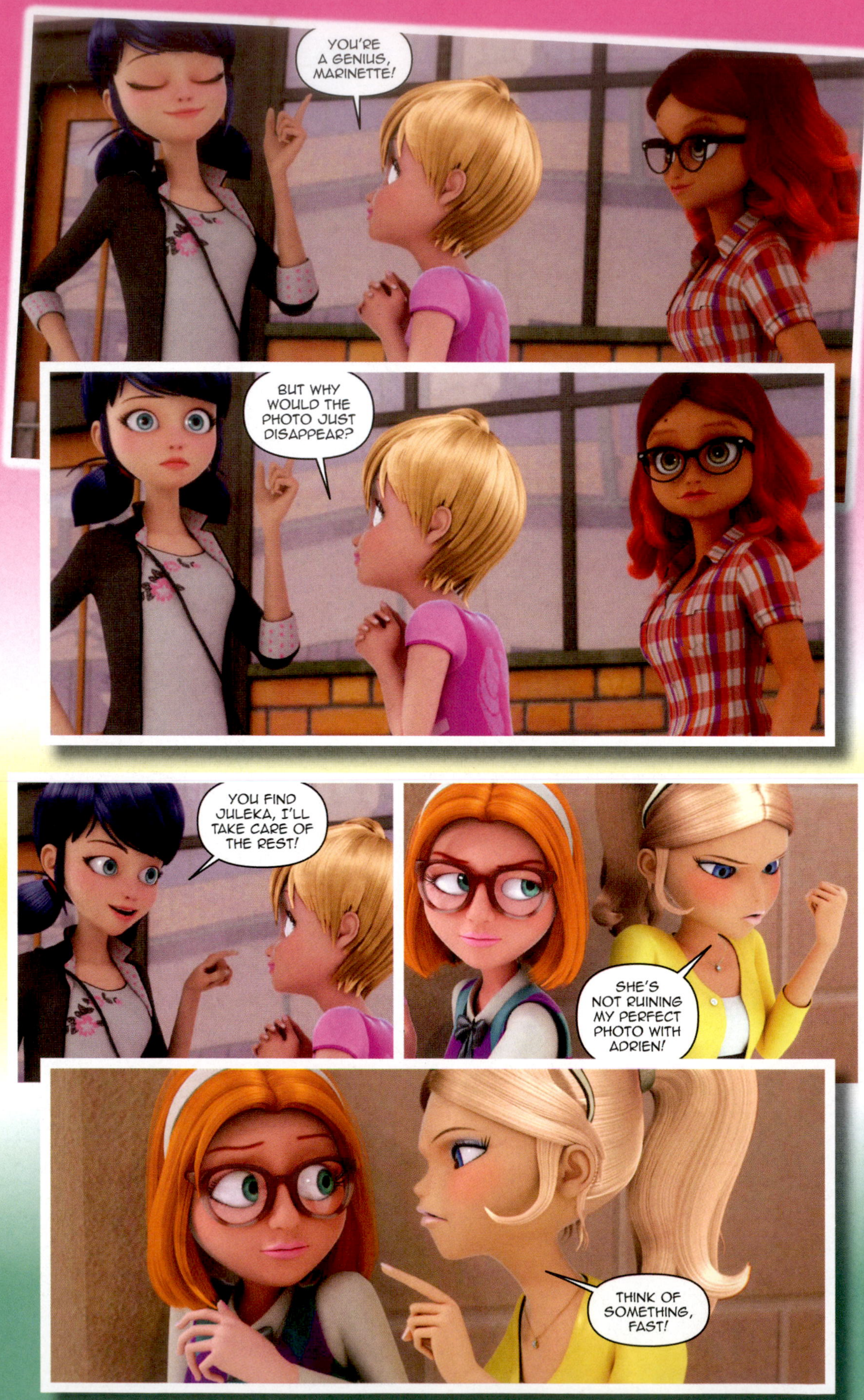
YOU'RE A GENIUS, MARINETTE!
BUT WHY WOULD THE PHOTO JUST DISAPPEAR?
YOU FIND JULEKA, I'LL TAKE CARE OF THE REST!
SHE'S NOT RUINING MY PERFECT PHOTO WITH ADRIEN!
THINK OF SOMETHING, FAST!

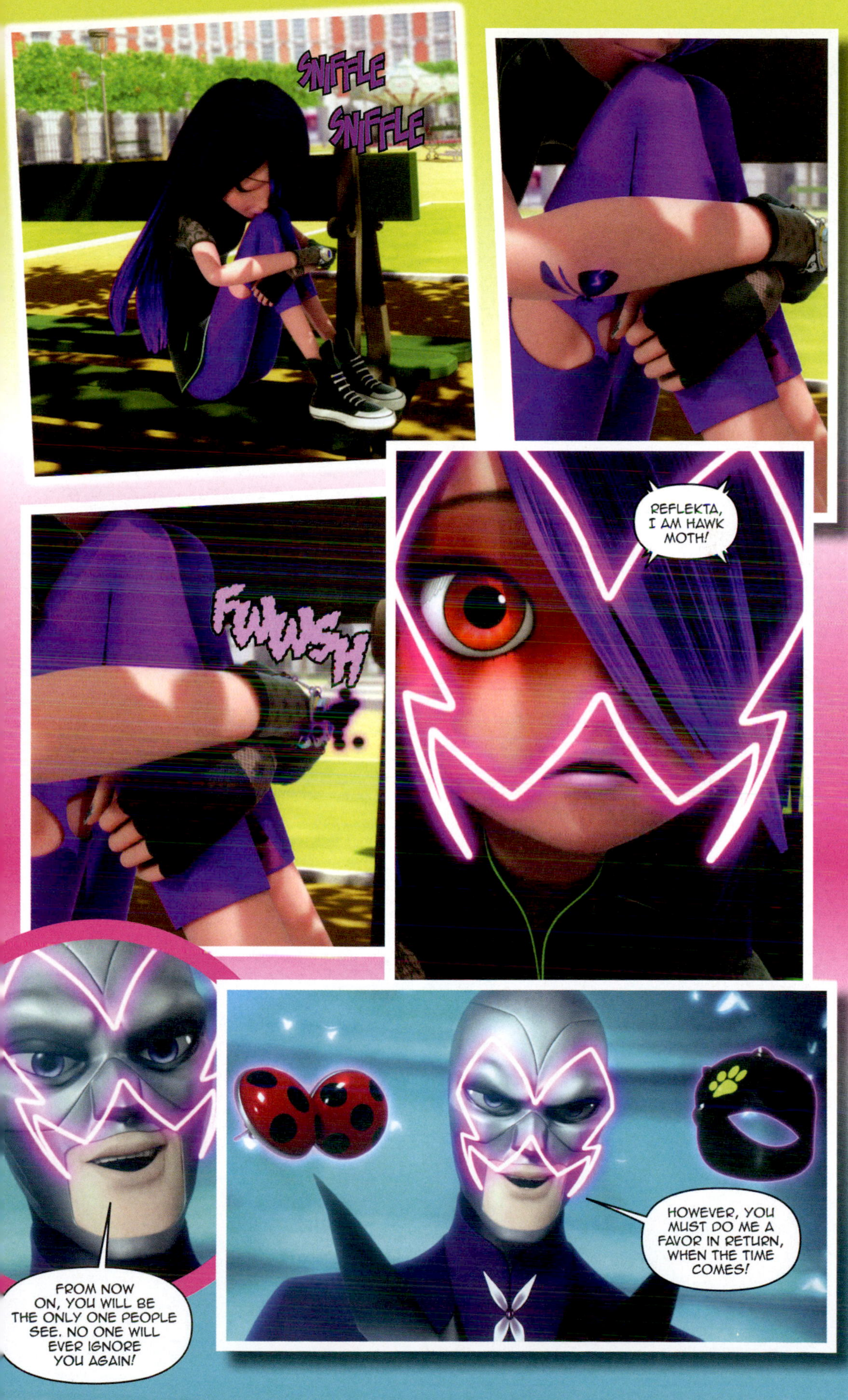
SNIFFLE
SNIFFLE
FWUSH
REFLEKTA, I AM HAWK MOTH!
FROM NOW ON, YOU WILL BE THE ONLY ONE PEOPLE SEE. NO ONE WILL EVER IGNORE YOU AGAIN!
HOWEVER, YOU MUST DO ME A FAVOR IN RETURN, WHEN THE TIME COMES!

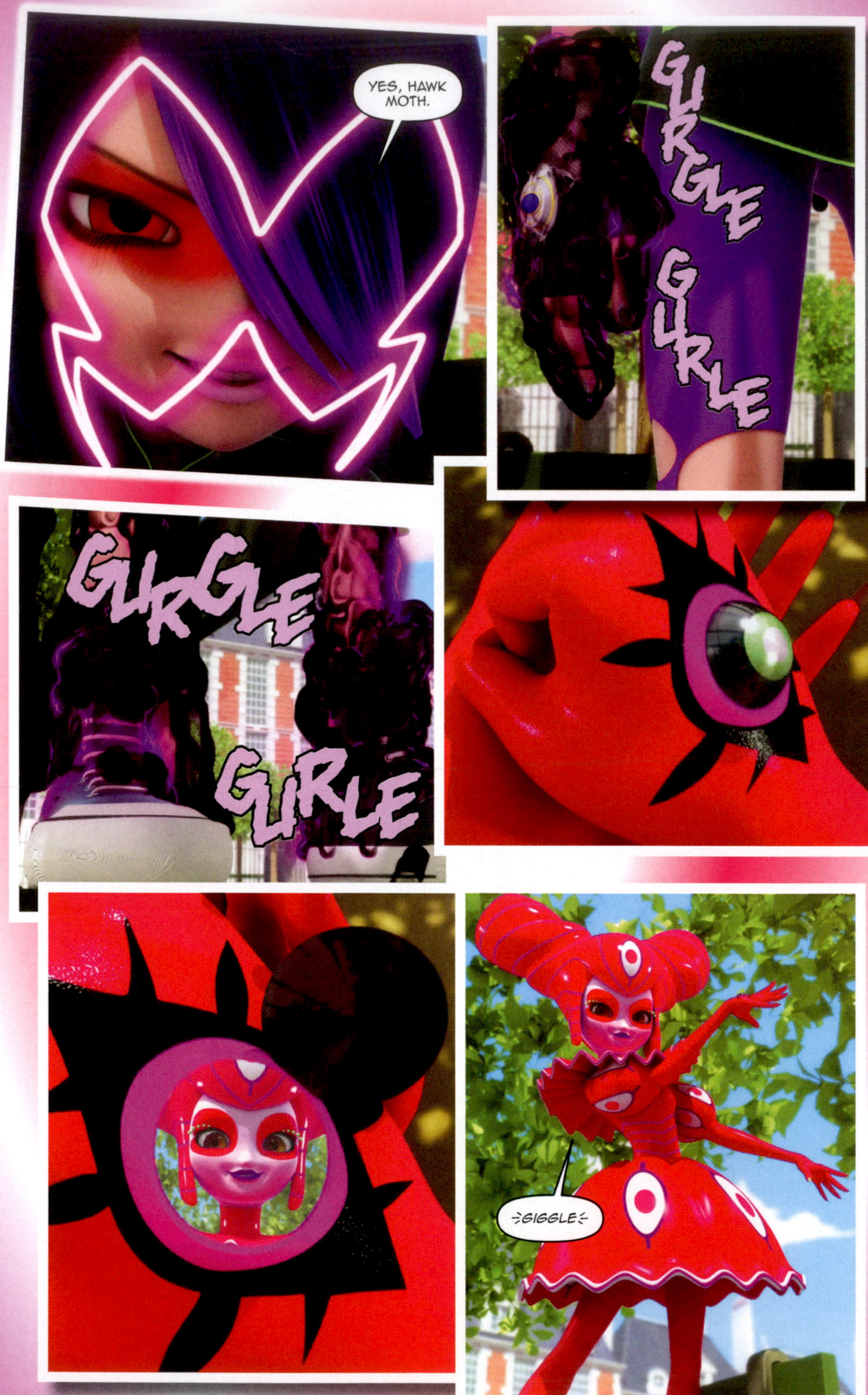
YES, HAWK MOTH.
GURGLE
GURLE
GURGLE
GURLE
GIGGLE

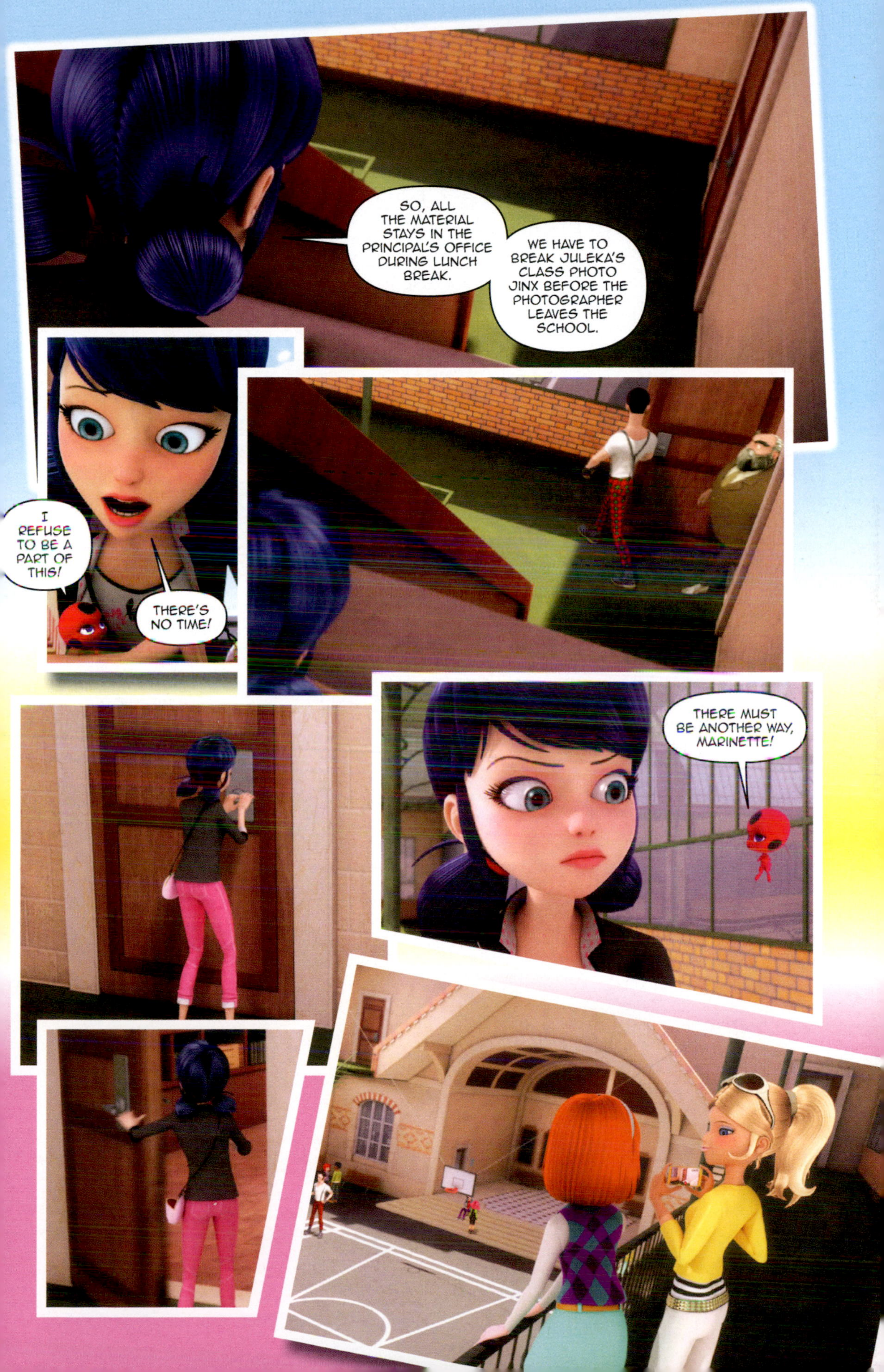
SO, ALL THE MATERIAL STAYS IN THE PRINCIPAL'S OFFICE DURING LUNCH BREAK.
WE HAVE TO BREAK JULEKA'S CLASS PHOTO JINX BEFORE THE PHOTOGRAPHER LEAVES THE SCHOOL.
I REFUSE TO BE A PART OF THIS!
THERE'S NO TIME!
THERE MUST BE ANOTHER WAY, MARINETTE!

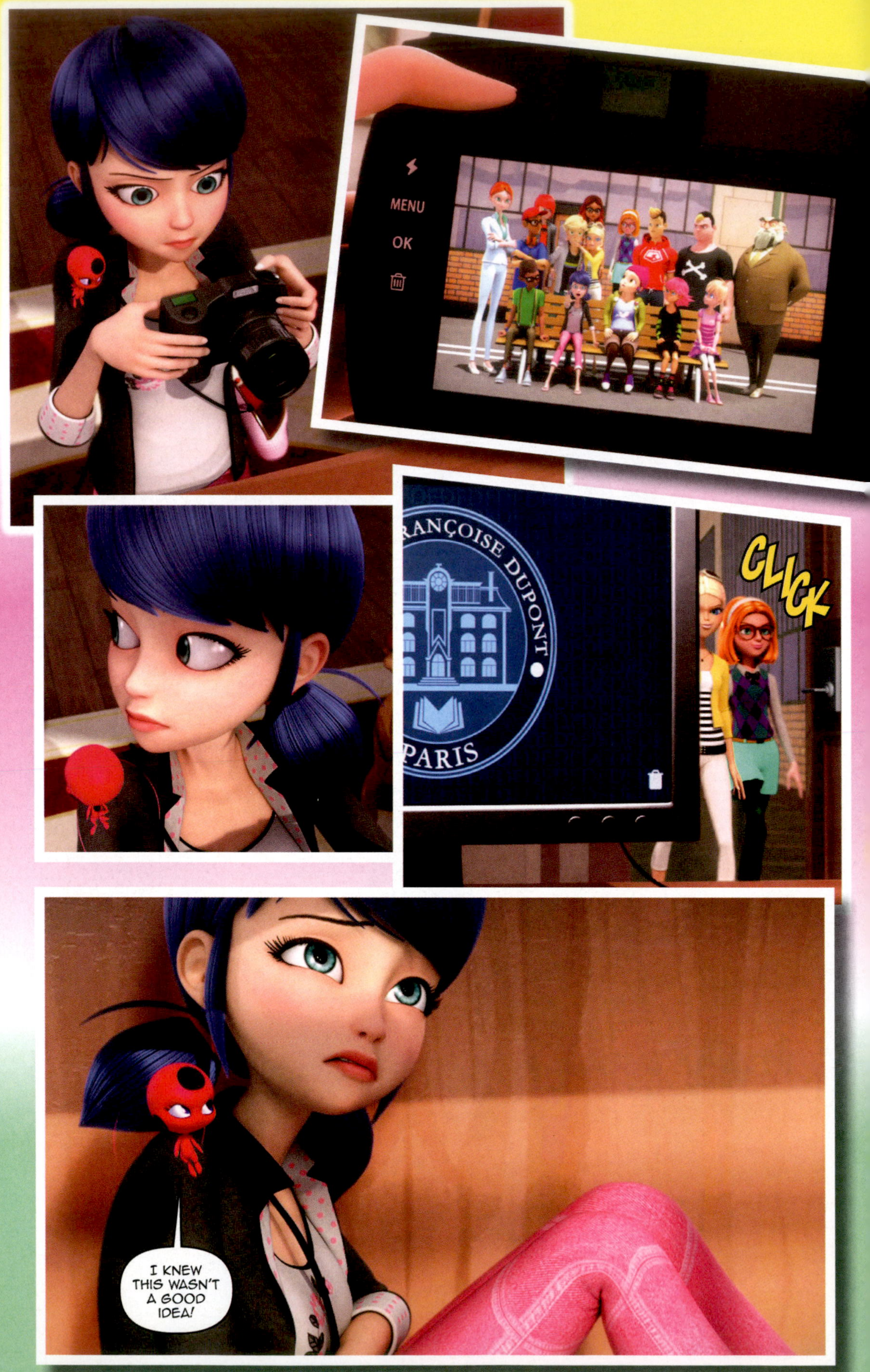
MENU
OK
FRANÇOISE DUPONT
PARIS
CLICK
I KNEW THIS WASN'T A GOOD IDEA!

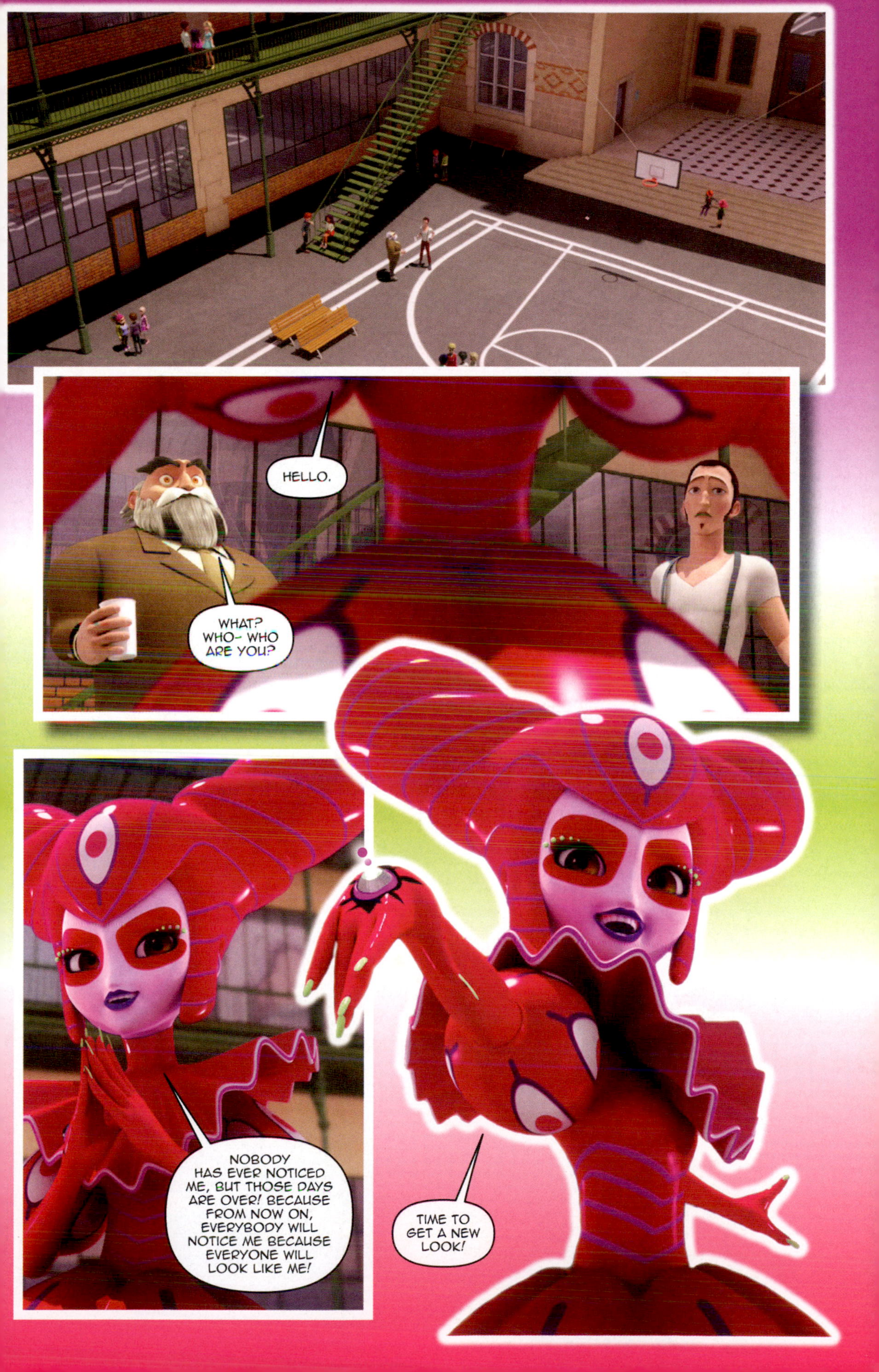
HELLO.
WHAT? WHO- WHO ARE YOU?
NOBODY HAS EVER NOTICED ME, BUT THOSE DAYS ARE OVER! BECAUSE FROM NOW ON, EVERYBODY WILL NOTICE ME BECAUSE EVERYONE WILL LOOK LIKE ME!
TIME TO GET A NEW LOOK!

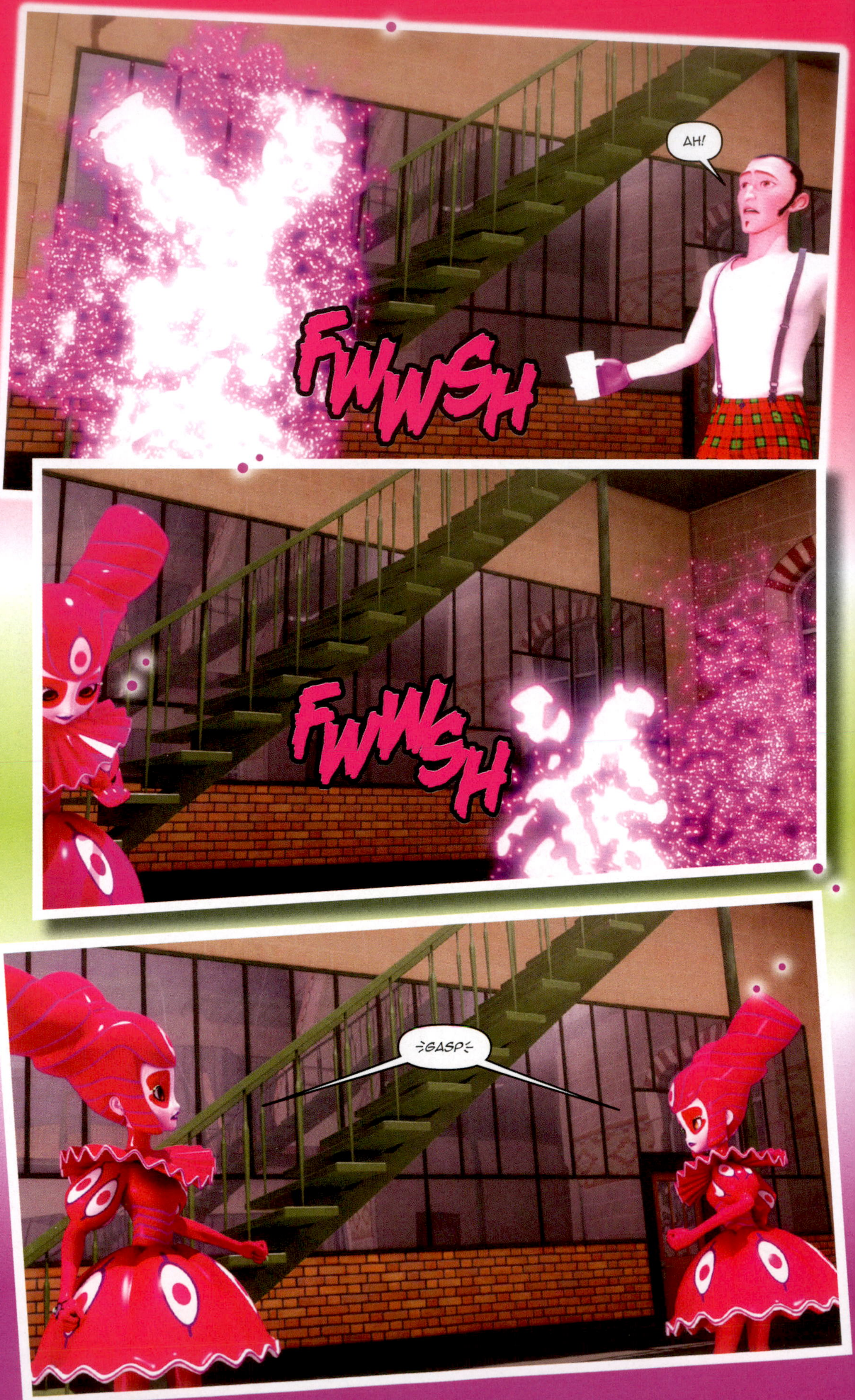
AH!
FWWSH
FWWSH
GASP

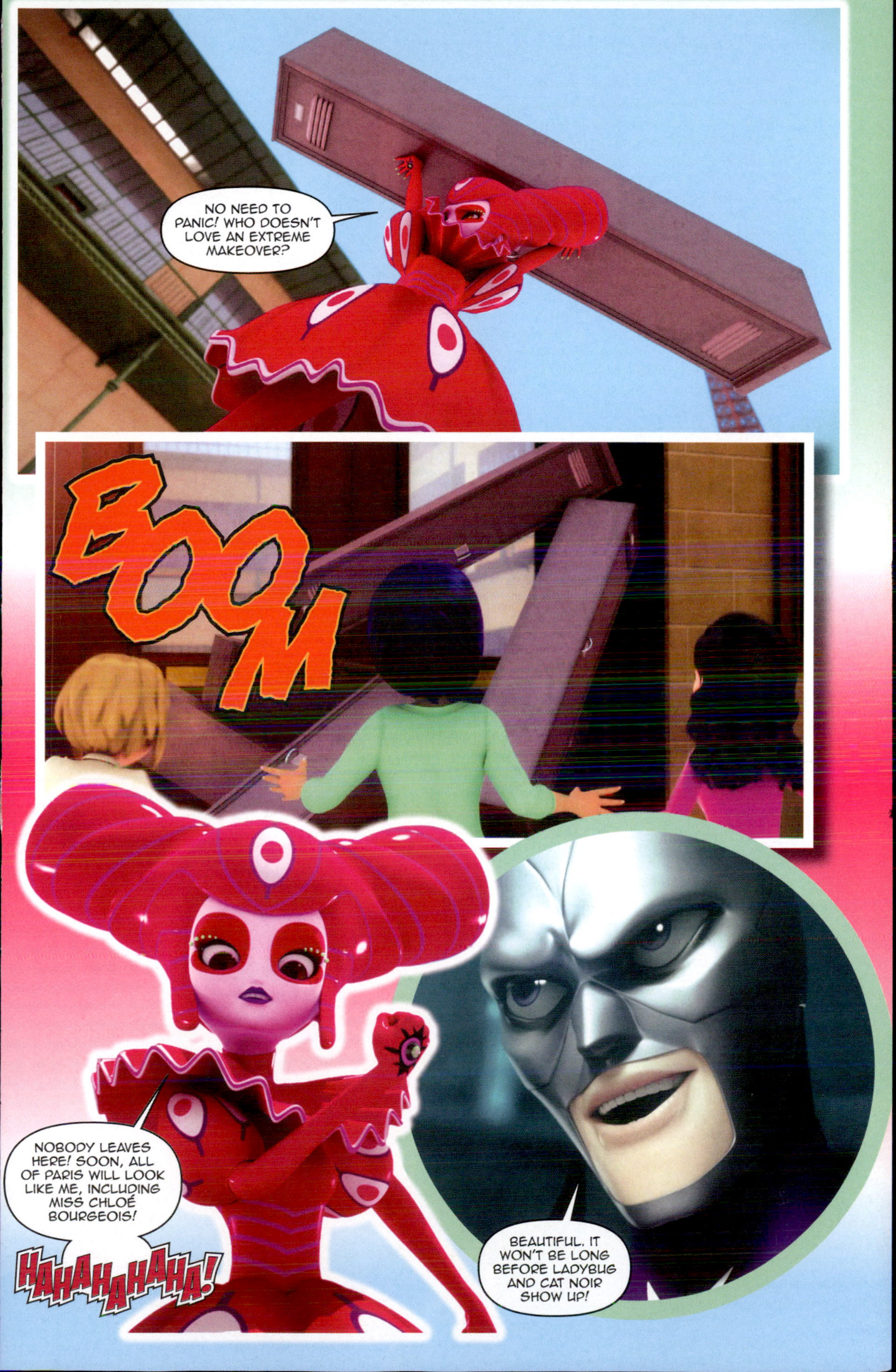
NO NEED TO PANIC! WHO DOESN'T LOVE AN EXTREME MAKEOVER?
BOOM
NOBODY LEAVES HERE! SOON, ALL OF PARIS WILL LOOK LIKE ME, INCLUDING MISS CHLOÉ BOURGEOIS!
HAHAHAHAHA!
BEAUTIFUL. IT WON'T BE LONG BEFORE LADYBUG AND CAT NOIR SHOW UP!

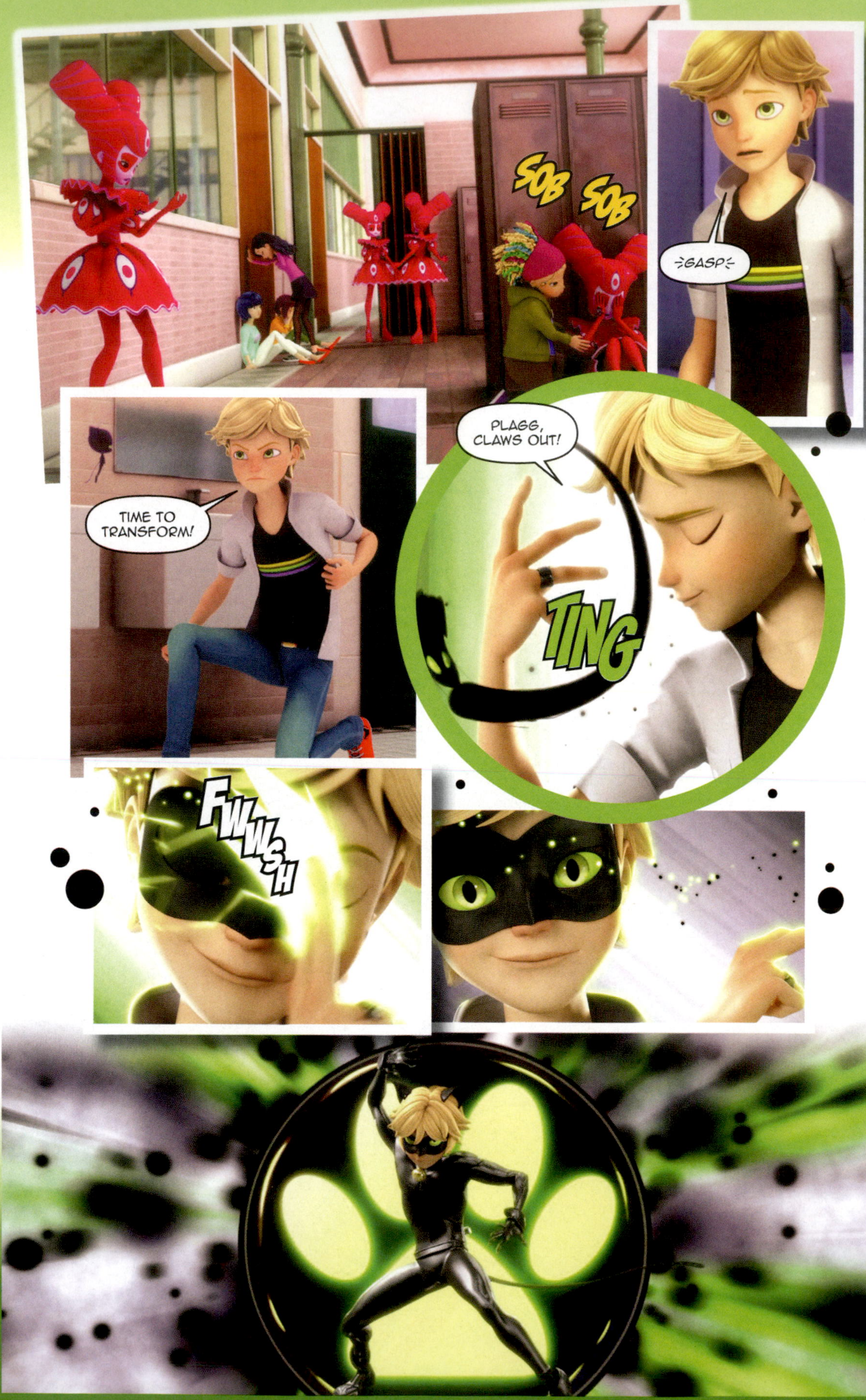
SOB
SOB
GASP
TIME TO TRANSFORM!
PLAGG, CLAWS OUT!
TING
FWWSH

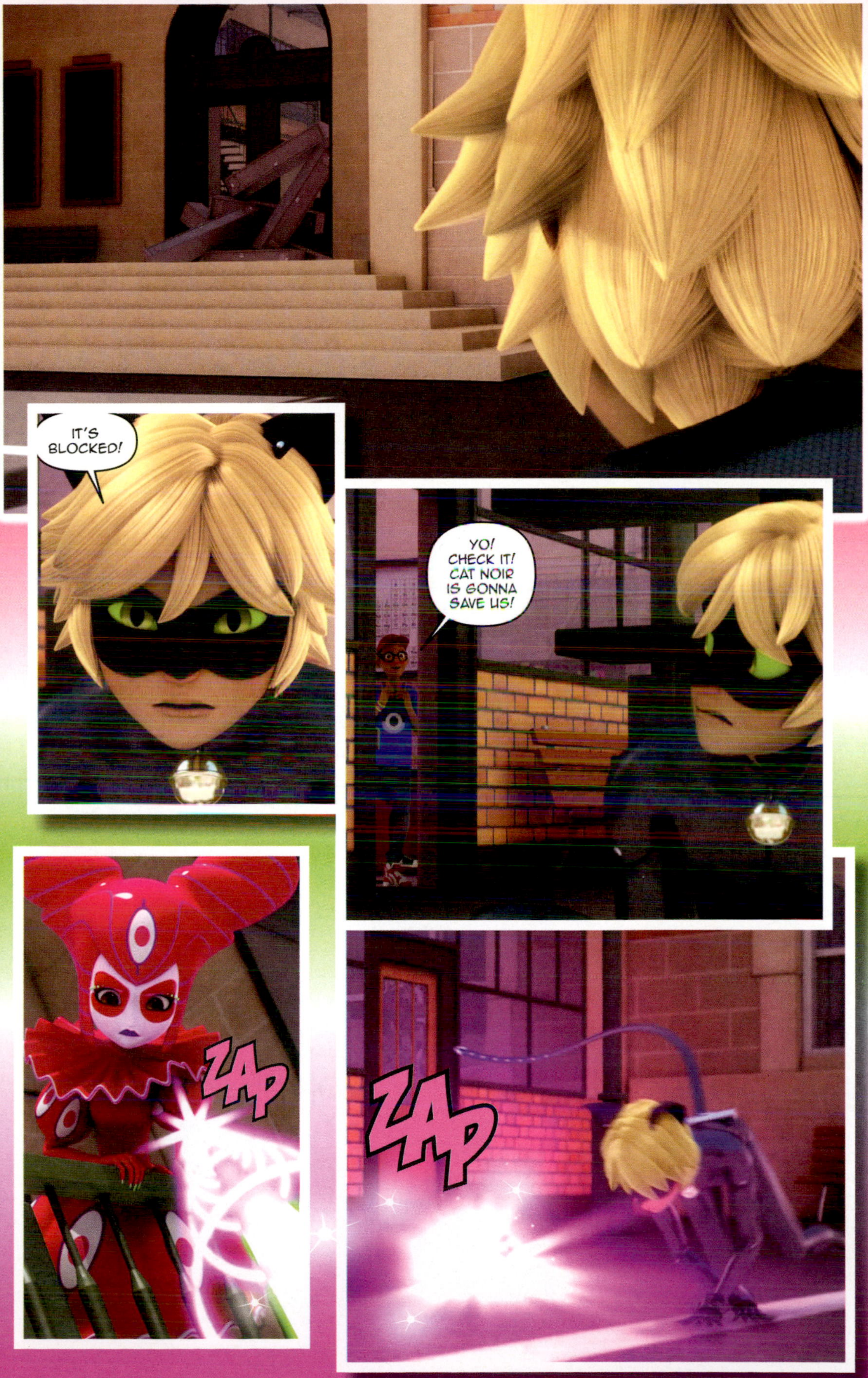
IT'S BLOCKED!
YO! CHECK IT! CAT NOIR IS GONNA SAVE US!
ZAP
ZAP

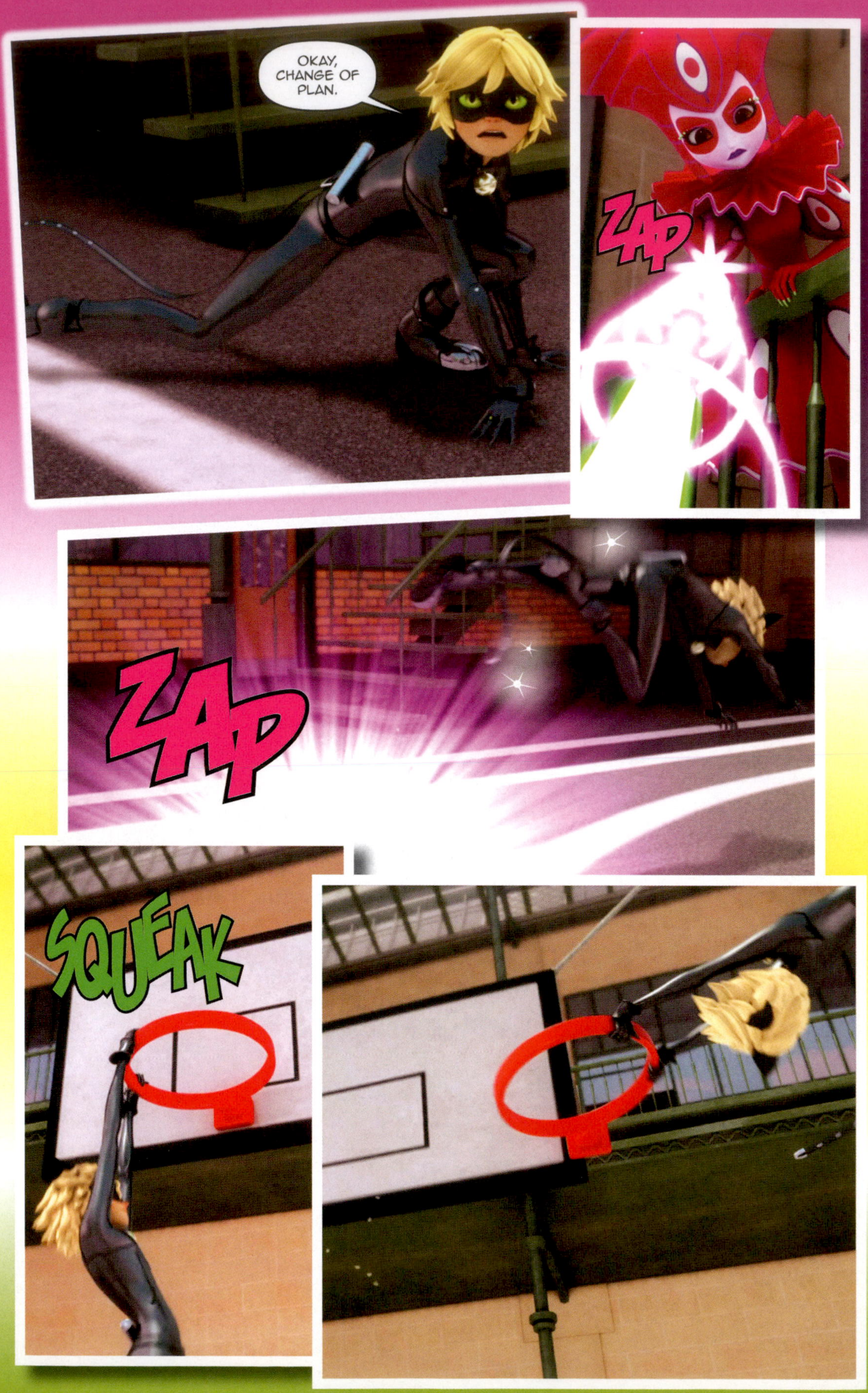
OKAY, CHANGE OF PLAN.
ZAP
ZAP
SQUEAK

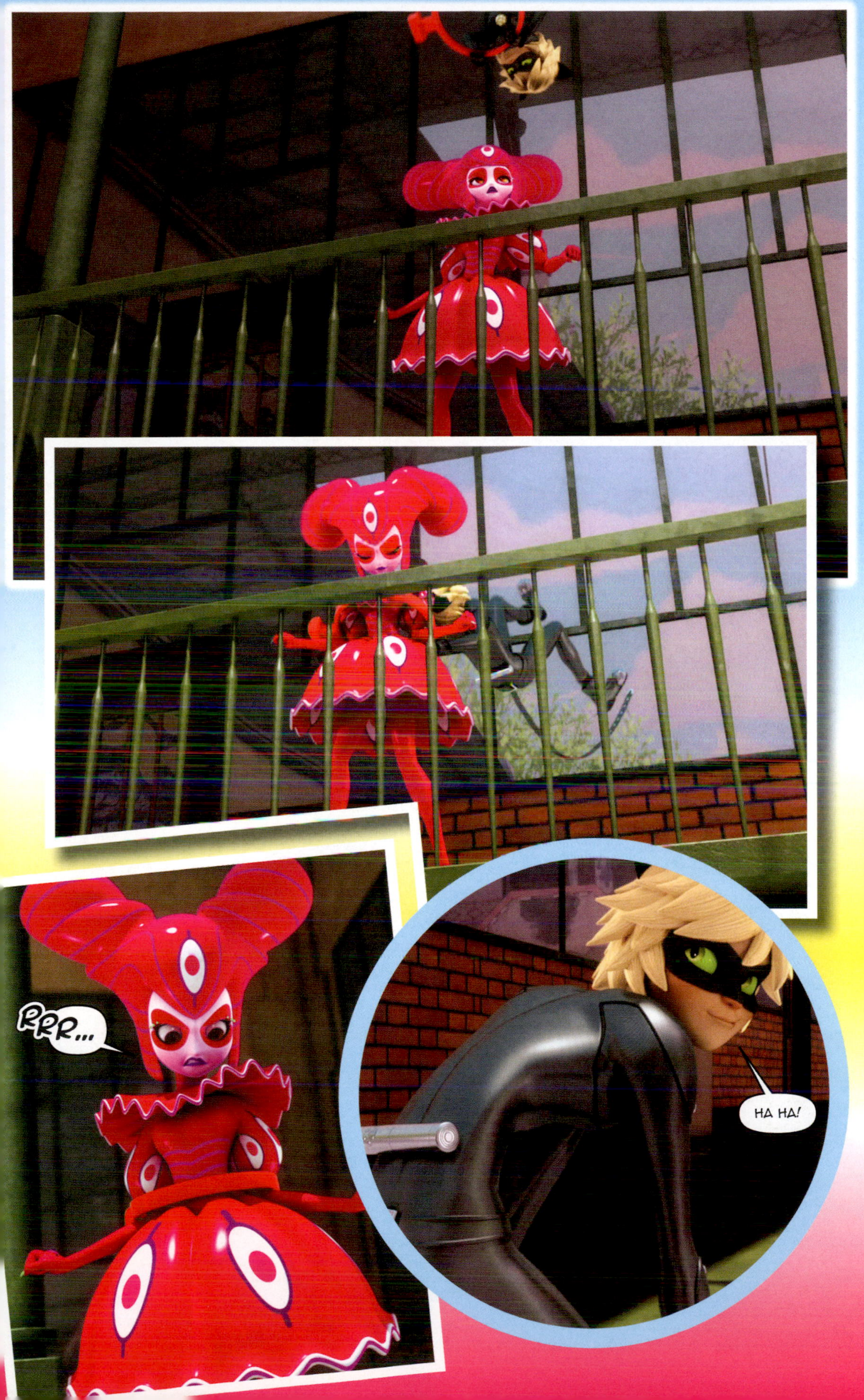
RRR...
HA HA!

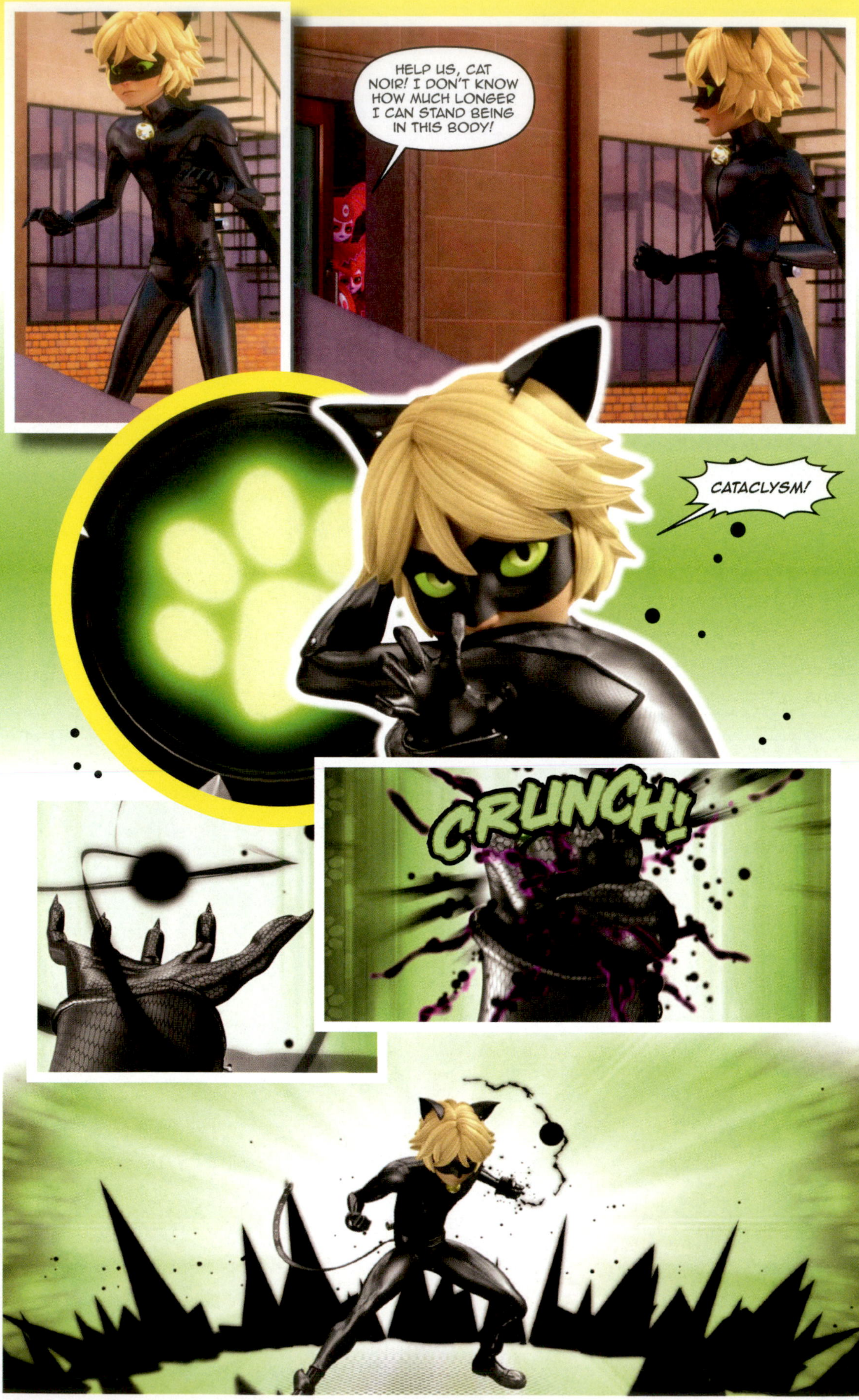
HELP US, CAT NOIR! I DON'T KNOW HOW MUCH LONGER I CAN STAND BEING IN THIS BODY!
CATACLYSM!
CRUNCH!

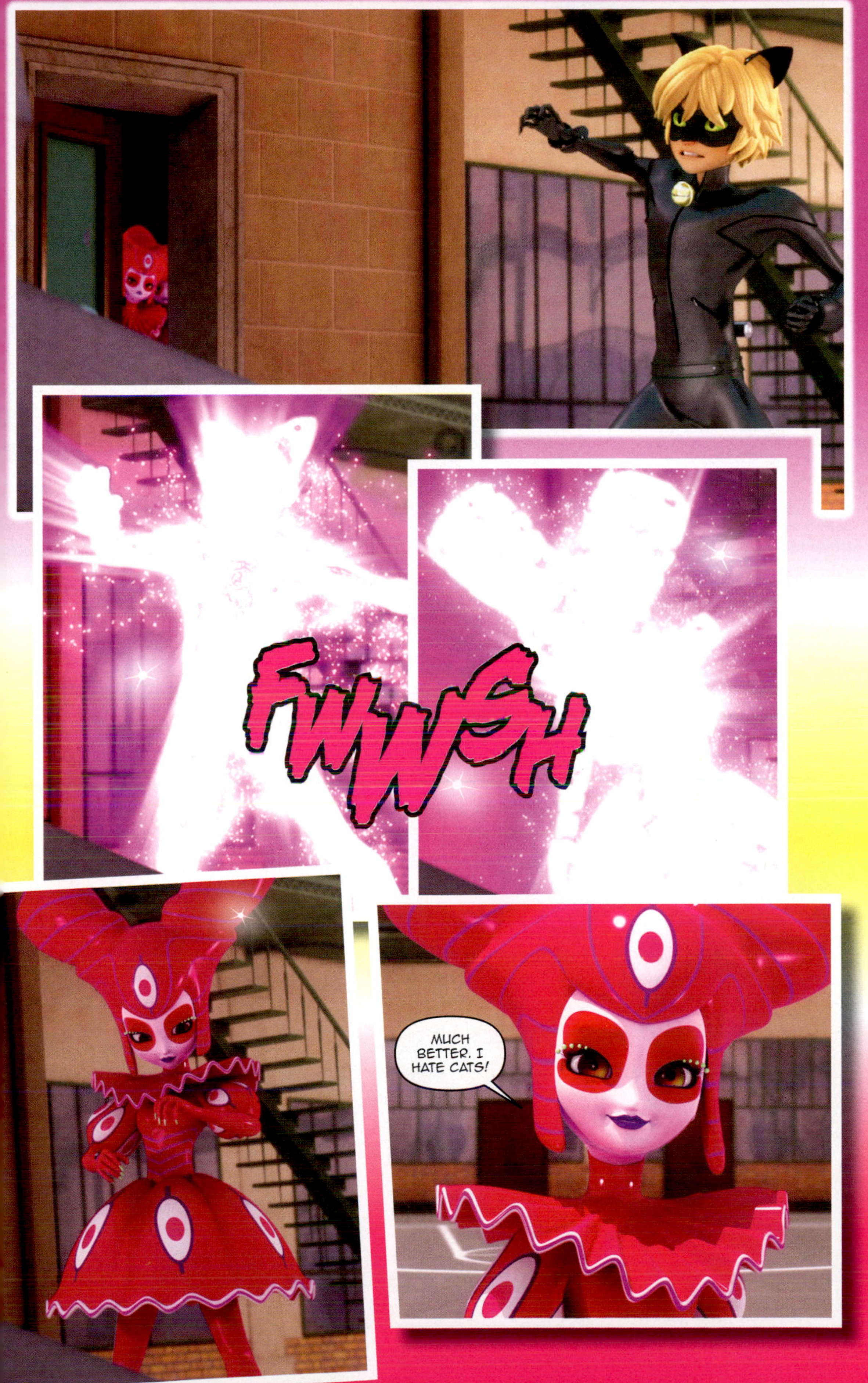
FWWSH
MUCH BETTER. I HATE CATS!

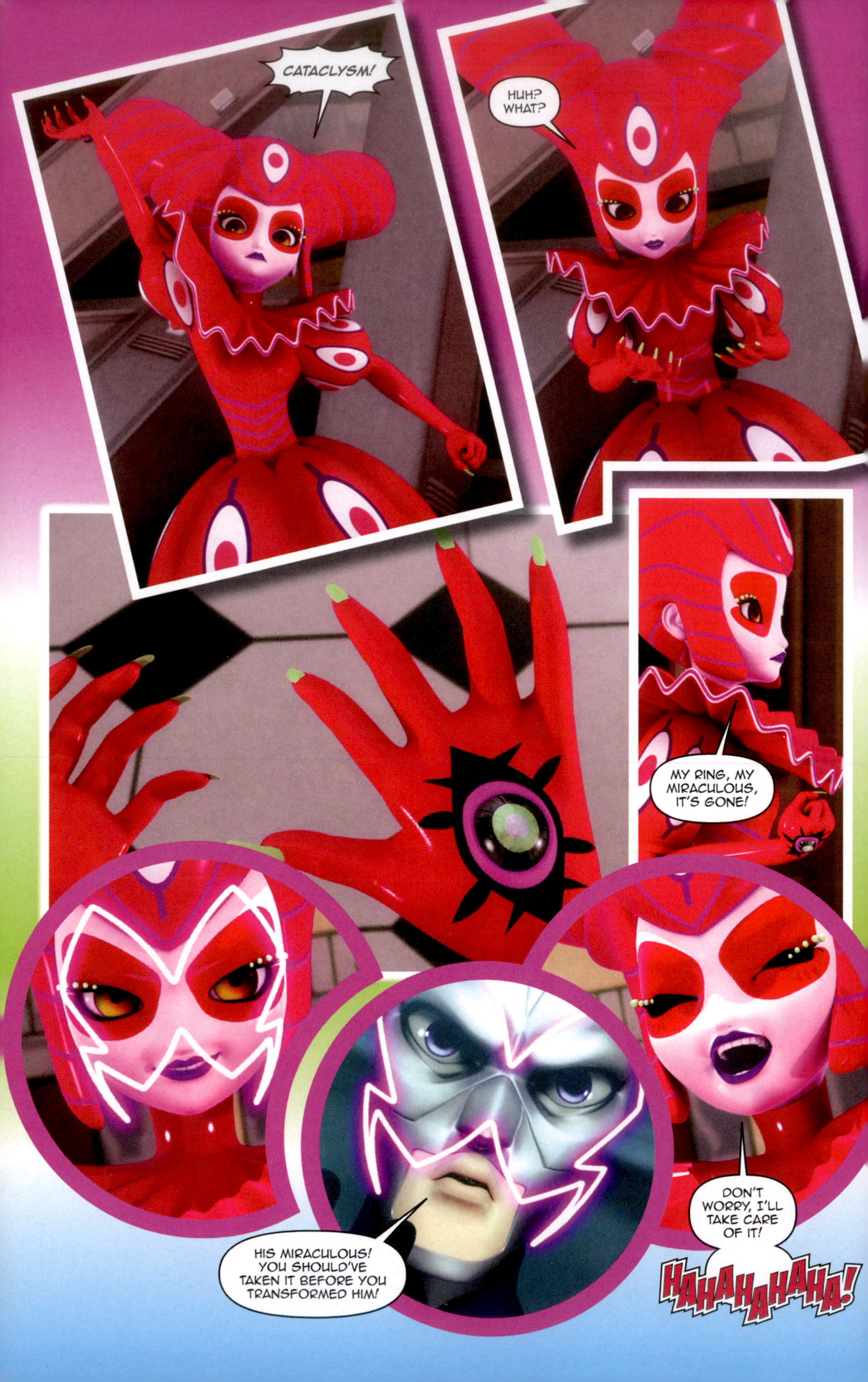
CATACLYSM!
HUH? WHAT?
MY RING, MY MIRACULOUS, IT'S GONE!
HIS MIRACULOUS! YOU SHOULD'VE TAKEN IT BEFORE YOU TRANSFORMED HIM!
DON'T WORRY, I'LL TAKE CARE OF IT!
HAHAHAHAHA!

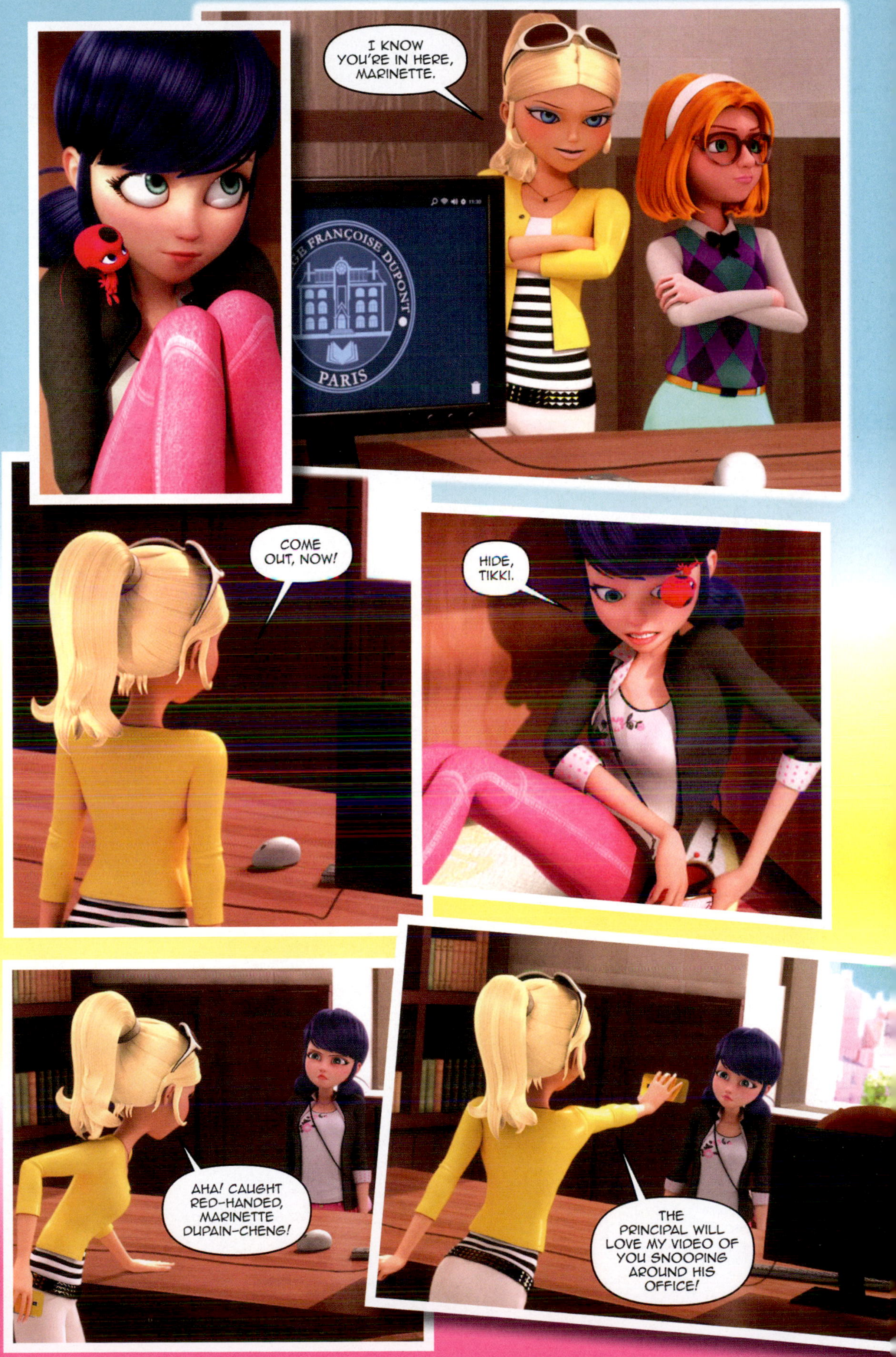
I KNOW YOU'RE IN HERE, MARINETTE.
COLLÈGE FRANÇOISE DUPONT
PARIS
COME OUT, NOW!
HIDE, TIKKI.
AHA! CAUGHT RED-HANDED, MARINETTE DUPAIN-CHENG!
THE PRINCIPAL WILL LOVE MY VIDEO OF YOU SNOOPING AROUND HIS OFFICE!

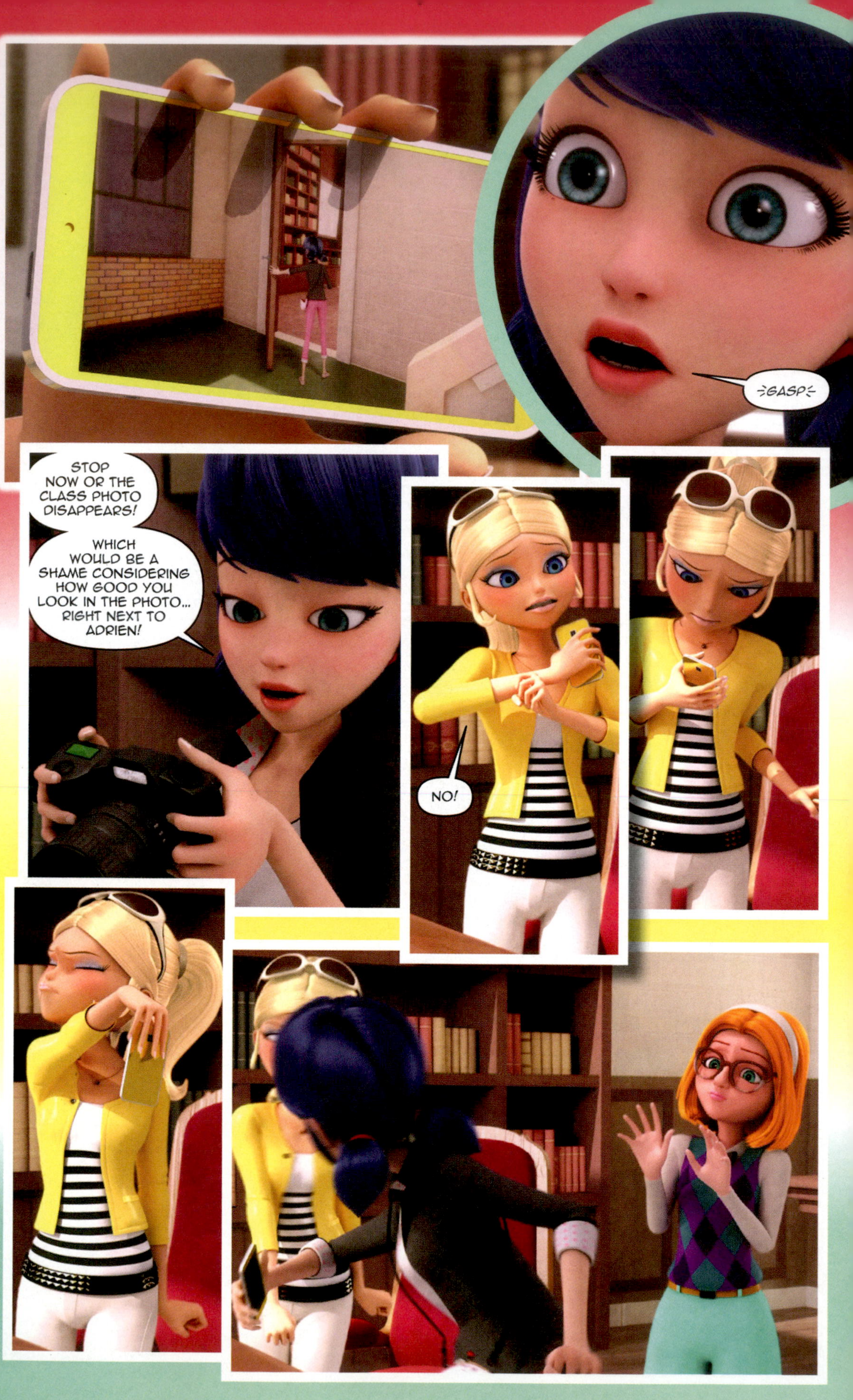
GASP
STOP NOW OR THE CLASS PHOTO DISAPPEARS!
WHICH WOULD BE A SHAME CONSIDERING HOW GOOD YOU LOOK IN THE PHOTO... RIGHT NEXT TO ADRIEN!
NO!

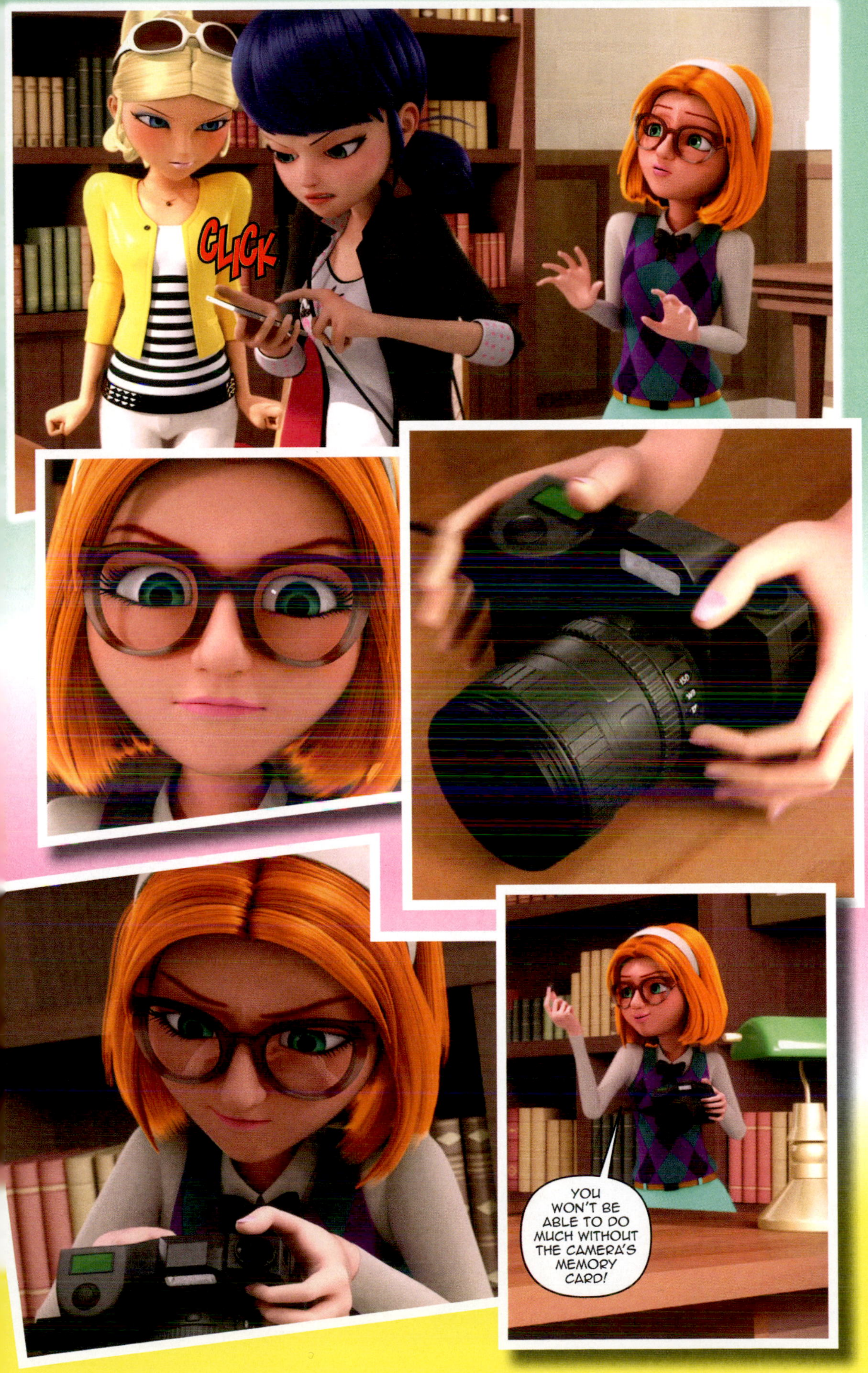
CLICK
YOU WON'T BE ABLE TO DO MUCH WITHOUT THE CAMERA'S MEMORY CARD!

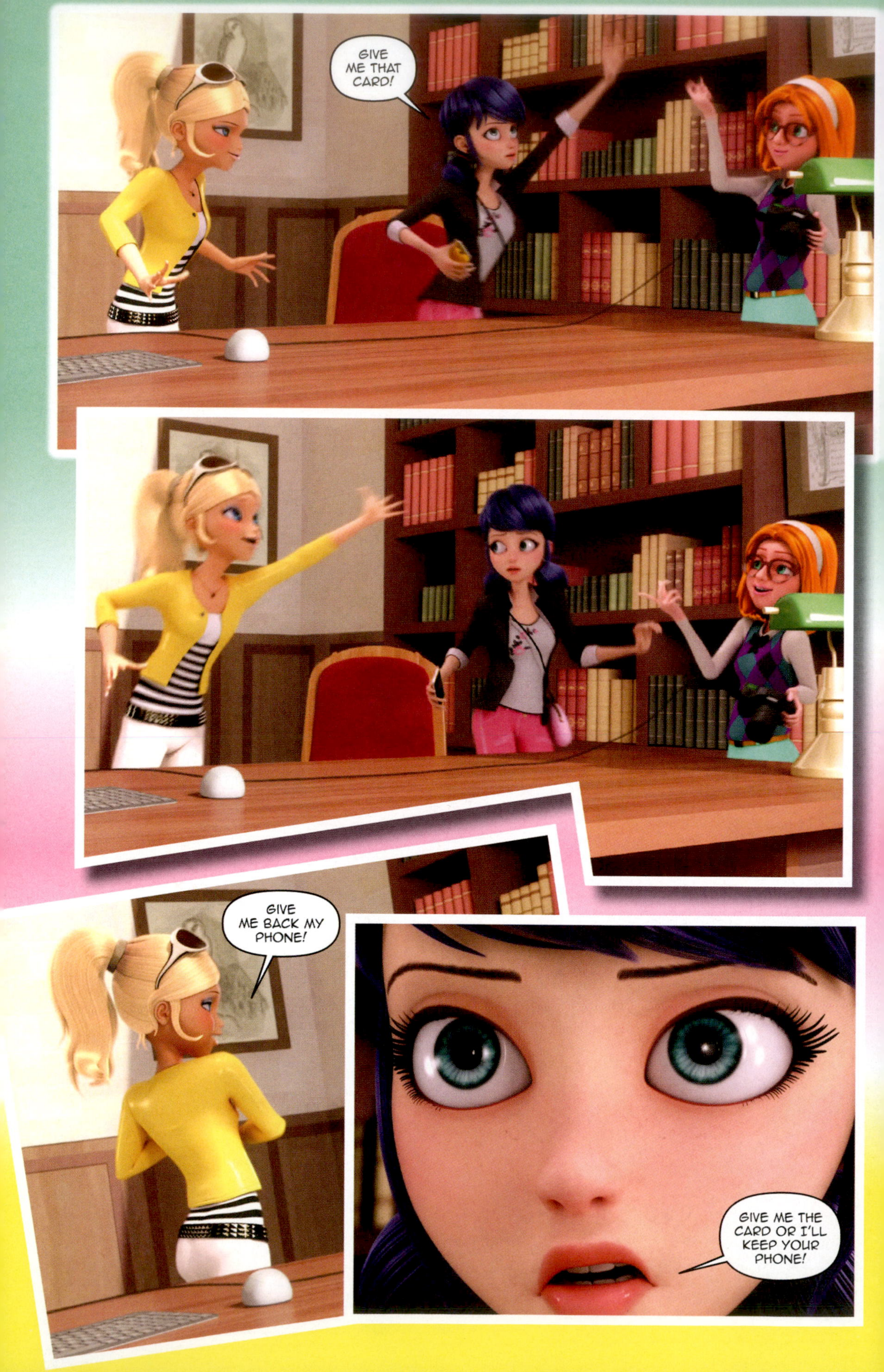
GIVE ME THAT CARD!
GIVE ME BACK MY PHONE!
GIVE ME THE CARD OR I'LL KEEP YOUR PHONE!

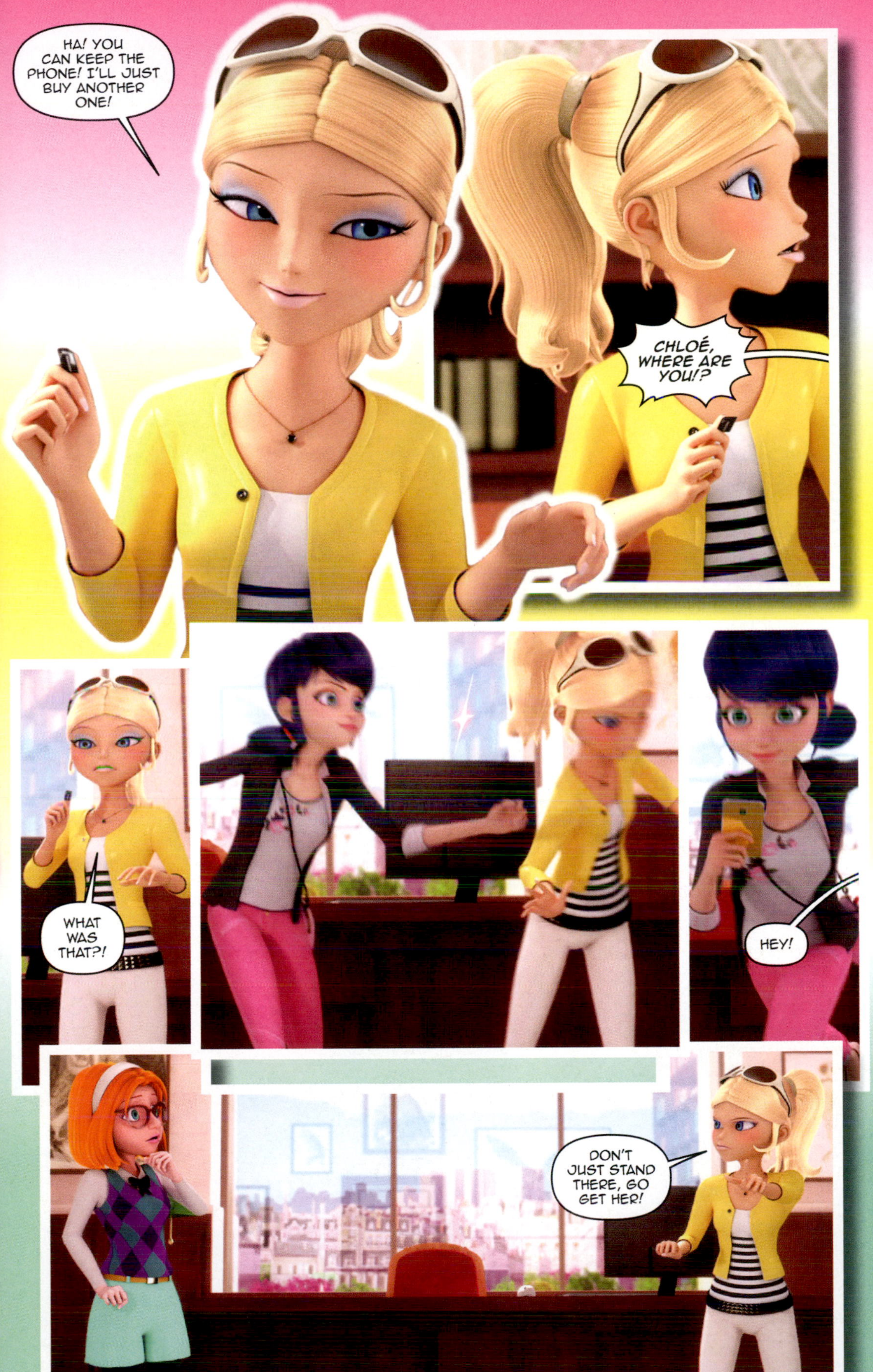
HA! YOU CAN KEEP THE PHONE! I'LL JUST BUY ANOTHER ONE!
CHLOÉ, WHERE ARE YOU!?
WHAT WAS THAT?!
HEY!
DON'T JUST STAND THERE, GO GET HER!

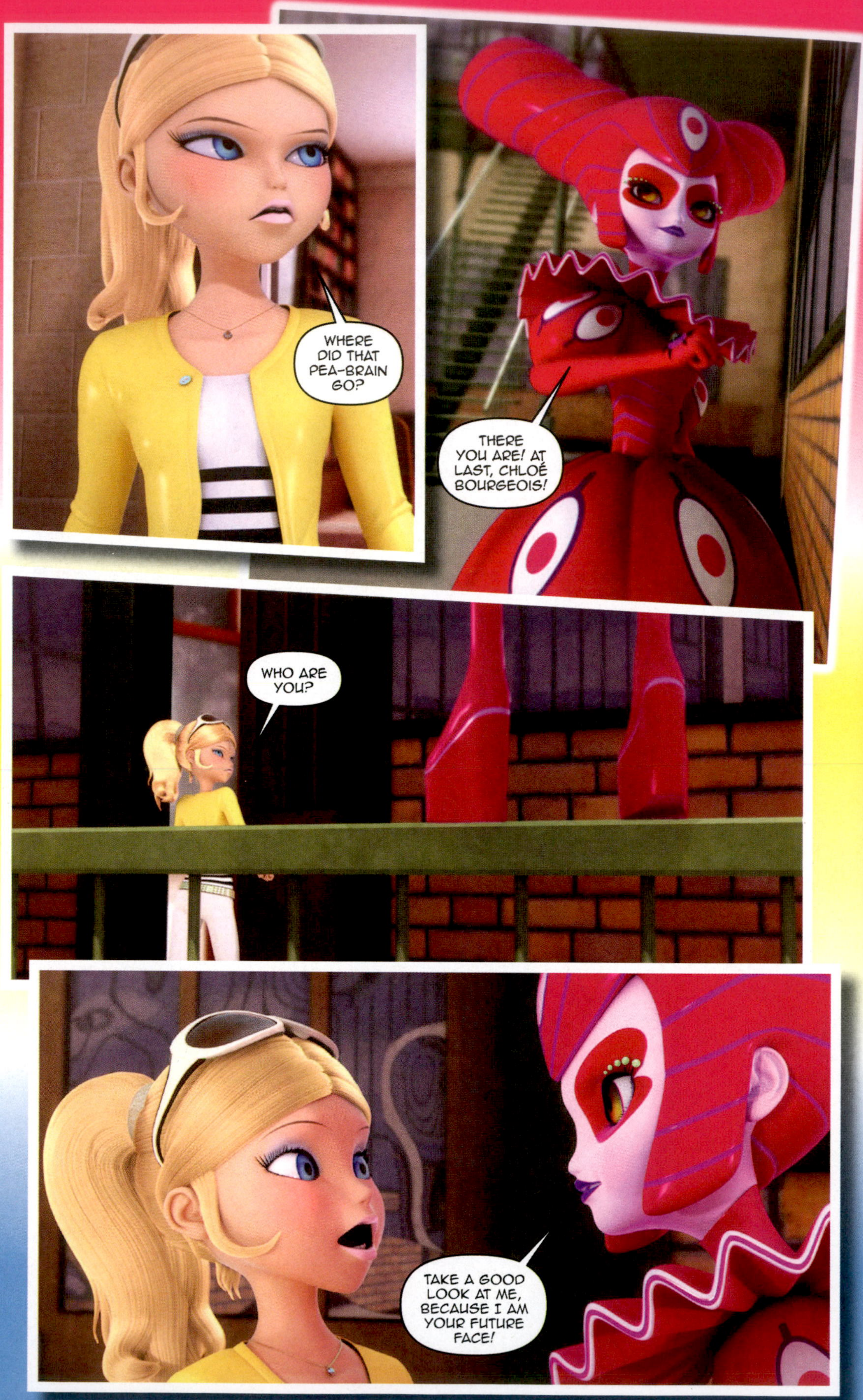
WHERE DID THAT PEA-BRAIN GO?
THERE YOU ARE! AT LAST, CHLOÉ BOURGEOIS!
WHO ARE YOU?
TAKE A GOOD LOOK AT ME, BECAUSE I AM YOUR FUTURE FACE!

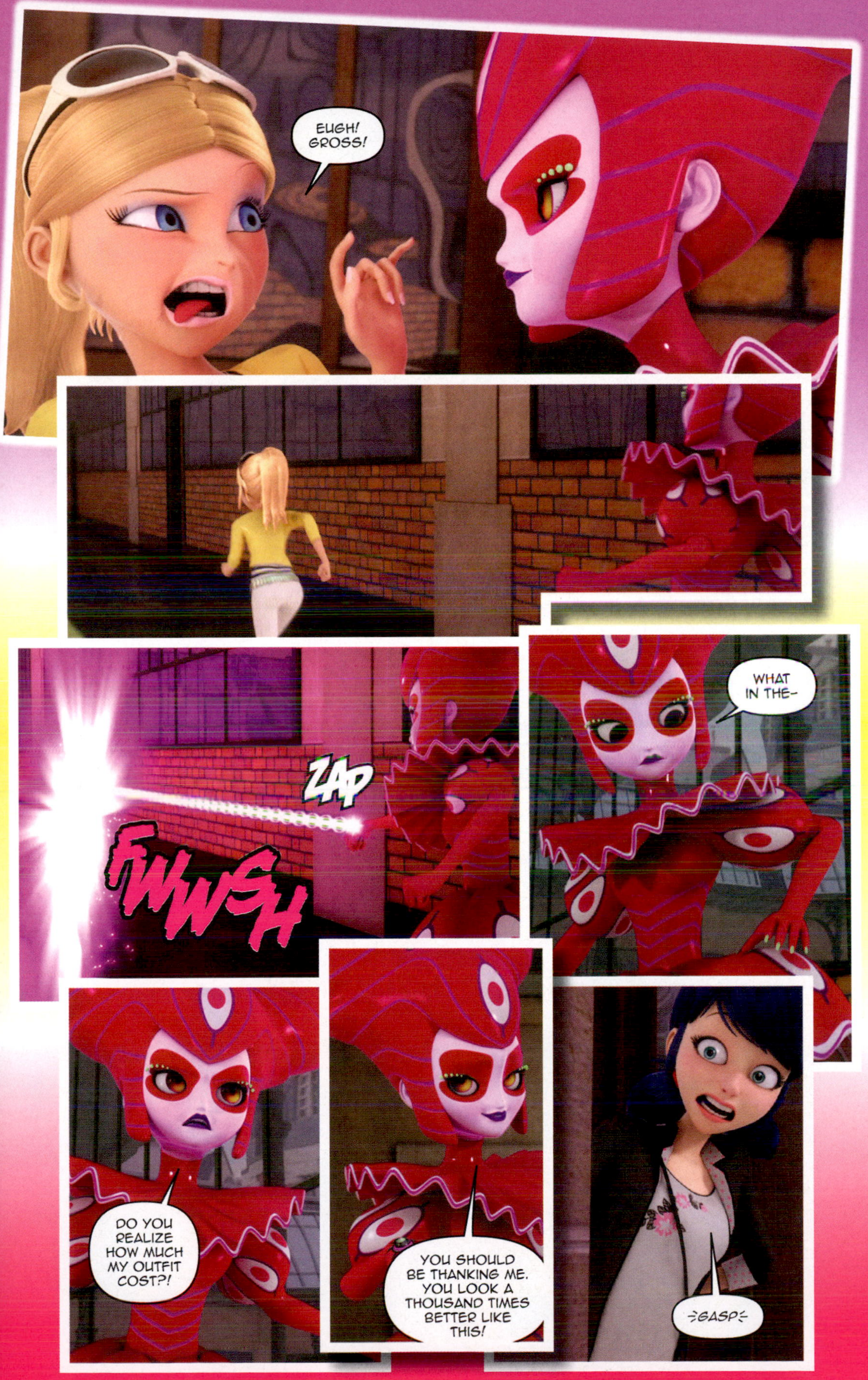
EUGH! GROSS!
ZAP
FWWSH
WHAT IN THE-
DO YOU REALIZE HOW MUCH MY OUTFIT COST?!
YOU SHOULD BE THANKING ME. YOU LOOK A THOUSAND TIMES BETTER LIKE THIS!
GASP

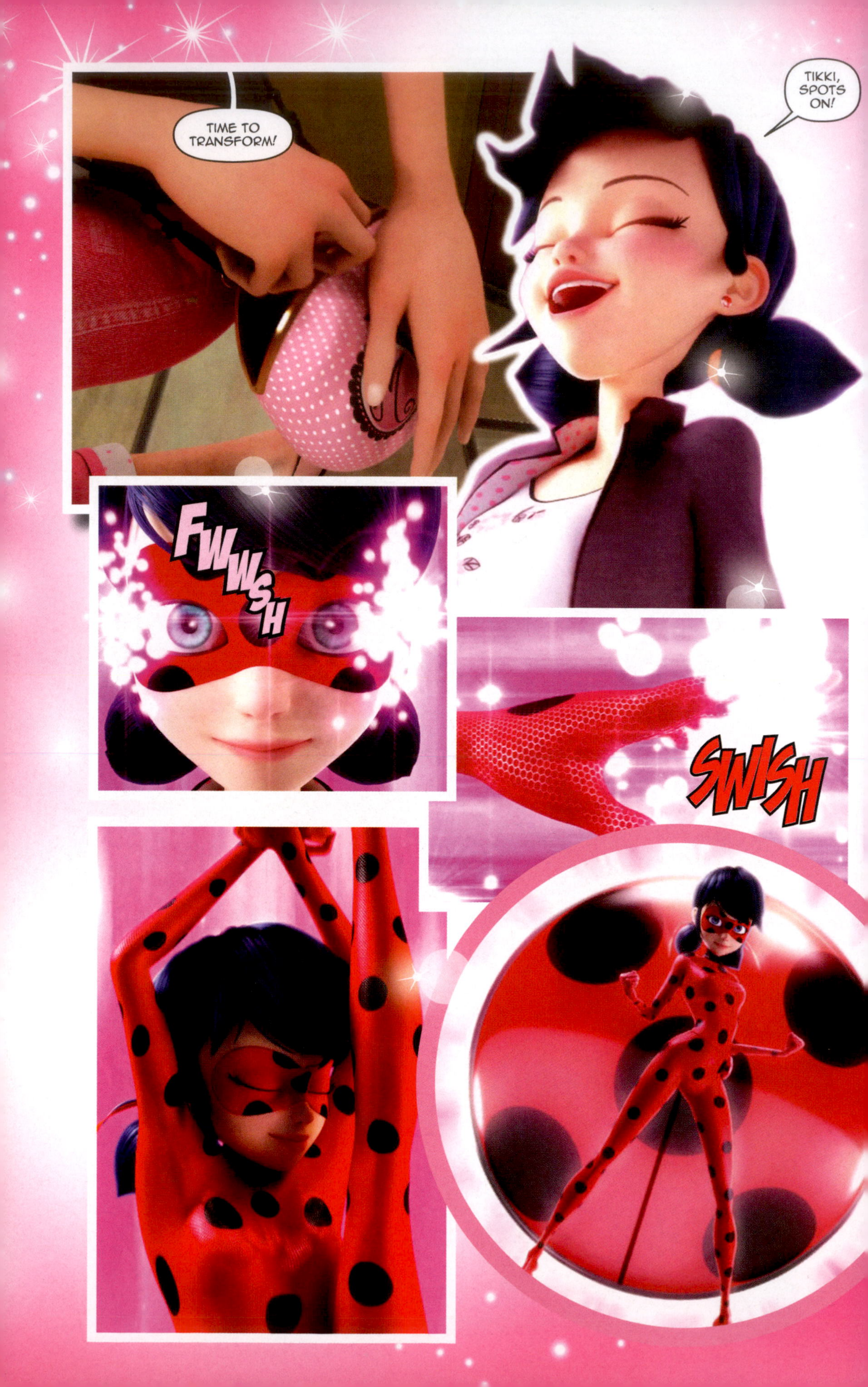
TIME TO TRANSFORM!
TIKKI, SPOTS ON!
FWWSH
SWISH

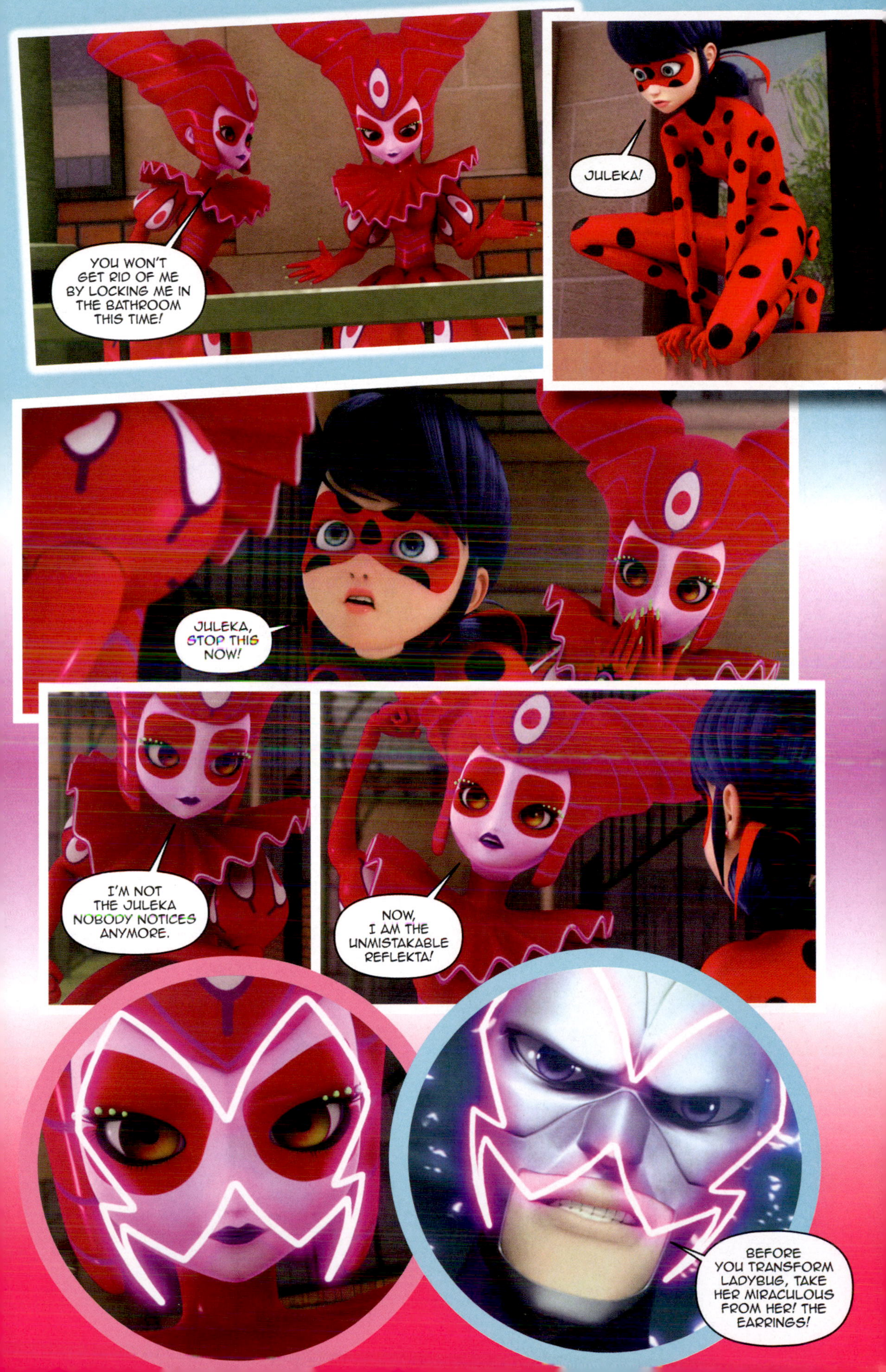
YOU WON'T GET RID OF ME BY LOCKING ME IN THE BATHROOM THIS TIME!
JULEKA!
JULEKA, STOP THIS NOW!
I'M NOT THE JULEKA NOBODY NOTICES ANYMORE.
NOW, I AM THE UNMISTAKABLE REFLEKTA!
BEFORE YOU TRANSFORM LADYBUG, TAKE HER MIRACULOUS FROM HER! THE EARRINGS!

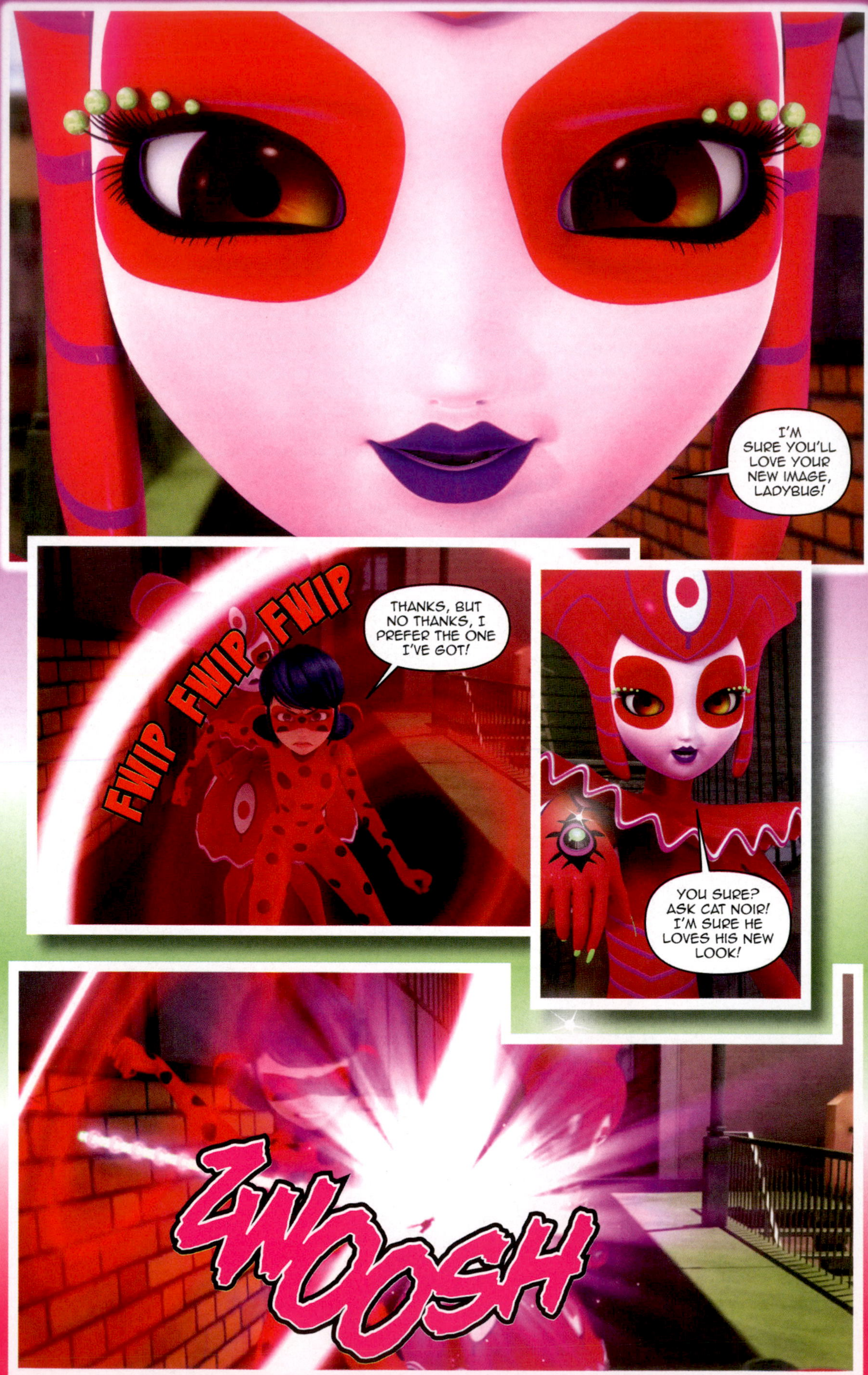
I'M SURE YOU'LL LOVE YOUR NEW IMAGE, LADYBUG!
FWIP FWIP FWIP
THANKS, BUT NO THANKS, I PREFER THE ONE I'VE GOT!
YOU SURE? ASK CAT NOIR! I'M SURE HE LOVES HIS NEW LOOK!
ZWOOSH

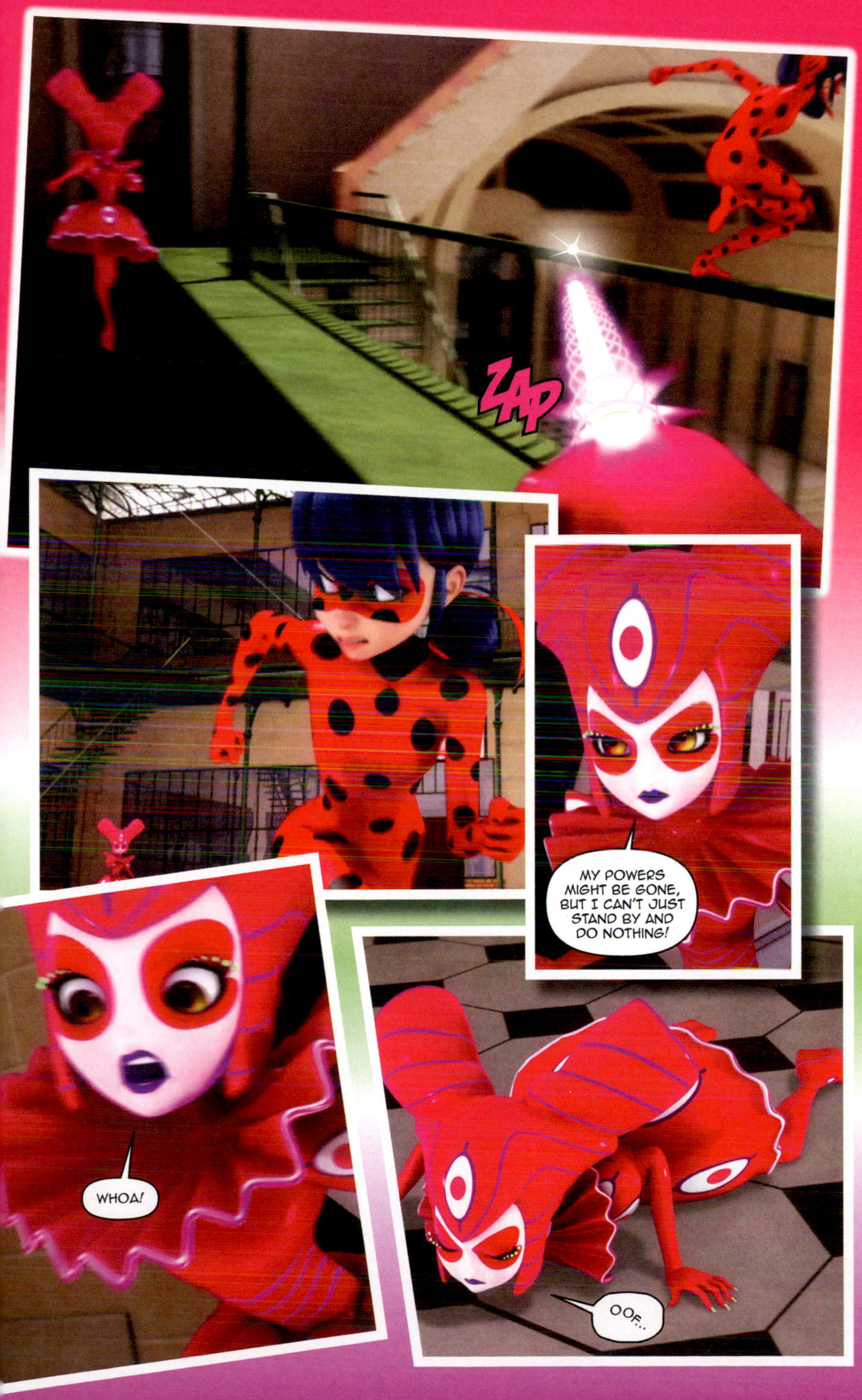
ZAP
MY POWERS MIGHT BE GONE, BUT I CAN'T JUST STAND BY AND DO NOTHING!
WHOA!
OOF...

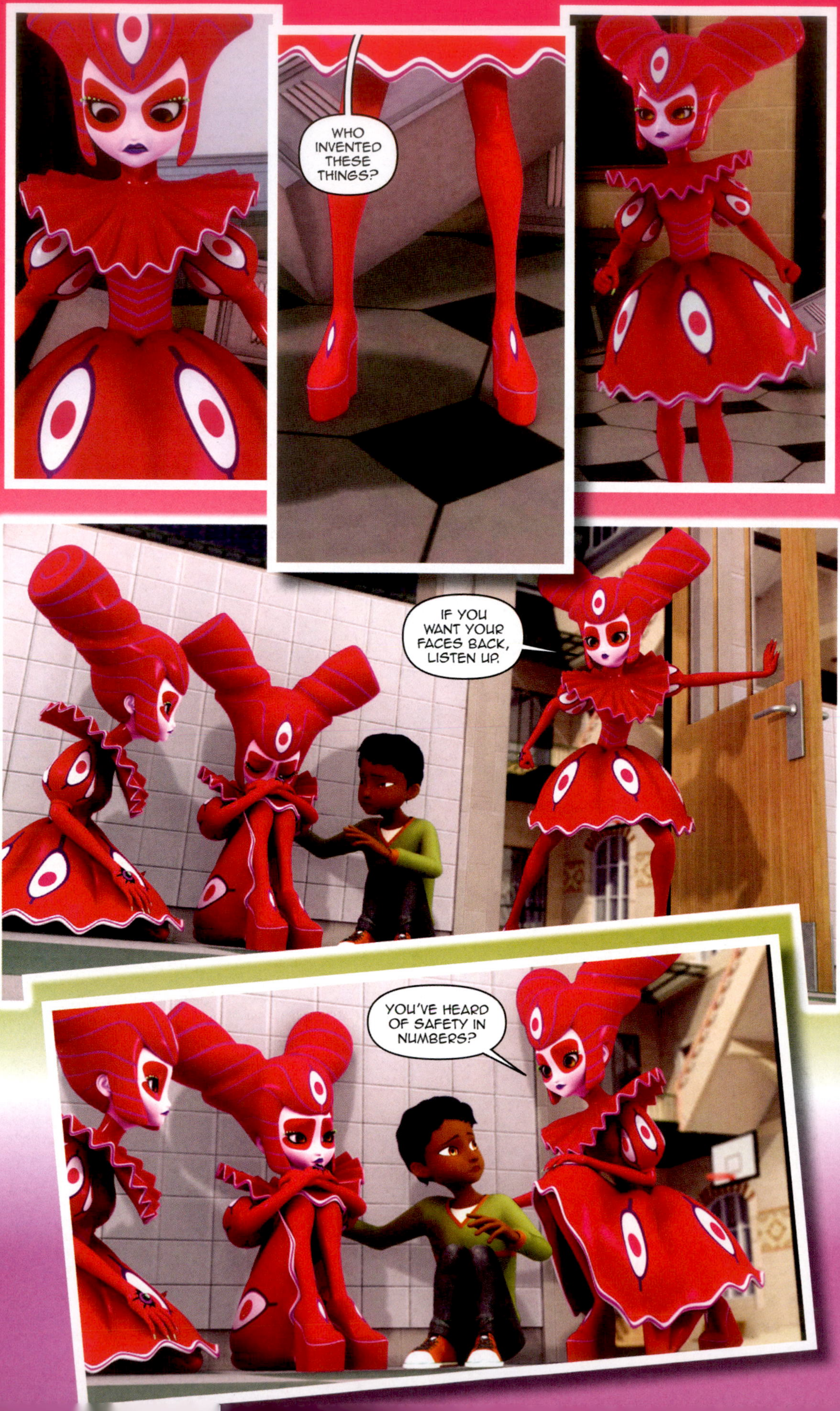
WHO INVENTED THESE THINGS?
IF YOU WANT YOUR FACES BACK, LISTEN UP.
YOU'VE HEARD OF SAFETY IN NUMBERS?

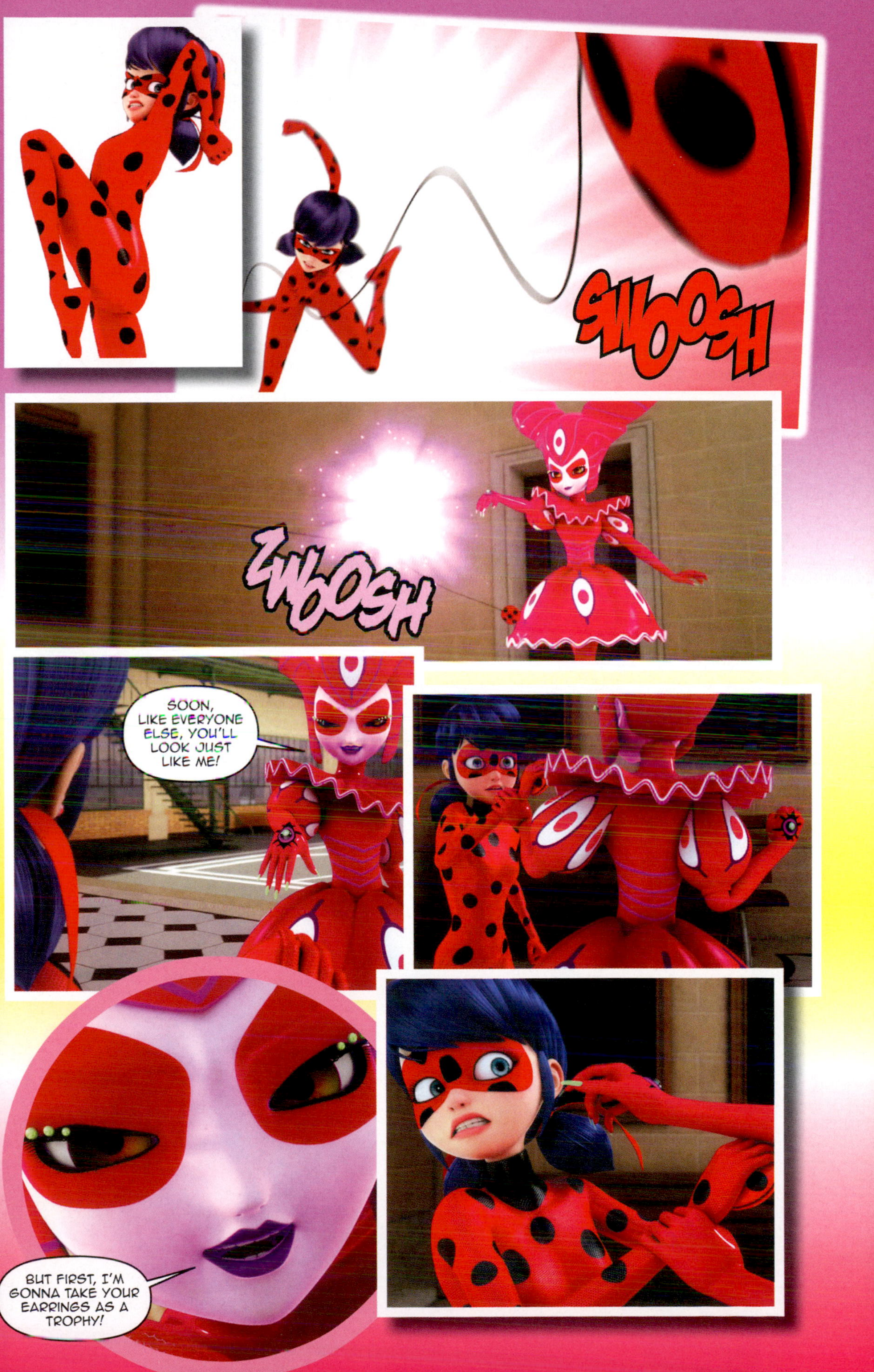
SWOOSH
ZWOOSH
SOON, LIKE EVERYONE ELSE, YOU'LL LOOK JUST LIKE ME!
BUT FIRST, I'M GONNA TAKE YOUR EARRINGS AS A TROPHY!

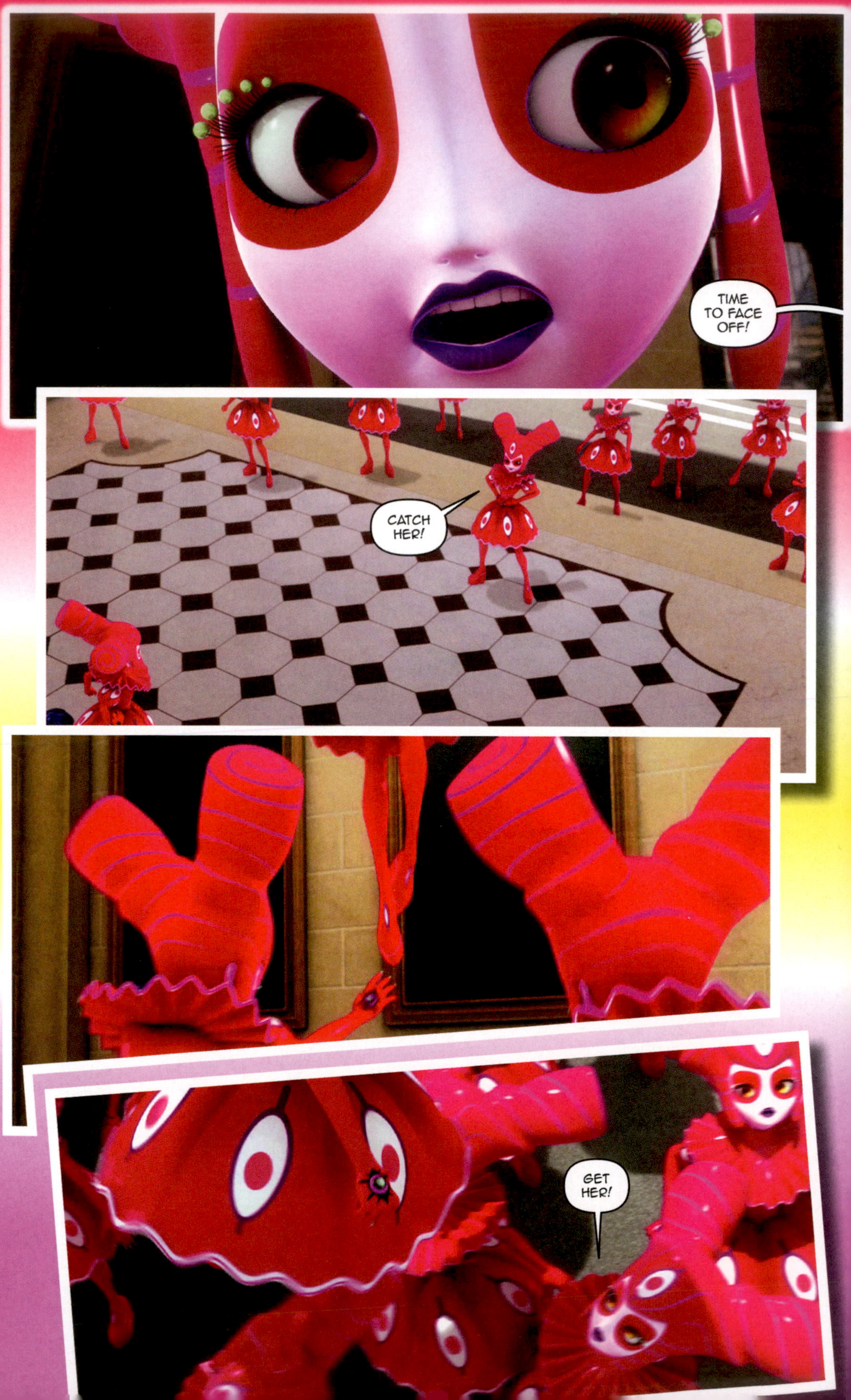
TIME TO FACE OFF!
CATCH HER!
GET HER!

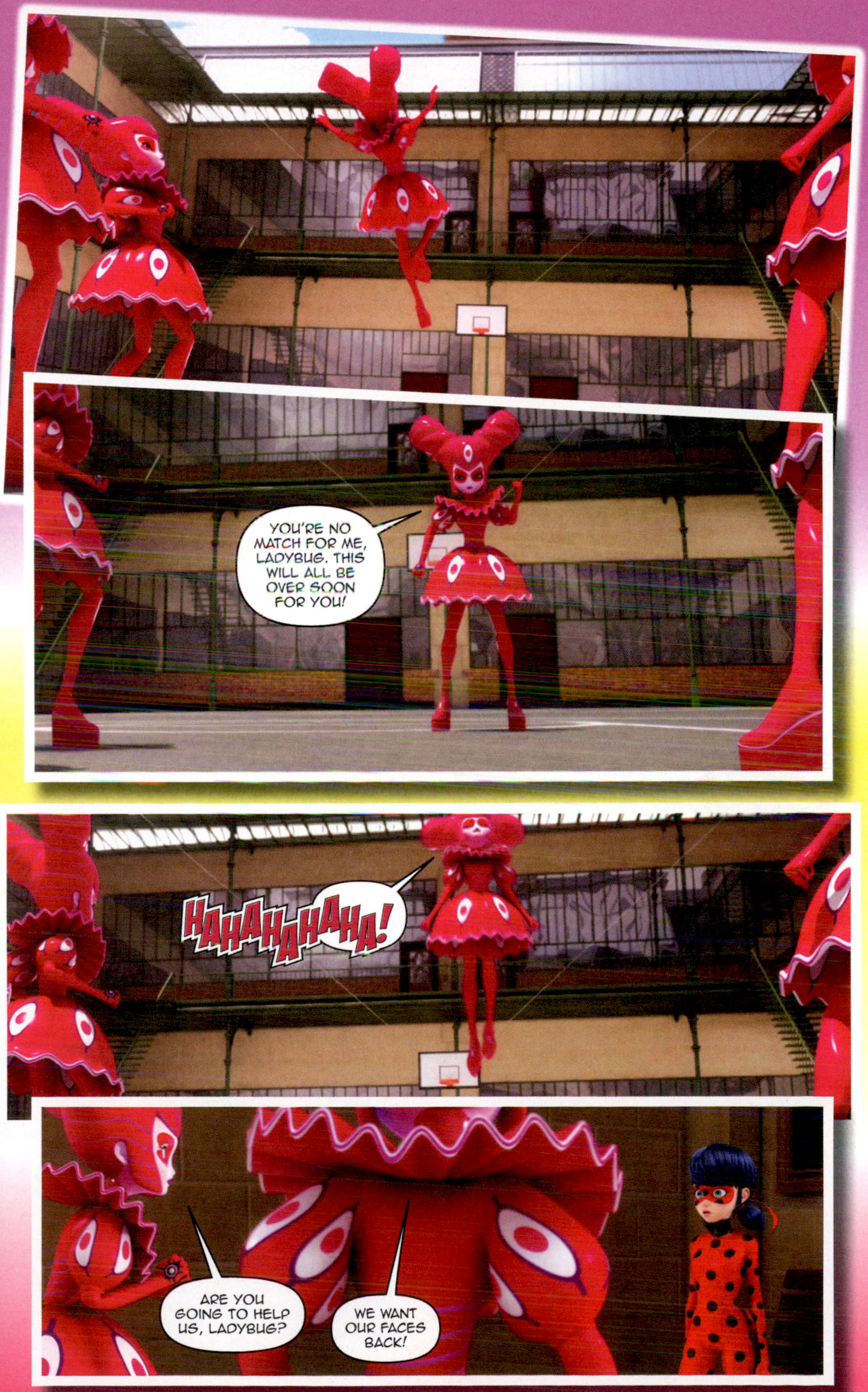
YOU'RE NO MATCH FOR ME, LADYBUG. THIS WILL ALL BE OVER SOON FOR YOU!
HAHAHAHAHAHA!
ARE YOU GOING TO HELP US, LADYBUG?
WE WANT OUR FACES BACK!

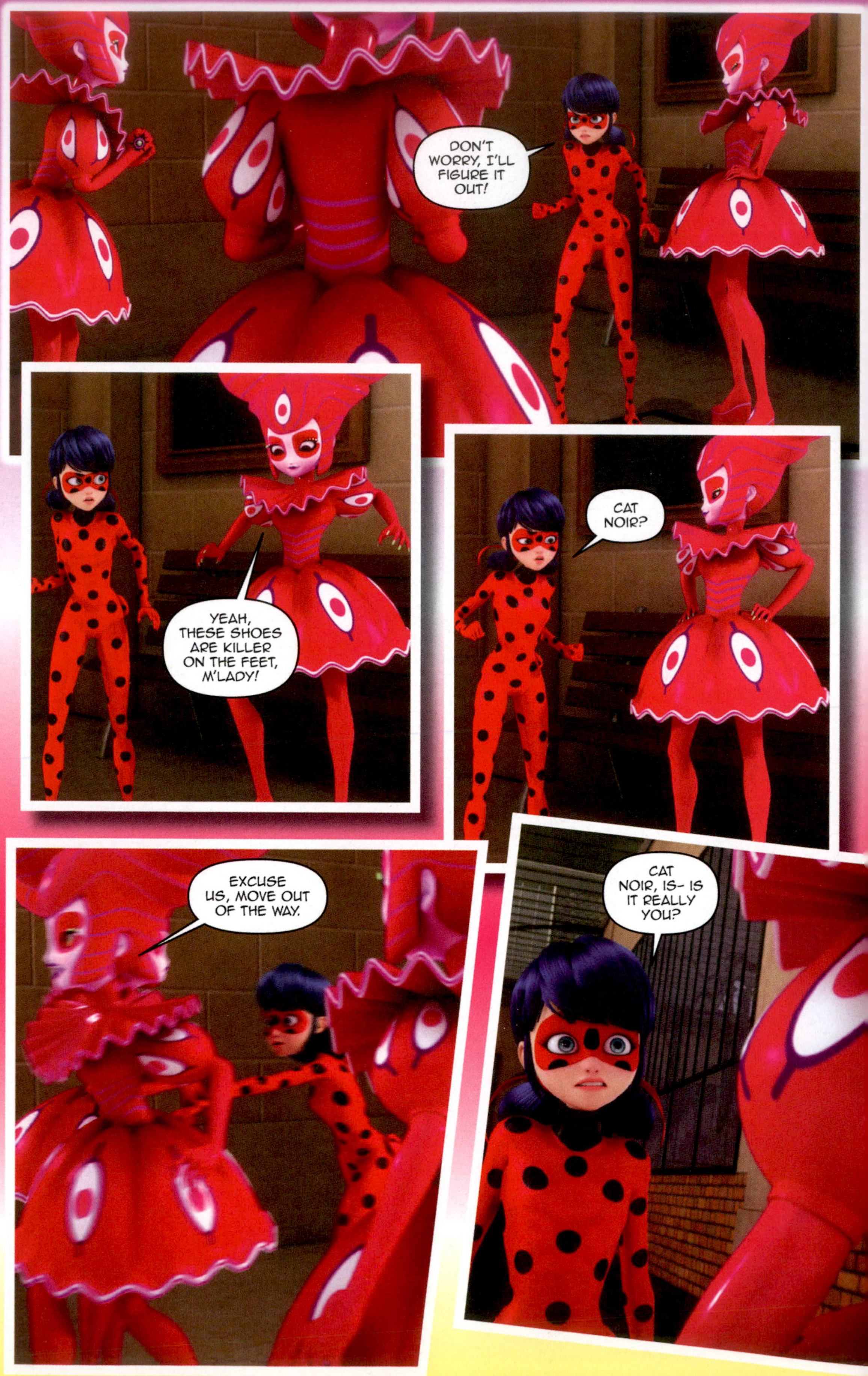
DON'T WORRY, I'LL FIGURE IT OUT!
YEAH, THESE SHOES ARE KILLER ON THE FEET, M'LADY!
CAT NOIR?
EXCUSE US, MOVE OUT OF THE WAY.
CAT NOIR, IS- IS IT REALLY YOU?

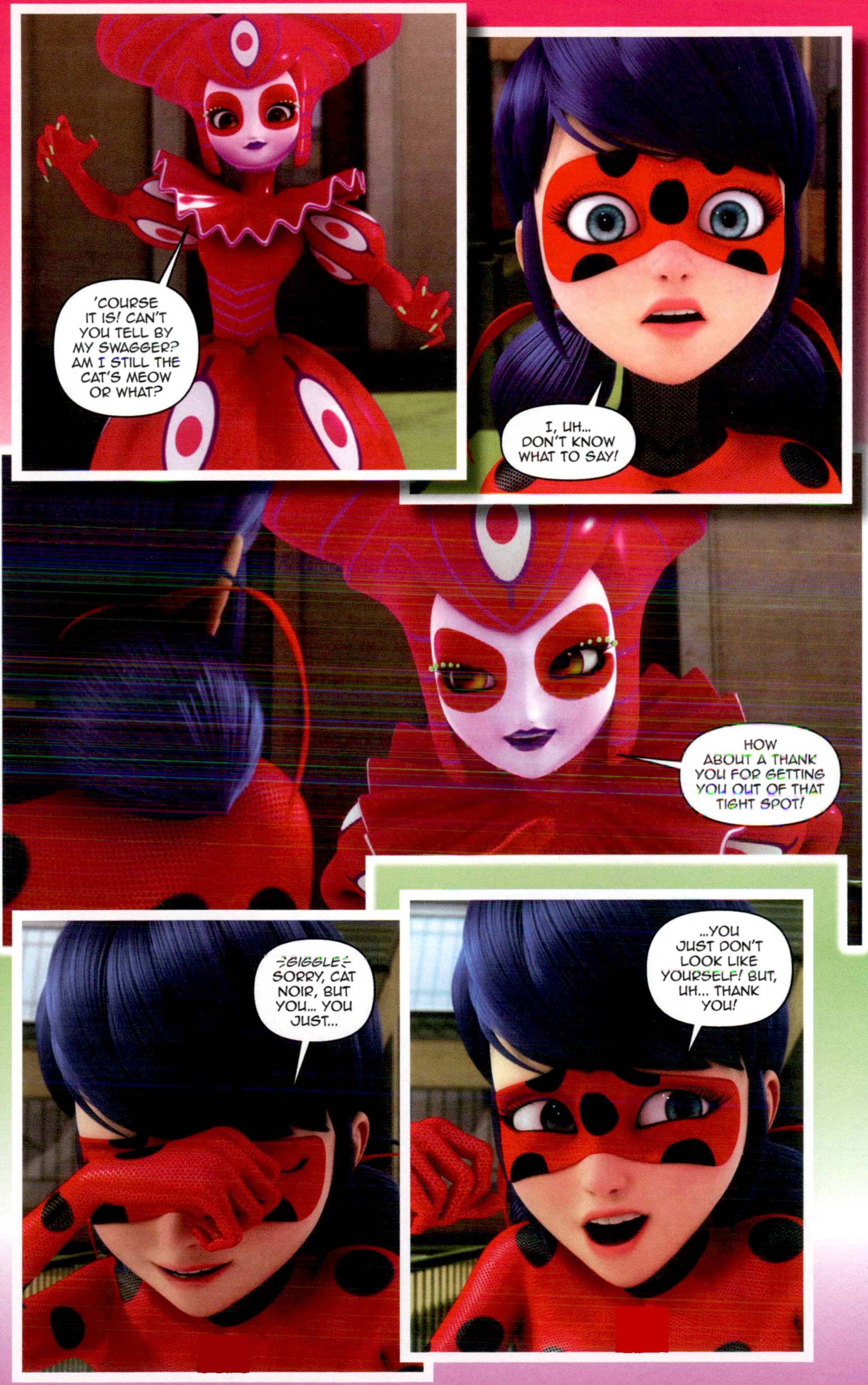
'COURSE IT IS! CAN'T YOU TELL BY MY SWAGGER? AM I STILL THE CAT'S MEOW OR WHAT?
I, UH... DON'T KNOW WHAT TO SAY!
HOW ABOUT A THANK YOU FOR GETTING YOU OUT OF THAT TIGHT SPOT!
-GIGGLE- SORRY, CAT NOIR, BUT YOU... YOU JUST...
...YOU JUST DON'T LOOK LIKE YOURSELF! BUT, UH... THANK YOU!

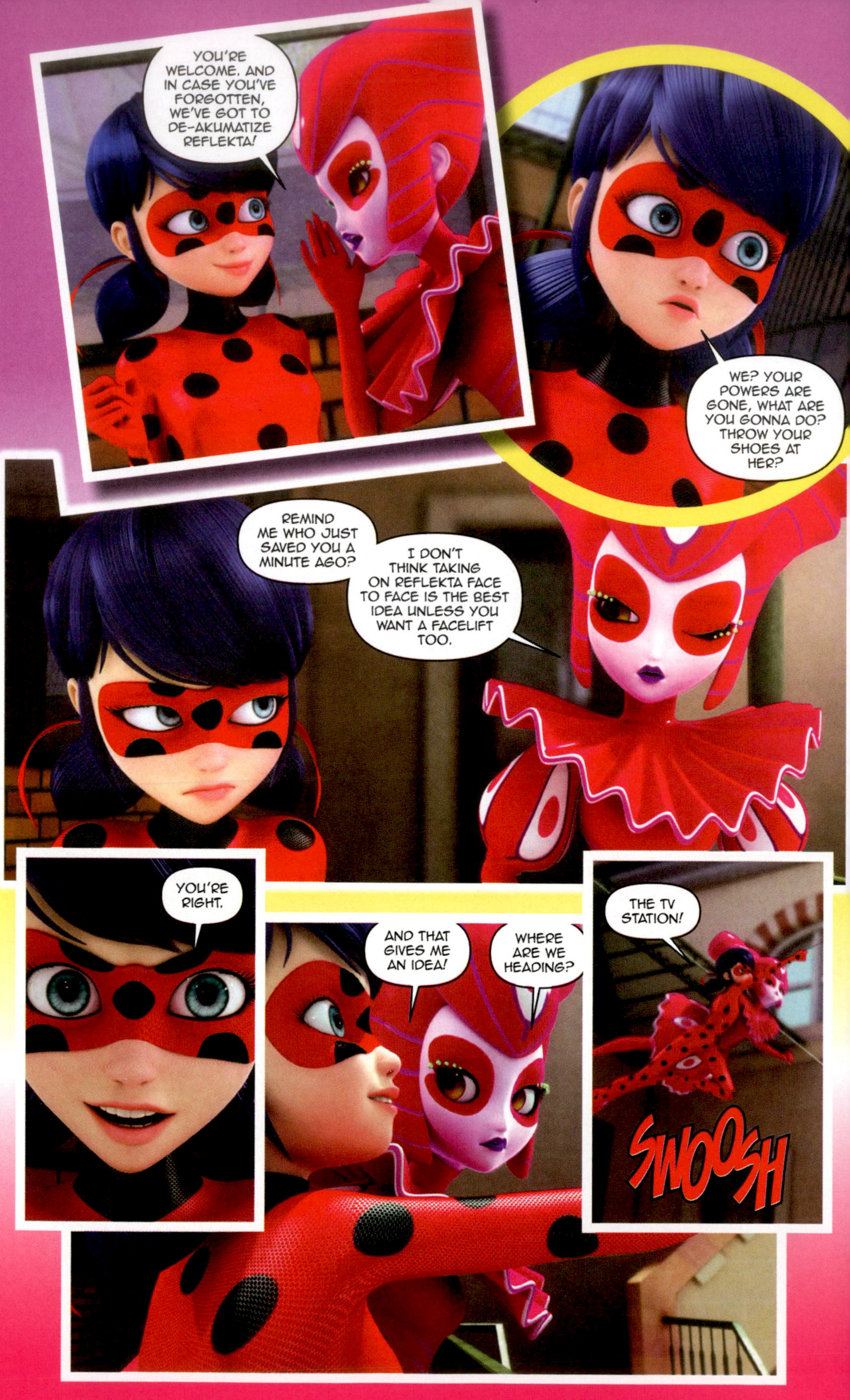

YOU'RE WELCOME. AND IN CASE YOU'VE FORGOTTEN, WE'VE GOT TO DE-AKUMATIZE REFLEKTA!
WE? YOUR POWERS ARE GONE, WHAT ARE YOU GONNA DO? THROW YOUR SHOES AT HER?
REMIND ME WHO JUST SAVED YOU A MINUTE AGO?
I DON'T THINK TAKING ON REFLEKTA FACE TO FACE IS THE BEST IDEA UNLESS YOU WANT A FACELIFT TOO.
YOU'RE RIGHT.
AND THAT GIVES ME AN IDEA!
WHERE ARE WE HEADING?
THE TV STATION!
SWOOSH

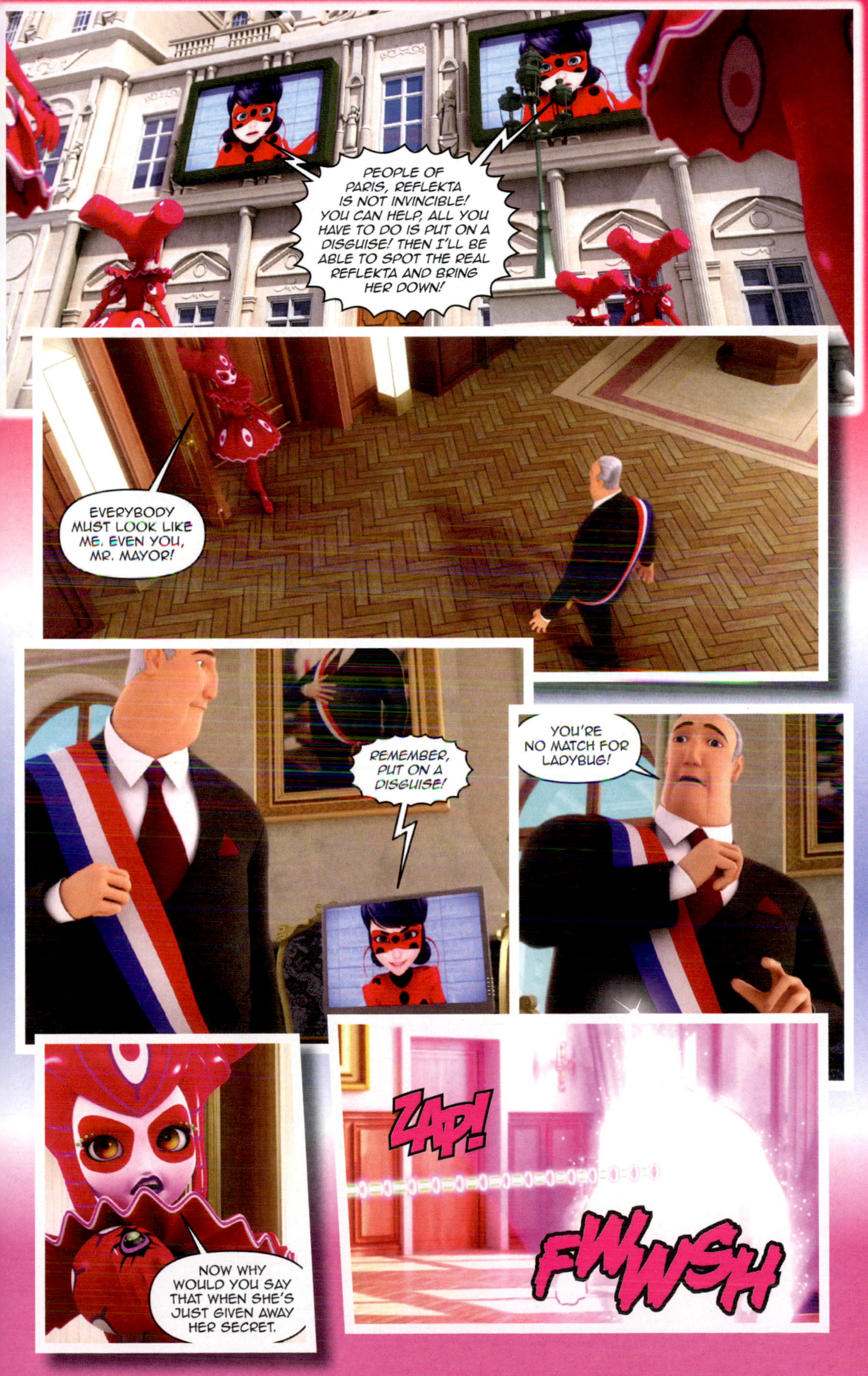
PEOPLE OF PARIS, REFLEKTA IS NOT INVINCIBLE! YOU CAN HELP, ALL YOU HAVE TO DO IS PUT ON A DISGUISE! THEN I'LL BE ABLE TO SPOT THE REAL REFLEKTA AND BRING HER DOWN!
EVERYBODY MUST LOOK LIKE ME. EVEN YOU, MR. MAYOR!
REMEMBER, PUT ON A DISGUISE!
YOU'RE NO MATCH FOR LADYBUG!
NOW WHY WOULD YOU SAY THAT WHEN SHE'S JUST GIVEN AWAY HER SECRET.
ZAP!
FWWSH

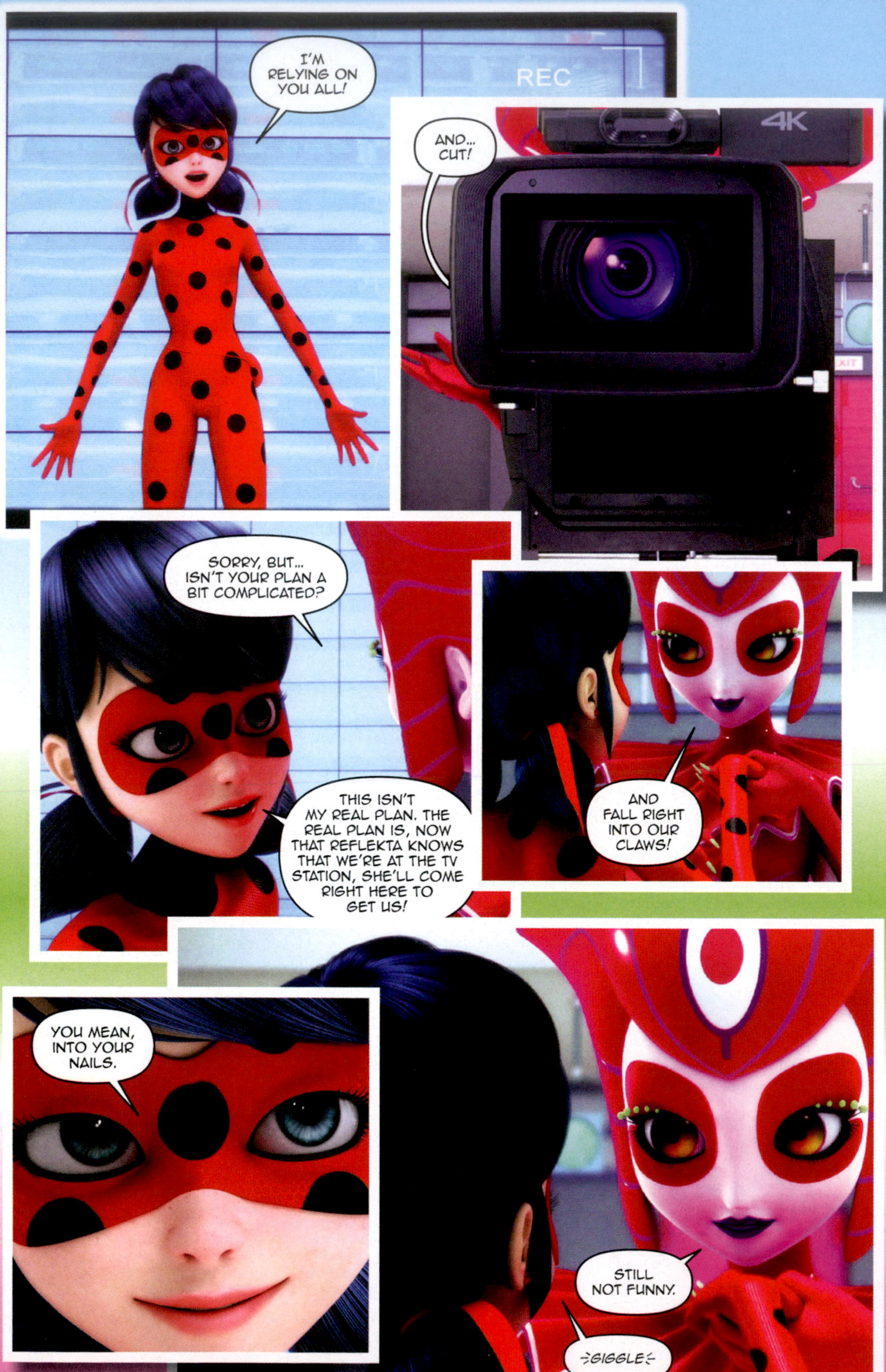
I'M RELYING ON YOU ALL!
REC
4K
AND... CUT!
SORRY, BUT... ISN'T YOUR PLAN A BIT COMPLICATED?
THIS ISN'T MY REAL PLAN. THE REAL PLAN IS, NOW THAT REFLEKTA KNOWS THAT WE'RE AT THE TV STATION, SHE'LL COME RIGHT HERE TO GET US!
AND FALL RIGHT INTO OUR CLAWS!
YOU MEAN, INTO YOUR NAILS.
STILL NOT FUNNY.
GIGGLE

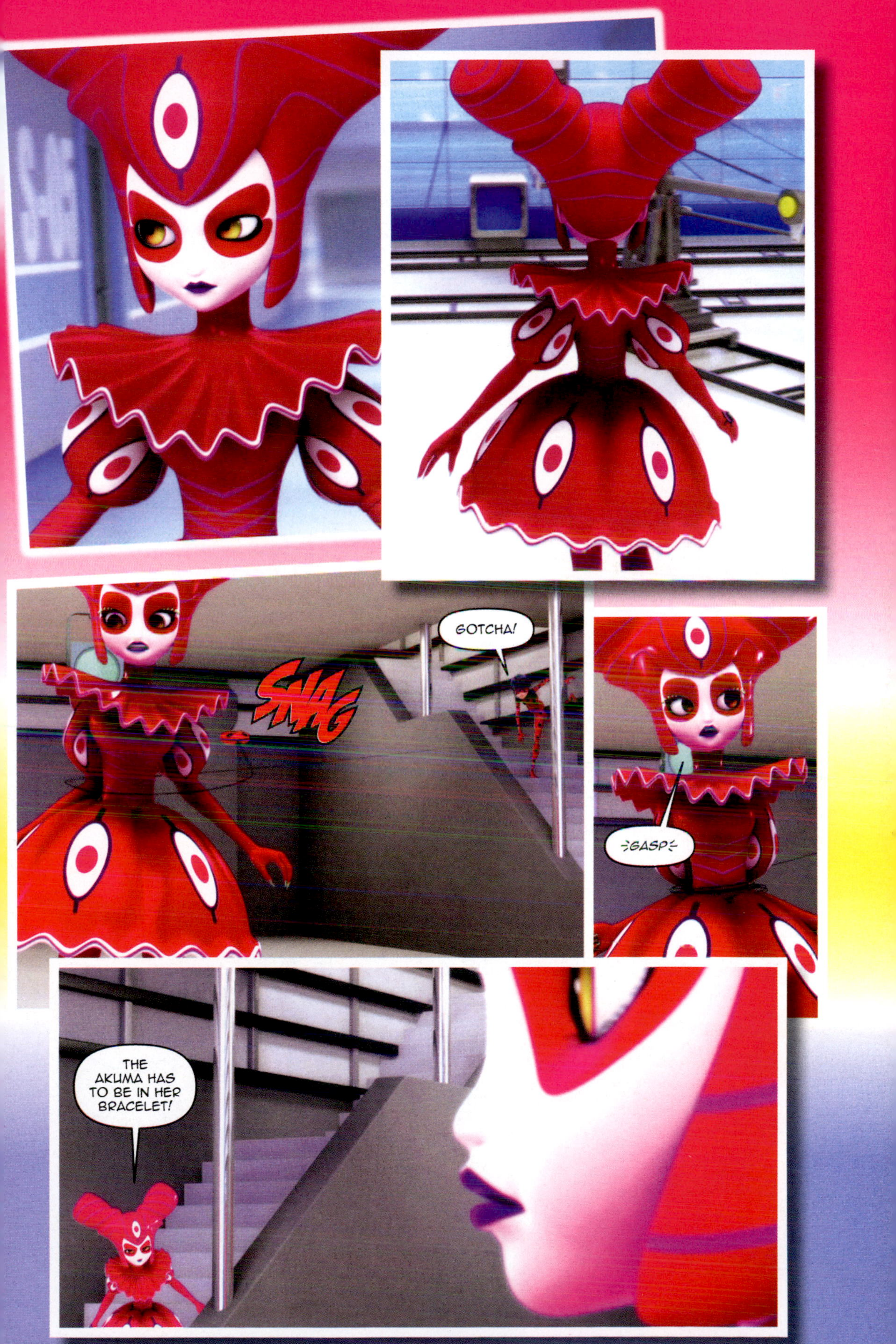
SNAG
GOTCHA!
GASP
THE AKUMA HAS TO BE IN HER BRACELET!

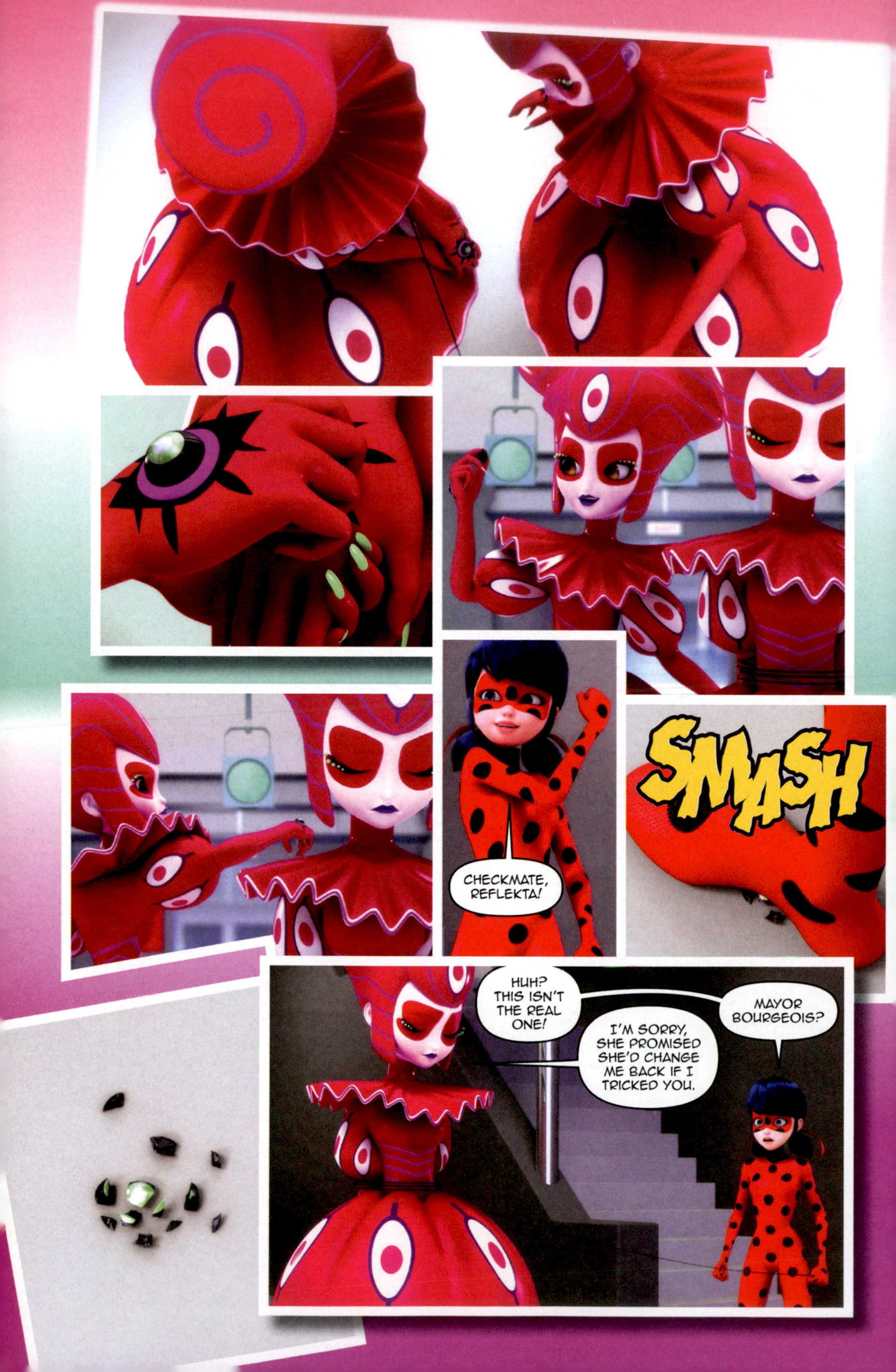
CHECKMATE, REFLEKTA!
SMASH
HUH? THIS ISN'T THE REAL ONE!
MAYOR BOURGEOIS?
I'M SORRY, SHE PROMISED SHE'D CHANGE ME BACK IF I TRICKED YOU.

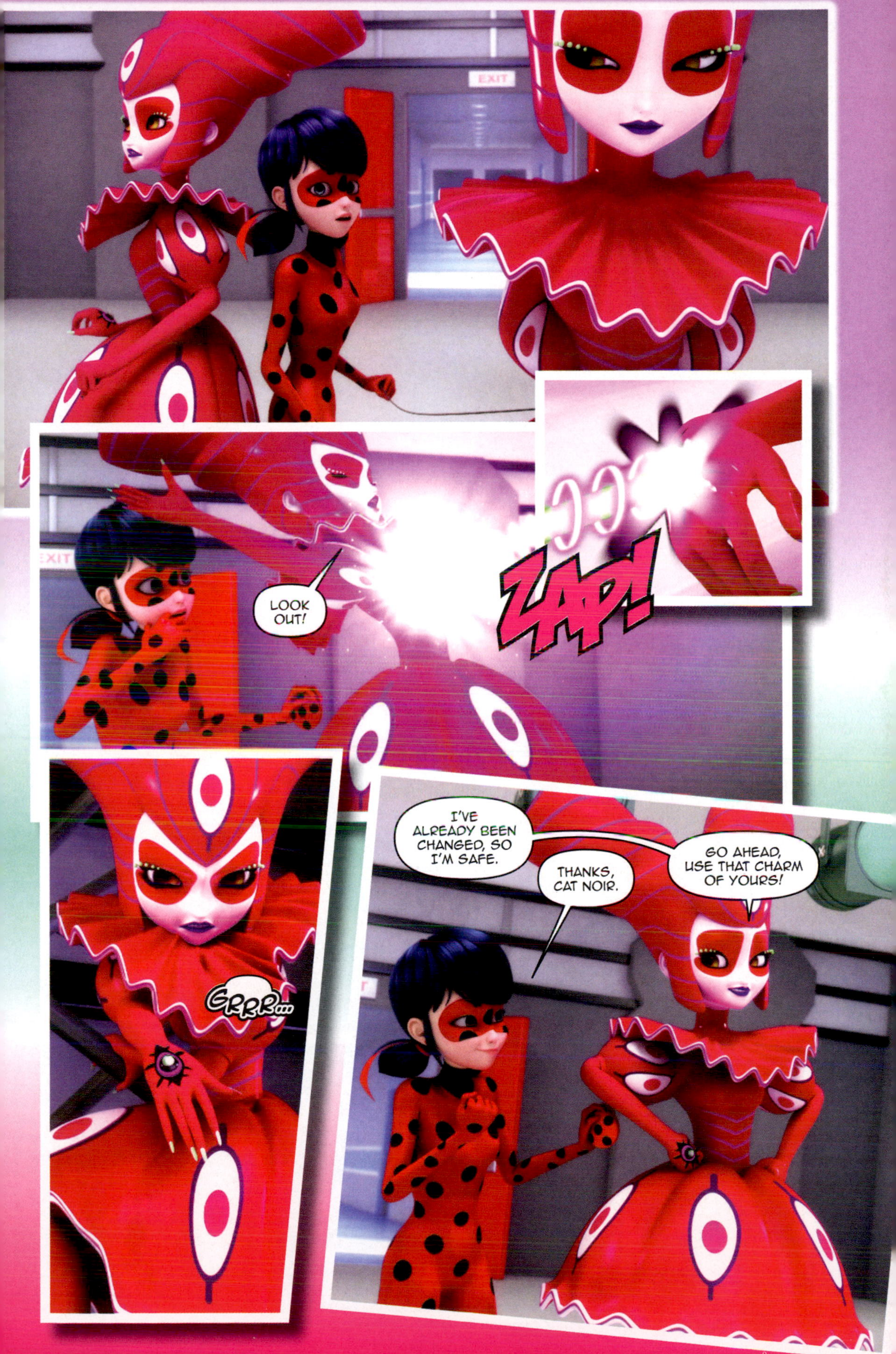
LOOK OUT!
ZAP!
GRRR...
I'VE ALREADY BEEN CHANGED, SO I'M SAFE.
GO AHEAD, USE THAT CHARM OF YOURS!
THANKS, CAT NOIR.

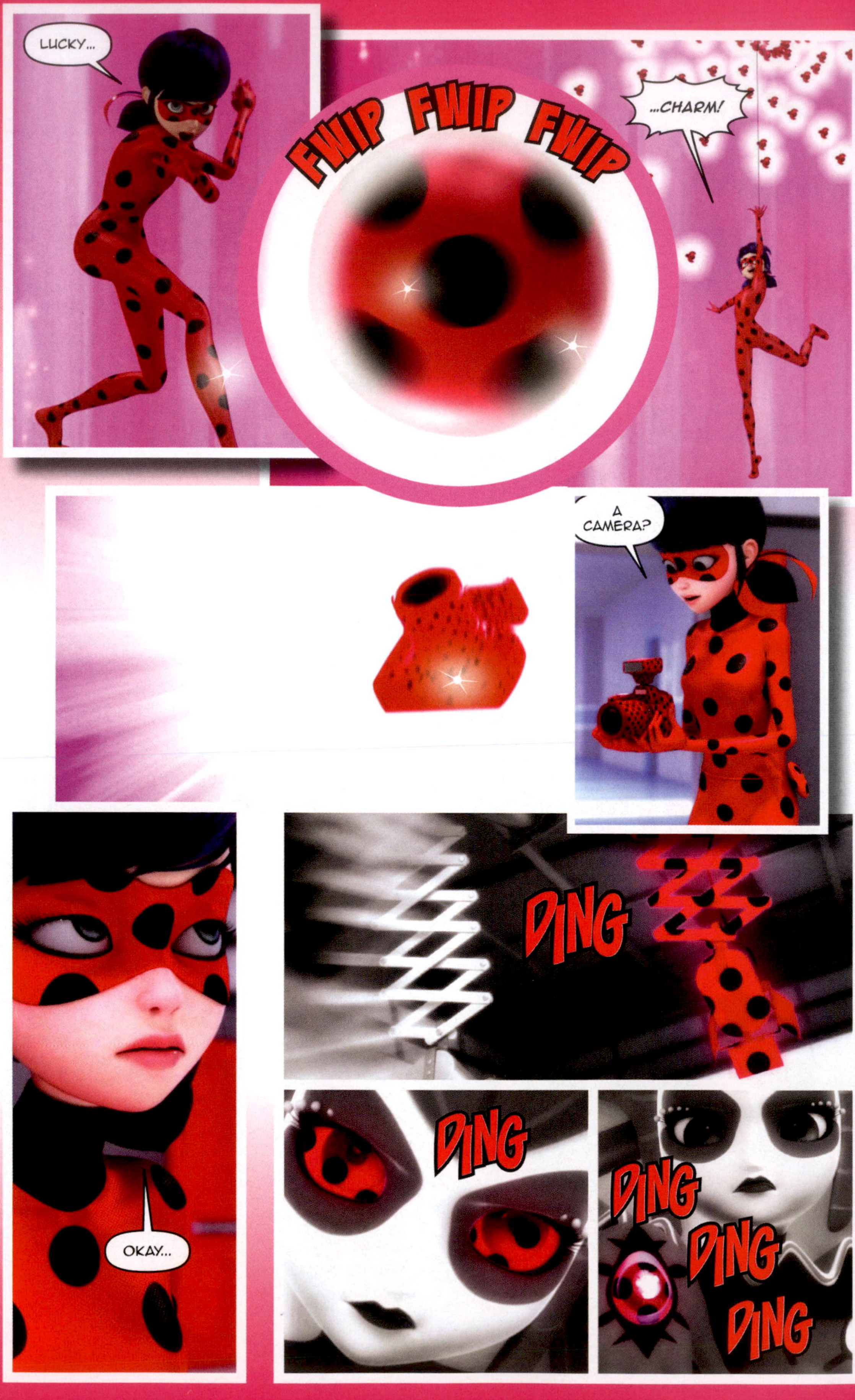
LUCKY...
FWIP FWIP FWIP
...CHARM!
A CAMERA?
OKAY...
DING
DING
DING
DING
DING

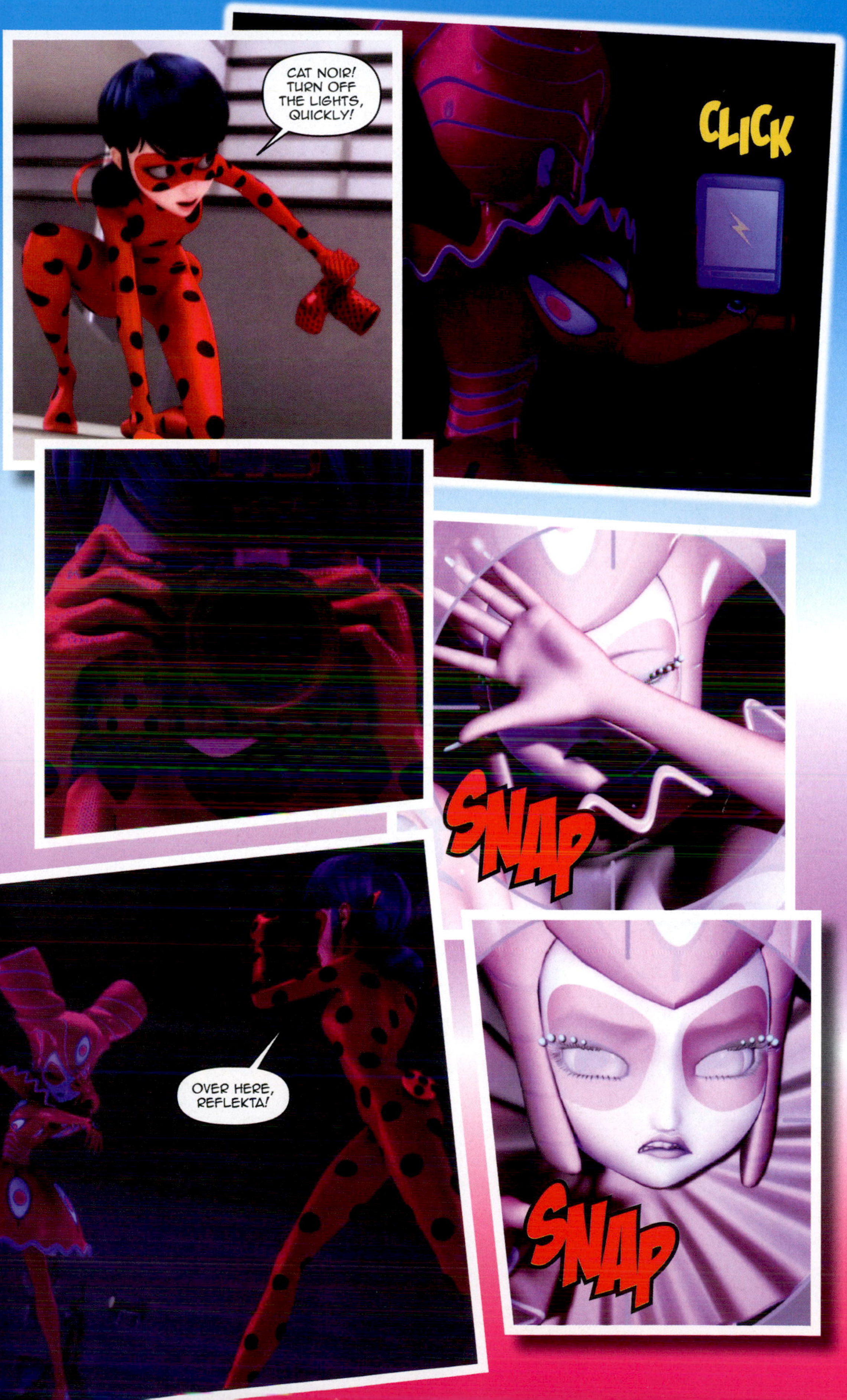
CAT NOIR! TURN OFF THE LIGHTS, QUICKLY!
CLICK
SNAP
OVER HERE, REFLEKTA!
SNAP

GASP
SNAP
WHAT?
MISSING SOMETHING?
SMASH

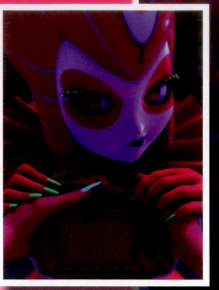

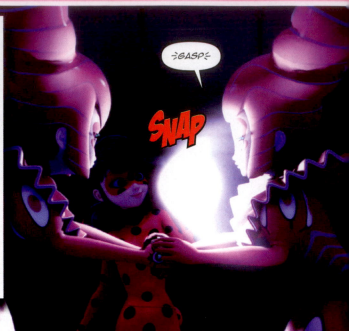

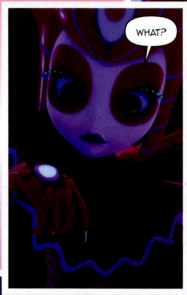

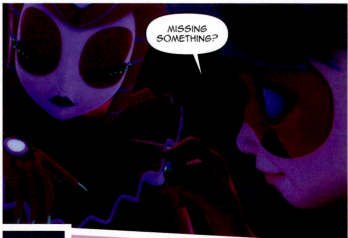

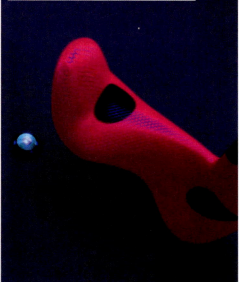

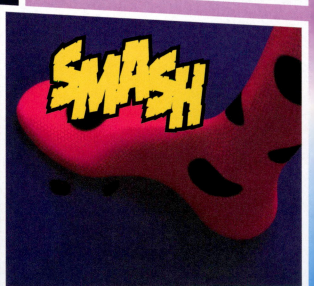

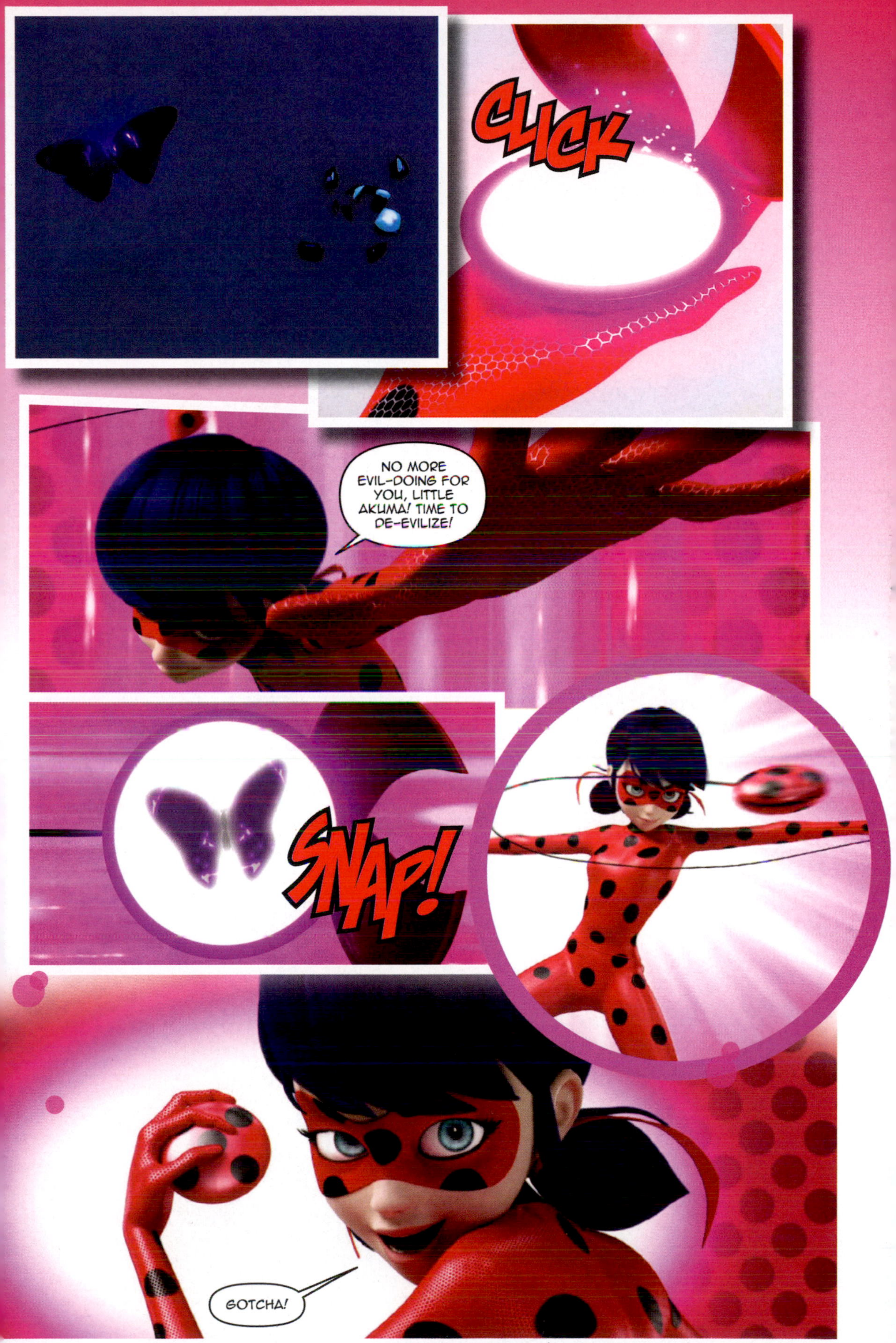
CLICK
NO MORE EVIL-DOING FOR YOU, LITTLE AKUMA! TIME TO DE-EVILIZE!
SNAP!
GOTCHA!

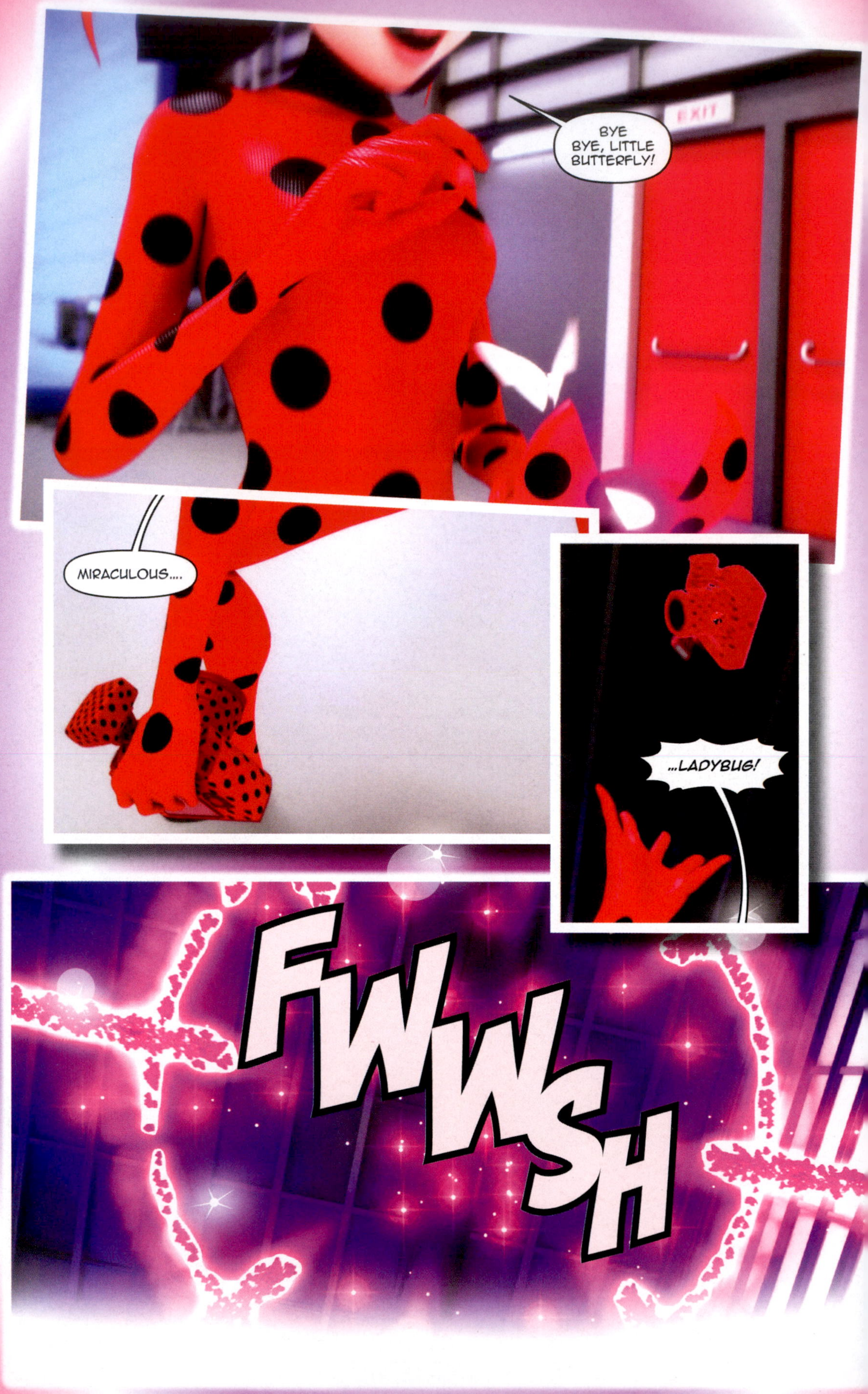
BYE BYE, LITTLE BUTTERFLY!
MIRACULOUS....
...LADYBUG!
FWWSH

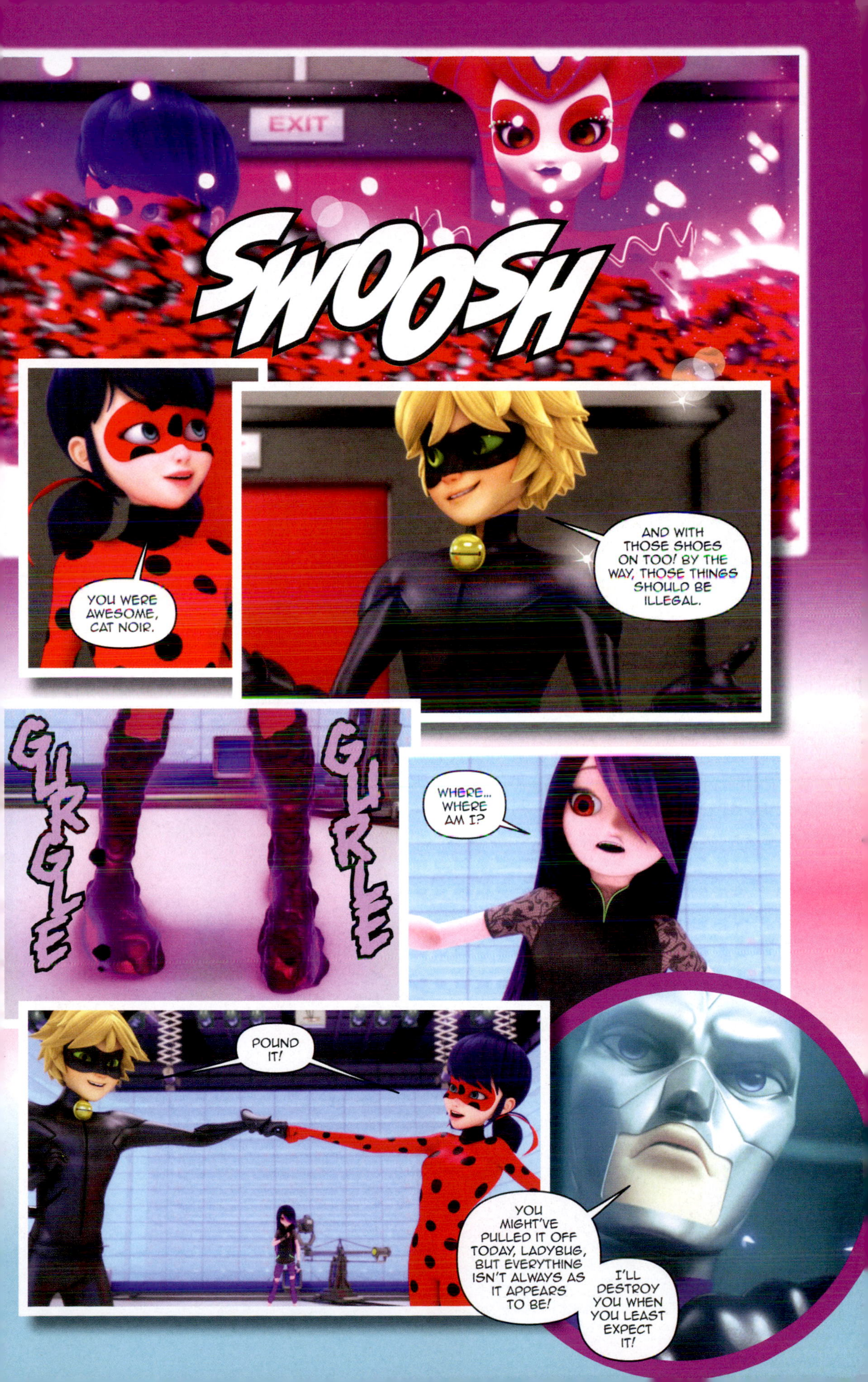
EXIT
SWOOSH
YOU WERE AWESOME, CAT NOIR.
AND WITH THOSE SHOES ON TOO! BY THE WAY, THOSE THINGS SHOULD BE ILLEGAL.
GURGLE
GURLE
WHERE... WHERE AM I?
POUND IT!
YOU MIGHT'VE PULLED IT OFF TODAY, LADYBUG, BUT EVERYTHING ISN'T ALWAYS AS IT APPEARS TO BE!
I'LL DESTROY YOU WHEN YOU LEAST EXPECT IT!

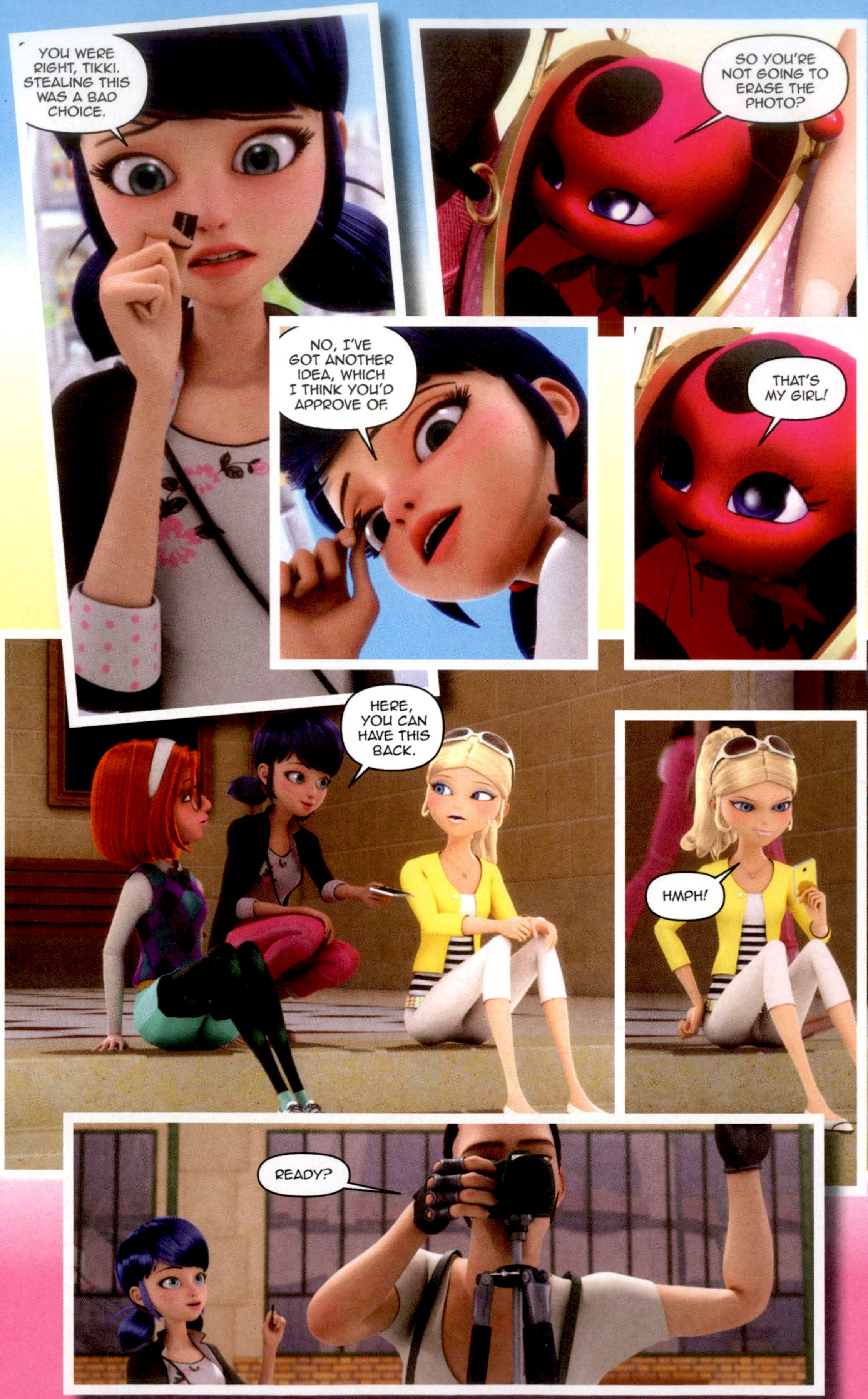
YOU WERE RIGHT, TIKKI. STEALING THIS WAS A BAD CHOICE.
SO YOU'RE NOT GOING TO ERASE THE PHOTO?
NO, I'VE GOT ANOTHER IDEA, WHICH I THINK YOU'D APPROVE OF.
THAT'S MY GIRL!
HERE, YOU CAN HAVE THIS BACK.
HMPH!
READY?

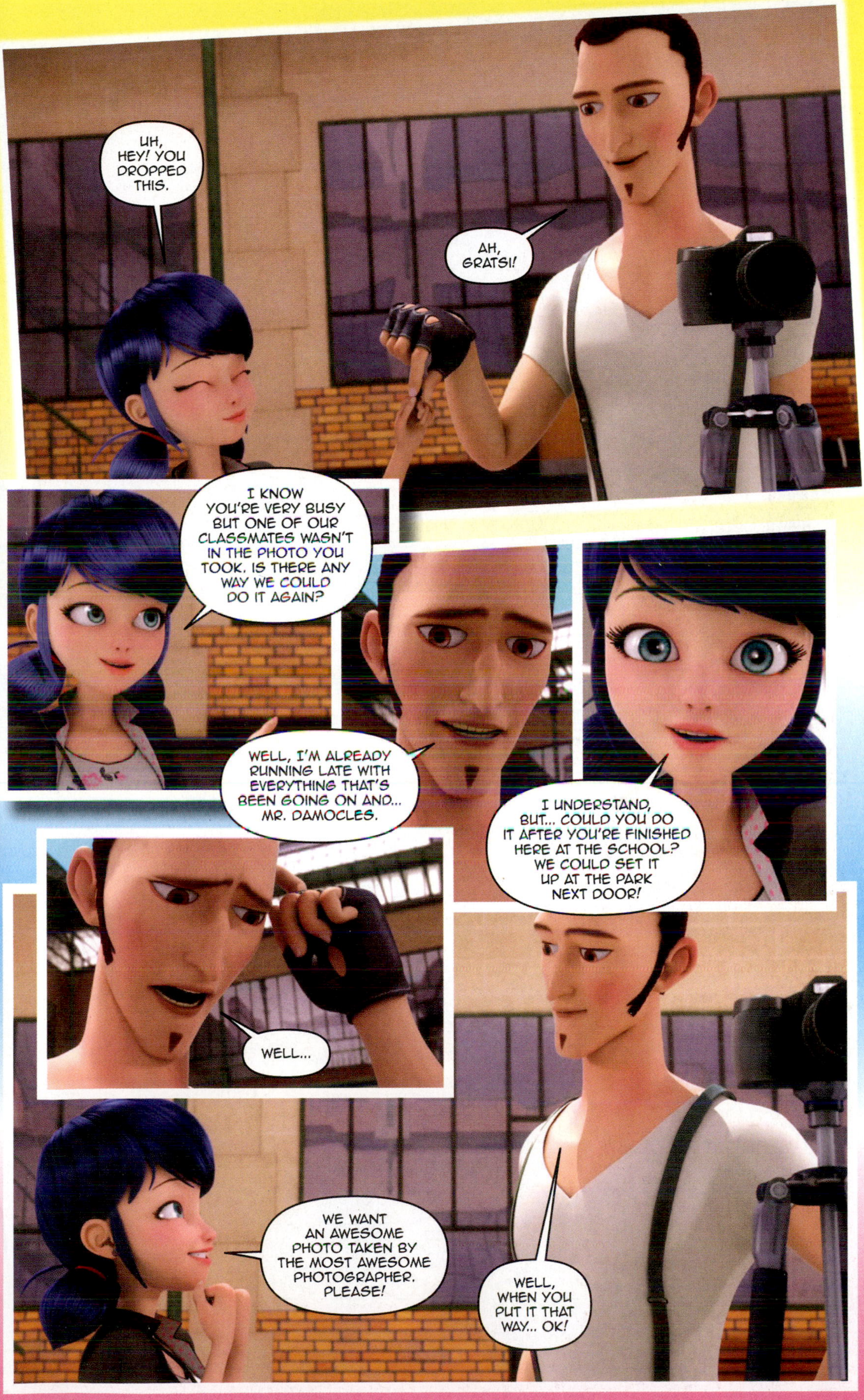
UH, HEY! YOU DROPPED THIS.
AH, GRATSI!
I KNOW YOU'RE VERY BUSY BUT ONE OF OUR CLASSMATES WASN'T IN THE PHOTO YOU TOOK. IS THERE ANY WAY WE COULD DO IT AGAIN?
WELL, I'M ALREADY RUNNING LATE WITH EVERYTHING THAT'S BEEN GOING ON AND... MR. DAMOCLES.
I UNDERSTAND, BUT... COULD YOU DO IT AFTER YOU'RE FINISHED HERE AT THE SCHOOL? WE COULD SET IT UP AT THE PARK NEXT DOOR!
WELL...
WE WANT AN AWESOME PHOTO TAKEN BY THE MOST AWESOME PHOTOGRAPHER. PLEASE!
WELL, WHEN YOU PUT IT THAT WAY... OK!

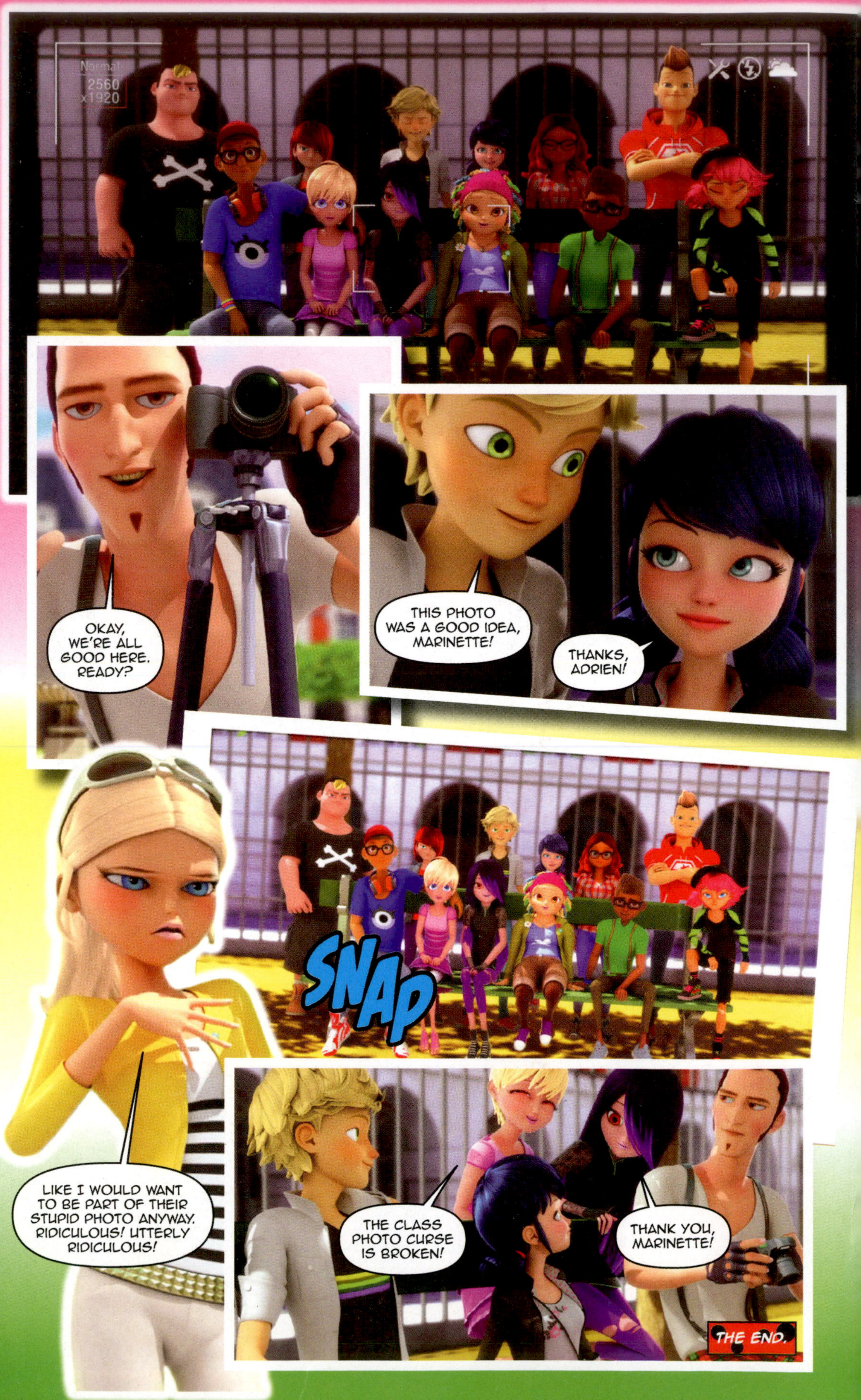

Normal
2560
x1920
OKAY, WE'RE ALL GOOD HERE. READY?
THIS PHOTO WAS A GOOD IDEA, MARINETTE!
THANKS, ADRIEN!
SNAP
LIKE I WOULD WANT TO BE PART OF THEIR STUPID PHOTO ANYWAY. RIDICULOUS! UTTERLY RIDICULOUS!
THE CLASS PHOTO CURSE IS BROKEN!
THANK YOU, MARINETTE!
THE END.